Thunder and Roses

Theodore Sturgeon circa 1946,
in New York City, with his sister-in-law.

Thunder and Roses

Volume IV:

The Complete Stories of

Theodore Sturgeon

Edited by
Paul Williams

Foreword by
James Gunn

North Atlantic Books
Berkeley, California

Thunder and Roses

Copyright © 1997 the Theodore Sturgeon Literary Trust. Previously published materials copyright © 1946, 1947, 1948, 1953, 1955 by Theodore Sturgeon and the Theodore Sturgeon Literary Trust. Foreword copyright © 1996 by Paramount Pictures; reprinted from *The Joy Machine* by kind permission of the publisher and the author. All rights reserved. No portion of this book, except for brief review, may be reproduced, stored in a retrieval system, or transmitted, in any form or by any means, electronic, mechanical, photocopying, recording or otherwise without the written permission of the publisher. For information contact North Atlantic Books.

Published by
North Atlantic Books
P.O. Box 12327
Berkeley, California 94712

Cover art *Sun Spots* © Jacek Yerka 1994
Cover and book design by Paula Morrison

Thunder and Roses is sponsored by the Society for the Study of Native Arts and Sciences, a nonprofit educational corporation whose goals are to develop an educational and crosscultural perspective linking various scientific, social, and artistic fields; to nurture a holistic view of arts, sciences, humanities, and healing; and to publish and distribute literature on the relationship of mind, body, and nature.

Library of Congress Cataloging-in-Publication Number

Sturgeon, Theodore.
Thunder and Roses / Theodore Sturgeon.
p. cm — (The complete stories of Theodore Sturgeon; v. 4)
ISBN 1-55643-328-X
I. Science fiction, American. I. Title. II. Series: Sturgeon, Theodore. Short Stories; v. 4
PS3569.T875A6 1997
813'.54—dc21

94-21610
CIP

1 2 3 4 5 6 7 8 9 / 03 02 01 00 99

EDITOR'S NOTE

THEODORE HAMILTON STURGEON was born February 26, 1918, and died May 8, 1985. This is the fourth of a series of volumes that will collect all of his short fiction of all types and all lengths shorter than a novel. The volumes and the stories within the volumes are organized chronologically by order of composition (insofar as it can be determined). This fourth volume contains stories written between early 1946 and the end of 1947. One is being published here for the first time; and three others have never before appeared in a Sturgeon collection.

Preparation of each of these volumes would not be possible without the hard work and invaluable participation of Noël Sturgeon, Debbie Notkin, and our publishers, Lindy Hough and Richard Grossinger. I would also like to thank, for their significant assistance with this volume, James Gunn, the Theodore Sturgeon Literary Trust, Marion Sturgeon, Jayne Williams, Dorothe Tunstall, Ralph Vicinanza, Kyle McAbee, Judith Merril, Faren Miller, Tom Whitmore, Angus MacDonald, Paula Morrison, Catherine Campaigne, T. V. Reed, Cindy Lee Berryhill, and all of you who have expressed your interest and support.

BOOKS BY THEODORE STURGEON

Without Sorcery (1948)
The Dreaming Jewels (1950)
More Than Human (1953)
E Pluribus Unicorn (1953)
Caviar (1955)
A Way Home (1955)
The King and Four Queens (1956)
I, Libertine (1956)
A Touch of Strange (1958)
The Cosmic Rape (1958)
Aliens 4 (1959)
Venus Plus X (1960)
Beyond (1960)
Some of Your Blood (1961)
Voyage to the Bottom of the Sea (1961)
The Player on the Other Side (1963)
Sturgeon in Orbit (1964)
Starshine (1966)
The Rare Breed (1966)
Sturgeon Is Alive and Well ... (1971)
The Worlds of Theodore Sturgeon (1972)
Sturgeon's West (with Don Ward) (1973)
Case and the Dreamer (1974)
Visions and Venturers (1978)
Maturity (1979)
The Stars Are the Styx (1979)
The Golden Helix (1979)
Alien Cargo (1984)
Godbody (1986)
A Touch of Sturgeon (1987)
The [Widget], the [Wadget], and Boff (1989)
Argyll (1993)
The Ultimate Egoist (1994)
Microcosmic God (1995)
Killdozer! (1996)
Star Trek, The Joy Machine (with James Gunn) (1996)
Thunder and Roses (1997)

CONTENTS

Foreword

by James Gunn

I MET TED Sturgeon because an editor called me. I had received letters from editors about my manuscripts, a couple of rejections and then a life-changing acceptance from Sam Merwin, Jr., but one day my telephone rang and a voice said, "This is Horace Gold calling from *Galaxy.*"

It was the fall of 1950. I was a graduate student at the University of Kansas, completing a master's degree in English, and I had been writing science fiction since 1948. I had gone back to graduate school under the G.I. Bill in the summer of 1949, after a year of freelancing in which I discovered that I could write and sell stories, though not fast enough to make a living at it. But I continued to write stories as a graduate student, and I had talked the English department into letting me write a science-fiction play called "Breaking Point" for academic credit. I had turned that into a novella. John Campbell rejected it at *Astounding,* and I sent it off to a new magazine whose first issue had just come out. It had attracted my attention by the variety of stories it was publishing and the skillful way they were written. It was called *Galaxy.*

I had published two stories in 1949, two so far in 1950, including one in what had been my favorite magazine for a dozen years, *Astounding,* and I would publish four more in 1951. It was enough to make me the envy of other graduate students, who had yet to be published, but I had made no particular impression on the science-fiction community. Now Horace Gold was calling. What he had to say could make a difference.

"I'd like to buy your story 'Breaking Point,'" Gold said, "but it's too long."

"I'll cut it," I said quickly. I knew the process of translating a play into fiction had left the story overburdened with dialogue.

"I don't trust you to do it," Gold said bluntly. He was either blunt or charming. "And I need it done in a hurry. Would you let Ted Sturgeon cut it by a third?"

I agreed without hesitation, even after I learned that Gold intended to compensate Sturgeon by giving him one cent a word of my three-cents-a-word payment. It still would be the longest story I had ever sold, and for more money than I had ever earned from writing, and Ted Sturgeon was a writer that I had admired, extravagantly, since I had become aware that particular kinds of stories were written by particular authors. I liked Asimov and Heinlein and van Vogt and De Camp and Simak for various reasons, often different, but Sturgeon's work was special. His offbeat characters were more believable and his prose was more carefully wrought. He was a writer's writer.

I recognized Sturgeon's touch in such early stories as "Ether Breather," "Microcosmic God," "Memorial," "Maturity," "Mewhu's Jet," and "Thunder and Roses" in *Astounding* and in "The Sky Was Full of Ships" in *Thrilling Wonder Stories.* When I occasionally came across a copy of *Astounding*'s sister fantasy magazine, *Unknown,* I found that special Sturgeon quality in "It," "The Ultimate Egoist," "Shottle Bop," "Yesterday Was Monday" and others. But I had missed out on a lot of magazines during World War II, and Sturgeon's work may have made the greatest impression when I saw the anthologies that began to appear after the war: "A God in a Garden" actually appeared in 1939, in Phil Stong's pioneer anthology *The Other Worlds,* but there was "Killdozer!" in Groff Conklin's *The Best of Science Fiction* and "Minority Report" in August Derleth's *Beyond Time and Space.*

Then Sturgeon's first novel, *The Dreaming Jewels,* was published in the February 1950 issue of *Fantastic Adventures.* The great short-story artist could write novels, too, I discovered, although to the end of his days he was at his best in the shorter lengths.

As a matter of fact Sturgeon had had a novelette, "The Stars Are the Styx," in the first issue of *Galaxy.* I waited anxiously to hear from

Sturgeon or Gold about "Breaking Point." I kept looking at issues of *Galaxy* as they came out, and at its forecasts for what would be published in the next issue, thinking that maybe my novella was going to get published without my being notified, or paid. I may have written to Sturgeon, finally; I remember a letter from Sturgeon telling me that he had put off working on the project for several months, and when he had got around to it Gold said he didn't want the story cut, he wanted it rewritten.

That might have been the end of it, but it wasn't: Lester del Rey published "Breaking Point" in the March 1953 issue of *Space Science Fiction,* and Piers Anthony wrote me a couple of decades later that reading it had made him realize that it was possible to write stories like that and get them published. It also was the title story for my 1972 collection. By the time "Breaking Point" was published, however, I had attended my first World Science Fiction Convention and I had met Sturgeon. He wasn't at the convention, but my agent was. My agent was Fred Pohl. Gold, who had disappointed me about my story, had recommended me to Fred. I had earned my degree and was working as an editor in Racine, Wisconsin, but I had continued to write and send stories to Fred. I also had persuaded my employers to send me to the convention in Chicago, had my first experience of meeting other writers and science-fiction enthusiasts, and talked with Fred, who told me he had just sold four stories for me. One of them, incidentally, was to *Galaxy,* "The Misogynist."

On the strength of that success, flimsy as it was, I quit my job and returned to freelance writing. It seems rash now but times, and needs, were simpler then. I made a trip to New York to meet editors, and I arranged to meet Ted (I was calling him Ted now). Ted's work had been appearing regularly in *Galaxy* (and in *Fantasy & Science Fiction,* as well), including the classic "Baby Is Three" in the October 1952 issue, which appeared just a couple of months before we met. I should have been in awe—though only five years older, he was a dozen years more experienced in writing and getting published—but Ted wouldn't let me. He was living in a house a former ship's captain had built on a hill overlooking the Hudson River, and he prepared lunch, and told me about his life and his writing, and the unusual relationships among the movers and shakers in New York science fiction.

Ted had a way of focusing his attention on people, of caring about them, that made them love him. *The St. James Guide to Science Fiction Writers* called him "the best loved of all SF writers." By the time I left that evening for a party at Horace Gold's apartment—Ted drove me to the Manhattan side of the George Washington Bridge—I felt as if Ted was a contemporary and maybe even a friend.

I followed Ted's career from a distance. We met one other time in the 1950s, at the World Science Fiction Convention in Philadelphia in 1953, when he gave a talk in which he announced what later came to be known as "Sturgeon's Law": "Ninety per cent of science fiction is crud, but then ninety per cent of everything is crud." *More Than Human,* the novel built around "Baby Is Three," was published in 1953, *The Cosmic Rape* in 1958, and *Venus Plus X* in 1960. That, except for a novelization of *Voyage to the Bottom of the Sea* and the posthumous *Godbody* (1986), made up his entire science-fiction novel production. He wrote five other non-SF novels, including the rakish *I, Libertine* and the sensitive psychological case study of vampirism *Some of Your Blood.*

But Ted published twenty-six collections of short stories, beginning in 1948 with *Without Sorcery* and continuing through such classics as *E Pluribus Unicorn* (1953), *Caviar* (1955), *A Touch of Strange* (1958), *Sturgeon in Orbit* (1964), *Sturgeon Is Alive and Well . . .* (1971), *The Golden Helix* (1979). In 1994, North Atlantic Books began publishing a ten-volume set of his complete short fiction. Ted also published a collection of the Western stories he had written, three in collaboration with Don Ward, *Sturgeon's West* (1973).

After a glorious flow of creativity in the 1950s, Ted faded from the science-fiction scene. Partly it was writer's block; in one famous instance, Robert Heinlein sent him a letter filled with story ideas and Ted turned at least two of them into stories. He also talked about the novel he had been working on for years; it may have been *Godbody.* Partly he was busy writing other things, including radio adaptations of his own stories in the 1950s and 1960s, and television scripts based on his work and that of others. All that came to a focus, it would seem, in the two scripts he wrote for *Star Trek,* the classics "Shore Leave" and "Amok Time." He also adapted "Killdozer!" as a television movie, but a revision by Ed MacKillop left him dissatisfied with the result. During the 1960s and 1970s Ted also reviewed books for the *New York Times* and wrote a column for the *National Review.*

His leave of absence from science fiction, broken by the publication of "Slow Sculpture" in 1970 and its Nebula and Hugo awards, was the reason his 1971 collection was titled *Sturgeon Is Alive and Well...* He also won the 1954 International Fantasy Award for *More Than Human,* was Guest of Honor at the 1962 World Science Fiction Convention in Chicago, and received the 1985 World Fantasy Convention Life Achievement Award the year he died.

He had hopes, periodically raised, regularly dashed, that his greatest novel, *More Than Human,* would become a feature film.

I created the Intensive English Institute on the Teaching of Science Fiction in 1974, as a response to the teachers who had written me during my term as president of the Science Fiction Writers of America saying, "I've just been asked to teach a science-fiction course. What do I teach?" The Institute became a regular summer offering in 1978, and I invited three writers to be guests for a week each: Gordon R. Dickson, with his enthusiasm for story structure and theme; Fred Pohl, with his broad range of experience as writer, editor, and agent; and Ted Sturgeon, with his charm and empathy and concern for style. All three accepted, and all three joined us every summer until Ted's death.

Those were the days when I really got to know Ted. He and his wife Jayne looked forward to a quiet week in Lawrence, I believe, and Ted liked the endless variety of students, from those of college age to the elderly, and from more than half a dozen foreign countries. They all loved Ted. That was Ted's greatest talent, and that was what he wrote about, the varieties of love, particularly the love of outcasts or the handicapped or the repressed. Love would save the world, he thought, if it ever got the chance. Ted's stories, John Clute wrote in *The Encyclopedia of Science Fiction,* "constituted a set of codes or maps capable of leading maimed adolescents out of alienation and into the light."

All three visiting writers had their special areas of interest. Ted's was craft and style, titles and opening sentences. He talked about "metric prose" and brought along an English translation of a book published in French, which told the same pointless story in dozens of different styles. He was good at titles; his favorite was "If All Men Were Brothers, Would You Let One Marry Your Sister?" And he recalled a contest with Don Ward (who by coincidence was my mentor as an editor in Racine, and attended the second Institute session) to invent the best opening sentence. Ted's was "At last they sat a dance out." [See "The Blue Letter," unpublished until this volume of *The Complete Stories of Theodore Sturgeon.*] But he thought Don's was better: "They banged through the cabin door and squared off in the snow outside." My favorite was Ted's opening sentence for *The Dreaming Jewels,* "They caught the kid doing something disgusting out under the bleachers at the high-school stadium." It turned out he was eating ants because he had a formic acid deficiency.

One of the projects that got started here at the University of Kansas after Ted's death, a decade ago, was a Writers Workshop in Science Fiction, and one of the early participants was a university student named John Ordover. A year later he told me he was going to return to his native New York to become an editor. He got his wish, first at Tor Books, then at Pocket Books, where he became editor of the *Star Trek* series. But he returned to the Workshop every summer as a guest editor and a vocal participant in the Campbell Conference, at which we sit around a table and discuss a single topic. In the summer of 1995 John brought something special along with him, the outline for a *Star Trek* episode that Ted Sturgeon had proposed back in the 1960s but that had never been produced. It was called "The Joy Machine," and he asked me if I would be interested in turning it into a novel.

I took a look at Ted's outline—his original outline, typos and all—and liked the idea. "The Joy Machine," after all, was a variation on the theme of 1962 novel, *The Joy Makers,* and I was still fascinated by the interplay between happiness and aspiration, between pleasure and struggle. In his outline, Ted saw pleasure, easily obtained and totally satisfying, as a threat to human existence, and I saw ways of building on Ted's situation to say some other things about happiness and the human condition. I agreed to write the novel. The result [*Star Trek, The Joy Machine,* a novel by James Gunn, based on the story by Theodore Sturgeon] was published in 1996.

My first contact with Ted Sturgeon came when Ted was asked to shorten my story. My last came when I was asked to lengthen his story. There must be a meaning in there somewhere.

James Gunn
Lawrence, Kansas

Maturity

DR. MARGARETTA WENZELL, she of the smooth face and wise eyes and flowing dark hair, and the raft of letters after her name in the medical "Who's Who," allowed herself to be called "Peg" only by her equals, of whom there were few. Her superiors did not, and her inferiors dared not. And yet Dr. Wenzell was not a forbidding person in any way. She had fourteen months to go to get to her thirtieth birthday; her figure hadn't changed since she was seventeen; her face, while hardly suited to a magazine cover, was designed rather for a salon study. She maintained her careful distance from most people for two reasons. One was that, as an endocrinologist, she had to make a fetish of objectivity; and the other was the fact that only by a consistent attitude of impersonality could she keep her personal charm from being a drawback to her work. Her work meant more to her than anything else in life, and she saw to it that her life stayed that way.

And yet the boy striding beside her called her "Peg." He had since he met her. He was neither her superior nor her inferior, and he was certainly not her equal. These subconscious divisions of Dr. Wenzell's had nothing to do with age or social position. Her standards were her own, and since Robin English could not be judged by any of them—or by anyone else's standards, for that matter—she had made no protest beyond a lift of the eyebrow. It couldn't be important.

He held her arm as they crossed the rainy street. He always did that, and he was one of the half-dozen men she had met in her life who did it unconsciously and invariably.

"There's a taxi!" she said.

He grinned. "So it is. Let's take the subway."

"Oh, Robin!"

"It's only temporary. Why, I've almost finished that operetta, and any day now I'll get the patent on that power brake of mine, and—"

He smiled down at her. His face was round and ruddy, and it hadn't quite enough chin, and Peg thought it was a delightful face. She wondered if it knew how to look angry or—purposeful.

"I know," she said. "I know. And you'll suddenly have bushels of money, and you won't have to worry about taxis—"

"I don't worry about 'em anyhow. Maybe such things'll bother me when your boy friend gets through with me."

"They will, and don't call him my boy friend."

"Sorry," he said casually.

They went down the steps at the subway terminal. Sorry. Robin could always dismiss things with that laconic expression. And he *could*. Whether he was sorry or not, wasn't important, somehow; it was the way he said it. It reduced the thing he was sorry for to so little value that it wasn't worth being sorry about.

Peg stood watching him as he swung up to the change booth. He walked easily, with an incredible grace. As graceful as a cat, but not at all like a cat. It was like the way he thought—as well as a human being, but not like a human being. She watched the way the light fell on his strange, planeless, open face, and his tousled head of sandy horsehair. He annoyed her ever so much, and she thought that it was probably because she liked him.

He stood aside to let her through the turnstile, smiling at her and whistling a snatch of a Bach fugue through his teeth. That was another thing. Robin played competent piano and absolutely knocked-out trumpet; but he never played the classics. He never whistled anything else.

There was no train in. They strolled up the platform slowly. Peg couldn't keep her eyes off Robin's face. His sensitive nostrils dilated, and she had the odd idea that he was smelling a sound—the echoing shuffle of feet and machinery in the quiet where there should be no quiet. As they passed the massive beam-and-coil-spring bumper at the end of the track, Robin paused, his eyes flickering over it, gauging its strength, judging its materials. It had never occurred to her to look at such a thing before. "What does that matter to you, Robin?"

He pointed. "First it knocks the trains pigeontoed. Then she'll nose into the beam there and the springs behind it will take up the shock. Now why do they use coils?"

"Why not?"

"Leaf springs would absorb the collision energy between the leaves, in friction. Coil springs store the energy and throw it right back ... oh! I see. They took for granted when they designed it that the brakes would be set. Big as those springs are, they're not going to shove the whole train back. And then, the play between the car couplings would—"

"But Robin—what does it matter? To you, I mean. No," she said quickly as a thick little furrow appeared and disappeared between his eyes. "I'm not saying you shouldn't be interested. I'm just wondering exactly what it is about such devices that fascinates you so."

"I don't know," he said. "The ... the integration, I suppose. The thought that went into it. The importance of the crash barrier to Mrs. Scholtz's stew and Sadie's date, and which ferry Tony catches, and all the other happenings that can happen to the cattle and the gods who use the subways."

Peg laughed delightedly. "And do you think about all of the meanings to all of the people of all of the things you see?"

"I don't have to think of them. They're there, right in front of me. Surely you can see homemade borscht and a goodnight kiss and thousands of other little, important things, all wrapped up in those big helical springs?"

"I have to think about it. But I do see them." She laughed again. "What do you think about when you listen to Bach?"

He looked at her quickly. "Did I say I listened to Bach?"

"My gremlins told me." She looked at him with puzzlement. He wasn't smiling. " 'You whistle it," she explained.

"Do I? Well, all right then. What do I think of? Architecture, I think. And the complete polish of it. The way old J. S. burnished every note, and the careful matching of all those harmonic voices. And ... and—"

"And what?"

He laughed, a burst of it, a compelling radiation which left little pieces of itself as smiles on the faces of the people around them. "And the sweating choirboys who had to pump the organ when he composed. How they must have hated him!"

A train came groaning into the station and stopped, snicking its doors open. "Watch them," said Robin, his quick eyes taking inventory of the people who jostled each other out of the train. "Not one in fifty is seeing anything. No one knows how far apart these pillars are, or the way all these rivets are set, or the cracks in the concrete under their feet. They're all looking at things separated from them in space and time—the offices they have left, the homes they're going to, the people they will see. Hardly any of them are consciously here, *now.* They're all ghosts, and we're a couple of Peeping Toms."

"Robin, Robin, you're such a *child!*"

"To you, of course. You're older than I am."

"Four days." It was a great joke between them.

"Four thousand years," he said soberly. They found a seat. "And I'm not a child. I'm a hyperthymus. You said so yourself."

"You won't be for very much longer," said Dr. Margaretta Wenzell. "Dr. Warfield and I will see to that."

"What are you doing it for?"

"You'll find out when we send the bill."

"I know it isn't that."

"Of course not," she said. Her remark tasted badly in her mouth. "It's just ... Robin, how long have you had that suit?"

"Uh ... suit?" He looked vaguely at the sleeve. "Oh, about three years. It's a good suit."

"Of course it is." It was, too. She remembered that he had gotten it with prize money from a poetry contest. "How many weeks room rent do you owe?"

"None!" he said triumphantly. "I rewired all the doorbells in the apartment house and fixed Mrs. Gridget's vacuum cleaner and composed a song for her daughter's wedding reception and invented a gadget to hold her cookbook under the kitchen shelf, with a little light that goes on when she swings it out. Next thing I knew she handed me a rent receipt. Wasn't that swell of her?"

"Oh," said Peg weakly. She clutched grimly at the point she was trying to make. "How much are you in debt?"

"Oh, that," he said.

"That."

"I guess ten-twelve thousand." He looked up. "Kcans Yppans. What are you driving at?"

"*What* did you say?"

He waved at the car card opposite. "Snappy Snack. Spelled backwards. Always spell things backward when you see them on car cards. If you don't, there's no telling what you might be mising."

"Oh, you blithering *idiot!*"

"Sorry. What were you saying?"

"I was getting to this," she said patiently. "There doesn't seem to be anything you can't do. You write, you paint, you compose, you invent things, you fix other things, you—"

"Cook," he said, as she stopped for breath; and he added idly, "I make love, too."

"No doubt," said the gland specialist primly. "On the other hand, there doesn't seem to be anything you've accomplished with all of these skills."

"They're not skills. They're talents. I have no skills."

Peg saw the distinction, and smiled. It was quite true. One had to spend a little time in practice to acquire a skill. If Robin couldn't do promisingly the first time he tried something, he would hardly try again. "A good point. And that is what Dr. Warfield and I want to adjust."

"'Adjust,' she says. Going to shrivel up all the pretty pink lobulae in my thymus. The only thymus I've got, too."

"And about time. You should have gotten rid of it when you were thirteen. Most people do."

"And then I'll be all grim and determined about everything, and generate gallons of sweat, and make thousands of dollars, so that at age thirty I can go back to school and get that high school diploma."

"Haven't you got a high school diploma?" asked Peg, her appalled voice echoing hollowly against her four post-graduate degrees.

"As a senior," smiled Robin, "I hadn't a thing but seniority. I'd been there six years. I didn't graduate from school; I was released."

"Robin, that's *awful!*"

"Why is it awful? Oh—I suppose it is." He looked puzzled and crestfallen.

Peg put her hand on his arm. It had nothing to do with logic, but something in her was wrenched when Robin looked hurt. "I suppose it doesn't matter, Robin. What you learn, and what you do with it, are really more important than *where* you learn."

"Yes ... but not *when*. I mean, you can learn too late. I know lots of things, but the things I don't know seem to have to do with getting along in the world. Isn't that what you mean by 'awful'? Isn't that what you and Dr. Warfield are going to change?"

"That's it. That's right. Robin. Oh, you're such a strange person!"

"Strange?"

"I mean ... you know, I was sure that Mel Warfield and I would have no end of trouble in persuading you to take these thymus treatments."

"Why?"

With a kind of exasperation she said, "I don't think you fully realize that the change in you will be drastic. You're going to lose a lot that's bad about you—I'm sure of that. But you'll see things quite differently. You ... you—" She fought for a description of what Robin would be like without his passionate interest in too many things, and her creative equipment bogged down. "You'll probably see things quite differently."

He looked into her eyes thoughtfully. "Is that bad?"

Bad? There never was a man who had less evil about him, she thought. "I think not," she said.

He spread his hands. "I don't think so either. So why hesitate? You have mentioned that I do a lot of things. Would that be true if I got all frothed up every time I tried something I'd never tried before?"

"No. No, of course not." She realized that it had been foolish of her to mix ordinary practical psychology into any consideration of Robin English. Obviously gland imbalances have frequent psychological symptoms, and in many of these cases the abnormal condition has its own self-justifying synapses which will set up a powerful defense mechanism when treatment is mentioned. Equally obviously, this wouldn't apply to Robin. Where most people seem to have an inherent dislike of being changed, Robin seemed to have a subconscious yearning for just that.

He said, "We get off at the next station."

"I know."

"I just wanted to tell you."

"Where to get off?"

In utter surprise, he said "Me?" and it was the most eloquent monosyllable she had ever heard. For the first time it occurred to her to wonder consciously what he thought of her. It hadn't seemed to matter, before. What was she, in his eyes? She suddenly realized that she, as a doctor meeting a man socially, had really no right to corner him, question him, analyze and diagnose the way she had over the past few weeks. She couldn't abide the existence of a correctable condition in her specialty, and this was probably the essence of selfishness. He probably regarded her as meddling and dominating. She astonished herself by asking him, point-blank.

"What do I think of you?" He considered, carefully. He appeared not to think it remarkable that she could have asked such a question. "You're a taffy-puller."

"I'm a *what?*"

"A taffy-puller. They hypnotize me. Didn't you ever see one?"

"I don't think so," she breathed. "But—"

"You see them down on the boardwalk. Beautifully machined little rigs, all chrome-plated eccentrics and cams. There are two cranks set near each other so that the 'handle' of each passes the axle of the other. They stick a big mass of taffy on one 'handle' and start the machine. Before that sticky, homogeneous mass has a chance to droop and drip off, the other crank has swung up and taken most of it. As the crank handles move away from each other the taffy is pulled out, and then as they move together again it loops and sags; and at the last possible moment the loop is shoved together. The taffy welds itself and is pulled apart again." Robin's eyes were shining and his voice was rapt. "Underneath the taffy is a stainless steel tray. There isn't a speck of taffy on it. Not a drop, not a smidgin. You stand there, and you look at it, and you wait for that lump of guff to slap itself all over those roller bearings and burnished con rods, but it never does. You wait for it to get tired of that fantastic juggling, and it never does. Sometimes gooey little bubbles get in the taffy and get carried around and pulled out and squashed flat, and when they break they do it slowly, leaving little soft craters that take a long time to fill up; and they're being mauled around the way the bubbles were." He sighed. "There's almost too much contrast—that competent, beautiful machinist's dream handling—what? Taffy—no definition, no boundaries, no predictable tensile strength. I feel somehow as if there ought to be an intermediate stage somewhere. I'd feel better if the machine handled one of Dali's limp watches, and the watch handled the mud. But that doesn't matter. How I feel, I mean. The taffy gets pulled. You're a taffy-puller. You've never done a wasteful or incompetent thing in your life, no matter what you were working with."

She sat quietly, letting the vivid picture he had painted fade away. Then, sharply, "Haven't I!" she cried. "I've let us ride past our station!"

Dr. Mellett Warfield let them in himself. Towering over his colleague, he bent his head, and the light caught his high white forehead, which, with his peaked hairline, made a perfect Tuscan arch. "Peg!"

"Hello, Mel. This is Robin English."

Warfield shook hands warmly. "I *am* glad to see you. Peg has told me a lot about you."

"I imagine she has," grinned Robin. "All about my histones and my albumins and the medullic and cortical tissues of my lobulae. I love that word. Lobulae. I lobule very much, Peg."

"Robin, for Pete's sake!"

Warfield laughed. "No—not only that. You see, I'd heard of you before. You designed that, didn't you?" He pointed. On a side table was a simple device with two multicolored disks mounted at the ends of a rotating arm, and powered by a little electric motor.

"The Whirltoy? Robin, I didn't know that!"

"I don't know a child psychologist or a pediatrician who hasn't got one," said Warfield. "I wouldn't part with that one for fifty times what it cost me—which is less than it's worth. I have yet to see the child, no matter how maladjusted, glandular, spoiled, or what have you, who isn't fascinated by those changing colors. Even the color-blind children can't keep their eyes off it because of the changing patterns it makes."

Peg looked at Robin as if he had just come in through the wall. "Robin ... the patent on that—"

"Doesn't exist," said Warfield. "He gave it to the Parents' Association."

"Well, sure. I made mine for fun. I had it a long time before a friend of mine said I ought to sell the idea to a toy manufacturer. But I heard that the Parents' Association sent toys to hospitals and I sort of figured maybe kids that needed amusement should have it, rather than only those whose parents could afford it."

"Robin, you're crazy. You could have—"

"No, Peg," said Warfield gently. "Don't try to make him regret it. Robin ... you won't mind if I call you Robin ... what led you to design the rotors so that they phase over and under the twentieth-of-a-second sight persistence level, so that the eye is drawn to it and then the mind has to concentrate on it?"

"I remember Zeitner's paper about that at the Society for Mental Sciences," said Peg in an awed tone. "'A brilliant application of optics to psychology.'"

"It wasn't brilliant," said Robin impatiently. "I didn't even know that that was what it was doing. I just messed with it until I liked it."

A look passed between Warfield and Peg. It said, "What would he accomplish if he ever really tried?"

Warfield shook his head and perched on the edge of a table. "Now listen to me, Robin," he said, gently and seriously. "I don't think Peg'll mind my telling you this; but it's important."

Peg colored slightly. "I think I know what you're going to say. But go ahead."

"When she first told me about you, and what she wanted to try, I was dead set against it. You see, we know infinitely more about the ductless glands nowadays than we did—well, even this time last year. But at the same time, their interaction is so complex, and their functions so subtle that there are dozens of unexplored mysteries. We're getting to them, one by one, as fast as they show themselves and as fast as we can compile data. The more I learn the less I like to take chances. When Peg just told me about you as a talented young man whose life history was a perfect example of hyper-thymus—infantilism, I think was the word she used—"

"Da! Also goo!" laughed Robin. "She might have been kind enough to call it, say, a static precocity."

"Please don't tease me about it, Robin."

"Oh. Sorry. Go on, Mel." Peg smiled at Warfield's slight start. She had done the same thing, for the same reason, the first time Robin called her "Peg."

"Anyhow, I certainly had no great desire to follow her suggestion—shoot you full of hormones and sterones to help you reorganize your metabolism and your psychology. After all, interesting as these cases are, a doctor has to ration his efforts. There are plenty of odd glandular situations walking around in the guise of a human beings. In addition, I had no personal interest in you. I have too much work to do to indulge a Messiah complex.

"But Peg was persistent. Peg can be *very* persistent. She kept bringing me late developments. I didn't know whether you were a hobby or an inverted phobia of hers. With some effort I managed to remain uninterested until she brought me those blood analyses."

"I'll never get over my disappointment about what she did with those blood specimens," said Robin soberly.

"Disappointment? Why?"

"I had hoped she was a vampire."

"Go on, Mel. Don't try to keep up with him."

"It wasn't until I found out that you wrote 'The Cellophane Chalice'—and mind you, I never did like poetry, but that was *different*—and that you also"—he ticked them off on his fingers—"wrote the original continuity for that pornographic horror of a comic strip 'Gertie and the Wolves,' did the pipe-cleaner figurines that were photographed to illustrate 'The Tiny Hans Anderson,' dropped a sackful of pine oil into the fountain at Radio City purely because you wanted to see thirty thousand gallons of bubbles, got thrown in the pen for it and while there saved the lives of two prisoners and a guard by slugging it out with a homicidal maniac in the bull pen; composed 'The Lullaby Tree' . . . by the way, how was it Rollo Vincente got all the credit—and the money—for that song? It was Number One on the hit list for sixteen weeks."

"He did a swell job," said Robin. "He wrote it down for me."

"Robin can't read music," Peg said tiredly.

"Oh Lord," said Warfield reverently. "I also learned that you invented that disgusting advertising disease 'Stoplight Acne' and gave it for free to an advertising copywriter—"

"Who is now making twenty thousand a year," said Peg.

"That guy was desperate," said Robin. "Besides, he gave me my gold trumpet."

"Which is in hock," said Peg.

"Oh, why go on?" said Warfield. "Most important, I learned that you didn't eat regularly, that you suffered from recurrent eviction, that you continually gave away your possessions, including your overcoats, with such bland illogic that once you spent four months in the hospital with pneumonia and complications—"

"Four winter months, I might point out," said Robin. "So help me, I don't know how I'd have gotten through that winter otherwise. That was well worth the price of an overcoat."

"So Peg began to make a social issue of it. She said that you were a fountainhead of art, science, and industry and that the dispersal of your talents was a crime against humanity. At this stage I would be inclined to agree with her even if she weren't Peg." Warfield looked at the girl, and the way he did it made Robin grin.

"So now that we have your cooperation, we'll go ahead, for the greater honor and glory of humanity and creative genius, as Dr. Wenzell here once phrased it. But I want you to understand that although there is every chance of success, there might be no result at all, or . . . or something worse."

"Like what?"

"How do I know?" said Warfield sharply, and only then did Peg realize what a strain this was to him.

"You're the doctor," said Robin. Suddenly he walked up to Warfield and touched his chest gently. He smiled. He said, "Mel, don't worry. I'll be all right."

Peg's emotional pop-valve let go a hysterical giggle. Warfield turned abruptly away and roughly tore a drawer open and pulled out a thin sheaf of documents. "You'll have to sign these," he said roughly. "I'm going to get the solutions ready. Come on, Peg."

In the laboratory, Peg leaned weakly against the centrifuge. "Don't worry, Mel," she quoted mistily.

"From the time of Hippocrates," growled Warfield, "it has been the duty and practice of the physician to do everything in his power to engender confidence in the patient. And he—"

"Made you feel better."

After a long pause Warfield said, "Yes, he did."

"Mel, I think he's right. I think he *will* be all right. I think that what he has can't be killed. There's too *much* of it!"

She suddenly noticed that Warfield's busy hands had become still, though he didn't turn to look at her. He said, "I was afraid of that."

"What?"

"Oh, I—skip it."

"Mel, what's the matter?"

"Nothing of any importance—especially to you. It's just the way you talk about Robin . . . the way your voice sounds—"

"That's utterly ridiculous!"

Warfield chuckled a little. "Not that I can blame you. Really I can't. That boy has, without exception, the most captivating—"

"Mel, you're being offensive. You certainly know me well enough to know that my interest in Robin English is purely professional—even if I have to include the arts among the professions. Personally he doesn't appeal to me. Why, he's a *child!*"

"A situation which I shall adjust for you."

"That was the n-nastiest thing anyone ever said to me!" she blazed.

"Oh, Peg." He came to her, wiping his hands on a towel. He threw it away—a most uncharacteristic gesture, for him—and put his hands gently on her shoulders. She would not meet his eyes.

"Your lower lip is twice as big as it ought to be," he said softly. "I am sorry, darling."

"Don't call me darling."

"I lost my good sense. May I ask you to marry me again?"

"M-marry you again?"

"Thank the powers for that sense of the ridiculous! May I ask you again? It's about time."

"Let's see—what is the periodicity?— You ask me every nineteen days, don't you?"

"Aloud," he said gravely.

"I—" At last she met his eyes. "No. No! Don't talk about it!"

He took his hands off her shoulders. "All right, Peg."

"Mel, I wish you wouldn't keep bringing this up. If I ever change my mind, I'll speak up."

"Yes, he said thoughtfully. "I believe you would."

"It's just that you— Oh Mel, everything's so balanced now! My work is finally going the way I want it to go, and I just don't *need* anything else." She held up a hand, quickly. "If you say anything about ductless glands I'll walk out of here and never see you again!"

"I won't, Peg."

There was a strained silence. Finally Peg said, "Are you almost ready?"

Mel nodded and went back to the bench. "You can bring him in now."

Peg went out into the reception office. Something white and swift swished past her face, went rocketing up into the corner of the ceiling, hovered, and then drifted down to the floor in slow spirals. "What in—"

"Oh— Sorry, Peg," Robin said, grinning sheepishly. He went and picked up the white object, and held it out to her. "Tandem monoplane," he explained. "The Langley principle. If Langley had only had a decent power plant, aviation history would have been drastically different. The thing is really airworthy."

"Robin, you're impossible. Mel's ready. Where's the thing he asked you to sign?"

"Hm-m-m? Oh, that—this is it."

"You made that airplane out of it?"

"Well, I wanted to see if I could do it without tearing the paper. I did, too." He disassembled the craft busily, and smoothed the papers. "They're all right, see?"

"I ought to make you stand in the corner," she said, half angrily. She looked at him and suddenly, violently, resented Mel for what he had intimated. "Come on, Robin," she said. She took his hand and led him into the laboratory.

"Sit down, Robin," said Warfield without looking up.

"Per–dition!" said Robin, wide-eyed. "You've got more glassware here than the Biltmore Bar. As the hot, cross Bunsen said to the evaporator, 'Be still, my love.' "

Peg moaned. Warfield said, "And what did the evaporator say to that?"

" 'Thank you very much.' You see," said Robin solemnly, "It was a retort courteous."

"Do you think," gasped Peg, "that we'll be able to put a stop to that kind of thing with these treatments?"

"Here," said Warfield, handing him a glass. "Bottoms up."

Robin rose, accepted the glass, bowed from the waist, and said, "Well, here's to champagne for my real friends and real pain for my sham friends. Exit wastrel." And he drained the glass.

"Now if you'll rope him and throw him," said Warfield, approaching with a hypodermic. Robin sat on the examining table, quite relaxed, as the needle sank into his arm.

"Never felt a thing," he said briskly, and then collapsed. Peg caught his head before it could strike the pillow and lowered it gently. She took his wrist. His pulse felt as if it had lost its flywheel.

"Post-pituitary syncope," said Warfield. "I half expected that. He'll be all right. It's compensated for. There just isn't any way of slowing down neopituitrin. Watch what happens when the pineal starts kicking up."

Peg suddenly clutched at the limp wrist. "He's . . . he's— Oh Mel, it's stopped."

"Hang on, Peg. Just a few more seconds, and it should—"

Under Peg's desperate fingers, the pulse beat came in full and strong, as suddenly as if it had been push button turned. With it, Peg began to breathe again. She saw Warfield wipe his eyes. Sweat, probably.

Robin's eyes opened slowly, and an utterly beatific expression crossed his face. He sighed luxuriously. "Beautiful," he said clearly.

"What is it, Robin?"

"Did you see it? I never thought of that before. It's the most perfectly functional, aesthetically balanced thing produced by the mind of man." Sheer wonder suffused his face. "I *saw* one!"

"What was it?"

"A baseball bat!"

Warfield's chin came up. "Well I'll be ... Peg, don't laugh." Peg was hardly likely to. "You know, he's about right?"

"I'll think about aesthetics later," said Peg with some heat. "Is he going to be all right?"

"That's all of the immediate reactions that I suspected. There'll be some accelerated mental states—melancholia and exuberance alternating pretty rapidly and pretty drastically. He'll have to have some outlet for stepped-up muscular energy. Then he'll sleep."

"I'm glad it's over."

"Over?" said Warfield, and went out. She called after him, but he went straight out through the office.

Robin sat up and shook his head violently. "How did—"

Peg took his upper arm. "Sit up, Robin. Up and go." She raised him, but instead of merely sitting up, he rose and pulled away from her. He paced rapidly down the laboratory, turned and came back. His face held that pitiable, puzzled look, with the deep crease between his brows. He walked past her, his eyes distant; then he whirled suddenly on her. His smile was brilliant. "Peg!" he shouted. "I didn't expect to see you here!" His eyes drifted past her face, gazed over her shoulder, and he turned and looked around the walls. "Where, incidentally, is 'here'?"

"Dr. Warfield's laboratory."

"Mel. Oh ... Mel. Yes, of course. I must be getting old."

"Perhaps you are."

He put his hand on his chest, just below his throat. "What would my thymus be doing about now? Trying to think of something quotable to say as its last words?"

"It may be some time," she smiled. "But I imagine it's on its way out. Get your coat on. I'll go home with you."

"What on earth for?"

She considered, and then decided to tell him the truth. "You're full of sterones and hormones and synthetic albuminoids, you know. It isn't dangerous, but glandular balance is a strange thing, and from the treatment you just got you're liable to do anything but levitate—and knowing you," she added, "even that wouldn't surprise me."

"Gosh. I didn't realize that I might be a nuisance to people."

"You didn't realize ... why, there was a pretty fair list of possibilities of what might happen to you in that release you signed."

"There was? I didn't read it."

"Robin English, I don't know what I'm supposed to do with you."

"Haven't you already done it?" he shrugged. "What's the odds? Mel said I'd have to sign it, and I took his word for it."

"I wish," said Peg fervently, "that I could guarantee the change in your sense of values the way I can the change in your hormone adjustment. You're going to have to be educated! And let this be the first lesson—*never* sign anything without reading it first! What are you laughing at, you idiot?"

"I was just thinking how I would stall things if I go to work for some big outfit and have to sign a payroll," he chuckled.

"Get your coat," said Peg, smiling. "And stop your nonsense."

They took a taxi, after all. In spite of Robin's protests, Peg wouldn't chance anything else after Robin:

Nearly fainted on the street from a sudden hunger, and when taken to a restaurant got petulant to the point of abusiveness when he found there was no Tabasco in the place, advancing a brilliant argument with the management to the effect that they should supply same to those who desired it even if what the customer *had* ordered was four pieces of seven-layer cake.

Ran half a block to give a small boy with a runny nose his very expensive embroidered silk handkerchief.

Bumped into a lamp-post, lost his temper and swung at it, fracturing slightly his middle phalanx annularis.

Indulged in a slightly less than admirable remorseful jag in which he recounted a series of petty sins—and some not too petty at that—and cast wistful eyes at the huge wheels of an approaching tractor-trailer.

Went into gales of helpless laughter over Peg's use of the phrase "Signs of the times" and gaspingly explained to her that he was suffering from sinus of the thymus.

And the payoff—the instantaneous composition of eleven verses of an original song concerning one "Stella with the Springy Spine," which was of far too questionable a nature for him to carol at the top of his voice the way he did. She employed a firmness just short of physical force and at last managed to bundle him into a cab, in which he could horrify no one but the driver, who gave Peg a knowing wink which infuriated her.

After getting in his rooms—a feat which required the assistance of Landlady Gridget's passkey, since he had lost his, and the sufferance of a glance of deep suspicion from the good lady—Robin, who had been unnaturally silent for all of eight minutes, shucked off his coat and headed for the studio couch in one continuous movement. He rolled off his feet and onto the couch with his head buried in the cushions.

"Robin—are you all right?"

"Mm-m-m."

She looked about her.

Robin's two-and-kitchenette was a fantastic place. She had never dreamed that the laws of gravity would permit such a piling-up of miscellany. There were two guitars on an easy-chair, one cracked across the head. A clarinet case with little holes punched in it lay on the floor by the wall. Curious, she bent and lifted the lid. It was lined with newspaper, and in it were two desiccated bananas and a live tarantula. She squeaked and dropped the cover.

Leaning against the far wall was a six-foot-square canvas, unfinished, of a dream-scape of rolling hills and pale feathery trees. She looked away, blinked, and looked back. It could have been a mistake.

She sincerely hoped that it was; but it seemed to her that the masses of those hills, and the foliage, made a pretty clear picture of a . . . a—

"No," she whispered. "I haven't got that kind of a mind!"

There was a beautifully finished clay figurine standing proudly amongst a litter of plasticine, modeling tools, a guitar tuner and a flat glass of beer. It was a nude, in an exquisitely taut pose; a girl with her head flung back and a rapt expression on her face, and she was marsupial. On the bookcase was a four-foot model of a kayak made of whalebone and sealskin. Books overflowed the shelves and every table and chair in the place. There were none in the sink; it was too full of dishes, being sung to by a light cloud of fruit flies. It was more than she could stand. She slipped out of her coat, moved a fishbowl with some baby turtles in it, and an 8 mm projector, off the drainboard and went to work. After she had done all the dishes and reorganized the china closet, where ivy was growing, she rummaged a bit and found a spray gun, with which she attacked the fruit flies. It seemed to be a fairly efficient insecticide, although it smelled like banana oil and coagulated all over the sink. It wasn't until the next day that she identified the distinctive odor of it. It was pastel fixatif.

She tiptoed over to the arch and looked in at Robin. He had hardly moved. She knew he was probably good for twelve hours' sleep.

She bent over him and gently pushed some of his rough hair away from his eyes. She had never seen eyes, before, which had such smooth lids.

Robin smiled while he slept. She wished she knew why.

Carefully she removed his shoes. She had to step very close to the couch to do it, and something crunched under her foot. It was a radio tube. She shook her head and sighed, and got a piece of cardboard—there was no dustpan—and a broom and swept up the pieces. Among them she found a stuffed canary and a fifty-dollar bill, both quite covered with "flug," or dust whiskers. She wondered how many times Robin had sat on that couch, over that bill, eating beans out of the can and thinking about some glorious fantasy of his own.

She sighed again and put on her coat. As she reached the door she paused, debating whether, if she left a note anywhere in this monumental clutter, he would find it. She wanted him to call her as soon as he awoke, so she could have an idea as to his prognosis. She knew well that in his condition, with his particular treatment, that the imbalances should be all adjusted within twelve hours. But still—

Then why not wake him and remind him to call?

She suddenly realized that she was afraid to—that she was glad he was asleep and … and harmless. She felt that she could name what it was she was afraid of if she tried. So she didn't try.

"Blast!" she said half aloud. She hated to be hesitant, ever, about anything.

She would leave word with the landlady to wake him early in the morning, she decided abruptly.

She felt like a crawling coward.

She turned to the door, and Robin said brightly, "Goodbye, Peg darling. Thanks for everything. You've been swell. I'll call you when I wake up."

"You young demon!" she ejaculated. "How long have you been awake?"

"I haven't been asleep," he said, coming to the archway. He chuckled. "I'm sorry to say you are right about the canvas. I forgot about the disgusting thing's being so conspicuous."

"Oh, that's all … why did you pretend to be asleep?"

"I felt something coming and didn't want it to."

"I … don't know what you mean; but why didn't you let it come?"

He looked at her somberly. Either it was something new, or she had never noticed the tinge of green in his eyes. "Because you wouldn't have fought me."

"I don't know what you're talking about."

The lower half of his face grinned. "You like most of the things I do," he said. "I like you to humor me in those things. Those things are"—he put his fingertips to his chest, then flung them outward—"like this—fun, from here out. I don't want to be humored from here *in*."

Over his shoulder she saw the big canvas. From this distance it was even more specific. She shuddered.

"Goodbye, Peg."

It was a dismissal. She nodded, and went out, closing the door softly behind her. Then she ran.

Dr. Margaretta Wenzell was highly intelligent, and she was just as sensitive. Twice she appeared at Mel Warfield's laboratory at the hour appointed for Robin's succeeding treatments. Once Robin did not speak to her. The second time she went, Robin did not show up. On inquiry, she learned from the information desk at the medical center that Robin had been there, had asked if she were in Dr. Warfield's office, and having been told that she was, had turned around and walked out. After that she did not go again. She called up Warfield and asked him to forward Robin's case history and each progress report. Mel complied without asking questions; and if Dr. Wenzell spent more time poring over them than their importance justified, it was the only sign she gave that it mattered to her.

It mattered—very much. Never had Peg, in consultation or out, turned a patient over to another doctor before. And yet, she was conscious of a certain relief. Somehow, she was deeply certain that Robin had not ceased to like her. Consciously, she refused to give any importance to his liking for her, but in spite of that she derived a kind of comfort from an arduously-reached conclusion that Robin had reasons of his own for avoiding her, and that they would come out in good time.

She was astonished at the progress reports. She could deduce the probable changes in Robin from the esoteric language of the reaction-listings. Here a sharp drop in the 17-ketosteroids; there a note of the extraordinary effect on the whole metabolism, making it temporarily immune to the depressing effect of the adrenal cortices in colossal overdoses. An entry in the third week of the course caused Peg two sleepless nights of research; the pituitrin production was fluctuating wildly, with no apparent balancing reaction from any other gland—and no appreciable effect on the patient. A supplementary report arrived then, by special messenger, which eased her mind considerably. It showed a slight miscalculation in a biochemical analysis of Robin's blood which almost accounted for the incredible activity of the pituitaries. It continued to worry her, although she knew that she could hardly pretend to criticize Mel Warfield's vast experience in the practice of hormone therapy.

But somehow, somewhere deep inside, she did question something else in Mel. Impersonality had to go very closely with the unpredictable psychosomatic and physiological changes that occurred during gland treatments; and in Robin's case, Peg doubted vaguely that Mel was able to be as detached as might be wished. She tried not to think about it, and was bothered by the effort of trying. And every time she felt able to laugh it off, she would remember Mel's odd statement in the laboratory that day—but then, he had taken such a quick and warm liking to the boy. Could he possibly resent him on her behalf? Again she felt that resurgence of fury at Mel and at herself; and again she wished that she could be left alone; she wanted to laugh at herself in the role of *femme fatale,* but laughter was out of order.

The progress reports were by no means the only source of information about Robin, however. In the tenth day of his treatment, she noticed an item in the "Man About Town" column in the *Daily Blazes.*

> Patrons of the Goose's Neck were treated to a startling sight this AM when Vincent (The Duke) Voisier came tearing into the place, literally bowling over a table-full of customers—and their table—in the process of hauling Vic Hill, songwriter extraordinary, out to the curb. The center of attention out there semed to be a tousled-headed character by the name of Robin English, who told this snooper mildly that Mr. Voisier was going to produce his show. At that moment The Duke and Hill came sailing out of the bistro, scooped up this Robin English and hurled him into a taxicab, leaving your reporter in a cloud of carbon monoxide and wild surmise. Now followers of this column know that Brother Voisier is usually as excitable as the occupant of Slab 3 at the City Morgue. My

> guess is missed if show business isn't about to be shown some business. Voisier is a rich man because of his odd habit of taking no wild chances....

And then there was a letter from a book publisher tactfully asking for a character reference prior to giving one Robin English an advance on an anthology of poems. She answered immediately, giving Robin an A-1 rating, and only after sending it off did she realize that a few short weeks ago she would not have considered such a thing. Robin's reliability was a strange and wonderful structure, and his record likewise.

At long last, then, came his phone call.

"Peg?"

"Wh ... oh, Robin! Robin, how are you?"

"Sharp as a marshmallow, and disgustingly productive. Will you come over?"

"Come over?" she asked stupidly. "Where?"

"Robin's Roost," he chuckled. "My McGee hall closet and bath. Home."

"But Robin, I ... you—"

"Safe as a tomb," he said solemnly.

Something within her rose delightedly at the overtone of amusement in his voice.

"I'm a big grown-up man now," he said. "Restrained, mature, reliable and thoroughly unappetizing. Come over and I won't be anything but repulsive. Impersonal. Detached. No ... say semi-detached. Like a brownstone front. A serious mien. Well, if it's before dinner I'll have a chow mein."

"Stop!" she gasped. "Robin, you're mad! You're delirious!"

"Delirious and repressing, like a certain soft drink. Four o'clock suit you?"

It so happened that it did not. "All right, Robin," she said helplessly, and hung up.

She discovered that she had cleared her afternoon so efficiently that she had time to go home and change. Well, of course she had to change. That princess neckline was—not daring, of course, but—

too demure. That was it; demure. She did not want to be demure. She wanted to be businesslike.

So she changed to a navy sharkskin suit with a wide belt and a starched dicky at the throat, the severest thing in her wardrobe. It was incidental that it fitted like clasped hands, and took two inches off her second dimension and added them to her third. As incidental as Robin's double-take when he saw it; she could almost sense his shifting gears.

"Well!" said Robin as he stepped back from the door. "A mannequin, kin to the manna from heaven. Come *in,* Peg!"

"Do you write your scripts out, Robin? You *can't* generate those things on the spur of the moment!"

"I can for moments like this," he said gallantly, handing her inside.

It was her turn for a double-take. The little apartment was scrupulously clean and neat. Books were in bookcases; it had taken the addition of three more bookcases to accomplish that. A set of shelves had been built in one corner, very cleverly designed to break up the boxlike proportions of the room, and in it were neatly stacked manuscripts and, up above, musical instruments. There was more livestock than ever, but it was in cages and a terrarium—she wondered where the white rats had been on her last visit. Imprisoned in the bathtub, no doubt. There was a huge and gentle pastel of a laughing satyr on the wall. She wondered where the big oil was.

"I painted ol' Splay-foot over it," said Robin.

"You include telepathy among your many talents?" she asked without turning.

"I include a guilty conscience among my many neuroses," he countered. "Sit down."

"I hear you're getting a play produced," she said conversationally, as he deftly set out a beautiful tray of exotic morsels—avocado mashed with garlic juice on little toast squares; stuffed olives sliced paper-thin on zwieback and chive cheese; stems of fennel stuffed with blue cheese; deviled eggs on rounds of pimento; and a strange and lovely dish of oriental cashews in blood-orange pulp.

"It isn't a play. It's a musical."

"Oh? Whose book?"

"Mine."

"Fine, Robin. I read that Vic Hill's doing the lyrics."

"Well, yes. Voisier seemed to think mine were— Well, to tell you the truth, he called in Hill for the name. Got to have a name people know. However, they are my lyrics."

"Robin. Are you letting him—"

"Ah—shush, Peg! No one's doing anything to me!" He laughed. "Sorry. I can't help laughing at the way you, looking like a Vassar p.g., ruffle up like a mother hen. The truth is that I'm getting plenty out of this. There just don't seem to be enough names to go around on the billing. I wrote the silly little thing at one sitting, and filled in the music and staging just to round it off—sort of an overall synopsis. Next thing you know this Voisier is all over me like a tent, wanting me to direct it as well; and since there's a sequence in there—sort of a duet between voice and drums in boogie-beat—that no one seems to be able to do right, he wants me to act that part too." He spread his hands. "Voisier knows what he is doing. Only you can't have one man's name plastered all over the production. The public doesn't take to that kind of thing. Voisier's treating the whole deal like a business. Show business is still business."

"Oh—that's better. And what about this anthology of poems?"

"Oh, that. Stuff I had kicking around the house here." His eyes traveled over the neat shelves and bookcases. "Remarkable what a lot of salable material I had, once I found it by cleaning up some."

"What else did you find?"

"Some gadgets. A centrifugal pump I designed using the business end of a meat grinder for the impeller. A way to take three-dimensional portraits with a head clamp and a swivel chair and a 35 mm camera. A formula for a quick-drying artist's oil pigment which can't contract the paint. A way to drill holes through glass—holes a twenty-five thousandth of an inch or less in diameter—with some scraps of wire and a No. 6 dry cell. You know—odds and ends."

"You've marketed all these?"

"Yes, or patented or copyrighted them."

"Oh Robin, I'm *so* glad! Are you getting results?"

"Am I?" The old, lovely, wondering look came into his face. "Peg, people are crazy. They just give money away. I honestly don't have to think about money any more. That is, I never did; but now I tell people my account number and ask them to send their check to it for deposit, and they keep piling it in, and I can't cash enough checks to keep up with it. When are you going to ask me why I've been keeping away from you?"

The abruptness of the question took Peg's breath away. It was all she had been thinking about, and it was the reason she had accepted his invitation. She colored. "Frankly, I didn't know how to lead up to it."

"You didn't have to lead up to it," he said, smiling gravely. "You know that, Peg."

"I suppose I know it. Well—why?"

"You like the eatments?" He indicated the colorful dishes on the coffee table.

"Delicious, and simply lovely to look at. But—"

"It's like that. This isn't food for hungry people. Canapés like these are carefully designed to appeal to all five senses—if you delight in the crunch of good zwieback the way I do, and include hearing."

She stared at him. "I think I'm being likened to a . . . a smörgasbord!"

He laughed. "The point I'm making is that a hungry man will go for this kind of food as happily as any other. The important thing to him is that it's food. If he happens to like the particular titillations offered by such food as this, he will probably look back on his gobbling with some regret, later, when his appetite for food is satisfied and his psychic—artistic, if you like—hungers can be felt." Robin grinned suddenly. "This is a wayward and wandering analogy, I know; but it does express why I kept away from you."

"It does?"

"Yes, of course. Look, Peg, I can see what's happening to me even if I am the patient. I wonder why so many doctors overlook that? You can play around with my metabolism and my psychology and ultimately affect such an abstract as my emotional maturity. But there's one thing you can't touch—and that is my own estimate of the things I have learned. My sense of values. You can change my approach to these things, but not the things themselves. One such thing is that I have a violent reaction against sordidness, no matter how well justified the sordidness may have been when I did the sordid thing, whatever it was. In the past, primarily the justification has been the important thing. Now—and by 'now' I mean since I started these treatments—the reaction is more important. So I avoid sordidness because I don't want to live through the reaction afterward, and not so much because I dislike doing a sordid thing."

"That's a symptom of maturity," said Peg. "But what has it to do with me?"

"I was hungry," he said simply. "So hungry I couldn't see straight. And suddenly so full of horse sense that I wouldn't reach for the pretty canapés until I could fully appreciate them. And now—sit down, Peg!"

"I . . . have to go," she said in a throttled voice.

"Oh, you're wrong," he said, not moving. He spoke very quietly. "You don't have to go. You haven't been listening to me. You're defensive when I've laid no siege. I have just said that I'm incapable of doing anything in bad taste—that is, anything which will taste bad to me, now or later. And you are behaving as if I had said the opposite. You are thinking with your emotions instead of your intellect."

Slowly, she sank back into her chair. "You take a great deal for granted," she said coldly.

"That, in effect, is what the bread and cheese and pimentos and olives told me when I told them about these trays," he said. "Oh, Peg, let's not quarrel. You know that all I've just said is true. I could candy-coat all my phrases, talk for twice as long, and say half as much; and if I did you'd resent it later; you know you would."

"I rather resent it now."

"Not really." He met her gaze, and held it until she began to smile.

"Robin, you're impossible!"

"Not impossible. Just highly unlikely."

He sprang to pour coffee for her—and how did he know that she preferred coffee to tea? he had both—and he said, "Now we can talk about the other thing that's bothering me. Mel."

"What about Mel?" she said sharply.

He smiled at her tone. "I gather that it's the other thing that's been bothering you?"

She almost swore at him.

"Sorry," he said with his quick grin, and was as quickly sober. "Warfield's very much in love with you, Peg."

"He—has said so."

"Not to me," said Robin. "I'm not intimating that he has poured out his soul to me. But he can't conceal it. What he mostly does is avoid talking about you. Under the circumstances, that begins to be repetitious and—significant." He shrugged. "Thing is, I have found myself a little worried from time to time. About myself."

"Since when did you start worrying about yourself?"

"Perhaps it's symptomatic. This induced maturity that I am beginning to be inflicted with has made me think carefully about a lot of things I used to pass off without a thought. No one can escape the basic urgencies of life—hunger, self-preservation, and so on. At my flightiest moments I was never completely unaware of hunger. The difference between a childish and a mature approach to such a basic seems to be that the child is preoccupied only with an immediate hunger. The adult directs most of his activities to overcoming tomorrow's hunger.

"Self-preservation is another basic that used to worry me not at all as long as danger was invisible. I'd dodge an approaching taxi, but not an approaching winter. Along come a few gland-treatments, and I find myself feeling dangers, not emotionally, and now, but intellectually, and in the future."

"A healthy sign," nodded Peg.

"Perhaps so. Although that intellectual realization is a handy thing to have around to ward off personal catastrophes, it is also the raw material for an anxiety neurosis. I don't think Mel Warfield is trying to kill me, but I think he has reason enough to."

"*What?*" Peg said, horrified.

"Certainly. He loves you. You—" he broke off, and smiled engagingly. She felt her color rising, as she watched his bright eyes, the round bland oval of his almost chinless face.

"Don't say it, Robin," she breathed.

"—you won't marry him," Robin finished easily. "Whom you love needn't enter into the conversation." He laughed. "What amounts of wind we use to avoid the utterance of a couple of syllables! Anyway, let it suffice that Mel, for his own reasons, regards me as a rival, or at least as a stumbling block." His eyes narrowed shrewdly. "I gather that he has also concluded that your chief objection to me has been my . . . ah . . . immaturity. No, Peg, don't bother to answer. So if I am right—and I think I am—he has been put in the unenviable position of working like fury to remove his chief rival's greatest drawback. His only drawback, if you'll forgive the phrase, ma'am," he added, with a twinkle and the tip of an imaginary hat. "No fun for him. And I don't think that Brother Mel is so constituted that he can get any pleasure out of the great sacrifice act."

"I think you're making a mountain out of—"

"Peg, Peg, certainly you know enough about psychology to realize that I am not accusing Mel of being a potential murderer, or even of consciously wanting to hurt me. But the compulsions of the subconscious are not civilized. Your barely expressed annoyance at the man who jostles you in a crowded bus is the civilized outlet to an impulse for raw murder. Your conditioned reflexes keep you from transfixing him with the nearest nail file; but what about the impulses of a man engaged in the subtle complexities of a thing like the glandular overhaul I'm getting? In the bus, your factor of safety with your reactions can run from no visible reaction through a lifted eyebrow to an acid comment, before you reach the point where you give him a tap on the noggin and actually do damage. Whereas Mel's little old subconscious just has to cause his hand to slip while doing a subcutaneous, or to cause his eye to misread a figure on the milligram scale, for me to be disposed of in any several of many horrible ways. Peg! What's the matter?"

Her voice quivering, she said quietly, "That is the most disgusting, conceited, cowardly drivel I have ever had to listen to. Mel Warfield may have the misfortune to be human, but he is one of the finest humans I have ever met. As a scientist, there is no one in this country—probably in the world—more skilled than he. He is also a gentleman, in the good old-fashioned meaning of the word—I *will* say it, no matter how much adolescent sneering you choose to do—and if he is engaged on a case, the case comes first." She rose. "Robin, I have had to take a lot from you, because as a specialist I knew what an advanced condition I had to allow for. That is going to stop. You are going to find out that one of the prices you must pay for the privilege of becoming an adult is the control of the noises your mouth makes."

Robin looked a little startled. "It would be a little dishonest of me to think these things without expressing them."

She went on as if she hadn't heard. "The kind of control I mean has to go back further than the antrums. All of us have mean, cowardly thoughts from time to time. Apparently the maturity you're getting is normal enough that you're developing a man-sized inferiority complex along with it. You are beginning to recognize that Mel is a better man than you'll ever be, and the only way you can rationalize that is to try to make him small enough to be taking advantage of you."

"Holy cow," breathed Robin. "Put down that knout, Peg! I'm not going to make a hobby of taking cracks at Mel Warfield behind his back. I'm just handing it to you straight, the way I see it, for just one reason—to explain why I am discontinuing the course of treatment."

She was halfway to the door as he spoke, and she brought up sharply as if she had been tied by a ten-foot rope. "Robin! You're not going to do anything of the kind!"

"I'm going to do exactly that," said Robin. "I'm not used to lying awake nights worrying about what someone else is likely to do. I'm doing all right. I've come as far in this thing as I intend to go. I'm producing more than I ever did in my life before, and I can live adequately on what I'm getting and will get for this music and these patents and plays and poems, to live for the rest of my life if I quit working tomorrow—and I'm not likely to quit working tomorrow."

"Robin! You're half hysterical! You don't know what you're talking about! In your present condition you can't depend on the biochemical balance of your glandular svstem. It can only be kept balanced artificially, until it gradually adjusts itself to operation without the thymus. In addition, the enormous but balanced overdoses of other gland extracts we have had to give you must be equalized as they recede to normalcy. You simply *can't* stop now!"

"I simply *will* stop now," he said, mimicking her tone. "I took the chance of starting with this treatment, and I'll take the chance of quitting. Don't worry; no matter what happens your beloved Mel's nose is clean, because of that release I signed. I'm not going to sue anybody."

She looked at him wonderingly. "You're really trying to be as offensive as you possibly can, aren't you? I wonder why?"

"It seems the only way for me to put over a point to you," he said irritably. "If you must know, there's another reason. The stuff I'm producing now is good, if I can believe what I read in the papers. It has occurred to me that whatever creativeness I have is largely compounded of the very immaturity you are trying to get rid of. Why should I cut off the supply of irrationality that produces a work of art like my musical comedy? Why should I continue a course of treatment that will ultimately lead me to producing nothing creative? I'm putting my art before my course, that's all."

"A good pun, Robin," said Peg stonily, "but a bad time for it. I think we'll let you stew in your own juice for a while. Watch your diet and your hours, and when you need professional help, get in touch with me and I'll see what I can do about getting Mel to take you on again."

"Nice of you. Why bother?"

"Partly sheer stubbornness; you make it so obvious you want nothing of the kind. Partly professional ethics, a thing which I wouldn't expect a child, however precocious, to understand fully."

He went slowly past her and opened the door. "Goodbye, Dr. Wenzell."

"Goodbye, Robin. And *good* luck."

Later, in her office at the hospital, Peg's phone rang.

"Yes?"

"Peg! I've just received a note, by messenger, from Robin English."

"Mel! What did he say?"

"He enclosed a check for just twice what I billed him for, and he says that he won't be back."

"Mel, is it safe?"

"Of course it's not safe! The pituitary reactions are absolutely unpredictable—you know that. I can't prognosticate anything at all without the seventy-two-hour check-ups. He might be all right; I really wouldn't know. He's strong and healthy and tremendously resilient. But to stop treatment now is taking unfair advantage of his metabolism. Can't you do anything about it?"

"Can't *I* do anything?"

"He'll listen to you, Peg. Try, won't you? I . . . well, in some ways I'm glad to have him off my neck, frankly. It's been . . . but anyway, I'll lose sleep over it, I know I will. Will you see if you can do anything with him?"

A long pause.

"Hello, Peg—are you still there?"

"Yes, Mel . . . let him go. It's what he wants."

"Peg! You . . . you mean you won't see him?"

"N-no, I—can't, Mel, I won't. Don't ask me to."

"I hardly know what to say. Peg, what's the matter?"

"*Nothing's* the matter. I won't see him, that's all, and if I did it wouldn't do any good. I don't care what hap— Oh, Mel, do watch him! Don't let anything . . . I mean, he's *got* to be all right. Read his stuff, Mel. Go see his plays. You'll be able to f-find out that way."

"And if I don't like the looks of what I find out, what am I supposed to do about it?"

"I don't know. I don't know. Call me up whenever you find out anything, Mel."

"I will, Peg. I'm—sorry. I didn't realize that you . . . I mean, I knew it, but I didn't know you felt so—"

"Goodbye, Mel."

She hung up and sat and cried without hiding her face.

Robin's first novel was published five months later, while his musical, *Too Humorous to Mention,* was eight weeks old and just at the brilliant beginning of its incredible run, while *The Cellophane Chalice,* his little, forgotten book of verse, went into its sixth printing, and while three new songs from *Too Humorous* were changing places like the shells in the old army game on the Hit Parade in the one-two-three spots. The title of one of them, "Born Tomorrow," had been bought at an astonishing figure by Hollywood, and royalties were beginning to roll in for Robin's self-tapping back-out drill bits.

The novel was a strange and compelling volume called *Festoon.* The ravings of the three critics who were fortunate enough to read it in manuscript made the title hit the top of the bestseller lists and stay there like a masthead. Robin English was made an honorary doctor of law by a college in Iowa, a Kentucky Colonel, a member of the Lambs Club, and a technical advisor to the American Society of Basement Inventors. He dazedly declined a projected nomination to the State Senate which was backed by a colossal petition; wrote a careful letter of thanks to the municipality of Enumclaw, Washington, for the baroque golden key to the city it sent him because of the fact that early in his life he had been born there; was photographed for the "Young Men of the Month" page of *Pic,* and bought himself a startlingly functional mansion in Westchester County. He wrote a skillful novella which was sold in Boston and banned in Paris, recorded a collection of *muezzin* calls, won a pie-eating contest at the Bucks County Fair, and made a radio address on the evolution of modern poetry which was called one of the most magnificent compositions in the history of the language. He bought a towboat and had a barge built in the most luxurious pleasure-yacht style and turned them over to the city hospital for pleasure cruises to Coney Island for invalid children. Then he disappeared.

He was a legend by then, and there was plenty of copy about him for the columnists and the press agents to run, so that in spite of his prominence, his absence was only gradually felt. But gradually the questions asked in the niteries and on the graveyard shifts at newspaper offices began to tell. Too often reporters came back empty-handed when assigned to a new R. E. story—*any* new R. E. story. An item in the "Man About Town" column led to a few reader's letters, mostly from women, asking his whereabouts; and then there was a landslide of queries. It was worth a stick or two on the front pages, and then it suddenly disappeared from the papers when all the editors were told in a mimeographed letter that Mr. English's business would be handled by his law firm, which had on proud exhibition a complete power of attorney—and which would answer no queries. All business mail was photostated and returned, bearing Robin's rubber-stamped signature and the name of his lawyers. All fan mail was filed.

The categories of men who can disappear in New York are extreme. The very poor can manage it. The very rich can manage it, with care. Robin did it. And then the rumors started. The rôle of "Billy-buffoon" which he had taken in his musical was a mask-and-wig part, and it was said that his understudy didn't work at every performance. English was reported to have been seen in Hollywood; in Russia; dead; and once even on Flatbush Avenue. Robin's extraordinary talents, in the gentle hands of idle rumor, took on fantastic proportions. He was advisor to three cabinet members. He had invented a space drive and was at the moment circling Mars. He was painting a mural in the City Morgue. He was working on an epic novel. He had stumbled on a method for refining U-235 in the average well-equipped kitchen, and was going crazy in trying to conceal that he knew it. He was the author of every anonymous pamphlet cranked out to the public everywhere, from lurid tracts through political apassionatae to out-and-out pornography. And of course murders and robberies were accredited to his capacious reputation. All of these things remained as engagingly fictional as his real activities had been; but since they had nothing like books and plays and inventions to perpetuate them, they faded from the press and from conversation.

But not from the thoughts of a few people. Drs. Wenzell and Warfield compiled and annotated Robin English's case history with as close a psychological analysis as they could manage. Ostensibly, the work was purely one of professional interest; and yet if it led to a rational conclusion as to where he was and what he was doing, who could say that such a conclusion was not the reason for the work? In any case, the book was not published, but rested neatly in the active files of Mel Warfield's case records, and grew. Here a flash of fantasy was a sure sign of suprarenal imbalance, there a line of sober thought was post-pituitary equilibrium. One couldn't know—but then, so little could be known....

Dr. Mellett Warfield was called, late one night, to the hospital, on a hormone case. It was one of the sedative and psychology sessions which he had always found so wearing; this one, however, was worse than usual. The consultation room was just down the corridor from Peg's office—the office into which he used to drop for a chat any time he was nearby. He had not seen the inside of it for three months now; he had not been forbidden to come in, nor had he been invited. Since Robin disappeared, a stretched and silent barrier had existed between the doctors.

And tonight, Mel Warfield had a bad time of it. It wasn't the patient—a tricky case, but not unusual. It was that silent office down the hall, empty now, and dark, empty and dark like Peg's telephone voice these days, like her eyes . . . inside the office it would be empty and dark, but there would be a pencil from her hand, a place on the blotter where she put her elbow when she paused to think of—of whatever she thought, these distant days.

Efficient and hurried, he rid himself of his patient and, leaving the last details to a night nurse, he escaped down the corridor. He was deeply annoyed with himself; that room had been more with him than his patient. That wouldn't do. Realizing this, he also recognized the fact that his recent isolation in his own laboratory had been just as bad, just as much preoccupation, for all the work he had done. "Overcompensation," he muttered to himself, and then wanted to kick himself; here he was dragging out labels to stick on his troubles like a damned parlor psychologist. He opened the half-glazed door and stepped into Peg's office.

He leaned back against the closed door and closed his eyes to accustom them to the dark. Peg seldom used scent, but somehow this room was full of her. He opened his eyes slowly. There was the heavy bookcase, with its prim rows of esoterica, green and gold, black and gold; some twin books, some triplets, some cousins to each other, but all of the same concise family, all pretending to be Fact in spite of having been written by human beings. . . . He shook himself impatiently.

The clock at the end of the desk sent him its dicrotic whisper, and glowed as faintly as it spoke. Half-past three . . . in twelve hours it would be like that again, only Peg would be sitting there, perhaps bowed forward, her chin on one hand, sadly pensive, thinking of—oh, a line of poetry and a ductless gland, a phrase from a song and a great, corrosive worry. If he opened his eyes wide to the desk in the darkness, he could all but see—

She sobbed, and it shocked him so that he cried out, and saw flames.

"Peg!"

Her shock was probably as great, but she made no sound.

"Peg! What is it? Why are you—it's half-past—what are you—" He moved.

"Don't turn on the light," she said grayly.

He went round to her, held out his hands. He thought she shook her head. He let his hands fall and stood stupidly for a moment. Then he knew, somehow, that she was trembling. He dropped on his knees beside her chair and held her close to him. She cried, then.

"You've seen him."

She nodded, moving her wet cheek against his neck. He thought, something has happened, and I've got to know what it it is—I'll go out of my mind if I have to guess. "Peg, what happened?"

She cried. It was hurtful crying, the crying which granulates the eyelids and wrenches the neck-tendons with its sawtoothed, shameless squeaks.

He thought, I'll ask her. I'll ask her right out, the worst possible thing it could be, and it won't be that. And then I'll ask her the next worst thing. He wet his lips. "Did—did he—" But it wouldn't come out that way. "He—asked you—"

She nodded again, her cheekbone hard and hot and wet against him. "I just said yes," she gasped hoarsely. "What else could I say? He knew . . . he must have known. . . ."

Mel Warfield's stomach twisted into a spastic knot, and his stopped breath made thunder in his ears.

He stood up, and spoke to himself levelly, with great care. He spoke silent, balanced things about behaviorism, about things which, after all, happen every day to people. . . . "God damn it!" Peg wasn't people! Peg was—was—

"This is crazy," he said. "This is completely insane, Peg. Listen to me. You're going to tell me the whole thing, every last little rotten detail, right from the very beginning."

"Why?"

"Because I want you to. Because you've got to." A detached part of his mind wondered what he would have to do to make his voice sound like that on purpose.

"If you like," she said, and he knew she was doing it because of him, and not at all for herself.

She had been looking for Robin. She had been looking for him for weeks—near the theaters which were showing his plays, at the libraries, the parks—anywhere. She had admitted to herself that although his development would follow logic of a sort, the logic would be of a kind, or in a direction, that would be beyond her. Therefore a haphazard search was her most direct course. Random radiation can interfere with any frequency. A siren touches every note on any scale.

There is a place in the Village which serves no food or hard liquor, but only wines and champagne. There are divans and easy-chairs and coffee tables; it is more like a living-room, thrice compounded, than a café. Dr. Margaretta Wenzell, bound for an obscure Italian place in the neighborhood whence emanated rumors of spaghetti and green sauce, had yielded to some impulse and found herself ordering a wine cooler here instead.

She sat near the corner and looked at the surprisingly good paintings which filled most of the space between windows. Out of her sight someone stroked a piano with dolorous perfection. Near her a man with a book studied its cover as if he saw all its contents. Opposite, a man with a girl studied her eyes as wordlessly, and as if he saw all her soul.

Peg sipped and felt alone. And then there was a burst of laughter from the hidden corner, and Peg came up out of her chair as if she had been physically snatched. "It wasn't that I recognized his voice," she told Mel, "or even the way it was used. I can't really describe what happened. It was like the impulse which had made me come into the place—a reasonless, vague tugging, the kind of thing that makes you say 'Why not?' . . . it was that, but a thousand times more intense. That's important, because it's one of the few things that shows how he's changed and—and what he is."

She ignored her spilled drink and, like a sleepwalker, went back toward the gentle drumming of voices and the casual piano.

He was there, facing her, leaning forward over a long, low coffee table, his hands—they seemed larger or heavier than she had remembered—spread on it, his head turned to the girl who sat at the end of the chesterfield at his right.

She looked at the girl, at the four other people in the group, at the bored man who played the piano, and back again at Robin and it was only in this second glance that she recognized him, though, oddly, she knew he was there.

He was different. His hair was different—darker, probably because he had used something to control its coarse rebelliousness. His eyes seemed longer, probably because in repose they were now kept narrow. But his face as a whole was the most different thing about him. It was stronger, better proportioned. The old diffidence was gone, gone with the charming bewilderment. But there was charm in the face—a new kind, a charm which she had never associated with him. In that instant of recognition, she knew that she could never couple the words "childish" and "Robin" together again.

She might have spoken, but her voice had quite deserted her. Robin looked up and rose in the same split second, with an apparent understanding of the whole situation and all of her feelings. "Miss Effingwell!" he said joyfully. He was at her side in three long strides, his strong hand under her elbow—and she needed it. "Remember me? I'm Freddy, from the Accounting Department." His left eyelid flickered.

Too faint to think, Peg said, "F-freddy. Of course."

He steered her to the chesterfield, into which she sank gratefully. "Miss Effingwell, I want you to meet my quaffing-cohorts. Left to right, Binnie Morrow, Missouri's gift to show business. Cortlandt—he's a real travelling salesman. Look out."

"I travel in hops," said Cortlandt surprisingly.

"The kind of hops they put in beer," Robin supplemented, and laughed that new, confident laugh again. "And those two gentlemen with spectacles and intense expressions are Doctors Pellegrini and Fels, who are psychiatrists."

"I'm still an intern," said Pellegrini, and blushed. He seemed very young.

"And this," said Robin, indicating a tweedy, thin little woman, "is Miss McCarthy, a member of the second oldest profession."

"He makes it sound very romantic," smiled Miss McCarthy. "Actually I'm a pawnbroker's assistant."

"Her motto is *'In hoc ferplenti,'*" said Robin, and sat down.

"How do you do?" murmured Peg faintly, with a small inclusive smile.

"We were in the middle of a fantastic argument," Robin said. "I just asked for a simple little definition, and caused no end of fireworks."

"Do go on," said Peg. "What were you trying to define?"

"Maturity," said Robin; and immediately, as if to attract attention away from Peg's white twisted face, "Cortlandt, where on earth do you buy your ties?"

The salesman dropped his sandy lashes and pulled up his blazing four-in-hand, which then and there served the only real function of its gorgeous life, by holding the eyes of the party until Peg could calm herself.

"Where were we?" asked Miss McCarthy at length.

"I had just said," answered Binnie Morrow, the showgirl, "that all psychiatrists were crazy." She blushed. It went well with the glossy frame of chestnut hair round her face. "And then Dr. Pellegrini said that he and Dr. Fels were psychiatrists. I'm sorry. I didn't know."

"Don't apologize," said Fels.

"No, don't," said Robin. "If it's true, it's true whether or not we have these madmen in our midst. If it's false, I'm sure they can defend themselves. What about it, Dr. Fels?"

Fels turned to the showgirl. "Why do you think psychiatrists are crazy?"

She twirled the stem of her glasses. "It's the company they keep. The stuff comes off on them."

Pellegrini laughed. "You know, I think you're right! In the clinic, we work in pairs and in groups. That way we can watch each other. Sometimes I think about the influences a psychiatrist must come under when he's on his own, and I get scared."

"What about that?" Robin asked the older doctor.

"I don't worry much. Few neurotics are particularly dominating. There are minor monomaniacs, of course, but many of those just stay on the single track and don't have operating conflicts. It's the ones with internal frictions who come under our hands mostly, and they're full of opposed or nearly opposed forces which work out to overall weakness."

"And immaturity," added Robin.

The salesman looked up. "There's a definition, then," he said. "Turn it around and make it positive, and you define maturity as strength and sanity."

Robin opened his mouth and closed it again. What was so very different about his face?

"Strength and sanity," said Miss McCarthy thoughtfully. "They don't mean anything. Strength—stronger than what? A man is stronger than an ant; an ant can move much more, for its size and weight, than a man can. And sanity—who knows what that is?"

Pellegrini said, "Sanity and maturity are the same thing."

"Are all children insane?" smiled Miss McCarthy.

"You know what I mean," said Pellegrini, almost irritably. "Maturity is the condition achieved when sanity exists within an organism at its ontogenetic peak."

"That'll hold you," grinned Robin.

"It won't hold me," said Cortlandt. "What do you mean by 'ontogenetic peak'? The fullest possible development of function and facilities in the animal concerned?"

"That's right."

Cortlandt shook his sandy head. "Seems to me I read somewhere that, according to comparative anatomies, among warm-blooded animals, homo sapiens is unique in the fact that physically, he dies of old age before he is fully mature."

"That's right," nodded Dr. Fels. "Just as anatomy comparisons indicate that man should have a period of gestation of eleven months instead of nine. The law recognizes that one—did you know? Anyhow, in psychiatry we run into immaturity all the time. I might almost say that our job is primarily to mature our patients ... man is the only animal which stays kittenish all its life. Maturity to a bull gorilla or a full-grown lion is a very serious thing. The basics become very close—procreation, self-preservation, the hunt. There isn't time for the playful amusements which preoccupy most of humanity."

"Ah," said Robin. "Poetry, then, and music and sculpture—they're all the results of the same impulses that make a kitten roll a ball of yarn around?"

Fels hesitated. "I—suppose they are, viewed objectively."

The sandy-haired Cortlandt broke in again. "You just came out with another definition, by implication, Doctor. You said that a psychiatrist's job is primarily to mature his patients. Maturity, then, would be what a psychiatrist would call adjustment?"

"Or psychic balance, or orgastic potency, or 'cured,'" grinned Robin, "depending on his school."

Fels nodded. "That would be maturity."

Miss McCarthy, the pawnbroker's assistant, had spoken next. "I'm interested," she said to Pellegrini, "in what you said a moment ago about the onto—uh—that fullest possible development of function and facilities that you were talking about. If it's true that humans die of old age before they can grow up—then what would one be like if he did fully mature?"

Pellegrini looked startled. The other psychiatrist, Fels, answered. "How can we extrapolate such a thing? It has never happened."

"Hasn't it?" asked Robin quietly. No one heard, apparently, but Peg. *What was so different about his face?*

Cortlandt said, "That's quite a thought. In terms of other animals, your fully developed man would be a silent, predatory, cautious, copulating creature to whom life and living was a deadly serious business."

"No!" said the showgirl unexpectedly and with violence. "You're turning him into a gorilla instead of a making him something better."

"Why must he be something better?" asked Robin.

"He would have to be," said the girl. "I just know it. Maybe he would be like that if he was just an animal; but a man is more than that. A man's got something else that—that—" She floundered to a stop, tried again. "I think he would become like—like Christ."

"Or Leonardo?" mused Cortlandt.

"Well, doctor?" Robin asked Fels.

"Don't ask me," said the psychiatrist testily. "You're out of my field with a thing like this. This is pure fantasy."

Robin grinned broadly. "Is it, now?"

"It is," said Fels, and rose. "If you'll excuse me, it's getting late, and I have a heavy day tomorrow. Coming, Pellegrini?"

The young doctor half-rose, sat down, blushed, and said, "If you don't mind, Fels, I'd just as soon—I mean, I'd kind of like to see where this is leading."

"Into pure fantasy," reiterated Dr. Fels positively. "Come on."

"Dr. Fels makes a good point," said Robin to Pellegrini, not unkindly. "You'd better take his advice."

Bewildered, not knowing whether he had been asked to leave, torn between his obvious respect for Fels and his desire to pursue the subject, Pellegrini got up and left the table. As he turned away, the elder doctor said to Robin, "You, sir, show an astonishing degree of insight. You should have been a psychologist."

Robin waved his hand. "I knew you'd understand me, doctor. Good night."

They all murmured their good-nights. When the psychiatrists were out of earshot, Cortlandt turned to Robin, "Hey," he said, frowning. "Something happened here that I missed. What was it?"

"Yes," said Miss McCarthy. "What did he mean by that remark about your insight?"

Robin laughed richly. "Dr. Fels was guarding the young Dr. Pellegrini against evil influences," he said through his laughter, "and I caught him at it."

"Evil—what are you talking about?" asked Binnie Morrow.

Robin said patiently, "Do you remember what Fels said a while back—that the business of psychiatry is to mature its patients? He's right, you know. A psychiatrist regards emotional balance and maturity as almost the same thing. And a patient who has achieved that kind of balance is one whose inner conflicts are under control. These inner conflicts aren't just born into a person. A clubfoot or a blind eye or a yearning for a womb with a view produce no conflicts *except in terms of other people;* the thing called society. So—" he spread his heavy hands—"what modern psychiatry strives to do is to mature its patients, not in ontogenetic terms, not on an individualized psychosomatic basis, but purely and necessarily in terms of society, which is in itself illogical, unfunctional, and immature."

"That makes sense," said Cortlandt. "Society as a whole gets away with things which are prohibited in any well-run kindergarten, in the violence, greed, injustice, and stupidity departments. We have to wear clothes when the weather's too hot for it; we have to wear the wrong kind of clothes when the weather's too cold. We can be excused of any crime if we do it on a large enough scale. We—but why go on? What was Fels protecting Pellegrini from?"

"Any further consideration of maturity in terms of the individual, completely disregarding society. When we started considering the end-product, the extrapolated curve on the graph, we were considering an end which negates everything that modern psychiatry is and is trying to do. So Fels called it fantasy and cleared out."

"You mean he didn't want Pellegrini's fresh young convictions in the worth of psychiatry upset," said Miss McCarthy sardonically.

"But—" Binnie Morrow's voice was anxious— "you mean that psychiatry and analysis are worthless?"

"No!" Robin exploded. "I didn't say that! The psychos are doing a noble job, considering what they're up against. The fact remains that their chief occupation is in fitting individuals to a smooth survival in a monstrous environment. Fels realizes that very clearly. I don't think Pellegrini does, yet. He will when he's been practicing for as long as Fels. But Fels is right; when a youngster has gone as far as an internship there's no point in shaking him to his roots. Not until he has been practicing long enough to learn the objectivity of competence."

Cortlandt whistled. "I see what Fels meant by your insight."

"Cut it out," smiled Robin. "Let's get back to maturity, just to sum up. Then I have a date with one Morpheus.... Binnie, you said that there's more to a man than his physiology. What's your idea on what a fully developed, truly mature man would be?"

"What I said before," murmured the girl. "Like Christ. Someone who would understand everything, and do what he could for people."

"Cortlandt?"

The salesman shifted his feet. "I don't know. Maybe Binnie's right. Maybe it would be like the grim gorilla, too." He wet his lips. "Maybe both. An extension of the basic urges—hunger and sex and self-preservation, but carried so far that in self-preservation he might try to save humanity purely to keep it from killing him off when everything went to blazes."

"That's interesting," said Robin. "Miss McCarthy?"

"I think," she said slowly, "that he would be something quite beyond our understanding. I think that physically he would be superb—not muscle-bound, no; but balanced and almost impervious to diseases, with the kind of reflexes which would make him almost invulnerable to any physical accident. But the big difference would be in the mind, and I can't describe that. He couldn't describe it himself. If he tried, he would be like a teacher—a really good teacher—trying to teach algebra to a class of well-trained, unusually intelligent—chimpanzees."

"Superman!" said Robin. "Miss Effingwell?"

He looked directly at Peg, who, just in time, checked herself from looking behind her to see whom he was talking to. "M-me?" she squeaked stupidly. "I really don't know, Ro—uh, Freddy. I think Miss McCarthy has the right idea. What do you think?"

Laughing, Robin rose and tossed a bill on the table. "It would be a man with such profound understanding that he could define maturity in a sentence. A simple sentence. He wouldn't be asking other people what they thought. Good night, chillun. Going my way, Miss Effingwell?"

Peg nodded mutely.

"We wus robbed!" Cortlandt called after them. "You have an answer tucked away in your insight, Freddy!"

"Sure I have," winked Robin, "and I'm taking it outsight with me!"

Followed by reverent groans, Robin and Peg departed.

Out on the street, Robin squeezed her upper arm and said, "Hello, Peg. . . ." When he spoke quietly, his voice was almost the same as the one she remembered.

She said, "Oh, Robin—"

"How long have you been looking for me?"

"Three months. Ever since you—"

"Yes. Why?"

"I wanted to know how you were. I wanted to know what was happening to you. Your glands—"

"I can assume your clinical interest. That's not what I meant by *why*. So—why?"

She said nothing. He shrugged. "I know. I just wanted to hear you say it. No—" he said hastily, "don't say it now. I was playing with you. I'm sorry."

The "I'm sorry," was an echo, too. "Where are we going?"

"That depends," said Robin. "We'll talk first."

He led the way across Washington Square South and up wandering West Fourth Street. Around the corner of Barrow Street was a dimly lit restaurant, once a stable, with flagstone flooring and fieldstone walls. The tables were candlelit, the candles set in multicolored holders made of the drippings of the countless candles which had glimmered there before. A speaker, high up, murmured classical music. They found a table and Robin ordered sherry. The sound of his voice brought sharply to her their silence with each other; she had never been silent with Robin before. She felt a togetherness, a sharing, which was a new thing; he was not so evident to her as *they* were, listening to the music and watching the tilt and twist of reflected candle flames in the meniscus of their wine.

When the music permitted, and a little after, she asked, "Where have you been?"

"Nowhere. Right here in New York. And in the back room of my Westchester place. Sandy Hook, for a while. You know—around."

"Why have you been hiding?"

He looked quickly at her and away. "Have I changed?"

"You certainly have."

"A lot," he agreed. "And I knew it. I didn't want anyone else to know it. I didn't want anyone to watch it happen. It's happened fast. It's happening fast. I—I don't know where it's going."

"Have you been sick?"

"Oh, no—well, some aches in my hands and face and feet, and vertigo once in a while. Otherwise I've never been better."

Peg frowned. "Aches . . . what have you been doing?"

"Oh—a little writing. A lot of reading. I holed up in Westchester with all the books I could think of that I'd ever wanted to read. I got right out of myself for a while. Not for long, though."

"What happened?"

"It was strange . . . I got bored. I got so that a paragraph would tell me an author's style, a page would give me the plot . . . maybe if I could have become interested in mathematics or something it would have been different. I was suddenly cursed with a thing you might call hyper-understanding. It made me quit working altogether. There was no challenge in anything. I could do anything I wanted to do. I knew how to do it well. I didn't need to publish anything, or even to write it down. I didn't need approbation. It was pretty bad for a while. I know what failure is like, and the what's-the-use feeling. This was worse. This was what's-the-use—it will succeed."

"I don't know that I understand that," said Peg thoughtfully.

"I hope you never do," he said fervently.

After a pause, she asked, "Then what did you do?"

"What you saw me doing tonight. Starting arguments."

"On maturity?" Suddenly she snapped her fingers. "But of course! I should have realized. You added nothing to that discussion—you just kept the ball rolling. But why, Robin?"

He rubbed his knuckles. "I'm—very alone, Peg. I'm a little like Stapledon's Sirius—I'm the only one of my kind. When I reached a stage of boredom at which I had to find some alternative for suicide, I began to look for something I could have in common with other people. It seemed a slim hope. At first glance, there was nothing which interested me which would interest enough different *kinds* of people to make me want their opinions."

"There's always sex," said Peg facetiously.

"Sex!" he said scornfully. "The American public is basically disinterested in sex."

"*What!* Robin, you're mad! Why, every magazine cover, every plot of every book and movie, practically, shouts sex. How can you say a thing like that?"

"If the public were really interested," he smiled, "do you think they'd need all that high-pressure salesmanship? No, Peg; people are most curious about the same thing that has been bothering me; I happen to be in the odd position of having to face it, which is where I differ from most people."

"Having to face what?"

"Maturity."

She stared at him. "And that's what most people are interested in?"

"Certainly. You heard the argument tonight. I've started the same one hundreds of times recently. It's about all I do, these days. I've heard it knocked around in bars, in parks, in subways and buses and parish houses. Try it yourself. Bear in mind, though, that not everyone calls it maturity. Some call it self-help, and where their self-help will get them; others call it wishful thinking. Coué was preaching maturity; so were Philip Wylie and the Federation of Atomic Scientists and Fletcher, with his disgusting idea of chewing each mouthful of food a hundred times; Santayana and Immanuel Kant and Thoreau and, in their twisted ways, Dr. Townsend and Schopenhauer and Adolf Hitler and Billy Sunday were striving toward maturity insofar as maturity represents a greater goal for humanity, or a part of it . . . it's a sorry mistake to think one part deserves it over the rest. . . ."

"Have you found out what true, complete maturity is?"

"True, complete maturity isn't," he said positively. "But I *think* I know what it would be if it happened along. And don't ask me. If I'm ever absolutely sure, I'll let you know. Now let's talk about you."

"Not yet," she said, "if at all. I want to know first why you are making these rounds."

"Research," he said shortly.

"Certainly you can find more authoritative sources outside of bars and buses."

"Can I? By reading the experts, I found out that with very few exceptions, the more erudite and articulate a man gets, the more he feels that the rest of the world lacks what he has, and that therefore maturity is his condition, immaturity is the state of those less gifted than he. The man on the street talks more sense, though he may do it with less polish. I run into blocks occasionally—remember the hesitant psychiatrist?—and sometimes people in the late thirties confuse 'maturity' with 'middle aged' so thoroughly that they are kept from thinking about it. But by and large a gentle push in the right direction will yield the most astonishing conclusions. A mature man would be a tough, naked swami, perched in the fork of a tree, living an indescribable psycho-cosmic existence. Or he would be a camouflaged man, superficially a nonentity, living with but not of society, leaving it meticulously alone in favor of a private, functional, hyper-sensual existence. Or he would be a mysterious gangster, pulling strings, making and stopping wars for amusement. It's fascinating, Peg. Most people describe maturity as an extension of themselves; some describe it as something hateful and terrible; occasionally one, like that boy Cortlandt tonight, will become objective enough to dream up something like the Messianic gorilla he described." Robin shrugged. "Research."

"I see. And—and you? What's happening to you?"

"I think I'm getting there. I think I'm going to be that thing that has never happened before."

"Let me make some tests," she begged.

Very slowly he put his right hand, palm down, on the table, and said "No." It was the most positive utterance imaginable.

"Robin, why not?"

"Remember my two reasons for quitting the treatments?"

"I remember," she said acidly. "You thought that if you matured any more you'd stop producing your glittering little works of art. And you were afraid of Mel Warfield."

He apparently took no offense, but simply nodded. "They both still apply—transmuted, extended; but still the same two excellent reasons."

"I don't understand. You're not composing or writing or inventing now."

"I'm doing something much bigger. I'm—maturing. Peg," he said with a flash of his old diffidence, "do pardon my colossal immodesty, but there's no other way to phrase it—I myself am becoming a work of art, a deeply important, complex, *significant* thing. I am more completely alive now, I think, in every one of my senses, and in new ways that I'm only beginning to understand, than any man has ever been. You don't want to aid that process. You want it stopped. I'm different now, but not so different that I couldn't be a man among men. My difference will increase, and you are afraid of it, and there's nothing more to your unease than the emotion which makes the brown monkeys tear apart the white one."

"I'm afraid of nothing except that you'll turn into a monster!" she said hotly. "You seem all right now, but you obviously haven't rid yourself of all your childishness. It's childish in the extreme to imagine that nothing bad can happen to you."

"You won't say that," Robin said softly, "when you've heard my definition of maturity."

"Maturity!" she spat. "Do you know what maturity is in a vegetable? It's death. Do you know what maturity is in a simple animal? It's nothing—it's the redivision of immature cells, indefinitely—it's everlasting life, and everlasting immaturity. What are you, that can find something between those extremes?"

"I am Robin English, ex-child, post-adolescent, pre—"

"Go on."

He grinned. "Can't. It's never happened. There's no word for it. Now may we talk about you—aside from endocrinology?"

She gazed at him, her glance touching his cheek, stroking down and back to nestle in the hollow of his neck.

"Remember what I said once," he mused, "about the amounts of wind we waste?"

She nodded. "Let's not."

He grunted approvingly. "I mentioned my senses."

"You said that they were—uh—hyperdeveloped."

"I like 'em," he said, and smiled. "Maybe Cortlandt's super-gorilla was a good guess. I like delicacy—by the bucketful. I don't experiment, I don't probe, I don't instruct, and I don't play around with sensual matters."

"I understand," she said thickly.

"I know what you want."

"I don't doubt it," she said. She was sure that, holding the overhang of the table so tightly, every tiny thread of the tablecloth would leave an impression on her fingers.

"You want devotion, and sharing, and growth-together, and all the other components of that four-letter Anglo-Saxon monosyllable called love."

"You're playing with me again."

"Sorry . . . I can't give you those things. I think you know that. I'm far too preoccupied with my own importance . . . you see? It sounds much more effective when I say it myself! Anyway, do you want as much as I can give you?"

"I think," she whispered, "that you had better be specific. . . ."

In her office, in the dark, as she told it all to Mel Warfield, Peg began to cry again. She tried to hold it in, tried to speak, and then gave up to it altogether.

Mel rose from his perch on the edge of the desk and swore. "Spit it out, Peg," he barked. "So he asked you and you said yes." His fist struck his palm with a frightening snap, like bones breaking. "I wish I *had* killed him. I wish I had the chance now."

"You *what?*" She was shocked out of her tears. "Why?"

"For what he did to you."

She stared at him in the darkness. "That's a new wrinkle in chivalry," she said, with the ghost of her old sense of humor.

"I don't understand you," said Mel irritably.

Suddenly she uttered an extraordinary sound, a sort of attenuated chirp of hysterical laughter. "Mel Warfield, what on earth do you think I—he—just what do you think he did?"

"That is perfectly obvious," he said. "What else could have driven you into such a state?"

Her voice was suddenly clear and cold. "What he asked me, you purblind idiot, was whether I was a virgin. And I said yes. And he looked at me with that damned twinkle in his eyes and said, 'Sorry, Peg.' And then I came straight here and you found me. Now gather up your shiny ideals and that sink you call a mind and take them out of here and leave me alone!"

When Mel had backed off almost to the door, he uttered a grunt, as if from a heavy blow, and then turned and fled.

He called three times before he realized that the hospital switchboard operator's bland "Dr. Wenzell is out, Dr. Warfield" was on Peg's orders. He wrote a letter of apology which she answered after ten days—just *"Let's forget it, Mel,"* on memo paper.

The year grew old, grew cold and died, and a new one rose from its frozen bones, to cling for months to its infantile frigidity. It robbed itself of its childhood, sliding through a blustery summer, and found itself growing old too early. What ides, what cusp, what golden day is a year in its fullness, grown to its maturity? Where is the peak in a certain cycle, the point of farthest travel in a course which starts and ends in ice, or one which ends in dust, or starts and circles, ending in its nascent dream?

The meteor, Robin English, had passed, and the papers put him in their morgues and gave themselves to newer wonders and war-talk. Margaretta Wenzell worked too much and began to grow thin. Mellett Warfield worked too much and began to grow grey. They had nothing to do with each other.

And when Peg burst into his laboratory one grey day, there was a moment when she paused in the doorway, shocked by his appearance as he was shocked by hers. He was gaunt and dishevelled, and she was thin and livid. The moment passed.

"Peg! Why, I'm so—"

"Never mind that," she said crisply. "Look at this." She threw down a glossy eight by ten print.

"What—" he picked it up. It was slightly out of focus, a picture of a man elbowing his way through a crowd. The people around him were craning their necks toward a point off the picture, behind and beyond the grim figure. "It's a blow-up of a picture from this week's *Day Magazine,*" said Peg. "People crowding around a dogfight on 48th Street. That doesn't matter. What does matter is the man who got caught in the crowd."

Warfield flicked the edge of the print in annoyance. "I'd hoped that this visit had something to do with me," he growled.

"It has," she said. "You know who that is?"

"Of course."

"What do you think?"

Mel glanced at the picture again. "Getting to be quite a glamor boy in his old age, isn't he?"

Peg closed her eyes. There was a strange movement of the lids as she rolled the eyes under them. "You call yourself a doctor," she hissed. "Look at his chin."

"Nice chin."

"You don't remember Robin. You don't remember that round baby face."

"I'm not in love with him."

Mel thought she was going to strike him. She jammed the picture under his nose. "Look, look," she breathed.

He sighed and looked. Then he saw what she meant. He went white. "Ac—" His voice failed him.

"Acromegaly," she said.

"Oh, my God."

"We've got to get to him. We've got to arrest that condition before he turns into a monster and dies."

"Why should we arrest the condition?"

"Why? Mel, are you out of your mind? When does your responsibility to a patient end?"

"When the patient stops cooperating."

"I'll find him myself. Somewhere, somehow or other, there's a way to find him. I had hoped you'd help." She turned away.

"I know where he is," he said dully. "I don't see him."

"I don't care. I'm going to every single—you *what?*"

"I've always known." He wet his lips. "He was under some sort of delusion, apparently. A week or so after he quit his treatments he came to see me. He ... explained carefully that he had—uh—no use for you, that there was no longer any reason for me to want to . . . to kill him, and—you don't seem surprised."

"He told me about it."

"You *knew* about that?"

"Did you try to kill him, Mel?"

"It was an accident, Peg. Really it was. And he compensated for it. Splendidly. I don't know how he found out. The man's incredibly sharp."

"It was that post-pituitrin excess, wasn't it?"

"Yes, but that couldn't have anything to do with this—this hypertrophy, I mean—" he faltered— "I don't think so—"

She stared coldly at him. "Take me to him."

"Now?"

"Now."

He looked at her marble face, her set lips, and then slipped into his coat. She said, as he locked his door, "Why didn't you tell me where he was?"

"You didn't ask me. And, frankly, I didn't want you to see him, not as long as he refused to take his treatments."

"You could have let me decide that."

"Why did he let you know where he was?"

"Part of his fixation. He told me I could—uh—kill him any time I wanted to, any way except with my needles. It seemed important to him. Oh, Peg—"

She turned her face away from him. Downstairs, they caught a cab almost immediately, and Warfield gave the driver a Riverside address. Peg sat staring blindly ahead. Mel slumped in a corner and looked at his wrists, dully.

Peg broke the silence only once—to ask in a deceptively conversational voice if anything had been learned that she didn't know about the treatment of acromegaly. Warfield shook his head vaguely. She made a sound, then, like a sob, but when Warfield looked at her she still sat, dry-eyed, staring at the driver's coat collar.

They pulled up in front of one of those stately old cell-blocks of apartment houses that perch on the slanted, winding approaches to the Drive. They got out, and a doorman, a bit over life-size, swung open both leaves of a huge plate-glass-and-bronze door to let them into the building.

"Mr. Wenzell," said Warfield to a wax-faced desk clerk.

"What?" said Peg.

"He . . . it amuses him to use your name," said Warfield, as if he were speaking out of a mouthful of sal ammoniac.

"Mr. Wenzell is out," said the clerk. "Can I take a message?"

"You can take a message right to Mr. Wenzell, who is not out," said Warfield. "Tell him his two doctors are here and must see him."

"Tell him," said Peg clearly, "that Margaretta Wenzell is here."

"Yes, Mrs. Wenzell," said the clerk with alacrity.

"Why must you make this painful as well as unpleasant?" gritted Warfield. Peg smiled with her teeth and said nothing.

The clerk returned from the phone looking as if he had learned how to pronounce a word he had only seen chalked on fences before. "Fourteen. Suite C. The elevators—"

"Yes," growled Warfield. He took Peg's elbow and walked her over to the elevators as if she were a window dummy.

"You're hurting me."

"I'm sorry. I'm—a little upset. Do you have to go through with this weird business?"

She didn't answer. Instead she said, "Stay down here, Mel."

"I will not!"

She looked at him, and said a thousand words—hot-acid ones—in the sweep of her eyes across his face.

"Well," he said, "all right. All right. Tell you what. I'll give you fifteen minutes and then I'm coming up." He paused. "Why are you looking at me like that? What are you thinking about?"

"That corny line about the fifteen minutes. I was thinking about how much better Robin would deliver it."

"I think I hate you," said Warfield hoarsely, quietly.

Peg stepped into the elevator. "That was *much* better done," she said, and pushed the button which closed the doors.

On the fourteenth floor she walked to the door marked "C" and touched the bell. The door swung open instantly.

"Come in!" grated a voice. There was no one standing in the

doorway at all. She hesitated. Then she saw that someone was peering through the crack at the hinge side of the door.

"Come in, Peg!" said the voice. It was used gently now, though it was still gravelly. She stepped through and into the room. The door closed behind her. Robin was there. "Peg! It's *so* good to see you!"

"Hello, Robin," she whispered. Just what gesture she was about to make she would never know for she became suddenly conscious of someone else in the room. She wheeled. There was a girl on the davenport, who rose as Peg faced her. The girl didn't look, somehow, like a person. She looked like too many colors.

"Janice," said Robin. It wasn't an introduction. Robin just said the one word and moved his head slightly. The girl came slowly across the room toward him, passed him, went to the hall closet and took out a coat and hat and a handbag with a long strap. She draped the coat over her arm and opened the door; and then she paused and shot Peg a look of such utter hatred that Peg gasped. The door closed and she was alone with Robin English.

"Is *that* the best you can do," she said, without trying to keep the loathing out of her voice.

"The very best," said Robin equably. "Janice has no conversation. What else she has to recommend her, you can see. She is a great convenience."

A silly, colorful little thought crept into Peg's mind. She looked around the room.

"You're looking for a smörgasbord tray," chuckled Robin, sinking into an easy-chair and regarding her with amusement. "Why won't you look at me?"

Finally, she did.

He was taller, a very little. He was much handsomer. She saw that, and it was as if something festering within her had been lanced. There was pain—but oh! the blessed relief of pressure! His face was— *Oh yes,* said Dr. Wenzell to herself, *pre-pituitary. Acromegaly.* She said, "Let me see your hands."

He raised his eyebrows, and put his hands in his pockets. He shook his head.

Peg turned on her heel and went to the hall closet. She dipped into the pockets of an overcoat, and then into a topcoat, until she found a pair of gloves. She came back into the room, examining them carefully. Robin got to his feet.

"As I thought," she said. She held up the left glove. The seam between the index and second finger was split. And they were new gloves. She threw them aside.

"So you know about that. You would, of course."

"Robin, I don't think this would have happened if you had continued your treatments."

He slowly took out his hands and stared at them. They were lumpy, and the fingers were too long, and a little crooked. "A phenomenal hypertrophy of the bony processes, according to the books," he said. "A development that generally takes years."

"There's nothing normal about this case. There never was," said Peg, her voice thick with pity. "Why did you let it go like this?"

"I got interested in what I was doing." Suddenly he got to his feet and began to stride restlessly about the room. She tried not to look at him, at his altered face, with the heavy, coarse jaw. She strained to catch the remnants of his mellow voice through the harshness she heard now.

"What is it, Robin—Mel? Are you still afraid of Mel Warfield?"

"Hm? Mel ... oh! Mel. I'd almost forgotten. No, Peg, not any more. That was a long time ago. I've been so busy."

"With what?"

He squinted at her, then resumed his pacing. She realized that he was here, and not here. "My mind is working on two levels," he said. "Maybe more."

"Wh—are you telepathic?"

"I don't know. No. I'm—it's too slowly to say it."

"Too hard to say it?"

"Too slowly. It isn't a thing you can say piece by piece. It's a whole picture; you see it all at once and it means something."

"I don't understand."

"No," he said.

"Do you have any palsy, Robin?"

He held up his misshapen hands. They were quite steady. "It isn't Parkinson's disease," he said, again speaking her thought. "My mind is very clear, but only to me. My brain isn't softening. It's—deepening. A Klein bottle has only one surface but can contain a liquid because it has a contiguity through a fourth direction; my mind has five surfaces, so how many different liquids can it contain at once?"

"Robin!"

He made some inner effort that twisted his heavy face. "I've found out what maturity is, Peg," he said.

"Sit down, Robin," she said gently, "and tell me."

"I won't sit down!" he said. He took a turn around the room, and in quite a different voice, said, "What made it so hard to find out was the haziness of the word, and the ambivalence of the human animal. You said that maturity, in a plant, is death. Laurence Manning said that a plant isn't a plant, and a man isn't a man; they are conspiracies of millions of separate cell animals with thousands of separate specialties. Cells mature and die, singly and in great masses; sometimes they reach a full function that is maturity of another kind, and perform it for a long time—microseconds or years ... so maturity is and isn't, all the time, within a man. The unit man, as an animal, has a maturity that can only be an approximation—that would be when most of the specialized cells were doing their cooperative best—not their best, but their cooperative best, within him. And that's maturity in man, but only in man the animal. Man is another thing too. Call it mind, keep it simple. . . ." He paused for a long time, stopped, opened and closed his hands. Peg resisted the impulse to interrupt.

At last Robin said, "Mind is different. When the old man in the Huxley book ate carp-guts and lived for centuries, the mind part died, and he wasn't a mature thing. The mind part does not mature because it can't. It doesn't complete a life with a culminating death like a plant cell, because it doesn't simply exchange nourishment for the performance of a specialty like that. Mind—not brain; mind—works and doesn't work. Some of it has to do with physical living, but most of it does—*other* work. And there's no necessity for this work, no reason to start it, within the animal; and there's no end to it when it does work, no place it cannot go. When is it mature? How high is up?

"But mind leads to wisdoms—precepts for mature conduct within any framework. These are the wisdoms which can produce a mature Democrat or Protestant or stock-broker or husband. And I've found the simple statement of maturity within the largest framework any ordinary human being can know. It is simple—all the wisdoms are simple, because, for their fields, they are basic. I'll tell you—"

He stopped, his great head up, listening. Peg heard nothing. "—later," Robin finished. The door-buzzer shrilled.

"Come in!"

"Peg!" Mel Warfield all but ran in. "Are you all right?"

"Hello, Mel."

Warfield spun. The change from frantic male to absorbed physician was so swift it would have been comic anywhere else. "Robin!" His eyes flickered to the face, the hands, the feet, which were in cut slippers. "You know what that condition is?"

"He knows," said Peg.

"Saving no one's presence," said Mel Warfield. "There are three damned fools in this room. English, we might be able to arrest that condition; we might even—well, I can't promise too much, you understand, but if you'll only start treatment again, we might at least—"

He was interrupted by quite the most horrible sound Peg had ever heard—a burst of thunderous laughter from Robin's distorted throat. "Sure, Mel, sure. Glad to."

"Robin!" cried Peg. "You will?"

He laughed again. "Of course I will. I'm—mature enough to know what to do. Not today, though. Tomorrow all right?"

"Fine, fine," said Mel. He looked as if some great burden had been lifted from him—something that had been strapped to his whole body. "Ten o'clock at my place—I'll have everything ready. We'll run the most exhaustive set of tests on you that can be found this side of the Mayo Clinic."

"I can't be sure about the time." Robin went to the desk in the corner. "My number's unlisted," he said, writing rapidly on a sheet of note-paper. He folded it, folded it again. "Call me tonight or in the morning, just to make sure." He chuckled again. "I feel better already. Arrest the condition? It will be easy . . . you've never had a mature patient before." He slipped the paper into Peg's envelope hand-bag, and laughed again.

"Is there a joke?" Peg asked painfully.

"Sorry . . . no, it isn't a joke. But the huge relief . . . I see an end at last to a thing that seemed to have none, a final adjustment of the two factors I mentioned, one of which is an approximation, and the other a thing with no upper limits. Why do you hate each other?"

Warfield sucked in his breath and looked at Peg. Peg looked at her feet.

"I have been my own damnation," said Robin, "like most damned souls. There isn't a thing you could have done to prevent it. Mel once made an honest mistake, and it wasn't even a serious one. Peg, you have no right to assume that it was made through a single motive, and that a base one. Nature never shows one motive or one law at a time, unaffected by any other. And Mel—to hate Peg because of the things she has felt is like hating a man for moving when a tornado has taken him away. I—want to say something like 'Bless you, my children.' Now get out of here. You'll see me soon enough."

He herded them toward the door. Mel, feeling that there was something unsaid, something important, unable to think clearly because of the sudden rush, tried to gain a moment. "When would be the best time to call?"

"You'll know. Hurry, now. I have things to do."

Through the closing door, Peg got a last glimpse of Robin's face, distorted and handsome, slipping into an inward-turning relaxation as he let go the concentration that he had assumed shortly after she had arrived. *Like a man leaving children,* she thought.

In the elevator, with wonder in his voice, Mel said, "He thinks he's mature. He's just—just sick. Sick and old."

"I don't know what he is," Peg said wearily. "Some of what he said sounded like a delirium. And yet—I suppose a discussion of the Döppler shift would sound fairly delirious to a fourth-grade child.

I don't know, Mel, I just don't know. I can't think. . . . He seems—quite sure. . . ."

"We'll do what we can," said Mel. The doors slid open. "Peg—"

"Shh." She took his arm.

Robin English had talents and, lately, skills.

His will divided a large fortune between Drs. Wenzell and Warfield. His body and his brain were a mystery and a treasure to the institute to which he donated them. The mystery lay in the cause of death; the body was aberrated but still healthy, and it had simply stopped. A skill . . . Robin English was not the first man in the world to have that power, nor the only one. All men have it to a degree; the will to live is its complement, and daily works greater miracles than this simple thing of saying "Stop."

There was a terrible time when Peg and Mel burst back into the apartment on Riverside Drive, and after. But when enough time had gone by, it was all part of the many things they shared, and sharing is good. They shared their pain and their pleasure in their memories of him, as they shared an ineradicable sense of guilt. In due season they shared an understanding of Robin's death; it came to them that his decision to die had been made with his frightening burst of laughter, that day. Later still they understood his reason, though that took longer, in spite of the fact that he had written it on the paper he had tucked into Peg's handbag.

And they share, now, the simple wisdom he wrote; not a definition of maturity, but a delineation of the Grail in which it is contained:

"Enough is maturity—"

Tiny and the Monster

SHE *had* TO find out about Tiny—*everything* about Tiny.

They were bound to call him Tiny. The name was good for a laugh when he was a pup, and many times afterward.

He was a Great Dane, unfashionable with his long tail, smooth and glossy in the brown coat which fit so snugly over his heavily muscled shoulders and chest. His eyes were big and brown and his feet were big and black; he had a voice like thunder and a heart ten times his own great size.

He was born in the Virgin Islands, on St. Croix, which is a land of palm trees and sugar, of soft winds and luxuriant undergrowth whispering with the stealthy passage of pheasant and mongoose. There were rats in the ruins of the ancient estate houses that stood among the foothills—ruins with slave-built walls forty inches thick and great arches of weathered stone. There was pasture land where the field mice ran, and brooks asparkle with gaudy blue minnows.

But where in St. Croix had he learned to be so strange?

When Tiny was a puppy, all feet and ears, he learned many things. Most of these things were kinds of respect. He learned to respect that swift, vengeful piece of utter engineering called a scorpion when one of them whipped its barbed tail into his inquiring nose. He learned to respect the heavy deadness of the air about him that preceded a hurricane, for he knew that it meant hurry and hammering and utmost obedience from every creature on the estate. He learned to respect the justice of sharing, for he was pulled from the teat and from the trough when he crowded the others of his litter. He was the largest.

These things, all of them, he learned as respects. He was never struck, and although he learned caution he never learned fear. The pain he suffered from the scorpion—it happened only once—the strong but gentle hands which curbed his greed, the frightful violence of the hurricane that followed the tense preparations—all these things and many more taught him the justice of respect. He half understood a basic ethic: namely, that he would never be asked to do something, or to refrain from doing something, unless there was a good reason for it. His obedience, then, was a thing implicit, for it was half reasoned; and since it was not based on fear, but on justice, it could not interfere with his resourcefulness.

All of which, along with his blood, explained why he was such a splendid animal. It did not explain how he learned to read. It did not explain why Alec was compelled to sell him—not only to sell him but to search out Alistair Forsythe and sell him to her.

She *had* to find out. The whole thing was crazy. She hadn't wanted a dog. If she had wanted a dog, it wouldn't have been a Great Dane. And if it had been a Great Dane, it wouldn't have been Tiny, for he was a Crucian dog and had to be shipped all the way to Scarsdale, New York, by air.

The series of letters she sent to Alec were as full of wondering persuasion as his had been when he sold her the dog. It was through these letters that she learned about the scorpion and the hurricane, about Tiny's puppyhood and the way Alec brought up his dogs. If she learned something about Alec as well, that was understandable. Alec and Alistair Forsythe had never met, but through Tiny they shared a greater secret than many people who have grown up together.

"As for why I wrote you, of all people," Alec wrote in answer to her direct question, "I can't say I chose you at all. It was Tiny. One of the cruise-boat people mentioned your name at my place, over cocktails one afternoon. It was, as I remember, a Dr. Schwellenbach. Nice old fellow. As soon as your name was mentioned, Tiny's head came up as if I had called him. He got up from his station by the door and lolloped over to the doctor with his ears up and his nose quivering. I thought for a minute that the old fellow was offering him food, but no—he must have wanted to hear Schwellenbach say your name again. So I asked about you. A day or so later I was telling a couple of friends about it, and when I mentioned the name again, Tiny came snuffling over and shoved his nose into my hand. He was shivering. That got me. I wrote to a friend in New York who got your name and address in the phone book. You know the rest. I just wanted to tell you about it at first, but something made me suggest a sale. Somehow, it didn't seem right to have something like this going on and not have you meet Tiny. When you wrote that you couldn't get away from New York, there didn't seem to be anything else to do but send Tiny to you. And now—I don't know if I'm too happy about it. Judging from those pages and pages of questions you keep sending me, I get the idea that you are more than a little troubled by this crazy business."

She answered, "*Please* don't think I'm troubled about this! I'm not. I'm interested, and curious, and more than a little excited; but there is nothing about the situation that frightens me. I can't stress that enough. There's something around Tiny—sometimes I have the feeling it's something outside Tiny—that is infinitely comforting. I feel protected, in a strange way, and it's a different and greater thing than the protection I could expect from a large and intelligent dog. It's strange, and it's mysterious enough; but it isn't at all frightening.

"I have some more questions. Can you remember exactly what it was that Dr. Schwellenbach said the first time he mentioned my name and Tiny acted strangely? Was there ever any time that you can remember when Tiny was under some influence other than your own, something which might have given him these strange traits? What about his diet as a puppy? How many times did he get . . ." and so on.

And Alec answered, in part, "It was so long ago now that I can't remember exactly; but it seems to me Dr. Schwellenbach was talking about his work. As you know, he's a professor of metallurgy. He mentioned Professor Nowland as the greatest alloy specialist of his time—said Nowland could alloy anything with anything. Then he went on about Nowland's assistant. Said the assistant was very highly qualified, having been one of these Science Search products and something of a prodigy; in spite of which she was completely feminine and as beautiful a redhead as had ever exchanged heaven for earth. Then he said her name was Alistair Forsythe. (I hope you're not blushing, Miss Forsythe; you asked for this!) And then it was that

Tiny ran over to the doctor in that extraordinary way.

"The only time I can think of when Tiny was off the estate and possibly under some influence was the day old Debbil disappeared for a whole day with the pup when he was about three months old. Debbil is one of the characters who hang around here. He's a Crucian about sixty years old, a piratical-looking old gent with one eye and elephantiasis. He shuffles around the grounds running odd errands for anyone who will give him tobacco or a shot of white rum. Well, one morning I sent him over the hill to see if there was a leak in the water line that runs from the reservoir. It would only take a couple of hours, so I told him to take Tiny for a run.

"They were gone for the whole day. I was short-handed and busy as a squirrel in a nuthouse and didn't have a chance to send anyone after him. But he drifted in toward evening. I bawled him out thoroughly. It was no use asking him where he had been; he's only about quarter-witted anyway. He just claimed he couldn't remember, which is pretty usual for him. But for the next three days I was busy with Tiny. He wouldn't eat, and he hardly slept at all. He just kept staring out over the cane fields at the hill. He didn't seem to want to go there at all. I went out to have a look. There's nothing out that way but the reservoir and the old ruins of the governor's palace, which have been rotting there in the sun for the last century and a half. Nothing left now but an overgrown mound and a couple of arches, but it's supposed to be haunted. I forgot about it after that because Tiny got back to normal. As a matter of fact, he seemed to be better than ever, although, from then on, he would sometimes freeze and watch the hill as if he were listening to something. I haven't attached much importance to it until now. I still don't. Maybe he got chased by some mongoose's mother. Maybe he chewed up some ganja-weed—marijuana to you. But I doubt that it has anything to do with the way he acts now, any more than that business of the compasses that pointed west might have something to do with it. Did you hear about that, by the way? Craziest thing I ever heard of. It was right after I shipped Tiny off to you last fall, as I remember. Every ship and boat and plane from here to Sandy Hook reported that its compass began to indicate due west instead of a magnetic north! Fortunately the effect only lasted a couple of hours so there were no serious difficulties. One cruise steamer ran aground, and there were a couple of Miami fishing-boat mishaps. I only bring it up to remind both of us that Tiny's behavior may be odd, but not exclusively so in a world where such things as the crazy compasses occur."

And in her next, she wrote. "You're quite the philosopher, aren't you? Be careful of that Fortean attitude, my tropical friend. It tends to accept the idea of the unexplainable to an extent where explaining, or even investigating, begins to look useless. As far as that crazy compass episode is concerned, I remember it very well indeed. My boss, Dr. Nowland—yes, it's true, he can alloy anything with anything!—has been up to his ears in that fantastic happenstance. So have most of his colleagues in half a dozen sciences. They're able to explain it quite satisfactorily, too. It was simply the presence of some quite quasi-magnetic phenomenon that created a resultant field at right angles to the earth's own magnetic influence. That solution sent the pure theorists home happy. Of course, the practical ones—Nowland and his associates in metallurgy, for example—only have to figure out what caused the field. Science is a wonderful thing.

"By the way, you will notice my change of address. I have wanted for a long time to have a little house of my own, and I was lucky enough to get this one from a friend. It's up the Hudson from New York, quite countrified, but convenient enough to the city to be practical. I'm bringing Mother here from Upstate. She'll love it. And besides—as if you didn't know the most important reason when you saw it—it gives Tiny a place to run. He's no city dog.... I'd tell you that he found the house for me, too, if I didn't think that, these days, I'm crediting him with even more than his remarkable powers. Gregg and Marie Weems, the couple who had the cottage before, began to be haunted. So they said, anyway. Some indescribably horrible monster that both of them caught glimpses of, inside the house and out of it. Marie finally got the screaming meemies about it and insisted on Gregg's selling the place, housing shortage or no. They came straight to me. Why? Because they—Marie, anyway; she's a mystic little thing—had the idea that someone with a large dog would be safe in that house. The odd part of that was that neither of them knew I had recently acquired a Great Dane. As soon as they saw Tiny they threw themselves on my neck and begged me to take the place. Marie couldn't explain the feeling she had; what she and Gregg came to my place for was to ask me to buy a big dog and take the house. Why me? Well, she just felt I would like it, that was all. It seemed the right kind of place for me. And my having the dog clinched it. Anyway, you can put that down in your notebook of unexplainables."

So it went for the better part of a year. The letters were long and frequent, and, as sometimes happens, Alec and Alistair grew very close indeed. Almost by accident they found themselves writing letters that did not mention Tiny at all, although there were others that concerned nothing else. And, of course, Tiny was not always in the role of *canis superior.* He was a dog—all dog—and acted accordingly. His strangeness came out only at particular intervals. At first it had been at times when Alistair was most susceptible to being astonished by it—in other words, when it was least expected. Later, he would perform his odd feats when she was ready for him to do it, and under exactly the right circumstances. Later still, he became the superdog only when she asked him to....

The cottage was on a hillside, such a very steep hillside that the view of the river skipped over the railroad, and the trains were a secret rumble and never a sight at all. There was a wild and clean air about the place—a perpetual tingle of expectancy, as though someone coming into New York for the very first time on one of the trains had thrown his joyous anticipation high in the air and the cottage had caught it and breathed it and kept it forever.

Up the hairpin driveway to the house, one spring afternoon, toiled a miniature automobile in its lowest gear. Its little motor grunted and moaned as it took the last steep grade, a miniature Old Faithful appearing around its radiator cap. At the foot of the brownstone porch steps it stopped, and a miniature lady slid out from under the wheel. But for the fact that she was wearing an aviation mechanic's coveralls, and that her very first remark—an earthy epithet directed at the steaming radiator—was neither ladylike nor miniature, she might have been a model for the more precious variety of Mother's Day greeting card.

Fuming, she reached into the car and pressed the horn button. The quavering wail that resulted had its desired effect. It was answered instantly by the mighty howl of a Great Dane at the peak of aural agony. The door of the house crashed open and a girl in shorts and a halter rushed out on the porch, to stand with her russet hair ablaze in the sunlight, her lips parted, and her long eyes squinting against the light reflected from the river.

"What— Mother! Mother, darling, is that you? Already? Tiny!" she rapped as the dog bolted out of the open door and down the steps. "Come back here!"

The dog stopped. Mrs. Forsythe scooped a crescent wrench from the ledge behind the driver's seat and brandished it. "Let him come, Alistair," she said grimly. "In the name of sense, girl, what are you doing with a monster like that? I thought you said you had a dog, not a Shetland pony with fangs. If he messes with me, I'll separate him from a couple of those twelve-pound feet and bring him down to my weight. Where do you keep his saddle? I thought there was a meat shortage in this part of the country. Whatever possessed you to take up your abode with that carnivorous dromedary, anyway? And what's the idea of buying a barn like this, thirty miles from nowhere and perched on a precipice to boot, with a stepladder for a driveway and an altitude fit to boil water at eighty degrees Centigrade? It must take you forever to make breakfast. Twenty-minute eggs, and then they're raw. I'm hungry. If that Danish basilisk hasn't eaten everything in sight, I'd like to nibble on about eight sandwiches. Salami on whole wheat. Your flowers are gorgeous, child. So are you. You always were, of course. Pity you have brains. If you had no brains, you'd get married. A lovely view, honey, lovely. I like it here. Glad you bought it. Come here, you," she said to Tiny.

He approached this small specimen of volubility with his head a little low and his tail down. She extended a hand and held it still to let him sniff it before she thumped him on the withers. He waved his unfashionable tail in acceptance and then went to join the laughing Alistair, who was coming down the steps.

"Mother, you're marvelous." She bent and kissed her. "What on earth made that awful noise?"

"Noise? Oh, the horn." Mrs. Forsythe busily went about lifting the hood of the car. "I have a friend in the shoelace business. Wanted to stimulate trade for him. Fixed this up to make people jump out of their shoes. When they jump they break the laces. Leave their shoes in the street. Thousands of people walking about in their stocking feet. More people ought to, anyway. Good for the arches." She pointed. There were four big air-driven horns mounted on and around the little motor. Over the mouth of each was a shutter, so arranged that it revolved about an axle set at right angles to the horn, so that the bell was opened and closed by four small DC motors. "That's what gives it the warble. As for the beat-note, the four of them are tuned a sixteenth-tone apart. Pretty?"

"Pretty," Alistair conceded with sincerity. "No, please don't demonstrate it again, Mother! You almost wrenched poor Tiny's ears off the first time."

"Oh, did I?" Contritely she went to the dog. "I didn't mean to, honey-poodle, really I didn't." The honey-poodle looked up at her with somber brown eyes and thumped his tail on the ground. "I like him," said Mrs. Forsythe decisively. She put out a fearless hand and pulled affectionately at the loose flesh of Tiny's upper lip. "Will you look at those tusks! Good grief, dog, reel in some of that tongue or you'll turn yourself inside out. Why aren't you married yet, chicken?"

"Why aren't you?" Alistair countered.

Mrs. Forsythe stretched. "I've *been* married," she said, and Alistair knew that now her casualness was forced. "A married season with the likes of Dan Forsythe sticks with you." Her voice softened. "Your daddy was all kinds of good people, baby." She shook herself. "Let's eat. I want to hear about Tiny. Your driblets and drablets of information about that dog are as tantalizing as Chapter Eleven of a movie serial. Who's this Alec creature in St. Croix? Some kind of native—cannibal, or something? He sounds nice. I wonder if you know how nice *you* think he is? Good heavens, the girl's blushing! I only know what I read in your letters, darling, and I never knew you to quote anyone by the paragraph before but that old scoundrel

Nowland, and that was all about ductility and permeability and melting points. Metallurgy! A girl like you mucking about with molybs and durals instead of heartbeats and hope chests!"

"Mother, sweetheart, hasn't it occurred to you at all that I don't *want* to get married? Not yet, anyway."

"Of course it has. That doesn't alter the fact that a woman is only forty percent a woman until someone loves her, and only eighty percent a woman until she has children. As for you and your precious career, I seem to remember something about a certain Marie Sklodowska who didn't mind marrying a fellow called Curie, science or no science."

"Darling," said Alistair a little tiredly as they mounted the steps and went into the cool house, "once and for all, get this straight. The career, as such, doesn't matter at all. The work does. I like it. I don't see the sense of being married purely for the sake of being married."

"Oh, for heaven's sake, child, neither do I," said Mrs. Forsythe quickly. Then, casting a critical eye over her daughter, she sighed, "But it's such a waste."

"What do you mean?"

Her mother shook her head. "If you don't get it, it's because there's something wrong with your sense of values, in which case there's no point in arguing. I love your furniture. Now, for pity's sake feed me and tell me about this canine Carnera of yours."

Moving deftly about the kitchen while her mother perched like a bright-eyed bird on a utility ladder, Alistair told the story of her letters from Alec and Tiny's arrival.

"At first he was just a dog. A very wonderful dog, of course, and extremely well trained. We got along beautifully. There was nothing remarkable about him but his history, as far as I could see, and certainly no indication of . . . of anything. I mean, he might have responded to my name the way he did because the syllabic content pleased him."

"It should," said her mother complacently. "Dan and I spent weeks at a sound laboratory graphing a suitable name for you. Alistair

Forsythe. Has a beat, you know. Keep that in mind when you change it."

"Mother!"

"All right, dear. Go on with the story."

"For all I knew, the whole thing was a crazy coincidence. Tiny didn't respond particularly to the sound of my name after he got here. He seemed to take a perfectly normal, doggy pleasure in sticking around, that was all.

"Then, one evening after he had been with me about a month, I found out he could read."

"Read!" Mrs. Forsythe toppled, clutched the edge of the sink, and righted herself.

"Well, practically that. I used to study a lot in the evenings, and Tiny used to stretch out in front of the fire with his nose between his paws and watch me. I was tickled by that. I even got the habit of talking to him while I studied. I mean, about the work. He always seemed to be paying very close attention, which, of course, was silly. And maybe it was my imagination, but the times he'd get up and nuzzle me always seemed to be the times when my mind was wandering or when I would quit working and go on to something else.

"This particular evening I was working on the permeability mathematics of certain of the rare-earth group. I put down my pencil and reached for my *Handbook of Chemistry and Physics* and found nothing but a big hole in the bookcase. The book wasn't on the desk, either. So I swung around to Tiny and said, just for something to say, 'Tiny, what have you done with my handbook?'

"He went *whuff,* in the most startled tone of voice, leaped to his feet, and went over to his bed. He turned up the mattress with his paw and scooped out the book. He picked it up in his jaws—I wonder what he would have done if he were a Scotty; that's a chunky piece of literature!—and brought it to me.

"I just didn't know what to do. I took the book and riffled it. It was pretty well shoved around. Apparently he had been trying to leaf through it with those big splay feet of his. I put the book down and took him by the muzzle. I called him nine kinds of a rascal and asked him what he was looking for." She paused, building a sandwich.

"Well?"

"Oh," said Alistair, as if coming back from a far distance. "He didn't say."

There was a thoughtful silence. Finally Mrs. Forsythe looked up with her odd birdlike glance and said, "You're kidding. That dog isn't shaggy enough."

"You don't believe me." It wasn't a question.

The older woman got up to put a hand on the girl's shoulder. "Honey-lamb, your daddy used to say that the only things worth believing were things you learned from people you trusted. Of course I believe you. Thing is—do *you* believe you?"

"I'm not—sick, Mum, if that's what you mean. Let me tell you the rest of it."

"You mean there's more?"

"Plenty more." She put the stack of sandwiches on the sideboard where her mother could reach it. Mrs. Forsythe fell to with a will. "Tiny has been goading me to do research. A particular kind of research."

"Hut hine uffefa?"

"Mother! I didn't give you those sandwiches just to feed you. The idea was to soundproof you a bit, too, while I talked."

"Hohay!" said her mother cheerfully.

"Well, Tiny won't let me work on any other project but the one he's interested in. Mum, I can't talk if you're going to gape like that! No ... I can't say he won't let me do *any* work. But there's a certain line of endeavor that he approves. If I do anything else, he snuffles around, joggles my elbow, grunts, whimpers, and generally carries on until I lose my temper and tell him to go away. Then he'll walk over to the fireplace and flop down and sulk. Never takes his eyes off me. So, of course, I get all soft-hearted and repentant and apologize to him and get on with what he wants done."

Mrs. Forsythe swallowed, coughed, gulped some milk, and exploded, "Wait a minute, you're away too fast for me! What is it that he wants done? How do you know he wants it? Can he read, or can't he? Make some sense, child!"

Alistair laughed richly. "Poor Mum. I don't blame you, darling. No, I don't think he can really read. He shows no interest at all in books or pictures. The episode with the handbook seemed to be an experiment that didn't bring any results. *But*—he knows the difference between my books, even books that are bound alike, even when I shift them around in the bookcase. Tiny!"

The Great Dane scrambled to his feet from the corner of the kitchen, his paws skidding on the waxed linoleum. "Get me Hoag's *Basic Radio,* old feller, will you?"

Tiny turned and padded out. They heard him going up the stairs.

"I was afraid he wouldn't do it while you were here," she said. "He generally warns me not to say anything about his powers. He growls. He did that when Dr. Nowland dropped out for lunch one Saturday. I started to talk about Tiny and just couldn't. He acted disgracefully. First he growled and then he barked. It was the first time I've ever known him to bark in the house. Poor Dr. Nowland. He was scared half out of his wits."

Tiny thudded down the stairs and entered the kitchen. "Give it to Mum," said Alistair. Tiny walked sedately over to the stool and stood before the astonished Mrs. Forsythe. She took the volume from his jaws.

"*Basic Radio,*" she breathed.

"I asked him for that because I have a whole row of technical books up there, all from the same publisher, all the same color and about the same size," said Alistair calmly.

"But . . . but . . . how does he do it?"

Alistair shrugged. "I don't know. He doesn't read the titles. That I'm sure of. He can't read anything. I've tried to get him to do it a dozen different ways. I've lettered instructions on pieces of paper and shown them to him—you know, 'Go to the door' and 'Give me a kiss' and so on. He just looks at them and wags his tail. But if I read them first—"

"You mean, read them aloud?"

"No. Oh, he'll do anything I ask him to, sure. But I don't have to say it. Just read it, and he turns and does it. That's the way he makes me study what he wants studied."

"Are you telling me that behemoth can read your mind?"

"What do you think? Here, I'll show you. Give me the book."

Tiny's ears went up. "There's something in here about the electrical flux in supercooled copper that I don't quite remember. Let's see if Tiny's interested."

She sat on the kitchen table and began to leaf through the book. Tiny came and sat in front of her, his tongue lolling out, his big brown eyes fixed on her face. There was silence as she turned pages, read a little, turned some more. And suddenly Tiny whimpered urgently.

"See what I mean, Mum? All right, Tiny. I'll read it over."

Silence again, while Alistair's long green eyes traveled over the page. All at once Tiny stood up and nuzzled her leg.

"Hm-m-m? The reference? Want me to go back?"

Tiny sat again, expectantly. "There's a reference here to a passage in the first section on basic electric theory that he wants," she explained. She looked up. "Mother, you read it to him." She jumped off the table, handed the book over. "Here. Section forty-five. Tiny! Go listen to Mum. Go on," and she shoved him towards Mrs. Forsythe, who said in an awed voice, "When I was a little girl, I used to read bedtime stories to my dolls. I thought I'd quit that kind of thing altogether, and now I'm reading technical literature to this ... this canine catastrophe here. Shall I read aloud?"

"No, don't. See if he gets it."

But Mrs. Forsythe didn't get the chance. Before she had read two lines Tiny was frantic. He ran to Mrs. Forsythe and back to Alistair. He reared up like a frightened horse, rolled his eyes, and panted. He whimpered. He growled a little.

"For pity's sakes, what's wrong?"

"I guess he can't get it from you," said Alistair. "I've had the idea before that he's tuned to me in more ways than one, and this clinches it. All right, then. Give me back the—"

But before she could ask him, Tiny had bounded to Mrs. Forsythe, taken the book gently out of her hands, and carried it to his mistress. Alistair smiled at her paling mother, took the book, and read until Tiny suddenly seemed to lose interest. He went back to his station by the kitchen cabinet and lay down, yawning.

"That's that," said Alistair, closing the book. "In other words, class dismissed. Well, Mum?"

Mrs. Forsythe opened her mouth, closed it again, and shook her head. Alistair loosed a peal of laughter.

"Oh, Mum," she gurgled through her laughter. "History has been made. Mum, darling, you're speechless!"

"I am not," said Mrs. Forsythe gruffly. "I ... I think ... well, what do you know! You're right! I *am!*"

When they had their breath back—yes, Mrs. Forsythe joined in, for Alistair's statement was indeed true—Alistair picked up the book and said, "Now look, Mum, it's almost time for my session with Tiny. Oh, yes; it's a regular thing, and he certainly is leading me into some fascinating byways."

"Like what?"

"Like the old impossible problem of casting tungsten, for example. You know, there is a way to do it."

"You don't say! What do you cast it in—a play?"

Alistair wrinkled her straight nose. "Did you ever hear of pressure ice? Water compressed until it forms a solid at what is usually its boiling point?"

"I remember some such."

"Well, all you need is enough pressure, and a chamber that can take that kind of pressure, and a couple of details like a high-intensity field of umpteen megacycles phased with ... I forget the figures; anyhow, that's the way to go about it."

" 'If we had some eggs we could have some ham and eggs if we had some ham,' " quoted Mrs. Forsythe. "And besides, I seem to remember something about that pressure ice melting pretty much right now, like so," and she snapped her fingers. "How do you know your molded tungsten—that's what it would be, not cast at all—wouldn't change state the same way?"

"That's what I'm working on now," said Alistair calmly. "Come along, Tiny. Mum, you can find your way around all right, can't you? If you need anything, just sing out. This isn't a séance, you know."

"Isn't it, though?" muttered Mrs. Forsythe as her lithe daughter and the dog bounded up the stairs. She shook her head, went into the kitchen, drew a bucket of water, and carried it down to her car, which had cooled to a simmer. She was dashing careful handfuls of it onto the radiator before beginning to pour when her quick ear caught the scrunching of boots on the steep drive.

She looked up to see a young man trudging wearily in the mid-morning heat. He wore an old sharkskin suit and carried his coat. In spite of his wilted appearance, his step was firm and his golden hair was crisp in the sunlight. He swung up to Mrs. Forsythe and gave her a grin, all deep-blue eyes and good teeth. "Forsythe's?" he asked in a resonant baritone.

"That's right," said Mrs. Forsythe, finding that she had to turn her head from side to side to see both of his shoulders. And yet she could have swapped belts with him. "You must feel like the Blue Kangaroo here," she added, slapping her miniature mount on its broiling flank. "Boiled dry."

"You cahl de cyah de Blue Kangaroo?" he repeated, draping his coat over the door and mopping his forehead with what seemed to Mrs. Forsythe's discerning eye a pure linen handkerchief.

"I do," she replied, forcing herself not to comment on the young man's slight but strange accent. "It's strictly a dry-clutch job and acts like a castellated one. Let the pedal out, she races. Let it out three thirty-seconds of an inch more, and you're gone from there. Always stopping to walk back and pick up your head. Snaps right off, you know. Carry a bottle of collodion and a couple of splints to put your head back on. Starve to death without a head to eat with. What brings you here?"

In answer he held out a yellow envelope, looking solemnly at her head and neck, then at the car, his face quiet, his eyes crinkling with a huge enjoyment.

Mrs. Forsythe glanced at the envelope. "Oh. Telegram. She's inside. I'll give it to her. Come on in and have a drink. It's hotter than the hinges of Hail Columbia, Happy Land. Don't go wiping your feet like that! By jeepers, that's enough to give you an inferiority complex! Invite a man in, invite the dust on his feet, too. It's good, honest dirt and we don't run to white broadlooms here. Are you afraid of dogs?"

The young man laughed. "Dahgs talk to me, ma'am."

She glanced at him sharply, opened her mouth to tell him he might just be taken at his word around here, then thought better of it. "Sit down," she ordered. She bustled up a foaming glass of beer and set it beside him. "I'll get her down to sign for the wire," she said. The man half lowered the glass into which he had been jowls-deep, began to speak, found he was alone in the room, laughed suddenly and richly, wiped off the mustache of suds, and dived down for a new one.

Mrs. Forsythe grinned and shook her head as she heard the laughter, and went straight to Alistair's study. "Alistair!"

"Stop pushing me about the ductility of tungsten, Tiny! You know better than that. Figures are figures, and facts are facts. I think I see what you're trying to lead me to. All I can say is that if such a thing is possible, I never heard of any equipment that could handle it. Stick around a few years and I'll hire you a nuclear power plant. Until then, I'm afraid—"

"Alistair!"

"—there just isn't ... hm-m-m? Yes, Mother?"

"Telegram."

"Oh. Who from?"

"I don't know, being only one fortieth of one percent as psychic as that doghouse Dunninger you have there. In other words, I didn't open it."

"Oh, Mum, you're silly. Of course you could have ... oh, well, let's have it."

"I haven't got it. It's downstairs with Discobolus Junior, who brought it. No one," she said ecstatically, "has a right to be so tanned with hair that color."

"What *are* you talking about?"

"Go on down and sign for the telegram and see for yourself. You will find the maiden's dream with his golden head in a bucket of suds, all hot and sweaty from his noble efforts in attaining this peak without spikes or alpenstock, with nothing but his pure heart and Western Union to guide him."

"This maiden's dream happens to be tungsten treatment," said Alistair with some irritation. She looked longingly at her work sheet, put down her pencil, and rose. "Stay here, Tiny. I'll be right back as soon as I have successfully resisted my conniving mother's latest scheme to drag my red hairing across some young buck's path to matrimony." She paused at the door. "Aren't you staying up here, Mum?"

"Get that hair away from your face," said her mother grimly. "I am not. I wouldn't miss this for the world. And don't pun in front of that young man. It's practically the only thing in the world I consider vulgar."

Alistair led the way down the stairs and through the corridor to the kitchen, with her mother crowding her heels, once fluffing out her daughter's blazing hair, once taking a swift tuck in the back of the girl's halter. They spilled through the door almost together. Alistair stopped and frankly stared.

For the young man had risen and, still with the traces of beer foam on his modeled lips, stood with his jaws stupidly open, his head a little back, his eyes partly closed as if against a bright light. And it seemed as if everyone in the room forgot to breathe for a moment.

"Well!" Mrs. Forsythe exploded after a moment. "Honey, you've made a conquest. Hey, you, chin up, chest out."

"I beg your humble pardon," muttered the young man, and the phrase seemed more a colloquialism than an affectation.

Alistair, visibly pulling herself together, said, "Mother, please," and drifted forward to pick up the telegram that lay on the kitchen table. Her mother knew her well enough to realize that her hands and her eyes were steady only by a powerful effort. Whether the effort was in control of annoyance, embarrassment, or out-and-out biochemistry was a matter for later thought. At the moment Mrs. Forsythe was enjoying the situation tremendously.

"Please wait," said Alistair coolly. "There may be an answer to this." The young man simply bobbed his head. He was still a little wall-eyed with the impact of seeing Alistair, as many a young man had been before. But there were the beginnings of his astonishing smile around his lips as he watched her rip the envelope open.

"Mother! Listen!

> ARRIVED THIS MORNING AND HOPE I CAN CATCH YOU AT HOME. OLD DEBBIL KILLED IN ACCIDENT BUT FOUND HIS MEMORY BEFORE HE DIED. HAVE INFORMATION WHICH MAY CLEAR UP MYSTERY—OR DEEPEN IT. HOPE I CAN SEE YOU FOR I DON'T KNOW WHAT TO THINK.
>
> ALEC.

"How old is this tropical savage?" asked Mrs. Forsythe.

"He's not a savage and I don't know how old he is and I can't see what that has to do with it. I think he's about my age or a little older." She looked up and her eyes were shining.

"Deadly rival," said Mrs. Forsythe to the messenger consolingly. "Rotten timing here, somewhere."

"I—" said the young man.

"Mother, we've got to fix something to eat. Do you suppose he'll be able to stay over? Where's my green dress with the ... oh, you wouldn't know. It's new."

"Then the letters weren't all about the dog," said Mrs. Forsythe with a Cheshire grin.

"Mum, you're impossible. This is ... is important. Alec is ... is ..."

Her mother nodded. "Important. That's all I was pointing out."

The young man said, "I—"

Alistair turned to him. "I do hope you don't think we're totally mad. I'm sorry you had such a climb." She went to the sideboard and took a quarter out of a sugar bowl. He took it gravely.

Thank you, ma'am. If you don't min', I'll keep this piece of silver for the rest o' my everlahstin'."

"You're wel— What?"

The young man seemed to get even taller. "I greatly appreciate your hospitality, Miss Forsythe. I have you at a disadvantage, ma'am, and one I shall correct." He put a crooked forefinger between his lips and blew out an incredible blast of sound.

"Tiny!" he roared. "Here to me, dahg, an' mek me known!"

There was an answering roar from upstairs, and Tiny came tumbling down, scrabbling wildly as he took the turn at the foot of the stairs and hurtled over the slick flooring to crash joyfully into the young man.

"Ah, you beast," crooned the man, cuffing the dog happily. His accent thickened. "You thrive yourself here wid de lady-dem, you gray-yut styoupid harse. You glad me, mon, you glad me." He grinned at the two astonished women. "Forgive me," he said as he pummeled Tiny, pulled his ears, shoved him away, and caught him by the jaws. "For true, I couldn't get in the first word with Mrs. Forsythe, and after that I couldn't help meself. Alec my name is, and the telegram I took from the true messenger, finding him sighing and sweating at the sight of the hill there."

Alistair covered her face with her hands and said, "Oooh."

Mrs. Forsythe whooped with laughter. When she found her voice she demanded, "Young man, what is your last name?"

"Sundersen, ma'am."

"Mother! Why did you ask him that?"

"For reasons of euphony," said Mrs. Forsythe with a twinkle. "Alexander Sundersen. Very good. Alistair—"

"Stop! Mum, don't you dare—"

"I was going to say, Alistair, if you and our guest will excuse me, I'll have to get back to my knitting." She went to the door.

Alistair threw an appalled look at Alec and cried, "Mother! What are you knitting?"

"My brows, darling. See you later." Mrs. Forsythe chuckled and went out.

It took almost a week for Alec to get caught up with the latest developments in Tiny, for he got the story in the most meticulous detail. There never seemed to be enough time to get in all the explanations and anecdotes, so swiftly did it fly when he and Alistair were together. Some days he went into the city with Alistair in the morning and spent the day buying tools and equipment for his estate. New York was a wonder city to him—he had been there only once before—and Alistair found herself getting quite possessive about the place, showing it off like the contents of a jewel box. And then Alec stayed at the house a couple of days. He endeared himself forever to Mrs. Forsythe by removing, cleaning, and refacing the clutch on the Blue Kangaroo, simplifying the controls on the gas refrigerator so it could be defrosted without a major operation, and putting a building jack under the corner of the porch that threatened to sag.

And the sessions with Tiny were resumed and intensified. At first he seemed a little uneasy when Alec joined one of them, but within half an hour he relaxed. Thereafter, more and more he would interrupt Alistair to turn to Alec. Although he apparently could not understand Alec's thoughts at all, he seemed to comprehend perfectly when Alec spoke to Alistair. And within a few days she learned to accept these interruptions, for they speeded up the research they were doing. Alec was almost totally ignorant of the advanced theory with which Alistair worked, but his mind was clear, quick, and very direct. He was no theorist, and that was good. He was one of those rare grease-monkey geniuses, with a grasp of the laws of cause and effect that amounted to intuition. Tiny's reaction to this seemed to be approval. At any rate, the occasions when Alistair lost track of what Tiny was after occurred less and less frequently. Alec instinctively knew just how far to go back, and then how to spot the turning at which they had gone astray. And bit by bit they began to identify what it was that Tiny was after. As to why—and how—he was after it, Alec's experience with old Debbil seemed a clue. It was certainly sufficient to keep Alec plugging away at a possible solution to the strange animal's stranger need.

"It was down at the sugar mill," he told Alistair, after he had become fully acquainted with the incredible dog's actions and they were trying to determine the why and the how. "He called me over to the chute where cane is loaded into the conveyors.

" 'Bahss,' he told me, 'dat t'ing dere, it not safe, sah.' And he pointed through the guard over the bull gears that drove the conveyor. Great big everlahstin' teeth it has, Miss Alistair, a full ten inches long, and it whirlin' to the drive pinion. It's old, but strong for good. Debbil, what he saw was a bit o' play on the pinion shaf'.

" 'Now, you're an old fool,' I told him.

" 'No, bahss,' " he says. 'Look now, sah, de t'ing wit' de teet'—dem, it not safe, sah. I mek you see,' and before I could move meself or let a thought trickle, he opens the guard up and thrus' his han' inside! Bull gear, it run right up his arm and nip it off, neat as ever, at the shoulder. I humbly beg your pardon, Miss Alistair."

"G-go on," said Alistair, through her handkerchief.

"Well, sir, old Debbil was an idiot for true, and he only died the way he lived, rest him. He was old and he was all eaten out with malaria and elephantiasis and the like, that not even Dr. Thetford could save him. But a strange thing happened. As he lay dyin', with the entire village gathered roun' the door whisperin' plans for the wake, he sent to tell me come quickly. Down I run, and for the smile on his face I glad him when I cross the doorstep."

As Alec spoke, he was back in the Spanish-wall hut, with the air close under the palm-thatch roof and the glare of the pressure lantern set on the tiny window ledge to give the old man light to die by. Alec's accent deepened. " 'How you feel, mon?' I ahsk him. 'Bahss, I'm a dead man now, but I got a light in mah hey-yud.'

" 'Tell me then, Debbil.'

" 'Bahss, de folk-dem say, ol' Debbil, him cyahn't remembah de taste of a mango as he t'row away de skin. Him cyahn't remembah his own house do he stay away t'ree day.'

" 'Loose talk, Debbil.'

" 'True talk, Bahss. Foh de Lahd give me a leaky pot fo' hol' ma brains. But Bahss, I do recall one t'ing now, bright an' clear, and you must know. Bahss, de day I go up the wahtah line, I see a great jumbee in de stones of de gov'nor palace dere.' "

"What's a jumbee?" asked Mrs. Forsythe.

"A ghost, ma'am. The Crucians carry a crawlin' heap of superstitions. Tiny! What eats you, mon?"

Tiny growled again. Alec and Alistair exchanged a look. "He doesn't want you to go on."

"Listen carefully. I want him to get this. I am his friend. I want to help you help him. I realize that he wants as few people as possible to find out about this thing. I will say nothing to anybody unless and until I have his permission."

"Well, Tiny?"

The dog stood restlessly, swinging his great head from Alistair to Alec. Finally he made a sound like an audible shrug, then turned to Mrs. Forsythe.

"Mother's part of me," said Alistair firmly. "That's the way it's got to be. No alternative." She leaned forward. "You can't talk to us. You can only indicate what you want said and done. I think Alec's story will help us to understand what you want and help you to get it more quickly. Understand?"

Tiny gazed at her for a long moment, said, "*Whuff,*" and lay down with his nose between his paws and his eyes fixed on Alec.

"I think that's the green light," said Mrs. Forsythe, "and I might add that most of it was due to my daughter's conviction that you're a wonderful fellow."

"Mother!"

"Well, pare me down and call me Spud! They're *both* blushing!" said Mrs. Forsythe blatantly.

"Go on, Alec," choked Alistair.

"Thank you. Old Debbil told me a fine tale of the things he had seen at the ruins. A great beast, mind you, with no shape at all, and a face ugly to drive you mad. And about the beast was what he called a 'feelin' good.' He said it was a miracle, but he feared nothing. 'Wet it was, Bahss, like a slug, an' de eye it have is whirlin' an' shakin', an' I standin' dar feelin' like a bride at de altar step an' no fear in me.' Well, I thought the old man's mind was wandering, for I knew he was touched. But the story he told was *that* clear, and never a single second did he stop to think. Out it all came like a true thing.

"He said that Tiny walked to the beast and that it curved over him like an ocean wave. It closed over the dog, and Debbil was rooted there the livelong day, still without fear, and feelin' no smallest desire to move. He had no surprise at all, even at the thing he saw restin' in the thicket among the old stones.

"He said it was a submarine, a mighty one as great as the estate house and with no break nor mar in its surface but for the glass part let in where the mouth is on a shark.

"And then when the sun begun to dip, the beast gave a shudderin' heave and rolled back, and out walked Tiny. He stepped up to Debbil and stood. Then the beast began to quiver and shake, and Debbil said the air aroun' him heavied with the work the monster was doing, tryin' to talk. A cloud formed in his brain, and a voice swept over him. 'Not a livin' word, Bahss, not a sound at all. But it said to forget. It said to leave dis place and forget, sah.' And the last thing old Debbil saw as he turned away was the beast slumping down, seeming all but dead from the work it had done to speak at all. 'An' de cloud live in mah hey-yud, Bahss, f'om dat time onward. I'm a dead man now, Bahss, but de cloud gone and Debbil know de story.'" Alec leaned back and looked at his hands. "That was all. This must have happened about fifteen months pahst, just before Tiny began to show his strange stripe." He drew a deep breath and looked up. "Maybe I'm gullible. But I knew the old man too well. He never in this life could invent such a tale. I troubled myself to go up to the governor's palace after the buryin'. I might have been mistaken, but something big had lain in the deepest thicket, for it was crushed into a great hollow place near a hundred foot long. Well, there you are. For what it's worth, you have the story of a superstitious an' illiterate old man, at the point of death by violence and many years sick to boot."

There was a long silence, and at last Alistair threw her lucent hair back and said, "It isn't Tiny at all. It's a . . . a thing outside Tiny." She looked at the dog, her eyes wide. "And I don't even mind."

"Neither did Debbil, when he saw it," said Alec gravely.

Mrs. Forsythe snapped, "What are we sitting gawking at each other for? Don't answer; I'll tell you. All of us can think up a story to fit the facts, and we're all too self-conscious to come out with it. Any story that fit those facts would really be a killer."

"Well said." Alec grinned. "Would you like to tell us your idea?"

"Silly boy," muttered Alistair.

"Don't be impertinent, child. Of course I'd like to tell you, Alec. I think that the good Lord, in His infinite wisdom, has decided that it was about time for Alistair to come to her senses, and, knowing that it would take a quasi-scientific miracle to do it, dreamed up this—"

"Some day," said Alistair icily, "I'm going to pry you loose from your verbosity and your sense of humor in one fell swoop."

Mrs. Forsythe grinned. "There is a time for jocularity, kidlet, and this is it. I hate solemn people solemnly sitting around being awed by things. What do you make of all this, Alec?"

Alec pulled his ear and said, "I vote we leave it up to Tiny. It's his show. Let's get on with the work and just keep in mind what we already know."

To their astonishment, Tiny stumped over to Alec and licked his hand.

The blowoff came six weeks after Alec's arrival. (Oh, yes, he stayed six weeks, and longer. It took some fiendish cogitation for him to think of enough legitimate estate business that had to be done in New York to keep him that long, but after six weeks he was so much one of the family that he needed no excuse.) He had devised a code system for Tiny, so that Tiny could add something to their conversations. His point: "Here he sits, ma'am, like a fly on the wall, seeing everything and hearing everything and saying not a word. Picture it for yourself, and you in such a position, full entranced as you are with the talk you hear." And for Mrs. Forsythe particularly, the mental picture was altogether too vivid. It was so well presented that Tiny's research went by the board for four days while they devised the code. They had to give up the idea of a glove with a pencil pocket in it, with which Tiny might write a little, or any similar device. The dog was simply not deft enough for such meticulous work; and besides, he showed absolutely no signs of understanding any written or printed symbolism. Unless, of course, Alistair thought about it.

Alec's plan was simple. He cut some wooden forms—a disk, a square, a triangle to begin with. The disk signified "yes" or any other affirmation, depending on the context; the square was "no" or any negation; and the triangle indicated a question or a change of subject. The amount of information Tiny was able to impart by moving from one to another of these forms was astonishing. Once a subject for discussion was established, Tiny would take a stand between the disk and the square, so that all he had to do was to swing his head to one side or the other to indicate a "yes" or a "no." No longer were there those exasperating sessions in which the track of his research was lost while they back-trailed to discover where they had gone astray. The conversations ran like this:

"Tiny, I have a question. Hope you won't think it too personal. May I ask it?" That was Alec, always infinitely polite to dogs. He had always recognized their innate dignity.

Yes, the answer would come, as Tiny swung his head over the disk.

"Were we right in assuming that you, the dog, are not communicating with us, that you are the medium?"

Tiny went to the triangle. "You want to change the subject?"

Tiny hesitated, then went to the square. *No.*

Alistair said, "He obviously wants something from us before he will discuss the question. Right, Tiny?"

Yes.

Mrs. Forsythe said, "He's had his dinner, and he doesn't smoke. I think he wants us to assure him that we'll keep his secret."

Yes.

"Good. Alec, you're wonderful," said Alistair. "Mother, stop beaming. I only meant—"

"Leave it at that, child. Any qualification will spoil it for the man."

"Thank you, ma'am," said Alec gravely, with that deep twinkle of amusement around his eyes. Then he turned back to Tiny. "Well, what about it, sah? Are you a superdog?"

No.

"Who ... no, he can't answer that. Let's go back a bit. Was old Debbil's story true?"

Yes.

"Ah." They exchanged glances. "Where is this—monster? Still in St. Croix?"

No.

"Here?"

Yes.

"You mean here, in this room or in the house?"

No.

"Nearby, though?"

Yes.

"How can we find out just where, without mentioning the countryside item by item?" asked Alistair.

"I know," said Mrs. Forsythe. "Alec, according to Debbil, that 'submarine' thing was pretty big, wasn't it?"

"That it was, ma'am."

"Good. Tiny, does he ... it ... have the ship here, too?"

Yes.

Mrs. Forsythe spread her hands. "That's it, then. There's only one place around here where you could hide such an object." She nodded her head at the west wall of the house.

"The river!" cried Alistair. "That right, Tiny?"

Yes. And Tiny went immediately to the triangle.

"Wait!" said Alec. "Tiny, beggin' your pardon, but there's one more question. Shortly after you took passage to New York, there was a business with compasses, where they all pointed to the west. Was that the ship?"

Yes.

"In the water?"

No.

"Why," said Alistair, "this is pure science fiction! Alec, do you ever get science fiction in the tropics?"

"Ah, Miss Alistair, not often enough, for true. But well I know it. The space ships are old Mother Goose to me. But there's a difference here. For in all the stories I've read, when a beast comes here from space, it's to kill and conquer; and yet—and I don't know why—I know that this one wants nothing of the sort. More, he's out to do us good."

"I feel the same way," said Mrs. Forsythe thoughtfully. "It's sort of a protective cloud which seems to surround us. Does that make sense to you, Alistair?"

"I know it from 'way back," said Alistair with conviction. She looked at the dog thoughtfully. "I wonder why he ... it ... won't show itself. And why it can communicate only through me. And why me?"

"I'd say, Miss Alistair, that you were chosen because of your metallurgy. As to why we never see the beast, well, it knows best. Its reason must be a good one."

Day after day, and bit by bit, they got and gave information. Many things remained mysteries, but, strangely, there seemed no real need to question Tiny too closely. The atmosphere of confidence and good will that surrounded them made questions seem not only unnecessary but downright rude.

And day by day, little by little, a drawing began to take shape under Alec's skilled hands. It was a casting with a simple enough external contour, but inside it contained a series of baffles and a chamber. It was designed, apparently, to support and house a carballoy shaft. There were no openings into the central chamber except those taken by the shaft. The shaft turned; *something* within the chamber apparently drove it. There was plenty of discussion about it.

"Why the baffles?" moaned Alistair, palming all the neatness out of her flaming hair. "Why carballoy? And in the name of Nemo, why tungsten?"

Alec stared at the drawing for a long moment, then suddenly clapped a hand to his head. "Tiny! Is there radiation inside that housing? I mean, hard stuff?"

Yes.

"There you are, then," said Alec. "Tungsten to shield the radiation. A casting for uniformity. The baffles to make a meander out of the shaft openings—see, the shaft has plates turned on it to fit between the baffles."

"And nowhere for anything to go in, nowhere for anything to come out—except the shaft, of course—and besides, you can't cast tungsten that way! Maybe Tiny's monster can, but we can't. Maybe with the right flux and with enough power—but that's silly. Tungsten won't cast."

"And we cahn't build a space ship. There must be a way!"

"Not with today's facilities, and not with tungsten," said Alistair. "Tiny's ordering it from us the way we would order a wedding cake at the corner bakery."

"What made you say 'wedding cake'?"

"You, too, Alec? Don't I get enough of that from Mother?" But she smiled all the same. "But about the casting—it seems to me that our mysterious friend is in the position of a radio fiend who understands every part of his set, how it's made, how and why it works. Then a tube blows, and he finds he can't buy one. He has to make one if he gets one at all. Apparently old Debbil's beast is in that kind of spot. What about it, Tiny? Is your friend short a part which he understands but has never built before?"

Yes.

"And he needs it to get away from Earth?"

Yes.

Alec asked, "What's the trouble? Can't get escape velocity?"

Tiny hesitated, then went to the triangle. "Either he doesn't want to talk about it or the question doesn't quite fit the situation," said Alistair. "It doesn't matter. Our main problem is the casting. It just can't be done. Not by anyone on this planet, as far as I know; and I think I know. It has to be tungsten, Tiny?"

Yes.

"Tungsten for what?" asked Alec. "Radiation shield?"

Yes.

He turned to Alistair. "Isn't there something just as good?"

She mused, staring at his drawing. "Yes, several things," she said thoughtfully. Tiny watched her, motionless. He seemed to slump as she shrugged dispiritedly and said, "But not anything with walls as thin as that. A yard or so of lead might do it, and have something like the mechanical strength he seems to want, but it would obviously be too big. Beryllium—" At the word, Tiny went and stood right on top of the square, a most emphatic *no.*

"How about an alloy?" Alec asked.

"Well, Tiny?"

Tiny went to the triangle. Alistair nodded. "You don't know. I can't think of one. I'll take it up with Dr. Nowland. Maybe—"

The following day Alec stayed home and spent the day arguing cheerfully with Mrs. Forsythe and building a grape arbor. It was a radiant Alistair who came home that evening. "Got it! Got it!" she caroled as she danced in. "Alec, Tiny! Come on!"

They flew upstairs to the study. Without removing the green "beanie" with the orange feather that so nearly matched her hair, Alistair hauled out four reference books and began talking animatedly. "Auric molybdenum, Tiny, what about that? Gold and molyb III should do it! Listen!" And she launched forth into a spatter of absorption data, Greek-letter formulae, and strength-of-materials comparisons that made Alec's head swim. He sat watching her without listening. Increasingly, this was his greatest pleasure.

When Alistair was quite through, Tiny walked away from her and lay down, gazing off into space.

"Well, strike me!" said Alec. "Look yonder, Miss Alistair. The very first time I ever saw him thinking something over."

"*Sh-h!* Don't disturb him, then. If that is the answer, and if he never thought of it before, it will take some figuring out. There's no knowing what fantastic kind of science he's comparing it with."

"I see the point. Like—well, suppose we crashed a plane in the Brazilian jungle and needed a new hydraulic cylinder on the landing gear. Now, then, one of the natives shows us ironwood, and it's up to us to figure out if we can make it serve."

"That's about it," breathed Alistair. "I—" She was interrupted by Tiny, who suddenly leaped up and ran to her, kissing her hands, committing the forbidden enormity of putting his paws on her shoulders, running back to the wooden forms and nudging the disk, the yes symbol. His tail was going like a metronome without its pendulum.

Mrs. Forsythe came in in the midst of all this rowdiness and demanded, "What goes on? Who made a dervish out of Tiny? What have you been feeding him? Don't tell me. Let me . . . You don't mean you've solved his problem for him? What are you going to do, buy him a pogo stick?"

"Oh, Mum, we've got it! An alloy of molybdenum and gold. I can get it alloyed and cast in no time."

"Good, honey, good. You going to cast the whole thing?" She pointed to the drawing.

"Why, yes."

"Humph!"

"Mother! Why, if I may ask, do you 'humph' in that tone of voice?"

"You may ask, Chicken, who's going to pay for it?"

"Why, that will—I—oh. *Oh!*" she said, aghast, and ran to the drawing. Alec came and looked over her shoulder. She figured in the corner of the drawing, oh-ed once again and sat down weakly.

"How much?" asked Alec.

"I'll get an estimate in the morning," she said faintly. "I know plenty of people. I can get it at cost—maybe." She looked at Tiny despairingly. He came and laid his head against her knee, and she pulled at his ears. "I won't let you down, darling," she whispered.

She got the estimate the next day. It was a little over thirteen thousand dollars.

Alistair and Alec stared blankly at each other and then at the dog.

"Maybe you can tell us where we can raise that much money?" said Alistair, as if she expected Tiny to whip out a wallet.

Tiny whimpered, licked Alistair's hand, looked at Alec, and then lay down.

"Now what?" mused Alec.

"Now we go and fix something to eat," said Mrs. Forsythe, moving toward the door. The others were about to follow, when Tiny leaped to his feet and ran in front of them. He stood in the doorway and whimpered. When they came closer, he barked.

"Sh-h! What is it, Tiny? Want us to stay here a while?"

"Say, who's the boss around here?" Mrs. Forsythe wanted to know.

"He is," said Alec, and he knew he was speaking for all of them. They sat down, Mrs. Forsythe on the studio couch, Alistair at her desk, Alec at the drawing table. But Tiny seemed not to approve of the arrangement. He became vastly excited, running to Alec, nudging him hard, dashing to Alistair, taking her wrist very gently in his jaws and pulling gently toward Alec.

"What is it, fellow?"

"Seems like matchmaking to me," remarked Mrs. Forsythe.

"Nonsense, Mum," said Alistair, coloring. "He wants Alec and me to change places, that's all."

Alec said, "Oh," and went to sit beside Mrs. Forsythe. Alistair sat at the drawing table. Tiny put a paw up on it, poked at the large tablet of paper. Alistair looked at him curiously, then tore off the top sheet. Tiny nudged a pencil with his nose.

Then they waited. Somehow, no one wanted to speak. Perhaps no one could, but there seemed to be no reason to try. And gradually a tension built up in the room. Tiny stood stiff and rapt in the center of the room. His eyes glazed, and when he finally keeled over limply, no one went to him.

Alistair picked up the pencil slowly. Watching her hand, Alec was reminded of the movement of the pointer on a ouija board. The pencil traveled steadily, in small surges, to the very top of the paper and hung there. Alistair's face was quite blank.

After that no one could say what happened, exactly. It was as if their eyes had done what their voices had done. They could see, but they did not care to. And Alistair's pencil began to move. Something, somewhere, was directing her mind—not her hand. Faster and faster her pencil flew, and it wrote what was later to be known as the Forsythe Formulae.

There was no sign then, of course, of the furor that they would cause, of the millions of words of conjecture that were written when it was discovered that the girl who wrote them could not possibly have had the mathematical background to write them. They were understood by no one at first, and by very few people ever. Alistair certainly did not know what they meant.

An editorial in a popular magazine came startlingly close to the true nature of the formulae when it said: "The Forsythe Formulae, which describe what the Sunday supplements call the 'Something-for-Nothing Clutch,' and the drawing that accompanies them, signify little to the layman. As far as can be determined, the formulae are the description and working principles of a device. It appears to be a power plant of sorts, and if it is ever understood, atomic power will go the way of gaslights.

"A sphere of energy is enclosed in a shell made of neutron-absorbing material. This sphere has inner and outer 'layers.' A shaft passes through the sphere. Apparently a magnetic field must be rotated about the outer casing of the device. The sphere of energy aligns itself with this field. The inner sphere rotates with the outer one and has the ability to turn the shaft. Unless the mathematics used are disproved—and no one seems to have come anywhere near doing that, unorthodox as they are—the aligning effect between the rotating field and the two concentric spheres, as well as the shaft, is quite independent of any load. In other words, if the original magnetic field rotates at 3000 r.p.m., the shaft will rotate at 3000 r.p.m., even if there is only 1/16 horsepower turning the field while there is 10,000 braking stress on the shaft.

"Ridiculous? Perhaps. And perhaps it is no more so than the apparent impossibility of 15 watts of energy pouring into the antenna of a radio station, and nothing coming down. The key to the whole problem is in the nature of those self-contained spheres of force inside the shell. Their power is apparently inherent, and consists of an ability to align, just as the useful property of steam is an ability to expand. If, as is suggested by Reinhardt in his 'Usage of the Symbol ß in the Forsythe Formulae,' these spheres are nothing but stable concentrations of pure binding energy, we have here a source of power beyond the wildest dreams of mankind. Whether or not we succeed in building such devices, it cannot be denied that whatever their mysterious source, the Forsythe Formulae are an epochal gift to several sciences, including, if you like, the art of philosophy."

After it was over, and the formulae written, the terrible tension lifted. The three humans sat in their happy coma, and the dog lay senseless on the rug. Mrs. Forsythe was the first to move, standing up abruptly. "Well!" she said.

It seemed to break a spell. Everything was quite normal. No hangovers, no sense of strangeness, no fear. They stood looking wonderingly at the mass of minute figures.

"I don't know," murmured Alistair, and the phrase covered a world of meaning. Then, "Alec—that casting. We've got to get it done. We've just got to, no matter what it costs us!"

"I'd like to," said Alec. "Why do we have to?"

She waved toward the drawing table. "We've been given that."

"You don't say!" said Mrs. Forsythe. "And what is that?"

Alistair put her hand to her head, and a strange, unfocused look came into her eyes. That look was the only part of the whole affair that ever really bothered Alec. It was a place she had gone to, a little bit; and he knew that no matter what happened, he would never be able to go there with her.

She said, "He's been . . . talking to me, you know. You do know that, don't you? I'm not guessing, Alec—Mum."

"I believe you, chicken," her mother said softly. "What are you trying to say?"

"I got it in concepts. It isn't a thing you can repeat, really. But the idea is that he couldn't give us any *thing*. His ship is completely functional, and there isn't anything he can exchange for what he wants us to do. But he has given us something of great value. . . ." Her voice trailed off; she seemed to listen to something for a moment. "Of value in several ways. A new science, a new approach to attack the science. New tools, new mathematics."

"But what is it? What can it do? And how is it going to help us pay for the casting?" asked Mrs. Forsythe.

"It can't, immediately," said Alistair decisively. "It's too big. We don't even know what it is. Why are you arguing? Can't you understand that he can't give us any gadgetry? That we haven't his techniques, materials, and tools, and so we couldn't make any actual machine he suggested? He's done the only thing he can; he's given us a new science, and tools to take it apart."

"That I know," said Alec gravely. "Well, indeed. I felt that. And I—I trust him. Do you, ma'am?"

"Yes, of course. I think he's—people. I think he has a sense of humor and a sense of justice," said Mrs. Forsythe firmly. "Let's get our heads together. We ought to be able to scrape it up some way. And why shouldn't we? Haven't we three got something to talk about for the rest of our lives?"

And their heads went together.

This is the letter that arrived two months later in St. Croix.

Honey-lamb,

Hold on to your seat. It's all over.

The casting arrived. I missed you more than ever, but when you have to go—and you know I'm glad you went! Anyway, I did as you indicated, through Tiny, before you left. The men who rented me the boat and ran it for me thought I was crazy, and said so. Do you know that once we were out on the river with the casting, and Tiny started whuffing and whimpering to tell me we were on the right spot, and I told the men to tip the casting over the side, they had the colossal nerve to insist on opening the crate? Got quite nasty about it. Didn't want to be a party to any dirty work. It was against my principles, but I let them, just to expedite matters. They were certain there was a body in the box! When they saw what it was, I was going to bend my umbrelly over their silly heads, but they looked so funny I couldn't do a thing but roar with laughter. That was when the man said I was crazy.

Anyhow, over the side it went, into the river. Made a lovely splash. About a minute later I got the loveliest feeling—I wish I could describe it to you. I was sort of overwhelmed by a feeling of utter satisfaction, and gratitude, and, oh, I don't know. I just felt *good,* all over. I looked at Tiny, and he was trembling. I think he felt it, too. I'd call it a thank you, on a grand psychic scale. I think you can rest assured that Tiny's monster got what it wanted.

But that wasn't the end of it. I paid off the boatmen and started up the bank. Something made me stop and wait, and then go back to the water's edge.

It was early evening, and very still. I was under some sort of compulsion, not an unpleasant thing, but an unbreakable one. I sat down on the river wall and watched the water. There was no one around—the boat had left—except one of those snazzy Sunlounge cruisers anchored a few yards out. I remember how still it was, because there was a little girl playing on the deck of the yacht, and I could hear her footsteps as she ran about.

Suddenly I noticed something in the water. I suppose I should have been frightened, but somehow I wasn't at all. Whatever the thing was, it was big and gray and slimy and quite shapeless. And somehow, it seemed to be the source of this aura of well-being and protectiveness that I felt. It was staring at me. I knew it was before I saw that it had an eye—a big one, with something whirling inside of it. I don't know. I wish I could write. I wish I had the power to tell you what it was like. I know that by human standards it was infinitely revolting. If this was Tiny's monster, I could understand its being sensitive to the revulsion it might cause. And wrongly, for I felt to the core that the creature was good.

It winked at me. I don't mean blinked. It winked. And then everything happened at once.

The creature was gone, and in seconds there was a disturbance in the water by the yacht. Something gray and wet reached up out of the river, and I saw it was going for that little girl. Only a tyke—about three, she was. Red hair just like yours. And it thumped that child in the small of the back just enough to knock her over into the river.

And can you believe it? I just sat there watching and said never a word. It didn't seem right to me that that baby could be struggling in the water. *But it didn't seem wrong, either!*

Well, before I could get my wits together, Tiny was off the wall like a hairy bullet and streaking through the water. I have often wondered why his feet are so big; I never will again. The hound is built like the lower half of a paddle wheel! In two shakes he had the baby by the scruff of the neck and was bringing her back to me. No one had seen that child get pushed, Alistair! No one but me. But there was a man on the yacht who must have seen her fall. He was all over the deck, roaring orders and getting in the way of things, and by the time he had his wherry in the water, Tiny had reached me with the little girl. She wasn't frightened, either, she thought it was a grand joke! Wonderful youngster.

So the man came ashore, all gratitude and tears, and wanted to gold-plate Tiny or something. Then he saw me. "That your dog?" I said it was my daughter's. She was in St. Croix on her honeymoon. Before I could stop him, he had a checkbook out and was scratching away at it. He said he knew my kind. Said he knew I'd never accept a thing for myself, but wouldn't refuse something for my daughter. I enclose the check. Why he picked a sum like thirteen thousand I'll never know. Anyhow, I know it'll be a help to you, and since the money really comes from Tiny's monster, I'm sure you'll use it. I suppose I can confess now. The idea that letting Alec put up the money even though he had to clean out his savings and mortgage his estate—would be all right if he were one of the family, because then he'd have you to help him make it all back again—well, that was all my inspiration. Sometimes, though, watching you, I wonder if I really had to work so all-fired hard to get you two married to each other.

Well, I imagine that closes the business of Tiny's monster. There are a lot of things we'll probably never know. I can guess some things, though. It could communicate with a dog but not with a human, unless it half killed itself trying. Apparently a dog is telepathic with humans to a degree, though it probably doesn't understand a lot of what it gets. I don't speak French, but I could probably transcribe French phonetically well enough so a Frenchman could read it. Tiny was transcribing that way. The monster could "send" through him and control him completely. It no doubt indoctrinated the dog—if I can use the term—the day old Debbil took him up the waterline. And when the monster caught, through Tiny, the mental picture of you when Dr. Schwellenbach mentioned you, it went to work through the dog to get you working on its problem. Mental pictures—that's probably what the monster used. That's how Tiny could tell one book from another without being able to read. You visualize everything you think about. What do you think? I think that mine's as good a guess as any.

You might be amused to learn that last night all the compasses in this neighborhood pointed west for a couple of hours! 'By, now, chillun. Keep on being happy.

Love and love, and a kiss for Alec,
Mum

P.S. Is St. Croix really a nice place to honeymoon? Jack—he's the fellow who signed the check—is getting very sentimental. He's very like your father. A widower, and—oh, I don't know. Says fate, or something, brought us together. Said he hadn't planned to take a trip upriver with his granddaughter, but something drove him to it. He can't imagine why he anchored just there. Seemed a good idea at the time. Maybe it was fate. He is very sweet. I wish I could forget that wink I saw in the water.

The Sky Was Full Of Ships

SYKES DIED, AND after two years they tracked Gordon Kemp down and brought him back, because he was the only man who knew anything about the death. Kemp had to face a coroner's jury in Switchpath, Arizona, a crossroads just at the edge of the desert, and he wasn't too happy about it, being city-bred and not quite understanding the difference between "hicks" and "folks."

The atmosphere in the courtroom was tense. Had there been great wainscoted walls and a statue of blind Justice, it would have been more impersonal and, for Kemp, easier to take. But this courtroom was a crossroads granger's hall in Switchpath, Arizona.

The presiding coroner was Bert Whelson, who held a corncob pipe instead of a gavel. At their ease around the room were other men, dirt farmers and prospectors like Whelson. It was like a movie shot. It needed only a comedy dance number and somebody playing a jug.

But there was nothing comic about it. These hicks were in a position to pile trouble on Kemp, trouble that might very easily wind up in the gas chamber.

The coroner leaned forward. "You got nothin' to be afeard of, son, if your conscience is clear."

"I still ain't talking. I brought the guy in, didn't I? Would I done that if I'd killed him?"

The coroner stroked his stubble, a soft rasping sound like a rope being pulled over a wooden beam.

"We don't know about that, Kemp. *Hmm.* Why can't you get it through your head that nobody's accusing you of anything? You're jest a feller knows something about the death of this here Alessandro Sykes. This court'd like to know exactly what happened."

He hesitated, shuffled.

"Sit down, son," said the coroner.

That did it. He slumped into the straight chair that one of the men pushed up for him, and told this story.

I guess I better go right back to the beginning, the first time I ever saw this here Sykes.

I was working in my shop one afternoon when he walked in. He watched what I was doing and spoke up.

"You Gordon Kemp?"

I said yes and looked him over. He was a scrawny feller, prob'ly sixty years old and wound up real tight. He talked fast, smoked fast, moved fast, as if there wasn't time for nothin', but he had to get on to somethin' else. I asked him what he wanted.

"You the man had that article in the magazine about the concentrated atomic torch?" he said.

"Yeah," I told him. "Only that guy from the magazine, he used an awful lot of loose talk. Says my torch was three hundred years ahead of its time." Actually it was something I stumbled on by accident, more or less. The ordinary atomic hydrogen torch—plenty hot.

I figured out a ring-shaped electro-magnet set just in front of the jet, to concentrate it. It repelled the hydrogen particles and concentrated them. It'll cut anything—anything. And since it got patented, you'd be surprised at the calls I get. You got no idea how many people want to cut into bank vaults an' the side doors of hock shops. Well, about Sykes...

I told him this magazine article went a little too far, but I did have quite a gadget. I give him a demonstration or two, and he seemed satisfied. Finally I told him I was wasting my time unless he had a proposition.

He's lookin' real happy about this torch of mine, an' he nods.

"Sure. Only you'll have to take a couple of weeks off. Go out west. Arizona. Cut a way into a cave there."

"Cave, huh?" I said. "Is it legal?" I didn't want no trouble.

"Sure it's legal," he tells me.

"How much?"

He says he hates to argue.

"If you'll get me into that place—and you can satisfy yourself as to whether it's legal—I'll give you five thousand dollars," he said.

Now, five thousand berries cuts a lot of ice for me. Especially for only two weeks' work. And besides, I liked the old guy's looks. He was queer as a nine-dollar bill, mind you, and had a funny way of carryin' on, but I could see he was worth the kind of money he talked.

He looked like he really needed help, too. Aw, maybe I'm just a boy scout at heart. As I say, I liked him, money or no money, and chances are I'd have helped him out for free.

He came to see me a couple more times and we sweated out the details. It wound up with him and me on the train and my torch and the other gear in the baggage car up front. Maybe some of you remember the day we arrived here. He seemed to know a lot of people here. Mm? I thought so. He told me how many years he had been coming out to Switchpath.

He told me lots of things. He was one of the talkin'est old geezers I ever did see. I understood about one ninth of what he said. He was lonely, I guess. I was the first man he ever called in to help him with his work, and he spilled the overflow of years of workin' by himself.

About this Switchpath proposition, he told me that when he was just a punk out of college, he was a archyologist roamin' around the desert lookin' for old Indian stuff, vases and arrowheads and such stuff. And he run across this here room in the rock, at the bottom of a deep cleft.

He got all excited when he told me about this part of it. Went on a mile a minute about plasticine ages and messy zorics and pally o' lithographs or something. I called him down to earth and he explained to me that this room was down in rock that was very old—a couple of hundred thousand years, or maybe a half million.

He said that rock had been there either before mankind had a start here on earth, or maybe about the same time as the missing link. Me, I don't care about dead people or dead people's great grandfathers, but Sykes was all enthusiastic.

Anyhow, it seems that this cave had been opened by some sort of an earthquake or something, and the stuff in it must have been there all that time. What got him excited was that the stuff was machinery of some kind and must have been put there 'way *before there was any human beings on earth at all!*

That seemed silly to me. I wanted to know what kind of machinery.

"Well," he says, "I thought at first that it was some sort of a radio transmitter. Get this," he says. "Here is a machine with an antenna on top of it, just like a microwave job. And beside it is another machine.

"This second machine is shaped like a dumbbell standing on one end. The top of it is a sort of covered hopper, and at the waist of the machine is a arrangement of solenoids made out of some alloy that was never seen before on this earth.

"There's gearing between this machine and the other, the transmitter. I have figured out what this dumbbell thing is. It's a recorder."

I want to know what is it recording. He lays one finger on the side of his nose and winks at me.

"Thought," he says. "Raw thought. But that isn't all. Earthquakes, continental shifts, weather cycles, lots more stuff. It integrates all these things with thought."

I want to know how he knows all this. That was when told me that he had been with this thing for the better part of the last thirty years. He'd figured it out all by himself. He was real touchy about that part of it.

Then I began to realize what was the matter with the poor old guy. He really figured he had something big here and he wanted to find out about it. But it seems he was a ugly kid and a shy man, and he wanted to make the big splash all by himself. It wouldn't do for him just to be known as the man who discovered this thing.

"Any dolt could have stumbled across it," he'd say. He wanted to find out everything there was about this thing before he let a soul know about it. "Greater than the Rosetta Stone," he used to say. "Greater than the nuclear hypotheses." Oh, he was a great one for slinging the five-dollar words.

"And it will be Sykes who gave this to the world," he would say. "Sykes will give it to humanity, complete and provable, and history will be reckoned from the day I speak." Oh, he was wacky, all right. I didn't mind, though. He was harmless, and a nicer little character you'd never want to meet.

Funny guy, that Sykes. What kind of a life he led I can only imagine. He had dough—inherited an income or something, so he didn't have the problem that bothers most of the rest of us. He would spend days in that cavern, staring at the machines. He didn't want to touch them. He only wanted to find out what they were doing there. One of them was running.

The big machine, the dumbbell-shaped one, was running. It didn't make no noise. Both machines had a little disk set into the side. It was half red, half black. On the big machine, the one he called the recorder, this here disk was turning. Not fast, but you could see it was moving. Sykes was all excited about that.

On the way out here, on the train, he spouted a lot of stuff. I don't know why. Maybe he thought I was too dumb to ever tell anybody about it. If that's what he thought, he had the right idea. I'm just a grease monkey who happened to have a bright idea. Anyway, he showed me something he had taken from the cave.

It was a piece of wire about six feet long. But wire like I have never seen before or since. It was about 35 gauge—like a hair. And crooked. Crimped, I mean. Sykes said it was magnetized too. It bent easy enough, but it wouldn't kink at all, and you couldn't put a tight bend in it. I imagine it'd dent a pair of pliers.

He asked me if I thought I could break it. I tried and got a gash in my lunch-hook for my trouble. So help me, it wouldn't break, and it wouldn't cut, and you couldn't get any of those crimps out of it. I don't mean you'd pull the wire and it would snap back. No. You couldn't pull it straight at all.

Sykes told me on the train that it had taken him eight months to cut that piece loose. It was more than just tough. It fused with itself. The first four times he managed to cut it through, he couldn't get the ends apart fast enough to keep them from fusing together again.

He finally had to clamp a pair of steel blocks around the wire, wait for enough wire to feed through to give him some slack and then put about twelve tons on some shears to cut through the wire.

Forged iridium steel, those cutters were, and that wire left a heck of a hole in them.

But the wire parted. He had a big helical spring hauling the wire tight, so that the instant it parted it was snapped out of the way. It had to be cut twice to get the one piece out, and when he put the ends together they fused. I mean, both on the piece he took out and the two free ends in the machine—not a mark, not a bulge.

Well, you all remember when we arrived here with that equipment, and how we hired a car and went off into the desert. All the while the old man was happy as a kid.

"Kemp, my boy," he says, "I got it decoded. I can read that tape. Do you realize what that means? Every bit of human history—I can get it in detail. Every single thing that ever happened to this earth or the people in it.

"You have no idea in what detail that tape records," he says. "Want to know who put the bee on Alexander the Great? Want to know what the name of Pericles' girlfriend really was? I have it all here. What about these Indian and old Greek legends about a lost continent? What about old Fort's fireballs? Who was the man in the iron mask? I have it, son, I have it."

That was what went on all the way out there, to that place in the dry gulch where the cave was.

You wouldn't believe what a place that was to get to. How that old guy ever had the energy to keep going back to it I'll never know. We had to stop the car about twenty miles from here and hoof it.

The country out there is all tore up. If I hadn't already seen the color of his money I'd 'a said the heck with it. Sand an' heat an' big rocks an' more places to fall into and break your silly neck—*Lord!*

Me with a pack on my back too, the torch, the gas and a power supply and all. We got to this cleft, see, and he outs with a length of rope and makes it fast to a stone column that's eroded nearby. He has a slip-snaffle on it. He lowers himself into the gulch and I drop the gear down after him, and then down I go.

Brother, it's dark in there. We go uphill about a hundred and fifty yards, and then Sykes pulls up in front of a facing. By the light of his flash I can see the remains of a flock of campfires he's made there over the years.

"There it is," he says. "It's all yours, Kemp. If that three-hundred-years-in-the-future torch of yours is any good—prove it."

I unlimbered my stuff and got to work, and believe me it was hard, slow goin'. But I got through. It took nine hours before I had a hole fit for us to crawl through, and another hour for it to cool enough so's we could use it.

All that time the old man talked. It was mostly bragging about the job he'd done decoding the wire he had. It was mostly Greek to me.

"I have a record here," he says, swishin' his hunk of wire around, "of a phase of the industrial revolution in Central Europe that will have the historians gnashing their teeth. But have I said anything? Not me. Not Sykes!

"I'll have the history of mankind written in such detail, with such authority, that the name of Sykes will go into the language as a synonym for the miraculously accurate." I remember that because he said it so much. He said it like it tasted good.

I remember once I asked him why it was we had to bother cutting in. Where was the hole he had used?

"That, my boy," he says, "is an unforeseen quality of the machines. For some reason they closed themselves up. In a way I'm glad they did. I was unable to get back in and I was forced to concentrate on my sample. If it hadn't been for that, I doubt that I would ever have cracked the code."

So I asked him what about all this—what were the machines and who left them there and what for? All this while I was cutting away at that rock facing. And, man! I never seen rock like that. If it *was* rock, which now, I doubt.

It come off in flakes, in front of my torch. *My* torch, that'll cut anything. Do you know that in those nine hours I only got through about seven and a half inches of that stuff! And my torch'll walk into laminated bank vaults like the door was open.

When I asked him he shut up for a long time, but I guess he wanted to talk. He sure was enthusiastic. And besides, he figured I was too dumb to savvy what he was talking about. As I said before, he was right there. So he run off about it, and this is about how it went—

"Who left these machines here or how they operate, we may never know. It would be interesting to find out, but the important thing is to get the records and decode them all."

It had taken him a while to recognize that machine as a recorder. The tipoff was that it was running and the other one, the transmitter, was not.

He thought at first that maybe the transmitter was busted, but after a year or two of examining the machines without touching them he began to realize that there was a gear train waiting by the tape where it fed through the gismo that crimped it.

This gear train was fixed to start the transmitter, see? But it was keyed to a certain crimp in the tape. In other words, when something happened somewhere on earth that was just the right thing, the crimper would record it and the transmitter would get keyed off.

Sykes studied that set-up for years before he figured the particular squiggle in that wire that would start that transmitter to sending. Where was it sending to? Why? Sure, he thought about that. But that didn't matter to him.

What was supposed to happen when the tape ran out? Who or what would come and look at it when it was all done? You know, he didn't care. He just wanted to read that tape, is all. Seems there's a lot of guys write history books and stuff. And he wanted to call them liars. He wanted to tell them the way it really was. Can you imagine? So there I am, cutting away with my super-torch on what seems to be a solid wall made out of some stuff has no right to be so tough. I can still see it.

So dark, and me with black goggles on, and the doc with his back to me so's he won't wreck his eyes, spoutin' along about history and the first unbiased account of it. And how he was going to thrust it on the world and just kill all those guys with all those theories.

I remember quitting once for a breather and letting the mercury cells juice up a bit while I had a smoke. Just to make talk I ask Sykes when does he think that transmitter is going to go to work.

"Oh," he says. "It already did. It's finished. That's how I knew that my figuring was right. That tape has a certain rate through the machine. It's in millimeters per month. I have the figure. It wouldn't matter to you. But something happened a while ago that made it possible to check. July sixteenth, nineteen hundred and forty-five, to be exact."

"You don't tell me," I says.

"Oh," he says, real pleased, "but I do! That day something happened which put a wiggle in the wire there—the thing I was looking for all along. It was the crimp that triggered the transmitter. I happened to be in the cave at the time.

"The transmitter started up and the little disk spun around like mad. Then it stopped. I looked in the papers the next week to see what it was. Nothing I could find. It wasn't until the following August that I found out."

I suddenly caught wise.

"Oh—the atom bomb! You mean that rig was set up to send something as soon as an atomic explosion kicked off somewhere on earth!"

He nodded his head. By the glare of the red-hot rock he looked like a skinny old owl.

"That's right. That's why we've got to get in there in a hurry. It was after the second Bikini blast that the cave got sealed up. I don't know if that transmission is ever going to be picked up.

"I don't know if anything is going to happen if it is picked up. I do know that I have the wire decoded and I mean to get those records before anybody else does."

If that wall had been any thicker I never would've gotten through. When I got my circle cut and the cut-out piece dropped inside, my rig was about at its last gasp. So was Sykes. For the last two hours he'd been hoppin' up an' down with impatience.

"Thirty years' work," he kept saying. "I've waited for this for thirty years and I won't be stopped now. Hurry up! Hurry up!"

And when we had to wait for the opening to cool I thought he'd go wild. I guess that's what built him up to his big breakdown. He sure was keyed up.

Well, at last we crawled into the place. He'd talked so much about it that I almost felt I was comin' back to something instead of seeing it for the first time.

There was the machines, the big one about seven feet tall, dumbbell shaped, and the little one sort of a rounded cube with a bunch of macaroni on top that was this antenna he was talking about.

We lit a pressure lantern that flooded the place with light—it was small, with a floor about nine by nine—and he jumped over to the machines.

He scrabbles around and hauls out some wire. Then he stops and stands there looking stupid at me.

"What's the matter, Doc?" I say. I called him Doc.

He gulps and swallows.

"The reel's empty. It's empty! There's only eight inches of wire here. Only—" and that was when he fainted.

I jumped up right away and shook him and shoved him around a little until his eyes started to blink. He sits up and shakes himself.

"Refilled," he says. He is real hoarse. "Kemp! They've been here!"

I began to get the idea. The lower chamber is empty. The upper one is full. The whole set-up is arranged to run off a new recording. And where is Sykes' thirty years' work?

He starts to laugh. I look at him. I can't take that. The place is too small for all that noise. I never heard anybody laugh like that. Like short screams, one after the other, fast. He laughs and laughs.

I carry him out. I put him down outside and go in for my gear. I can hear him laughing out there and that busted-up voice of his echoing in the gulch. I get everything onto the backpack and go to put out the pressure lantern when I hear a little click.

It's that transmitter. The little red and black disk is turning around on it. I just stand there watching it. It only runs for three or four minutes. And then it begins to get hot in there.

I got scared. I ducked out of the hole and picked up Sykes. He didn't weigh much. I looked back in the hole. The cave was lit up. Red. The machines were cherry-red, straw-colored, white, just that quick. They melted. I saw it. I ran.

I don't hardly remember getting to the rope and tying Sykes on and climbing up and hauling him up after me. He was quiet then, but conscious. I carried him away until the light from the gulch stopped me. I turned around to watch.

I could see a ways down into the gulch. It was fillin' up with lava. It was lightin' up the whole desert. And I never felt such heat. I ran again.

I got to the car and dumped Sykes in. He shifted around on the seat some. I asked him how he felt. He didn't answer that but mumbled a lot of stuff.

Something like this.

"They knew we'd reached the atomic age. They wanted to be told when. The transmitter did just that. They came and took the recordings and refilled the machine.

"They sealed off the room with something they thought only controlled atomic power could break into. This time the transmitter was triggered to human beings in that room. Your torch did it, Kemp—that three-hundred-years-in-the-future torch! They think we have atomic power! They'll come back!"

"Who, Doc? Who?" I says.

"I don't know," he mumbles. "There'd be only one reason why someone—some creature—would want to know a thing like that. And that's so they could stop us."

I laughed at him. I got in and started the car and laughed at him.

"Doc," I said, "we ain't goin' to be stopped now. Like the papers say, we're in the atomic age if it kills us. But we're in for keeps. Why, humanity would have to be killed before it'd get out of this atomic age."

"I know that, Kemp—I know—that's what I mean! What have we done? What have we done?"

After that he's quiet a while and when I look at him again I see he's dead. So I brought him in. In the excitement I faded. It just didn't look good to me. I knew nobody would listen to a yarn like that.

There was silence in the courtroom until somebody coughed, and then everyone felt he had to make a sound with his throat or his feet. The coroner held up his hand.

"I kin see what Brother Kemp was worried about. If that story is true I, for one, would think twice about tellin' it."

"He's a liar!" roared a prospector from the benches. "He's a murderin' liar! I have a kid reads that kind of stuff, an' I never did like to see him at it. Believe me, he's a-goin' to cut it out as of right now. I think this Kemp feller needs a hangin'!"

"Now, Jed!" bellowed the coroner. 'If we kill off this man we do it legal, hear?" The sudden hubbub quieted, and the coroner turned to the prisoner.

"Listen here, Kemp—somethin' jest occurred to me. How long was it from the time of the first atom blast until the time that room got sealed up?"

"I dunno. About two years. Little over. Why?"

"An' how long since that night you been talking about, when Sykes died?"

"Or was murdered," growled the prospector.

"Shut up, Jed. Well, Kemp?"

"About eighteen mon— No. Nearer two years."

"Well then," said the coroner, spreading his hands. "If there was anything in your story, or in that goofy idea of the dead man's about someone comin' to kill us off—well, ain't it about time they did?"

There were guffaws, and the end of the grange hall disappeared in a burst of flame. Yelling, cursing, some screaming, they pushed and fought their way out into the moonlit road.

The sky was full of ships.

Largo

THE CHANDELIERS ON the eighty-first floor of the Empire State Building swung wildly without any reason. A company of soldiers marched over a new, well-built bridge, and it collapsed. Enrico Caruso filled his lungs and sang, and the crystal glass before him shattered.

And Vernon Drecksall composed his Largo.

He composed it in hotel rooms and scored it on trains and ships, and it took more than twenty-two years. He started it in the days when smoke hung over the city, because factories used coal instead of broadcast power; when men spoke to men over wires and never saw each other's faces; when the nations of earth were ruled by the greed of a man or the greed of men. During the Thirty Days War and the Great Change which followed it, he labored; and he finished it on the day of his death.

It was music. That is a silly, inarticulate phrase. I heard a woman say "Thank you" to the doctor who cured her cancer, and then she cried, for the words said so little. I knew a man who was born lonely, and whose loneliness increased as he lived until it was a terrible thing. And then he met the girl he was to marry, and one night he said, "I love you." Just words; but they filled the incredibly vast emptiness within him; filled it completely, so that there was enough left over to spill out in three syllables, eight letters.... The Largo—it was music. Break away from individual words; separate yourself from the meaning of them strung together, and try to imagine music like Drecksall's Largo in E Flat. Each note was more than polished—burnished. As music is defined as a succession of notes, so the Largo was a thing surpassing music; for its rests, its upbeats, its melodic pauses were silences blended in harmony, in discord. Only Drecksall's genius could give tangible, recognizable tone to silence. The music created scales and keys and chords of silence, which played in exquisite counterpoint with the audible themes.

It was dedicated to Drecksall himself, because he was a true genius, which means that everything in the universe which was not a part of him existed for him. But the Largo was written for Wylie, and inspired by Gretel.

They were all young when they met. It was at a summer resort, one of those strange outposts of city settlement houses. The guests were plumbers and artists and bankers and stenographers and gravicab drivers and students. Pascal Wylie was shrewd and stocky, and came there to squander a small inheritance at a place where people would be impressed by it. He had himself convinced that when the paltry thousands were gone he could ease himself into a position where more could be gotten by someone else's efforts. Unfortunately this was quite true. It is hardly just, but people like that can always find a moneymaker to whom their parasitism is indispensable.

Gretel was one of the students. Without enthusiasm, she attended a school in the city which taught a trade for which she was not fitted and which would not have supported her if she had been. Wylie's feminine counterpart, she was spending her marriageable years as he spent his money, in places where it would impress others less fortunate. Like him, she lived in a passively certain expectation that when her unearned assets were gone, the future would replace them. Her most valuable possession was a quick smile and a swifter glance, which she used very often—whenever, in fact, a remark was made in her presence which she did not understand. The smile and the glance were humorous and understanding and completely misleading. The subtler the remark, the quicker her reaction. Her rather full lips she held slightly parted, and one watched them to catch the brilliantly wise thought they were about to utter. They never did. She was always surrounded by quasi-sophisticates, and pseudo-intellectuals whose conversation got farther and farther above her silly head until she retreated behind one slightly raised golden eyebrow, her whole manner indicating that the company was clever, but a bit below her. She was unbelievably dumb and an utterly fascinating person to know slightly.

Vernon Drecksall washed pots and groomed vegetables for the waspish cook. He had a violin and he cared about little else, but he had discovered that to be able to play he must eat, and this job served to harness his soul to earth, where it did not belong. He got as many dollars each week as he worked hours each day, an arrangement which was quite satisfactory by his peculiar standards.

Each night after Drecksall had scoured the last of his eight dozen pots, disposed of his three bushels of garbage, and swabbed down an acre and a half of floor-space, he went to his room for his violin and then headed for the privacy of distance. Up into the forest on a rocky trail that took him to the brink of a hilltop lake he would go; beating through thick undergrowth he reached a granite boulder that shouldered out into the water at the end of a point. Night after night he stood there on that natural stage and played with almost heartbreaking abandon. Before him stretched the warm, black water, studded with starlight, like the eyes of an audience. Like the glow of an usher's torch the riding lights of a passing heliplane would move over the water. Like the breathing of twenty thousand spell-bound people, the water pressed and stroked and rustled on the bank. But there was never any applause. That suited his mood. They didn't applaud Lincoln at Gettysburg either.

Every ten days the pot-walloper was given a day off, which meant that he worked only until noon, which, again, generally turned out to be four in the afternoon after various emergency odds and ends had been taken care of. Then he had the privilege of circulating among people who disliked him on sight while he mourned that the woods were full of vandals and the lake was full of boats and the telejuke box was incapable of anything but rhythmically insincere approaches to total discord. He didn't look forward to his days off, until he saw Gretel.

She was sitting on an ancient Hammond electric organ, staring off into space, and thinking about absolutely nothing. The mountain sunset streamed through a window behind her, making her hair a halo and her profiled body the only thing in the universe fit to be framed by that glorious light. Drecksall was unprepared for the sight; he was blinded and enslaved. He didn't believe her. She must be music. It was, for him, a perfectly rational conclusion, for she was past all understanding, and until now nothing not musical had struck him that way. He moved over to her and told her so. He was not trying to be poetic when he said, "Someone played you on the organ, and you were too lovely to come out as sound." He was simply stating what he believed.

She sat above him and turned her head. She gave him an unfathomable half-smile, and as she drew her breath the golden glow from behind her crept around her cheek and tinted the arched flesh of her nostrils. It was an exquisite gesture; she saw in his eyes that she had pleased him and thought, He stinks of grease and ammonia.

He put out his hand and touched her. He was actually afraid that she would slip back into a swelling of symphonic sound, sweep over him and be gone past all remembering.

"Are you a real woman who will be alive?" he faltered.

Stupid questions are not always stupid to stupid people. "Of course," she said.

Then he asked her to marry him.

She looked at his craggy face and boniness and his hollow chest and mad-looking eyes and shook her head. He backed away from her, turned and ran. He looked once over his shoulder, and caught the picture of her that lighted his brain until the day he died. For there, in light and shade, in warm flesh and cool colors, was the Largo; and he would have to live until he turned her back into music. He could not command her as she was; but if he could duplicate her in sharps and flats and heart-stopping syncopation, then she would be his. As he ran, staring back, his head *thwacked* on the doorpost, and he staggered on, all blood and tears.

Gretel looked pensively at her fingernails. "Good God," she said, "what a dope." And she went back to her cow-like mental vacancy.

A couple of nights later Gretel and Pascal Wylie were in a canoe on the hilltop lake, blandly violating the sacredness Drecksall had invested in her, when they heard music.

"What's that?" said Wylie sharply.

"Vi'lin," said Gretel. For her the subject closed with an almost audible snap, but Wylie's peering mind was diverted; and seeing this, she accepted it without protest, as she accepted all things. "Wonder who it is?" said Wylie. He touched a lever, and the silent solenoid-impulse motor in the stern of the canoe wafted them toward the sound.

"It's that kitchen-boy!" whispered Wylie a moment later.

Gretel roused herself enough to look. "He's crazy," she said coldly. She wished vaguely that Wylie would take her away from the sound of the violin, or that Drecksall would stop playing. Or—play something else. She had never heard these notes before, which was not surprising considering the kind of music Drecksall played. But such music had never bothered her until now. Very little ever bothered her. She made an almost recognizable effort to understand why she didn't like it, realized that it made her feel ashamed, assumed that she was ashamed because she was out with Wylie, and dropped the matter. Having reasoned past the music itself, she was no longer interested. She might have been had she realized that it was her own portrait in someone else's eyes that she had listened to.

Wylie felt himself stirred too, but differently. It didn't matter to him why this scullery lad was scraping a fiddle on the lakeshore when he should have been asleep. The thing that struck him was that the man could make that violin talk. He made it get inside you—inside people who didn't give a damn, like Wylie. Wylie began to wonder why the hands that performed that way had taken on a duty of washing pots. He had learned early that the best way to get along (to him that meant to get rich) was to find your best talent and exploit it. Here was a man wasting a talent on trees and fish.

Music is a science as well as an art, and it is a shocking thing to those who think that musicians are by nature incompetent and impractical, to discover that more often than not a musician has a strong mechanical flair. Conversely, a person who is unmechanical is seldom musical. Drecksall's playing on this particular night was careful, thoughtful, precise. He was building something quite as tangible to him as a bridge is to an engineer. The future whole was awe-inspiring, beautiful, but, like the bridge, it was composed of quite unromantic essentials—tonal nuts, bolts and rivets. It was the skillful machining of these that intrigued Wylie, possibly far more than would the completed work.

Drecksall paused at the end of a bewildering arpeggio, and stood with his violin in his hand, staring puzzledly across the water. He had just realized the enormity of his task, and was completely wrapped up in it, so was totally unprepared for Wylie's sudden burst of clapping. It was not applause, exactly; Wylie was gladhanding, following the birth of a bright idea. He had an idea he would butter up the violinist, befriend him, get him to someone who would know if he was really any good or not from a commercial point of view. If he was, Wylie could take a cut, maybe. Ten percent—forty—seventy-five? Drecksall was young. He would last a long time, and he looked like a dope.

So he cracked his lean hands together and whistled shrilly, like a grandfather at a burlesque house. Surely the ape would appreciate enthusiasm!

Drecksall leapt like a startled moose, nearly lost his footing, and then froze, peering toward the dark canoe, a hot smoke of anger curling into his brain. He felt stripped, imposed upon. He felt kicked. His night playing demanded infinitely more privacy than his body, and it was being rudely stared at. He suddenly broke the violin over his knee, hurled the pieces at the canoe, and ran into the dark woods.

"I told you he was crazy," said Gretel complacently.

It was a long time before Pascal Wylie could puff the wind back into his sails.

Two days later Drecksall was returning from a copse a hundred yards from the resort's main building, carrying a couple of large garbage pails. There was an incinerator back there, and as he left it he heard the whirring of rotary wings. He looked up and saw a cab descending, and would have ignored it altogether had he not noticed that the man who climbed out and paid the driver had a violin-case under his arm. Drecksall looked at it the way a prep-school boy looks at a soft-drink calendar.

"Hi," said Pascal Wylie. Drecksall nodded.

"I want to talk to you," said Wylie.

"Me?" Drecksall couldn't take his eyes off the violin.

"Yeh. Heard you lost your fiddle."

Drecksall just stared. Wylie grinned and handed over the instrument. Drecksall dropped his garbage cans, clasped the case and clawed it open. The violin was a good one, complete with three bows, spare strings, and a pitch pipe. Drecksall stood helplessly, his wide mouth trying fruitlessly to say the same thing his eyes were saying.

"You want that violin?" asked Wylie briskly. The question needed no answer. "It's yours if you'll do me a favor."

"What?"

Wylie gestured toward the cab. "Just hop in there with me. We'll run into the city, and you'll play that thing for a friend of mine. Chances are that after he hears you you can go right on playing as long as you want to, and you'll never wash another pot. How's it strike you?"

Drecksall looked at the tumbled garbage cans. "I can't leave here," he said. "I'd lose my job."

Wylie was not thinking about that. If the violinist failed the audition, he would starve—and he could, for all Wylie cared. But he thought the man had a chance. He snatched the violin and walked toward the cab. "Okay, then."

Drecksall picked up the cans and stared after Wylie. His would-be manager climbed in, giving not a backward glance. With elaborate carelessness, however, he did manage to have a great deal of difficulty in getting the violin-case in after him. It hung, black and shining and desirable, for seconds; and suddenly Drecksall realized just how badly those cans smelled. He ran to the cab and climbed in.

"Good boy," said Wylie.

Drecksall took the violin-case from him and opened it. "I never had a violin as nice as this before," he said simply.

The audition went off smoothly. Drecksall was led into a soundproof room containing a novachord and an unpleasing female organist. He was handed a sheaf of sheet music which, but for the individual titles, he thereafter ignored. A red light flashed, a speaker baffle said boredly, "Go ahead, please," and Drecksall played. He played for an hour, stopping twice in the middle of selections to tune his violin, which was new and springy, and once to upbraid the organist, who, after the first few bars, had never played better in her life.

Afterward, in another room, Wylie was called in to speak to an official. He crossed the room and, with his hat on, perched easily on the edge of the man's desk and looked at his fingernails until the man spoke.

"You're this fellow's manager?"

"Mmm."

"Eight hundred for thirty minutes five times weekly, thirteen weeks." He dragged a contract form out of the desk, filled in some spaces, and shoved it over to Wylie. Wylie looked at it gingerly as if it was one of Drecksall's garbage pails, took the pen, crossed out the $800 and wrote in $5000. Then he yawned and looked out of the window.

"Don't be silly," said the radio executive. He looked keenly at Wylie, sighed, and drew up another contract. It was for two thousand. Wylie signed with alacrity. "Make that out in two checks, payable to cash," he said. "One eighteen hundred, and one two hundred."

The man behind the desk made out the checks. "Yours is the ten percent check?" he asked. Wylie smiled.

"I think you're a heel," said the exec, and handed the papers over.

At the door, Wylie tipped his hat and grinned. "Thank you very much, sir," he said. He went and found Drecksall and gave him his check. "Go buy yourself some clothes," he said. Drecksall looked at it and gasped.

"Two hundred dollars?"

Wylie nodded. "You're hired. Let's get out of here."

That was only the beginning. Wylie knew an amazing number of people, and before the year was out, Drecksall was nationally known. Money poured in, and, as Wylie was shrewd as well as slick, he saw to it that Drecksall got plenty. Since there was so much always on hand, Drecksall never questioned the cut that Wylie took, and Wylie was remarkably secretive about where he put his own money.

And one other thing of importance happened.

One afternoon Drecksall hurried home to the apartment he shared with Wylie in Safrisco. It was a quietly elaborate place, and it included the one thing Drecksall demanded—a totally soundproofed practice room. Flinging open the door, Drecksall was halfway across the sumptuous living room before he quite realized that on entering he had seen someone else in the room. He swung around, staring.

"Hello," said Gretel. She set down her drink and swung her feet off the couch. "Remember me?"

Drecksall nodded silently, watching her, stripping gloves off his hands.

"You're changed," he said after a bit, looking at her clothes, her hair.

"I should be." She smiled vapidly. "I'm married."

"Oh." It penetrated slowly. "Who to?"

"Pascal."

"He—he changed you?"

Gretel's bird-brain manufactured a bird's laugh. "Sure."

"Good God," whispered Drecksall in disgust. He went into his room and closed the door. He had just begun to hate Wylie.

Gretel picked up her drink again. "He's still crazy," she said.

In nearly all things Vernon Drecksall was as reasonably sane as the rest of us; but he was a monomaniac, and he could hardly be blamed for assuming the things he did. He and his odd conception of Gretel were made for each other. He was the form-fitting husk for his vision of her, and she had filled it completely. She could never do so again, because so much of that vision was composed of sunset gold and purple shadow and that unforgettable tinge of pink when the light shone through her nostril. He could not be expected to understand that. He only knew that the vision didn't fit any more; that something had happened to change her from that utter perfection. And he had her own word for it that Pascal Wylie was that thing. He slumped into the most driving kind of misery. He couldn't see that there was anything he could do about it except to go ahead with his building. Some day he would have her back. Some day she would emerge from his violin in a great bubble of melody which would settle before him, open up and reveal her there as she had been on that summer evening. And she would be his. Toward that iridescent ideal, he strove. Hour upon hour, alone in his soundproofed cell, he wrought the Largo. Sometimes he was rewarded by sustained flashes of completion. He had a phrase for her hair, a swift run for her strange eyes as she turned her head, a dazzling contrapuntal passage for the sound of her voice. Each little detail that was mastered was carefully scored, and he would play them jealously now and again, seeing his visions, spurring himself on to represent the duller notes which represented the more prosaic part of the picture—the window frame behind her, the scratched surface of the old Hammond organ, the crack at the side of her shoe.

During the war, and the ruinous period afterward, he was glad that there was no longer any time for concerts or broadcasts or public appearances, for it left him time to work. Deep in the heart of a half-ruined hotel he labored by candlelight, while the three great counter-revolutions rolled and swirled around his little citadel of silence. Twice he saw Pascal Wylie in a gibbering state of fear; both times he had thrown him bodily out of his practice-room, ignoring his pleading and his warning that they were all going to be shot. Wylie was in politics up to his ears and over, though fortunately for him he had stayed in the background and let dollars speak for him. When it was all over and the exhausted world began to build again, Drecksall was possibly the only man alive who neither knew nor cared what had happened. He had been touched by it too; his investments were completely wiped out, but that meant nothing to him. He was certain that there would be more, and he was right. The Great Change was on, and with the nation's rebirth there was plenty for such as he.

And so the years swept by him as had the violence of war and revolution and renascence. Time left him alone, and it was with something of a shock that Wylie, during that rocky period, realized that the strange creature was the only solid, unchanging thing in the universe. Gretel changed by the day, for hers was the scintillant peasant beauty that fades early. She gave every promise of finally occupying some chimney-corner until she grew into a gargoyle and became part of the mantel. Wylie cared for her casually from force of habit, and bent his efforts to rebuilding his fortune. And Drecksall played.

Something else was creeping into the building of the Largo. The central theme itself, that breathing, mutant reproduction of Gretel, was being framed in a darker, deeper mass of tones. It was a thing like hatred, like vengeance, that frame. It was Pascal Wylie, and it wound round and about the thing that was Gretel. This was not mere music. This was something more definite than even Drecksall's crazed kind of music. It was the outline, the detailed description, of a definite plan of action. The same impulse that drove him to do something about his vanished Gretel was forcing him to deal, in his own way, with Wylie.

There came a time when Drecksall felt that the Largo was nearly complete. It would need more than scoring for the composition to be fully rounded. It would need an audience, and it would need a setting. It couldn't be played in any ordinary concert hall, nor in the open air. For its full effect, it must needs be played in an auditorium built for it, and it alone.

A building like that never existed, nor did Drecksall expect it to. He built it himself. It took two years or more. It cost thousands—so much, indeed, that he went to Wylie for more; and Wylie, fearing that he would begin asking questions, gave him more and more of his own earnings, telling him blandly that theater managers and the broadcasting chains were paying more these days. Drecksall didn't care, as long as he got enough for his purpose.

He had no end of trouble. It was months before he found an engineer who would dare attempt the auditorium, more months before he found one who could be convinced that he meant what he said when he gave his specifications. They were to be followed to the thousandth of a millimeter, and Drecksall's rages when he saw tiny variations on the blueprints were really beautiful to behold. In time, the indignant words, "After all, Mr. Drecksall, I'm a graduate engineer, and while you may be the world's foremost violinist, you are not qualified to—" became real poison to him. After breaking up a few expensive violins and accessories over their erudite heads, he gave up personal visits from architects and contractors and handled the thing vitriolically, by mail.

But when the auditorium was finished, it was what he had ordered, from the bedrock and soil he had specified to the top of the heavy square tower. It was certainly a strange affair. It was not very large, and looked like the conventionalized nose of a space cruiser. Its walls were thin at the bottom, thick and massive at its domed top. Inside, the basic construction was easily seen. It was made of thirty-eight arches all joining at the top and forming the circular walls at the sides and base. The tower was squat and massive; solid, steel-reinforced concrete. There were no windows, and the door was self-sealing, an integral part of its wall. It was lighted from a fixture which also was built into the contours of the wall. The only thing that detracted from that symphony of metrical lines on the interior wall was a heavy concrete block that jutted out over a stone chair—high over it. On the other side of the chamber was another such chair, but the wall over it was like all the others. At the exact center of the building was a tiny red tile, set into the floor, and this was the only indication of a stage, a place from which to perform. It was certainly a strange creation; but then, it had been built for a strange purpose.

Drecksall made his demands several weeks before he intended to play the Largo, because he expected resistance. He got it. Wylie failed to see why he should sit through a highly involved musical masterpiece when he had never cared particularly for music; why he should go out into the wilds, miles from the nearest city, to hear it; why it couldn't be played in the apartment or at their country place; and most particularly, why he should rouse Gretel from the intellectual stupor she had fallen into these last years and drag her out there to the auditorium. Drecksall heard him out patiently, said, "It really isn't much to ask," and left the room. He was back in a moment with the concert violin which he wrapped carefully in a plexiskin and put away in its case. "I'm not going to play again," he said quietly, "until I play the Largo for you and Gretel, in my auditorium." Then, leaving Wylie to give puzzled shrugs at the violin-case, he went out.

It took just forty-eight hours for Wylie to discover that Drecksall was really serious, for it was that long before the violinist had an engagement. Wylie got into his soup and fish, went to call Drecksall, and found him sprawled smiling on the couch of his practice room. He refused to go. Fuming, Wylie canceled the concert. He didn't give in on that occasion, nor on the next, but when he read a note on one of the facsi-papers to the effect that the Old Master was at long last developing temperament, and that perhaps the word "maybe" should be inserted before the date of each of his scheduled concerts, Wylie broke down, at last asking himself why he had made an issue of it at all. Drecksall had been easy enough to get along with.

And at long last they hired a heliplane and whirred the long miles out to the auditorium. As they landed, Wylie broke his glum silence to ask, "How long'll we be here?"

"I couldn't say," grinned Drecksall happily.

"How long will it take to play the thing?"

"About an hour."

"Shall I tell him to come back in about that time?" asked Wylie, nodding toward the cab-driver.

Drecksall alighted from the cab and helped Gretel out. "If you like," he said.

The plane shot away and they walked up the rough trail toward the auditorium. "That the place?" asked Wylie.

"That's the place."

Wylie looked at it. "Hell! What did you go and spend all that jack on that place for? Why, it wouldn't hold fifty people!"

"It wasn't meant to," said Drecksall gently.

They reached the door—that is, the point where the path ended against the wall. Drecksall paused and looked at them.

"You have a hard collar on," he said. "Take it off."

"Take—what for?"

"This building is the last word—*my* last word—in acoustics. I can't have anything spoiling it." He looked at Gretel. She was standing there, uncomplaining as ever. "Tell her to take off those stockings, too. They're sheer plastic, and might echo."

Wylie glanced over his shoulder at the speck that was the retreating heliplane, shrugged, and took off his collar. "Take your stockings off," he said to Gretel.

The spasm that signified mental activity crossed Gretel's bland face. "He's crazy," she said, looking at Drecksall.

"You're kiddin'," said Wylie. "Go on—take 'em off."

Once that was disposed of, Drecksall opened the door and followed them in. He turned on the lights, closed the door. "Sit over there," he said to Wylie, indicating the stone seat under the jutting block. He led Gretel over to the other chair. Then he took his violin out and put the case into a recess in the wall. A panel slid over it.

"This is a looney sort of place," said Wylie. His voice echoed so that it hurt his ears. For his own comfort, he whispered. "What gave you the idea for it?"

Drecksall stopped rubbing his bow with rosin to stare at his manager. "What gave me the idea? Study, you fool. Years of it. Infinite patience in going into the laws and phenomena and—and tricks of acoustics. Be quiet. I'm going to play."

He snuggled the tail of the violin into the hollow of his throat, bowed the open strings, flattened one of them microscopically. Then, without another word, he began to play.

Little else could be said here than that he played his Largo. It began stridently, weaving that dreadful flaming frame for the vision of Gretel; and Wylie was whisked deep into it. One part of his brain ticked busily away, still wondering about this auditorium, the fact that it was built for an audience of two, the surprise in discovering that for years Drecksall had had a secret activity, the realization that the acoustics of the place were indeed amazing. The notes spread out from his inspired violin, were gathered at the top of the dome and hurled back with a force that made the building tremble. Yes, the building echoed; soon, it had far more echoed sound in it than original, so that Drecksall could slip into a thin, sweet piping and be accompanied by a tumultuous background of sound that he had created long seconds before.

The music suddenly took an ear-shattering turn, and then began a theme—a theme that caught both Wylie and the comatose Gretel the same way, made them both stretch their memories back and back until they settled on a dark lake. They saw again a figure on a rock, pressing notes out through the warm air on a hilltop lake. The same theme—and then again that crashing series of bass runs; and then, before the listeners had time to be startled by it, that almost telepathic theme again. Back and back again he returned to it, the roar of the bass strings and the compelling measures of the memory theme; and always they were faster, and louder, and closer together. They blended finally into a great crescendo, a monster welling of sound that gathered in the dome and came crashing down, pressing the stone block away from the wall, sending its massive tons down on Pascal Wylie. Its crash was symphonic, precisely blended with the mood and rhythm of the music; and as the echoes died away, that whole section of floor sank out of sight, bearing Wylie's crushed body and the pile of rubble that hid it; and a panel slid across the opening. Now the auditorium was acoustically perfect for the greater task that was at hand.

Gretel sat in a paralysis of fear, and Drecksall played earnestly on. This part of the Largo was justice. He had long wanted to kill Wylie because Wylie, he felt, had killed the Gretel he pictured. But artistic integrity forbade the use of any weapon but music, for music was so deeply involved.

And now began the recreation of his old, old vision. He did not look at the unmoving Gretel, but sketched in the essentials of his tone-portrait, and then went over them and over them, filling in. He never lost sight of the shades he had already drawn, but all the while he strove for more and more perfect completion. Even Gretel began to see it. The music moved, with mechanical perfection, across her mental screen, burning indelibly wherever it touched. It moved with speed, slowly, the way the darting photoelectric beam slowly draws a transmitted photograph. It moved as indirectly and as purposefully and as implacably.

The laboring strings hummed and crackled, and Drecksall's fingers were a blur. Gretel, shockingly, felt the fabric of the clothes she had worn that day, all over her body; she felt the warmth of the setting sun on her back, and her lips began to move in the words she had spoken then, so vivid was the music.

And then, shrilly, the thing was complete. The picture was there, sustained by one thin, high note that fell and fell until it became low and vibrant and infinitely compelling. It continued unbearably, filling the room, filling it again at twice the pressure, again and again. A trickle of powdered stone came down from the tower's base, and then the tortured stone could stand no more. The upper walls cracked and the tower burst through.

And as it did, Vernon Drecksall saw and claimed his reward. The mass of masonry opened high over his head and a shaft of golden sunlight speared through, and in the roaring, dust-filled auditorium Gretel sat spotlighted. Her pose, her hair, her very expression, were, to his crazed and triumphant mind, the Largo, come alive. With a glad cry he hurled his violin away and caught her in his arms on the very instant that the great tower crushed down on them both. He had his revenge, and he had his consummation.

The chandeliers on the eighty-first floor of the Empire State Building swung wildly without any reason. A company of soldiers marched over a new, well-built bridge, and it collapsed. Enrico Caruso filled his lungs and sang, and the crystal glass before him shattered.

And Vernon Drecksall composed his Largo.

Thunder and Roses

When Pete Mawser learned about the show, he turned away from the GHQ bulletin board, touched his long chin, and determined to shave. This was odd, because the show would be video, and he would see it in his barracks.

He had an hour and a half. It felt good to have a purpose again—even shaving before eight o'clock. Eight o'clock Tuesday, just the way it used to be. Everyone used to catch that show on Tuesday. Everyone used to say, Wednesday morning, "How about the way she sang 'The Breeze and I' last night?" "Hey, did you hear Starr last night?"

That was a while ago, before all those people were dead, before the country was dead. Starr Anthim, institution, like Crosby, like Duse, like Jenny Lind, like the Statue of Liberty.

(Liberty had been one of the first to get it, her bronze beauty volatilized, radioactive, and even now being carried about in vagrant winds, spreading over the earth—)

Pete Mawser grunted and forced his thoughts away from the drifting, poisonous fragments of a blasted Liberty. Hate was first. Hate was ubiquitous, like the increasing blue glow in the air at night, like the tension that hung over the base.

Gunfire crackled sporadically far to the right, swept nearer. Pete stepped out of the street and made for a parked ten-wheeler. There's a lot of cover in and around a ten-wheeler.

There was a Wac sitting on the short running-board.

At the corner a stocky figure backed into the intersection. The man carried a tommy gun in his arms, and he was swinging to and fro with the gentle, wavering motion of a weathervane. He staggered toward them, his gun muzzle hunting. Someone fired from a building and the man swiveled and blasted wildly at the sound.

"He's—blind," said Pete Mawser, and added, "He ought to be," looking at the tattered face.

A siren keened. An armored jeep slewed into the street. The full-throated roar of a brace of .50-caliber machine guns put a swift and shocking end to the incident.

"Poor crazy kid," Pete said softly. "That's the fourth I've seen today." He looked down at the Wac. She was smiling.

"Hey!"

"Hello, Sarge." She must have identified him before, because now she did not raise her eyes or her voice. "What happened?"

"You know what happened. Some kid got tired of having nothing to fight and nowhere to run to. What's the matter with you?"

"No," she said. "I don't mean that." At last she looked up at him. "I mean all of this. I can't seem to remember."

"You . . . well, gee, it's not easy to forget. We got hit. We got hit everywhere at once. All the big cities are gone. We got it from both sides. We got too much. The air is becoming radioactive. We'll all—" He checked himself. She didn't know. She'd forgotten. There was nowhere to escape to, and she'd escaped inside herself, right here. Why tell her about it? Why tell her that everyone was going to die? Why tell her that other, shameful thing: that we hadn't struck back?

But she wasn't listening. She was still looking at him. Her eyes were not quite straight. One held his but the other was slightly shifted and seemed to be looking at his temples. She was smiling again. When his voice trailed off she didn't prompt him. Slowly he moved away. She did not turn her head, but kept looking up at where he had been, smiling a little. He turned away, wanting to run, walking fast.

(How long can a guy hold out? When you're in the Army they try to make you be like everybody else. What do you do when everybody else is cracking up?)

He blanked out the mental picture of himself as the last one left sane. He'd followed that one through before. It always led to the conclusion that it would be better to be one of the first. He wasn't ready for that yet.

Then he blanked that out, too. Every time he said to himself that he wasn't ready for that yet, something within him asked, "Why not?" and he never seemed to have an answer ready.

(How long could a guy hold out?)

He climbed the steps of the QM Central and went inside.

There was nobody at the reception switchboard. It didn't matter. Messages were carried by guys in jeeps, or on motorcycles. The Base Command was not insisting that anybody stick to a sitting job these days. Ten desk men would crack up for every one on a jeep, or on the soul-sweat squads. Pete made up his mind to put in a little stretch on a squad tomorrow. Do him good. He just hoped that this time the adjutant wouldn't burst into tears in the middle of the parade ground. You could keep your mind on the manual of arms just fine until something like that happened.

He bumped into Sonny Weisefreund in the barracks corridor. The tech's round young face was as cheerful as ever. He was naked and glowing, and had a towel thrown over his shoulder.

"Hi, Sonny. Is there plenty of hot water?"

"Why not?" grinned Sonny. Pete grinned back, cursing inwardly. Could anybody say anything about anything at all without one of these reminders? Sure there was hot water. The QM barracks had hot water for three hundred men. There were three dozen left. Men dead, men gone to the hills, men locked up so they wouldn't—

"Starr Anthim's doing a show tonight."

"Yeah. Tuesday night. Not funny, Pete. Don't you know there's a war—"

"No kidding," Pete said swiftly. "She's here—right here on the base."

Sonny's face was joyful. "Gee." He pulled the towel off his shoulder and tied it around his waist. "Starr Anthim here! Where are they going to put on the show?"

"HQ, I imagine. Video only. You know about public gatherings." And a good thing, too, he thought. Put on an in-person show, and some torn-up GI would crack during one of her numbers. He himself would get plenty mad over a thing like that—mad enough to do something about it then and there. And there would probably be a hundred and fifty or more like him, going raving mad because someone had spoiled a Starr Anthim show. That would be a dandy little shambles for her to put in her memory book.

"How'd she happen to come here, Pete?"

"Drifted in on the last gasp of a busted-up Navy helicopter."

"Yeah, but why?"

"Search me. Get your head out of that gift horse's mouth."

He went into the washroom, smiling and glad that he still could. He undressed and put his neatly folded clothes down on a bench. There were a soap wrapper and an empty toothpaste tube lying near the wall. He went and picked them up and put them in the catch-all. He took the mop which leaned against the partition and mopped the floor where Sonny had splashed after shaving. Got to keep things squared away. He might say something if it were anyone else but Sonny. But Sonny wasn't cracking up. Sonny always had been like that. Look there. Left his razor out again.

Pete started his shower, meticulously adjusting the valves until the pressure and temperature exactly suited him. He didn't do anything slapdash these days. There was so much to feel, and taste, and see now. The impact of water on his skin, the smell of soap, the consciousness of light and heat, the very pressure of standing on the soles of his feet—he wondered vaguely how the slow increase of radioactivity in the air, as the nitrogen transmuted to Carbon Fourteen, would affect him if he kept carefully healthy in every way. What happens first? Do you go blind? Headaches, maybe? Perhaps you lose your appetite. Or maybe you get tired all the time.

Why not go look it up?

On the other hand, why bother? Only a very small percentage of the men would die of radioactive poisoning. There were too many other things that killed more quickly, which was probably just as well. That razor, for example. It lay gleaming in a sunbeam, curved and clean in the yellow light. Sonny's father and grandfather had used it, or so he said, and it was his pride and joy.

Pete turned his back on it and soaped under his arms, concentrating on the tiny kisses of bursting bubbles. In the midst of a recurrence of disgust at himself for thinking so often of death, a staggering truth struck him. He did not think of such things because he was morbid, after all! It was the very familiarity of things that brought death-thoughts. It was either "I shall never do this again" or "This is one of the last times I shall do this." You might devote yourself completely to doing things in different ways, he thought madly. You might crawl across the floor this time, and next time walk across on your hands. You might skip dinner tonight, and have a snack at two in the morning instead, and eat grass for breakfast.

But you had to breathe. Your heart had to beat. You'd sweat and you'd shiver, the same as always. You couldn't get away from that. When those things happened, they would remind you. Your heart wouldn't beat out its *wunklunk, wunklunk* any more. It would go *one-less, one-less,* until it yelled and yammered in your ears and you had to make it stop.

Terrific polish on that razor.

And your breath would go on, same as before. You could sidle through this door, back through the next one and the one after, and figure out a totally new way to go through the one after that, but your breath would keep on sliding in and out of your nostrils like a razor going through whiskers, making a sound like a razor being stropped.

Sonny came in. Pete soaped his hair. Sonny picked up the razor and stood looking at it. Pete watched him, soap ran into his eye, he swore, and Sonny jumped.

"What are you looking at, Sonny? Didn't you ever see it before?"

"Oh, sure. Sure. I was just—" He shut the razor, opened it, flashed light from its blade, shut it again. "I'm tired of using this, Pete. I'm going to get rid of it. Want it?"

Want it? In his foot locker, maybe. Under his pillow. "Thanks no, Sonny. Couldn't use it."

"I like safety razors," Sonny mumbled. "Electrics, even better. What are we going to do with it?"

"Throw it in the . . . no." Pete pictured the razor turning end over end in the air, half open, gleaming in the maw of the catchall. "Throw it out the—" No. Curving out into the long grass. You might want it. You might crawl around in the moonlight looking for it. You might find it.

"I guess maybe I'll break it up."

"No," Pete said. "The pieces—" Sharp little pieces. Hollow-ground fragments. "I'll think of something. Wait'll I get dressed."

He washed briskly, toweled, while Sonny stood looking at the razor. It was a blade now, and if you broke it, there would be shards and glittering splinters, still razor sharp. You could slap its edge into an emery wheel and grind it away, and somebody could find it and put another edge on it because it was so obviously a razor, a fine steel razor, one that would slice so— "I know. The laboratory. We'll get rid of it," Pete said confidently.

He stepped into his clothes, and together they went to the laboratory wing. It was very quiet there. Their voices echoed.

"One of the ovens," said Pete, reaching for the razor.

"Bake ovens? You're crazy!"

Pete chuckled. "You don't know this place, do you? Like everything else on the base, there was a lot more went on here than most people knew about. They kept calling it the bake shop. Well, it *was* research headquarters for new high-nutrient flours. But there's lots else here. We tested utensils and designed beet peelers and all sorts of things like that. There's an electric furnace in here that—" He pushed open a door.

They crossed a long, quiet, cluttered room to the thermal equipment. "We can do everything here from annealing glass, through glazing ceramics, to finding the melting point of frying pans." He clicked a switch tentatively. A pilot light glowed. He swung open a small, heavy door and set the razor inside. "Kiss it good-bye. In twenty minutes it'll be a puddle."

"I want to see that," said Sonny. "Can I look around until it's cooked?"

"Why not?"

(Everybody around here always said "Why not?")

They walked through the laboratories. Beautifully equipped, they were, and too quiet. Once they passed a major who was bent over a complex electronic hook-up on one of the benches. He was watching a little amber light flicker, and he did not return their salute. They tiptoed past him, feeling awed at his absorption, envying it. They saw the models of the automatic kneaders, the vitaminizers, the remote-signal thermostats and timers and controls.

"What's in there?"

"I dunno. I'm over the edge of my territory. I don't think there's anybody left for this section. They were mostly mechanical and electronic theoreticians. The only thing I know about them is that if we ever needed anything in the way of tools, meters, or equipment, they had it or something better, and if we ever got real bright and figured out a startling new idea, they'd already built it and junked it a month ago. Hey!"

Sonny followed the pointing hand. "What?"

"That wall section. It's loose, or . . . well, what do you know?"

He pushed at the section of wall, which was very slightly out of line. There was a dark space beyond.

"What's in there?"

"Nothing, or some semiprivate hush-hush job. These guys used to get away with murder."

Sonny said, with an uncharacteristic flash of irony, "Isn't that the Army theoretician's business?"

Cautiously they peered in, then entered.

"Wh . . . *hey!* The door!"

It swung swiftly and quietly shut. The soft click of the latch was accompanied by a blaze of light.

The room was small and windowless. It contained machinery—a "trickle" charger, a bank of storage batteries, an electric-powered dynamo, two small self-starting gas-driven light plants and a Diesel complete with sealed compressed-air starting cylinders. In the corner was a relay rack with its panel-bolts spot-welded. Protruding from it was a red-top lever. Nothing was labeled.

They looked at the equipment wordlessly for a time and then Sonny said, "Somebody wanted to make awful sure he had power for something."

"Now, I wonder what—" Pete walked over to the relay rack. He looked at the lever without touching it. It was wired up; behind the handle, on the wire, was a folded tag. He opened it cautiously. "To be used only on specific orders of the Commanding Officer."

"Give it a yank and see what happens."

Something clicked behind them. They whirled. "What was that?"

"Seemed to come from that rig by the door."

They approached it cautiously. There was a spring-loaded solenoid attached to a bar which was hinged to drop across the inside of the secret door, where it would fit into steel gudgeons on the panel.

It clicked again. "A Geiger," said Pete disgustedly.

"Now why," mused Sonny, "would they design a door to stay locked unless the general radioactivity went beyond a certain point? That's what it is. See the relays? And the overload switch there? And this?"

"It has a manual lock, too," Pete pointed out. The counter clicked again. "Let's get out of here. I got one of those things built into my head these days."

The door opened easily. They went out, closing it behind them. The keyhole was cleverly concealed in the crack between two boards.

They were silent as they made their way back to the QM labs. The small thrill of violation was gone and, for Pete Mawser at least, the hate was back, that and the shame. A few short weeks before, this base had been a part of the finest country on earth. There was a lot of work here that was secret, and a lot that was such purely progressive and unapplied research that it would be in the way anywhere else but in this quiet wilderness.

Sweat stood out on his forehead. They hadn't struck back at their murderers! It was quite well known that there were launching sites all over the country, in secret caches far from any base or murdered city. Why must they sit here waiting to die, only to let the enemy—"enemies" was more like it—take over the continent when it was safe again?

He smiled grimly. One small consolation. They'd hit too hard: that was a certainty. Probably each of the attackers underestimated what the other would throw. The result—a spreading transmutation of nitrogen into deadly Carbon Fourteen. The effects would not be limited to the continent. What ghastly long-range effect the muted radioactivity would have on the overseas enemies was something that no one alive today could know.

Back at the furnace, Pete glanced at the temperature dial, then kicked the latch control. The pilot winked out and then the door swung open. They blinked and started back from the raging heat within, then bent and peered. The razor was gone. A pool of brilliance lay on the floor of the compartment.

"Ain't much left. Most of it oxidized away," Pete grunted.

They stood together for a time with their faces lit by that small shimmering ruin. Later, as they walked back to the barracks, Sonny broke his long silence with a sigh. "I'm glad we did that, Pete. I'm awful glad we did that."

At a quarter to eight they were waiting before the combination console in the barracks. All hands except Pete and Sonny and a wiry-haired, thick-set corporal named Bonze had elected to see the show on the big screen in the mess hall. The reception was better there, of course, but, as Bonze put it, "you don't get close enough in a big place like that."

"I hope she's the same," said Sonny, half to himself.

Why should she be? thought Pete morosely as he turned on the set and watched the screen begin to glow. There were many more of the golden speckles that had killed reception for the past two weeks. Why should anything be the same, ever again?

He fought a sudden temptation to kick the set to pieces. It, and Starr Anthim, were part of something that was dead. The country was dead, a real country—prosperous, sprawling, laughing, grabbing, growing and changing, leprous in spots with poverty and injustice, but healthy enough to overcome any ill. He wondered how the murderers would like it. They were welcome to it, now. Nowhere to go. No one to fight. That was true for every soul on earth now.

"You hope she's the same," he muttered.

"The show, I mean," said Sonny mildly. "I'd like to just sit here and have it like ... like—"

Oh, thought Pete mistily. Oh—that. Somewhere to go, that's what it is, for a few minutes. "I know," he said, all the harshness gone from his voice.

Noise receded from the audio as the carrier swept in. The light on the screen swirled and steadied into a diamond pattern. Pete adjusted the focus, chromic balance, and intensity. "Turn out the lights, Bonze. I don't want to see anything but Starr Anthim."

It *was* the same, at first. Starr Anthim had never used the usual fanfares, fade-ins, color, and clamor of her contemporaries. A black screen, then *click,* a blaze of gold. It was all there, in focus; tremendously intense, it did not change. Rather, the eye changed to take it in. She never moved for seconds after she came on; she was there, a portrait, a still face and a white throat. Her eyes were open and sleeping. Her face was alive and still.

Then, in the eyes which seemed green but were blue flecked with gold, an awareness seemed to gather, and they came awake. Only then was it noticeable that her lips were parted. Something in the eyes made the lips be seen, though nothing moved yet. Not until she bent her head slowly, so that some of the gold flecks seemed captured in the golden brows. The eyes were not, then, looking out at an audience. They were looking at me, and at *me,* and at ME.

"Hello—you," she said. She was a dream, with a kid sister's slightly irregular teeth.

Bonze shuddered. The cot on which he lay began to squeak rapidly. Sonny shifted in annoyance. Pete reached out in the dark and caught the leg of the cot. The squeaking subsided.

"May I sing a song?" Starr asked. There was music, very faint. "It's an old one, and one of the best. It's an easy song, a deep song, one that comes from the part of men and women that is mankind—the part that has in it no greed, no hate, no fear. This song is about joyousness and strength. It's—my favorite. Isn't it yours?"

The music swelled. Pete recognized the first two notes of the introduction and swore quietly. This was wrong. This song was not for ... this song was part of—

Sonny sat raptly. Bonze lay still.

Starr Anthim began to sing. Her voice was deep and powerful, but soft, with the merest touch of vibrato at the ends of the phrases. The song flowed from her without noticeable effort, seeming to come from her face, her long hair, her wide-set eyes. Her voice, like her face, was shadowed and clean, round, blue and green but mostly gold:

"When you gave me your heart, you gave me the world,
You gave me the night and the day,
And thunder, and roses, and sweet green grass,
The sea, and soft wet clay.

"I drank the dawn from a golden cup,
From a silver one, the dark,
The steed I rode was the wild west wind,
My song was the brook and the lark."

The music spiraled, caroled, slid into a somber cry of muted, hungry sixths and ninths; rose, blared, and cut, leaving her voice full and alone:

"With thunder I smote the evil of earth,
With roses I won the right,
With the sea I washed, and with clay I built,
And the world was a place of light!"

The last note left a face perfectly composed again, and there was no movement in it; it was sleeping and vital while the music curved off and away to the places where music rests when it is not heard.

Starr smiled.

"It's so easy," she said. "So simple. All that is fresh and clean and strong about mankind is in that song, and I think that's all that need concern us about mankind." She leaned forward. "Don't you see?"

The smile faded and was replaced with a gentle wonder. A tiny furrow appeared between her brows; she drew back quickly. "I can't seem to talk to you tonight," she said, her voice small. "You hate something."

Hate was shaped like a monstrous mushroom. Hate was the random speckling of a video plate.

"What has happened to us," said Starr abruptly, impersonally, "is simple, too. It doesn't matter who did it—do you understand that? *It doesn't matter.* We were attacked. We were struck from the east and from the west. Most of the bombs were atomic—there were blast bombs and there were dust bombs. We were hit by about five hundred and thirty bombs altogether, and it has killed us."

She waited.

Sonny's fist smacked into his palm. Bonze lay with his eyes open, quiet. Pete's jaws hurt.

"We have more bombs than both of them put together. We *have* them. We are not going to use them. *Wait!*" She raised her hands suddenly, as if she could see into each man's face. They sank back, tense.

"So saturated is the atmosphere with Carbon Fourteen that all of us in this hemisphere are going to die. Don't be afraid to say it. Don't be afraid to think it. It is a truth, and it must be faced. As the transmutation effect spreads from the ruins of our cities, the air will become increasingly radioactive, and then we must die. In months, in a year or so, the effects will be strong overseas. Most of the people there will die, too. None will escape completely. A worse thing will come to them than anything they gave us, because there will be a wave of horror and madness which is impossible to us. We are merely going to die. They will live and burn and sicken, and the children that will be born to them—" She shook her head, and her lower lip grew full. She visibly pulled herself together.

"Five hundred and thirty bombs— I don't think either of our attackers knew just how strong the other was. There has been so much secrecy." Her voice was sad. She shrugged slightly. "They have killed us, and they have ruined themselves. As for us—we are not blameless, either. Neither are we helpless to do anything—yet. But what we must do is hard. We must die—without striking back."

She gazed briefly at each man in turn, from the screen. "We must *not* strike back. Mankind is about to go through a hell of his own making. We can be vengeful—or merciful, if you like—and let go with the hundreds of bombs we have. That would sterilize the planet so that not a microbe, not a blade of grass could escape, and nothing new could grow. We would reduce the earth to a bald thing, dead and deadly.

"No, it just won't do. We can't do it.

"Remember the song? *That* is humanity. That's in all humans. A disease made other humans our enemies for a time, but as the generations march past, enemies become friends and friends enemies.

The enmity of those who have killed us is such a tiny, temporary thing in the long sweep of history!"

Her voice deepened. "Let us die with the knowledge that we have done the one noble thing left to us. The spark of humanity can still live and grow on this planet. It will be blown and drenched, shaken and all but extinguished, but it will live if that song is a true one. It will live if we are human enough to discount the fact that the spark is in the custody of our temporary enemy. Some—a few—of his children will live to merge with the new humanity that will gradually emerge from the jungles and the wilderness. Perhaps there will be ten thousand years of beastliness; perhaps man will be able to rebuild while he still has his ruins."

She raised her head, her voice tolling. "And even if this is the end of humankind, we dare not take away the chances some other life form might have to succeed where we failed. If we retaliate, there will not be a dog, a deer, an ape, a bird or fish or lizard to carry the evolutionary torch. In the name of justice, if we must condemn and destroy ourselves, let us not condemn all life along with us! We are heavy enough with sins. If we must destroy, let us stop with destroying ourselves!"

There was a shimmering flicker of music. It seemed to stir her hair like a breath of wind. She smiled.

"That's all," she whispered. And to each man there she said, "Good night—"

The screen went black. As the carrier cut off—there was no announcement—the ubiquitous speckles began to swarm across it.

Pete rose and switched on the lights. Bonze and Sonny were quite still. It must have been minutes later when Sonny sat up straight, shaking himself like a puppy. Something besides the silence seemed to tear with the movement.

He said softly, "You're not allowed to fight anything, or to run away, or to live, and now you can't even hate any more, because Starr says 'no.'"

There was bitterness in the sound of it, and a bitter smell to the air.

Pete Mawser sniffed once, which had nothing to do with the

smell. He froze, sniffed again. "What's that smell, Son'?"

Sonny tested it. "I don't— Something familiar. Vanilla—no . . . no.

"Almonds. Bitter— *Bonze!*"

Bonze lay still with his eyes open, grinning. His jaw muscles were knotted, and they could see almost all his teeth. He was soaking wet.

"Bonze!"

"It was just when she came on and said 'Hello—you,' remember?" whispered Pete. "Oh, the poor kid. That's why he wanted to catch the show here instead of in the mess hall."

"Went out looking at her," said Sonny through pale lips. "I can't say I blame him much. Wonder where he got the stuff."

"Never mind that." Pete's voice was harsh. "Let's get out of here."

They left to call the meat wagon. Bonze lay watching the console with his dead eyes and his smell of bitter almonds.

Pete did not realize where he was going, or exactly why, until he found himself on the dark street near GHQ and the communications shack. It had something to do with Bonze. Not that he wanted to do what Bonze had done. But then he hadn't thought of it. What would he have done if he'd thought of it? Nothing, probably. But still—it might be nice to be able to hear Starr, and see her, whenever he felt like it. Maybe there weren't any recordings, but her musical background was recorded, and the Sig might have dubbed the show off.

He stood uncertainly outside the GHQ building. There was a cluster of men outside the main entrance. Pete smiled briefly. Rain, nor snow, nor sleet, nor gloom of night could stay the stage-door Johnny.

He went down the side street and up the delivery ramp in the back. Two doors along the platform was the rear exit of the communications section.

There was a light on in the communications shack. He had his hand out to the screen door when he noticed someone standing in the shadows beside it. The light played daintily on the golden margins of a head and face.

He stopped. "Starr Anthim!"

"Hello, soldier. Sergeant."

He blushed like an adolescent. "I—" His voice left him. He swallowed, reached up to whip off his hat. He had no hat. "I saw the show," he said. He felt clumsy. It was dark, and yet he was very conscious of the fact that his dress shoes were indifferently shined.

She moved toward him into the light, and she was so beautiful that he had to close his eyes. "What's your name?"

"Mawser. Pete Mawser."

"Like the show?"

Not looking at her, he said stubbornly, "No."

"Oh?"

"I mean ... I liked it some. The song."

"I ... think I see."

"I wondered if I could maybe get a recording."

"I think so," she said. "What kind of a reproducer have you got?"

"Audiovid."

"A disk. Yes; we dubbed off a few. Wait, I'll get you one."

She went inside, moving slowly. Pete watched her, spellbound. She was a silhouette, crowned and haloed; and then she was a framed picture, vivid and golden. He waited, watching the light hungrily. She returned with a large envelope, called good night to someone inside, and came out on the platform.

"Here you are, Pete Mawser."

"Thanks very—" he mumbled. He wet his lips. "It was very good of you."

"Not really. The more it circulates, the better." She laughed suddenly. "That isn't meant quite as it sounds. I'm not exactly looking for new publicity these days."

The stubbornness came back. "I don't know that you'd get it, if you put on that show in normal times."

Her eyebrows went up. "Well!" she smiled. "I seem to have made quite an impression."

"I'm sorry," he said warmly. "I shouldn't have taken that tack. Everything you think and say these days is exaggerated."

"I know what you mean." She looked around. "How is it here?"

"It's O.K. I used to be bothered by the secrecy, and being buried miles away from civilization." He chuckled bitterly. "Turned out to be lucky after all."

"You sound like the first chapter of *One World or None*."

He looked up quickly. "What do you use for a reading list—the Government's own *'Index Expurgatorius'?*"

She laughed. "Come now—it isn't as bad as all that. The book was never banned. It was just—"

"—Unfashionable," he filled in.

"Yes, more's the pity. If people had paid more attention to it when it was published, perhaps this wouldn't have happened."

He followed her gaze to the dimly pulsating sky. "How long are you going to be here?"

"Until ... as long as ... I'm not leaving."

"You're not?"

"I'm finished," she said simply. "I've covered all the ground I can. I've been everywhere that ... anyone knows about."

"With this show?"

She nodded. "With this particular message."

He was quiet, thinking. She turned to the door, and he put out his hand, not touching her. "Please—"

"What is it?"

"I'd like to ... I mean, if you don't mind, I don't often have a chance to talk to— Maybe you'd like to walk around a little before you turn in."

"Thanks, no, Sergeant. I'm tired." She did sound tired. "I'll see you around."

He stared at her, a sudden fierce light in his brain. "I know where it is. It's got a red-topped lever and a tag referring to orders of the commanding officer. It's really camouflaged."

She was quiet so long that he thought she had not heard him. Then, "I'll take that walk."

They went down the ramp together and turned toward the dark parade ground.

"How did you know?" she asked quietly.

"Not too tough. This 'message' of yours; the fact that you've been all over the country with it; most of all, the fact that somebody finds it necessary to persuade us not to strike back. Who are you working for?" he asked bluntly.

Surprisingly, she laughed.

"What's that for?"

"A moment ago you were blushing and shuffling your feet."

His voice was rough. "I wasn't talking to a human being. I was talking to a thousand songs I've heard, and a hundred thousand blond pictures I've seen pinned up. You'd better tell me what this is all about."

She stopped. "Let's go up and see the colonel."

He took her elbow. "No. I'm just a sergeant, and he's high brass, and that doesn't make any difference at all now. You're a human being, and so am I, and I'm supposed to respect your rights as such. I don't. You're a woman, and—"

She stiffened. He kept her walking, and finished, "—and that will make as much difference as I let it. You'd better tell me about it."

"All right," she said, with a tired acquiescence that frightened something inside him. "You seem to have guessed right, though. It's true. There are master firing keys for the launching sites. We have located and dismantled all but two. It's very likely that one of the two was vaporized. The other one is—lost."

"Lost?"

"I don't have to tell you about the secrecy," she said disgustedly. "You know how it developed between nation and nation. You must know that it existed between State and Union, between department and department, office and office. There were only three or four men who knew where all the keys were. Three of them were in the Pentagon when it went up. That was the third blast bomb, you know. If there was another, it could only have been Senator Vandercook, and he died three weeks ago without talking."

"An automatic radio key, hm-m-m?"

"That's right. Sergeant, must we walk? I'm so tired—"

"I'm sorry," he said impulsively. They crossed to the reviewing stand and sat on the lonely benches. "Launching racks all over, all hidden, and all armed?"

"Most of them are armed. Enough. Armed and aimed."

"Aimed where?"

"It doesn't matter."

"I think I see. What's the optimum number again?"

"About six hundred and forty; a few more or less. At least five hundred and thirty have been thrown so far. We don't know exactly."

"Who are *we?*" he asked furiously.

"Who? Who?" She laughed weakly. "I could say, 'The Government,' perhaps. If the President dies, the Vice President takes over, and then the Speaker of the House, and so on and on. How far can you go? Pete Mawser, don't you realize yet what's happened?"

"I don't know what you mean."

"How many people do you think are left in this country?"

"I don't know. Just a few million, I guess."

"How many are here?"

"About nine hundred."

"Then as far as I know, this is the largest city left."

He leaped to his feet. *"NO!"* The syllable roared away from him, hurled itself against the dark, empty buildings, came back to him in a series of lower-case echoes: nonono*no* ... *no*-no—n ...

Starr began to speak rapidly, quietly. "They're scattered all over the fields and the roads. They sit in the sun and die in the afternoon. They run in packs, they tear at each other. They pray and starve and kill themselves and die in the fires. The fires—everywhere, if anything stands, it's burning. Summer, and the leaves all down in the Berkshires, and the blue grass burnt brown; you can see the grass dying from the air, the death going out wider and wider from the bald spots. Thunder and roses ... I saw roses, new ones, creeping from the smashed pots of a greenhouse. Brown petals, alive and sick, and the thorns turned back on themselves, growing into the stems, killing. Feldman died tonight."

He let her be quiet for a time. "Who is Feldman?"

"My pilot." She was talking hollowly into her hands. "He's been dying for weeks. He's been on his nerve ends. I don't think he had any blood left. He buzzed your GHQ and made for the landing strip. He came in with the motor dead, free rotors, giro. Smashed the landing gear. He was dead, too. He killed a man in Chicago so he could steal gas. The man didn't want the gas. There was a dead girl by the pump. He didn't want us to go near. I'm not going anywhere. I'm going to stay here. I'm tired."

At last she cried.

Pete left her alone, and walked out to the center of the parade ground, looking back at the faint huddled glimmer on the bleachers. His mind flickered over the show that evening, and the way she had sung before the merciless transmitter. "Hello—you." "If we must destroy, let us stop with destroying ourselves!"

The dimming spark of humankind—what could it mean to her? How could it mean so much?

"Thunder and roses." Twisted, sick, nonsurvival roses, killing themselves with their own thorns.

"And the world was a place of light!" Blue light, flickering in the contaminated air.

The enemy. The red-topped lever. Bonze. "They pray and starve and kill themselves and die in the fires."

What creatures were these, these corrupted, violent, murdering humans? What right had they to another chance? What was in them that was good?

Starr was good. Starr was crying. Only a human being could cry like that. Starr was a human being.

Had humanity anything of Starr Anthim in it?

Starr *was* a human being.

He looked down through the darkness for his hands. No planet, no universe, is greater to a man than his own ego, his own observing self. These hands were the hands of all history, and like the hands of all men, they could by their small acts make human history or end it. Whether this power of hands was that of a billion hands, or whether it came to a focus in these two—this was suddenly unimportant to the eternities which now infolded him.

He put humanity's hands deep in his pockets and walked slowly back to the bleachers.

"Starr."

She responded with a sleepy-child, interrogative whimper.

"They'll get their chance, Starr. I won't touch the key."

She sat straight. She rose, and came to him, smiling. He could see her smile because, very faintly in this air, her teeth fluoresced. She put her hands on his shoulders. "Pete."

He held her very close for a moment. Her knees buckled then, and he had to carry her.

There was no one in the Officers' Club, which was the nearest building. He stumbled in, moved clawing along the wall until he found a switch. The light hurt him. He carried her to a settee and put her down gently. She did not move. One side of her face was as pale as milk.

There was blood on his hands.

He stood looking stupidly at it, wiped it on the sides of his trousers, looking dully at Starr. There was blood on her shirt.

The echo of no's came back to him from the far walls of the big room before he knew he had spoken. Starr wouldn't do this. She couldn't!

A doctor. But there was no doctor. Not since Anders had hung himself. Get somebody. *Do* something.

He dropped to his knees and gently unbuttoned her shirt. Between the sturdy, unfeminine GI bra and the top of her slacks, there was blood on her side. He whipped out a clean handkerchief and began to wipe it away. There was no wound, no puncture. But abruptly there was blood again. He blotted it carefully. And again there was blood.

It was like trying to dry a piece of ice with a towel.

He ran to the water cooler, wrung out the bloody handkerchief and ran back to her. He bathed her face carefully, the pale right side, the flushed left side. The handkerchief reddened again, this time with cosmetics, and then her face was pale all over, with great blue shadows under the eyes. While he watched, blood appeared on her left cheek.

There must be *somebody*— He fled to the door.

"Pete!"

Running, turning at the sound of her voice, he hit the doorpost stunningly, caromed off, flailed for his balance, and then was back at her side. "Starr! Hang on, now! I'll get a doctor as quick as—"

Her hand strayed over her left cheek. "You found out. Nobody else knew, but Feldman. It got hard to cover properly." Her hand went up to her hair.

"Starr, I'll get a—"

"Pete, darling, promise me something?"

"Why, sure; certainly, Starr."

"Don't disturb my hair. It isn't—all mine, you see." She sounded like a seven-year-old, playing a game. "It all came out on this side, you see? I don't want you to see me that way."

He was on his knees beside her again. "What is it? What happened to you?" he asked hoarsely.

"Philadelphia," she murmured. "Right at the beginning. The mushroom went up a half mile away. The studio caved in. I came to the next day. I didn't know I was burned, then. It didn't show. My left side. It doesn't matter, Pete. It doesn't hurt at all, now."

He sprang to his feet again. "I'm going for a doctor."

"Don't go away. Please don't go away and leave me. Please don't." There were tears in her eyes. "Wait just a little while. Not very long, Pete."

He sank to his knees again. She gathered both his hands in hers and held them tightly. She smiled happily. "You're good, Pete. You're so good."

(She couldn't hear the blood in his ears, the roar of the whirlpool of hate and fear and anguish that spun inside him.)

She talked to him in a low voice, and then in whispers. Sometimes he hated himself because he couldn't quite follow her. She talked about school, and her first audition. "I was so scared that I got a vibrato in my voice. I'd never had one before. I always let myself get a little scared when I sing now. It's easy." There was something about a windowbox when she was four years old. "Two real live tulips and a pitcherplant. I used to be sorry for the flies."

There was a long period of silence after that, during which his muscles throbbed with cramp and stiffness, and gradually became numb. He must have dozed; he awoke with a violent start, feeling her fingers on his face. She was propped up on one elbow. She said clearly, "I just wanted to tell you, darling. Let me go first, and get everything ready for you. It's going to be wonderful. I'll fix you a special tossed salad. I'll make you a steamed chocolate pudding and keep it hot for you."

Too muddled to understand what she was saying, he smiled and pressed her back on the settee. She took his hands again.

The next time he awoke it was broad daylight, and she was dead.

Sonny Weisefreund was sitting on his cot when he got back to the barracks. He handed over the recording he had picked up from the parade ground on the way back. "Dew on it. Dry it off. Good boy," he croaked, and fell face downward on the cot Bonze had used.

Sonny stared at him. "Pete! Where've you been? What happened? Are you all right?"

Pete shifted a little and grunted. Sonny shrugged and took the audiovid disk out of its wet envelope. Moisture would not harm it particularly, though it could not be played while wet. It was made of a fine spiral of plastic, insulated between laminations. Electrostatic pickups above and below the turntable would fluctuate with changes in the dielectric constant which had been impressed by the recording, and these changes were amplified for the video. The audio was a conventional hill-and-dale needle. Sonny began to wipe it down carefully.

Pete fought upward out of a vast, green-lit place full of flickering cold fires. Starr was calling him. Something was punching him, too. He fought it weakly, trying to hear what she was saying. But someone else was jabbering too loud for him to hear.

He opened his eyes. Sonny was shaking him, his round face pink with excitement. The audiovid was running. Starr was talking. Sonny got up impatiently and turned down the audio gain. "Pete! Pete! Wake up, will you? I got to tell you something. Listen to me! Wake up, will yuh?"

"Huh?"

"That's better. Now listen. I've just been listening to Starr Anthim—"

"She's dead," said Pete. Sonny didn't hear. He went on explosively,

"I've figured it out. Starr was sent out here, and all over, to *beg* someone not to fire any more atom bombs. If the government was sure they wouldn't strike back, they wouldn't have taken the trouble. Somewhere, Pete, there's some way to launch bombs at those murdering cowards—and I've got a pret-ty shrewd idea of how to do it."

Pete strained groggily toward the faint sound of Starr's voice. Sonny talked on. "Now, s'posing there was a master radio key, an automatic code device something like the alarm signal they have on ships, that rings a bell on any ship within radio range when the operator sends four long dashes. Suppose there's an automatic code machine to launch bombs, with repeaters, maybe, buried all over the country. What would it be? Just a little lever to pull; thass all. How would the thing be hidden? In the middle of a lot of other equipment, that's where; in some place where you'd expect to find crazy-looking secret stuff. Like an experiment station. Like right here. You beginning to get the idea?"

"Shut up. I can't hear her."

"The hell with her! You can hear her some other time. You didn't hear a thing I said!"

"She's dead."

"Yeah. Well, I figure I'll pull that handle. What can I lose? It'll give those murderin' ... *what?*"

"She's dead."

"Dead? Starr Anthim?" His young face twisted, Sonny sank down to the cot. "You're half asleep. You don't know what you're saying."

"She's dead," Pete said hoarsely. "She got burned by one of the first bombs. I was with her when she ... she— Shut up, now, and get out of here and let me listen!" he bellowed hoarsely.

Sonny stood up slowly. "They killed her, too. They killed her. That does it. That just fixes it up." His face was white. He went out.

Pete got up. His legs weren't working right. He almost fell. He brought up against the console with a crash, his outflung arm sending the pickup skittering across the record. He put it on again and turned up the gain, then lay down to listen.

His head was all mixed up. Sonny talked too much. Bomb launchers, automatic code machines—

"You gave me your heart," sang Starr. *"You gave me your heart. You gave me your heart. You—"*

Pete heaved himself up again and moved the pickup arm. Anger, not at himself, but at Sonny for causing him to cut the disk that way, welled up.

Starr was talking, stupidly, her face going through the same expression over and over again. *"Struck from the east and from the Struck from the east and from the—"*

He got up again wearily and moved the pickup.

"You gave me your heart. You gave me—"

Pete made an agonized sound that was not a word at all, bent, lifted, and sent the console crashing over. In the bludgeoning silence he said, "I did, too."

Then, "Sonny." He waited.

"Sonny!"

His eyes went wide then, and he cursed and bolted for the corridor.

The panel was closed when he reached it. He kicked at it. It flew open, discovering darkness.

"Hey!" bellowed Sonny. "Shut it! You turned off the lights!"

Pete shut it behind him. The lights blazed.

"Pete! What's the matter?"

"Nothing's the matter, Son'," croaked Pete.

"What are you looking at?" said Sonny uneasily.

"I'm sorry," said Pete as gently as he could. "I just wanted to find something out, is all. Did you tell anyone else about this?" He pointed to the lever.

"Why, no. I only just figured it out while you were sleeping, just now."

Pete looked around carefully while Sonny shifted his weight. Pete moved toward a tool rack. "Something you haven't noticed yet, Sonny," he said softly, and pointed. "Up there, on the wall behind you. High up. See?"

Sonny turned. In one fluid movement Pete plucked off a fourteen-inch box wrench and hit Sonny with it as hard as he could.

Afterward he went to work systematically on the power supplies. He pulled the plugs on the gas engines and cracked their cylinders with a maul. He knocked off the tubing of the Diesel starters—the tanks let go explosively—and he cut all the cables with bolt cutters. Then he broke up the relay rack and its lever. When he was quite finished, he put away his tools and bent and stroked Sonny's tousled hair.

He went out and closed the partition carefully. It certainly was a wonderful piece of camouflage. He sat down heavily on a workbench nearby.

"You'll have your chance," he said into the far future. "And by heaven, you'd better make good."

After that he just waited.

It Wasn't Syzygy

BETTER NOT READ it. I mean it. No—this isn't one of those "perhaps it will happen to you" things. It's a lot worse than that. It might very possibly be happening to you right now. And you won't know until it's over. You can't, by the very nature of things.

(I wonder what the population really is?)

On the other hand, maybe it won't make any difference if I do tell you about it. Once you get used to the idea, you might even be able to relax and enjoy it. Heaven knows there's plenty to enjoy—and again I say it—by the very nature of things.

All right, then, if you think you can take it . . .

I met her in a restaurant. You may know the place—Murphy's. It has a big oval bar and then a partition. On the other side of the partition are small tables, then an aisle, then booths.

Gloria was sitting at one of the small tables. All of the booths but two were empty; all the other small tables but one were unoccupied, so there was plenty of room in the place for me.

But there was only one place I could sit—at her table. That was because, when I saw Gloria, there wasn't anything else in the world. I have never been through anything like that. I just stopped dead. I dropped my briefcase and stared at her. She had gleaming auburn hair and olive skin. She had delicate high-arched nostrils and a carved mouth, lips that were curved above like gull's wings on the downbeat, and full below. Her eyes were as sealed and spice-toned as a hot buttered rum, and as deep as a mountain night.

Without taking my eyes from her face, I groped for a chair and sat opposite her. I'd forgotten everything. Even about being hungry. Helen hadn't, though. Helen was the head waitress and a swell person. She was fortyish and happy. She didn't know my name but used to call me "The Hungry Fella." I never had to order. When I came in she'd fill me a bar-glass full of beer and pile up two orders of that day's Chef's Special on a steak platter. She arrived with the beer, picked up my briefcase, and went for the fodder. I just kept on looking at Gloria, who, by this time, was registering considerable amazement, and a little awe. The awe, she told me later, was conceived only at the size of the beer-glass, but I have my doubts about that.

She spoke first. "Taking an inventory?"

She had one of those rare voices which makes noises out of all other sounds. I nodded. Her chin was rounded, with the barest suggestion of a cleft, but the hinges of her jaw were square.

I think she was a little flustered. She dropped her eyes—I was glad, because I could see then how very long and thick her lashes were—and poked at her salad. She looked up again, half smiling. Her teeth met, tip to tip. I'd read about that but had never actually seen it before. "What is it?" she asked. "Have I made a conquest?"

I nodded again. "You certainly have."

"Well!" she breathed.

"Your name's Gloria," I said positively.

"How did you know?"

"It had to be, that's all."

She looked at me carefully, at my eyes, my forehead, my shoulders. "If your name is Leo, I'll scream."

"Scream then. But why?"

"I—I've always thought I'd meet a man named Leo and—"

Helen canceled the effects of months of good relations between herself and me, by bringing my lunch just then. Gloria's eyes widened when she saw it. "You must be very fond of lobster hollandaise."

"I'm very fond of all subtle things," I said, "and I like them in great masses."

"I've never met anyone like you," she said candidly.

"No one like you ever has."

"Oh?"

I picked up my fork. "Obviously not, or there'd be a race of us." I scooped up some lobster. "Would you be good enough to watch carefully while I eat? I can't seem to stop looking at you, and I'm afraid I might stab my face with the fork."

She chortled. It wasn't a chuckle, or a gargle. It was a true Lewis Carroll chortle. They're very rare. "I'll watch."

"Thank you. And while you watch, tell me what you don't like."

"What I *don't* like? Why?"

"I'll probably spend the rest of my life finding out the things you do like, and doing them with you. So let's get rid of the nonessentials."

She laughed. "All right. I don't like tapioca because it makes me feel conspicuous, staring that way. I don't like furniture with buttons on the upholstery; lace curtains that cross each other; small flower-prints; hooks-and-eyes and snap fasteners where zippers ought to be; that orchestra leader with the candy saxophones and the yodeling brother; tweedy men who smoke pipes; people who can't look me in the eye when they're lying; night clothes; people who make mixed drinks with Scotch—my, you eat fast."

"I just do it to get rid of my appetite so I can begin eating for esthetic reasons. I like that list."

"What don't *you* like?"

"I don't like literary intellectuals with their conversations all dressed up in overquotes. I don't like bathing-suits that don't let the sun in and I don't like weather that keeps bathing-suits in. I don't like salty food; clinging-vine girls; music that doesn't go anywhere or build anything; people who have forgotten how to wonder like children; automobiles designed to be better streamlined going backwards than going forward; people who will try anything once but are afraid to try it twice and acquire a taste; and professional skeptics." I went back to my lunch.

"You bat a thousand," she said. "Something remarkable is happening here."

"Let it happen," I cautioned. "Never mind what it is or why. Don't be like the guy who threw a light-bulb on the floor to find out if it was brittle." Helen passed and I ordered a Slivovitz.

"Prune brandy!" cried Gloria. "I love it!"

"I know. It's for you."

"Some day you're going to be wrong," she said, suddenly somber, "and that will be bad."

"That will be good. It'll be the difference between harmony and contrast, that's all."

"Leo—"

"Mm?"

She brought her gaze squarely to me, and it was so warm I could feel it on my face. "Nothing. I was just saying it, Leo. *Leo!*"

Something choked me—not the lobster. It was all gone.

"I have no gag for that. I can't top it. I can match it, Gloria."

Another thing was said, but without words.

There are still no words for it. Afterward she reached across and touched my hand with her fingertips. I saw colors.

I got up to go, after scribbling on a piece of the menu. "Here's my phone number. Call me up when there's no other way out."

She raised her eyebrows. "Don't you want my phone, or my address, or anything?"

"No," I said.

"But—"

"This means too much," I said. "I'm sorry if I seem to be dropping it in your lap like this. But any time you are with me, I want it to be because you want to be with me, not because you think it's what I might want. We've got to be together because we are traveling in the same direction at approximately the same speed, each under his own power. If I call you up and make all the arrangements, it could be that I was acting on a conditioned reflex, like any other wolf. If you call, we can both be sure."

"It makes sense." She raised those deep eyes to me. Leaving her was coming up out of those eyes hand over hand. A long haul. I only just made it.

Out on the street I tried valiantly to get some sense of proportion. The most remarkable thing about the whole remarkable business was simply this: that in all my life before, I had never been able to talk to anyone like that. I had always been diffident, easy-going, unaggressive to a fault, and rather slow on the uptake.

I felt like the daydreams of the much advertised 97-pound weakling as he clipped that coupon.

"Hey—you!"

I generally answered to that as well as anything else. I looked up and recoiled violently. There was a human head floating in midair next to me. I was so startled I couldn't even stop walking. The head drifted along beside me, bobbing slightly as if invisible legs carried an invisible body to which the visible head was attached. The face was middle-aged, bookish, dryly humorous.

"You're quite a hell of a fellow, aren't you?"

Oddly, my tongue loosened from the roof of my mouth. "Some pretty nice people think so," I faltered. I looked around nervously, expecting a stampede when other people saw this congenial horror.

"No one can see me but you," said the head. "No one that's likely to make a fuss, at any rate."

"Wh-what do you want?"

"Just wanted to tell you something," said the head. It must have had a throat somewhere because it cleared it. "Parthenogenesis," it said didactically, "has little survival value, even with syzygy. Without it—" The head disappeared. A little lower down, two bony, bare shoulders appeared, shrugged expressively, and vanished. The head reappeared. "—there isn't a chance."

"You don't say," I quavered.

It didn't say. Not any more, just then. It was gone.

I stopped, spun around, looking for it. What it had told me made as little sense to me, then, as its very appearance. It took quite a while for me to discover that it had told me the heart of the thing I'm telling you. I do hope I'm being a little more lucid than the head was.

Anyway, that was the first manifestation of all. By itself, it wasn't enough to make me doubt my sanity. As I said, it was only the first.

I might as well tell you something about Gloria. Her folks had been poor enough to evaluate good things, well enough off to be able to have a sample or two of these good things. So Gloria could appreciate what was good as well as the effort that was necessary to get it. At twenty-two she was the assistant buyer of a men's department store. (This was toward the end of the war.) She needed some extra money for a pet project, so she sang at a club every night. In her "spare" time she practiced and studied and at the end of a year she had her commercial pilot's license. She spent the rest of the war ferrying airplanes.

Do you begin to get the idea of what kind of people she was?

She was one of the most dynamic women who ever lived. She was thoughtful and articulate and completely un-phony. She was strong. You can have no idea—no; some of you do know how strong. I had forgotten.... She radiated her strength. Her strength surrounded her like a cloud rather than like armor, for she was tangible through it. She influenced everything and everyone she came near. I felt, sometimes, that the pieces of ground which bore her footprints, the chairs she used, the doors she touched and the books she held, continued to radiate for weeks afterward, like the Bikini ships.

She was completely self-sufficient. I had hit the matter squarely when I insisted that she call me before we saw each other again. Her very presence was a compliment. When she was with me, it was, by definition, because that was where she would rather be than any other place on earth. When she was away from me, it was because to be with me at that time would not have been a perfect thing, and in her way she was a perfectionist.

Oh, yes—a perfectionist. I should know!

You ought to know something about me, too, so that you can realize how completely a thing like this is done, and how it is being done to so many of you.

I'm in my twenties and I play guitar for a living. I've done a lot of things and I carry around a lot of memories from each of them—things that only I could possibly know. The color of the walls in the rooming house where I stayed when I was "on the beach" in Port Arthur, Texas, when the crew of my ship went out on strike. What kind of flowers that girl was wearing the night she jumped off the cruise ship in Montego Bay, down in Jamaica.

I can remember, hazily, things like my brother's crying because he was afraid of the vacuum cleaner, when he was four. So I couldn't have been quite three then. I can remember fighting with a kid called Boaz, when I was seven. I remember Harriet, whom I kissed under a fragrant tulip poplar one summer dusk when I was twelve. I remember the odd little lick that drummer used to tear off when, and only when he was really riding, while I was playing at the hotel, and the way the trumpet man's eyes used to close when he heard it. I remember the exact smell of the tiger's wagon when I was pulling ropes on the Barnes Circus, and the one-armed roustabout who used to chantey us along when we drove the stakes, he swinging a twelve-pound maul with the rest of us—

> *Hit* down, *slap it* down, *haul* back, *snub,* bub,
> *Half* back, *quarter* back, *all* back, *whoa!*

—he used to cry, with the mauls rat-tatting on the steelbound peg and the peg melting into the ground, and the snubber grunting over his taut half-hitch while the six of us stood in a circle around the peg. And those other hammers, in the blacksmith's shop in Puerto Rico, with the youngster swinging a sledge in great full circles, clanging on the anvil, while the old smith touched the work almost delicately with his shaping hammer and then tinkled out every syncopation known to man by bouncing it on the anvil's horn and face between his own strokes and those of the great metronomic sledge. I remember the laboring and servile response of a power shovel under my hands as they shifted from hoist to crowd to swing to rehaul controls, and the tang of burning drum-frictions and hot crater compound. That was at the same quarry where the big Finnish blast foreman was killed by a premature shot. He was out in the open and knew he couldn't get clear. He stood straight and still and let it come, since it was bound to come, and he raised his right hand to his head. My mechanic said he was trying to protect his face but I thought at the time he was saluting something.

Details; that's what I'm trying to get over to you. My head was full of details that were intimately my own.

It was a little over two weeks—sixteen days, three hours, and twenty-three minutes, to be exact—before Gloria called. During that time I nearly lost my mind. I was jealous, I was worried, I was frantic. I cursed myself for not having gotten her number—why, I didn't even know her last name! There were times when I determined to hang up on her if I heard her voice, I was so sore. There were times when I stopped work—I did a lot of arranging for small orchestras—and sat before the silent phone, begging it to ring. I had a routine worked out: I'd demand a statement as to how she felt about me before I let her say another thing. I'd demand an explanation of her silence. I'd act casual and disinterested. I'd—

The phone did ring, though, and it was Gloria, and the dialogue went like so:

"Hello?"

"Leo."

"Yes, Gloria!"

"I'm coming up."

"I'm waiting."

And that was it. I met her at the door. I had never touched her before, except for that one brief contact of her hands; and yet, with perfect confidence, with no idea of doing anything different, I took her in my arms and kissed her. This whole thing has its terrible aspects, and yet, sometimes I wonder if moments like that don't justify the horror of it.

I took her hand and led her into the living room. The room wavered like an underwater scene because she was in it. The air tasted different. We sat close together with our hands locked, saying that wordless thing with our eyes. I kissed her again. I didn't ask her anything at all.

She had the smoothest skin that ever was. She had a skin smoother than a bird's throat. It was like satin-finished aluminum, but warm and yielding. It was smooth like Gran' Marnier between your tongue and the roof of your mouth.

We played records—Django Reinhardt and The New Friends of Rhythm, and Bach's *Passacaglia and Fugue* and *Tubby the Tuba*. I showed her the Smith illustrations from *Fantazius Mallare* and my folio of Ed Weston prints. I saw things and heard things in them all that I had never known before, though they were things I loved.

Not one of them—not a book, nor a record, nor a picture, was new to her. By some alchemy, she had culled the random flood of esthetic expression that had come her way, and had her choices; and her choices were these things that I loved, but loved in a way exclusively hers, a way in which I could share.

We talked about books and places, ideas and people. In her way, she was something of a mystic. "I believe that there is something behind the old superstitions about calling up demons and materializations of departed spirits," she said thoughtfully. "But I don't think it was ever done with mumbo-jumbo—witches' brew and pentagrams and toads' skins stuffed with human hair buried at the crossroads on a May midnight, unless these rituals were part of a much larger thing—a purely psychic and un-ghostly force coming from the 'wizard' himself."

"I never thought much about it," I said, stroking her hair. It is the only hair that was not fine that I have ever touched with pleasure. Like everything else about her, it was strong and controlled and glowing. "Have you ever tried anything like that? You're some sort of a sorceress. I know when I'm enchanted at any rate."

"You're not enchanted," she said gravely. "You're not a thing with magic on it. You're a real magic all by yourself."

"You're a darling," I said. "Mine."

"I'm not!" she answered, in that odd way she had of turning aside fantasy for fact. "I don't belong to you. I belong to *me!*"

I must have looked rather stricken, for she laughed suddenly and kissed my hand. "What belongs to you is only a large part of 'us,'" she explained carefully. "Otherwise you belong to you and I belong to me. Do you see?"

"I think I do," I said slowly. "I said I wanted us to be together because we were both travelling together under our own power. I—didn't know it was going to be so true, that's all."

"Don't try to make it any different, Leo. Don't *ever.* If I started to really belong to you, I wouldn't be *me* any more, and then you wouldn't have anything at all."

"You seem so sure of these hazy things."

"They aren't hazy things! They're important. If it weren't for these things, I'd have to stop seeing you. I—*would* stop seeing you."

I put my arms tight around her. "Don't talk about that," I

whispered, more frightened than I have ever been in my life before. "Talk about something else. Finish what you were saying about pentagrams and spirits."

She was still a moment. I think her heart was pounding the way mine was, and I think she was frightened too.

"I spend a lot of time reading and mulling over those things," she said after a quiet time. "I don't know why. I find them fascinating. You know what, Leo? I think too much has been written about manifestations of evil. I think it's true that good is more powerful than evil. And I think that far too much has been written and said about ghosties an' ghoulies an' things that go 'boomp' i' th' nicht, as the old Scottish prayer has it. I think those things have been too underlined. They're remarkable enough, but have you ever realized that things that are remarkable are, by definition, rare?"

"If the cloven-hoofed horrors and the wailing banshees are remarkable—which they are—then what's commonplace?"

She spread her hands—square, quite large hands, capable and beautifully kept. "The manifestations of good, of course. I believe that they're much easier to call up. I believe they happen all the time. An evil mind has to be very evil before it can project itself into a new thing with a life of its own. From all accounts I have read, it takes a tremendously powerful mind to call up even a little demon. Good things must be much easier to materialize, because they fall in the pattern of good living. More people live good lives than such thoroughly bad ones that they can materialize evil things."

"Well then, why don't more people bring more good things from behind this mystic curtain?"

"But they do!" she cried. "They must! The world is so full of good things! Why do you suppose they're so good? What put the innate goodness into Bach and the Victoria Falls and the color of your hair and Negro laughter and the way ginger ale tickles your nostrils?"

I shook my head slowly. "I think that's lovely, and I don't like it."

"Why not?"

I looked at her. She was wearing a wine-colored suit and a marigold silken kerchief tucked into the throat. It reflected on the warm olive of her chin. It reminded me of my grandmother's saying when I was very small. "Let's see if you like butter," as she held a buttercup under my chin to see how much yellow it reflected. "You are good," I said slowly, searching hard for the words. "You are about the—the goodest thing that ever happened. If what you say is really true, then you might be just a shadow, a dream, a glorious thought that someone had."

"Oh, you idiot," she said, with sudden tears in her eyes. "You big, beautiful hunk of idiot!" She pressed me close and bit my cheek so hard that I yelped. "Is that real?"

"If it isn't," I said, shaken, "I'll be happy to go on dreaming."

She stayed another hour—as if there were such a thing as time when we were together—and then she left. I had her phone number by then. A hotel. And after she was gone, I wandered around my apartment, looking at the small wrinkles in the couch-cover where she had sat, touching the cup she had held, staring at the bland black surface of a record, marvelling at the way its grooves had unwound the *Passacaglia* for her. Most wonderful of all was a special way I discovered to turn my head as I moved. Her fragrance clung to my cheek, and if I turned my face just so, I could sense it. I thought about every one of those many minutes with her, each by itself, and the things we had done. I thought, too, about the things we had not done—I know you wondered—and I gloried in them. For, without a word spoken, we had agreed that a thing worth having was a thing worth awaiting and that where faith is complete, exploration is uncalled for.

She came back next day, and the day after. The first of these two visits was wonderful. We sang, mostly. I seemed to know all her very favorite songs. And by a happy accident, my pet key on the guitar—B flat—was exactly within her lovely contralto range. Though I say it as shouldn't, I played some marvellous guitar behind and around what she sang. We laughed a lot, largely at things that were secret between us—is there a love anywhere without its own new language?—and we talked for a long time about a book called *The Fountainhead* which seemed to have had the same extraordinary effect on her that it had on me; but then, it's an extraordinary book.

It was after she left that day that the strangeness began—the strangeness that turned into such utter horror. She hadn't been gone more than an hour when I heard the frightened scramble of tiny claws in the front room. I was poring over the string-bass part of a trio arrangement I was doing (and not seeing it for my Gloria-flavored thoughts) and I raised my head and listened. It was the most panic-struck scurrying imaginable, as if a regiment of newts and salamanders had broken ranks in a wild retreat. I remember clearly that the little claw susurrus did not disturb me at all, but the terror behind the movement startled me in ways that were not pleasant.

What were they running from? *was infinitely more important than* What were they?

Slowly I put down the manuscript and stood up. I went to the wall and along it to the archway, not so much to keep out of sight as to surprise the *thing* that had so terrorized the possessors of those small frightened feet.

And that was the first time I have ever been able to smile while the hackles on the back of my neck were one great crawling prickle. For there was nothing there at all; nothing to glow in the dark before I switched on the overhead light, nothing to show afterward. But the little feet scurried away faster—there must have been hundreds of them—tapping and scrabbling out a perfect crescendo of horrified escape. That was what made my hackles rise. What made me smile—

The sounds radiated from *my* feet!

I stood there in the archway, my eyeballs throbbing with the effort to see this invisible rout; and from the threshold, to right and left and away into the far corners of the front room, ran the sounds of the little paws and tiny scratching claws. It was as if they were being generated under my soles, and then fleeing madly. None ran behind me. There seemed to be something keeping them from the living room. I took a cautious step further into the front room, and now they did run behind me, but only as far as the archway. I could hear them reach it and scuttle off to the side walls. You see what made me smile?

I was the horror that frightened them so!

The sound gradually lessened. It was not that it lessened in overall intensity. It was just there were fewer and fewer creatures running away. It diminished rapidly, and in about ninety seconds it had reduced to an occasional single scampering. One invisible creature ran around and around me, as if all the unseen holes in the walls had been stopped up and it was frantically looking for one. It found one, too, and was gone.

I laughed then and went back to my work. I remember that I thought quite clearly after that, for a while. I remember writing in a *glissando* passage that was a stroke of genius—something to drive the doghouse slapper crazy but guaranteed to drive the customers even crazier if it could be done at all. I remember zoom-zooming it off under my breath, and feeling mightily pleased with myself over it.

And then the reaction struck me.

Those little claws—

What was happening to me?

I thought instantly of Gloria. *There's some deadly law of compensation working here,* I thought. For every yellow light, a purple shadow. For every peal of laughter, a cry of anguish somewhere. For the bliss of Gloria, a touch of horror to even things up.

I licked my lips, for they were wet and my tongue was dry.

What was happening to me?

I thought again of Gloria, and the colors and sounds of Gloria, and most of all, the reality, the solid normalcy of Gloria, for all her exquisite sense of fantasy.

I couldn't go crazy. I *couldn't!* Not *now!* I'd be—unfit.

Unfit! As terrifying to me, then, as the old cry of "*Unclean*" was in the Middle Ages.

"*Gloria, darling,*" I'd have to say, "*Honey, we'll just have to call it quits. You see, I'm off my trolley. Oh, I'm quite serious. Yes indeedy. The men in the white coats will come around and back up their little wagon to the door and take me away to the laughing academy. And we won't see each other any more. A pity. A great pity. Just give me a hearty little old handshake, now, and go find yourself another fellow.*"

"Gloria!" I yelled. Gloria was all those colors, and the lovely sounds, and the fragrance that clung to my cheek and came to me when I moved and held my head just so.

"Oh, I dunno," I moaned. "I just don't know what to do! What is it? What is it?"

"Syzygy."

"Huh?" I came bolt upright, staring around wildly. Twenty inches over the couch hovered the seamed face of my jovial phantom of the street outside Murphy's. "You! Now I know I'm off my—hey! What is syzygy?"

"What's happening to you."

"Well, what is happening to me?"

"Syzygy." The head grinned engagingly. I put my head in my hands. There is an emotional pitch—an unemotional pitch, really—at which nothing is surprising, and I'd reached it. "Please explain," I said dully. "Tell me who you are, and what you mean by this sizz-sizz whatever-it-is."

"I'm not anybody," said the head, "and syzygy is a concomitant of parthenogenetic and certain other low types. I think what's happening *is* syzygy. If it isn't—" The head disappeared, a hand with spatulate fingers appeared and snapped its fingers explosively; the hand disappeared, the head reappeared and smiled, "—you're a gone goose."

"Don't *do* that," I said miserably.

"Don't do what?"

"That—that piecemeal business. Why do you do it?"

"Oh—that. Conservation of energy. It works here too, you know."

"Where is 'here'?"

"That's a little difficult to explain until you get the knack of it. It's the place where reverse ratios exist. I mean, if something stacks up in a three to five ratio there, it's a five to three ratio here. Forces must balance."

I almost had it. What he said almost made sense. I opened my mouth to question him but he was gone.

After that I just sat there. Perhaps I wept.

And Gloria came the next day, too. That was bad. I did two wrong things. First, I kept information from her, which was inexcusable. If you are going to share at all, you must share the bad things too. The other thing I did was to question her like a jealous adolescent.

But what else could be expected? Everything was changed. Everything was different. I opened the door to her and she brushed past me with a smile, and not a very warm one at that, leaving me at the door all outstretched arms and large clumsy feet.

She shrugged out of her coat and curled up on the couch.

"Leo, play some music."

I felt like hell and I know I looked it. Did she notice? Did she even care? Didn't it make any difference at all how I felt, what I was going through?

I went and stood in front of her. "Gloria," I said sternly, "where have you been?"

She looked up at me and released a small, retrospective sigh that turned me bright green and sent horns sprouting out of my scalp. It was such a happy, satisfied little sound. I stood there glowering at her. She waited a moment more and then got up, switched on the amplifier and turntable, dug out the "Dance of the Hours," turned the volume up, added too much bass, and switched in the volume expander, which is quite the wrong thing to use on that record. I strode across the room and turned the volume down.

"Please, Leo," she said in a hurt tone. "I like it that way."

Viciously I turned it back up and sat down with my elbows on my knees and my lower lip stuck out. I was wild. This was all wrong.

I know what I should do, I thought sullenly. *I ought to yank the plug on the rig and stand up and tell her off.*

How right I was! But I didn't do it. How could I do it? This was *Gloria!* Even when I looked up at her and saw her staring at me, saw the slight curl to her lip, I didn't do it. Well, it was too late then. She was watching me, comparing me with—

Yes, that was it. She was comparing me with somebody. Somebody who was different from her, someone who rode roughshod over everything delicate and subtle about her, everything about her that I liked and shared with her. And she, of course, ate it up.

I took refuge in the tactic of letting her make the first move. I think, then, that she despised me. And rightly.

A bit of cockney dialogue I had once heard danced through my mind:

"D'ye love us, Alf?"

"Yus."

"Well, knock us abaht a bit."

You see? I knew the right things to do, but—

But this was Gloria. I *couldn't.*

The record finished, and she let the automatic shut off the turntable. I think she expected me to turn it over. I didn't. She said, "All right, Leo. What is it?" tiredly.

I said to myself, "I'll start with the worst possible thing that could happen. She'll deny that, and then at least I'll feel better." So I said to her, "You've changed. There's somebody else."

She looked up at the picture molding and smiled sleepily. "Yes," she said. "There certainly is."

"Uff!" I said, because that caught me right in the solar plexus. I sat down abruptly.

"His name's Arthur," she said dreamily. "He's a real man, Leo."

"Oh," I said bitterly. "I can see it. Five o'clock shadow and a head full of white matter. A toupée on his chest and a vernacular like a boatswain. Too much shoulders, too little hips, and, to quote Thorne Smith, a voice as low as his intentions. A man who never learned the distinction between eating and dining, whose idea of a hot time consists of—"

"Stop it," she said. She said it quite casually and very quietly. Because my voice was raised, it contrasted enough to have a positively deafening effect. I stood there with my jaw swinging like the lower gate of a steam-shovel as she went on, "Don't be catty, Leo."

It was a studied insult for her to use such a woman-to-woman phrase, and we both knew it. I was suddenly filled with what the French call *esprit d'escalier*—the wit of the staircase; in other words, the belated knowledge of the thing you should have said if you'd only thought of it in time, which you mumble frustratedly to yourself as you go down the stairs on your way out. I should have caught her to me as she tried to brush past me when she arrived, smothered her with—what was that corny line? "kisses—hard tooth-raking kisses, that broke his lips and hers in exquisite, salty pain." Then I should have threatened her with pinking scissors—

And then I thought of the glittering, balanced structure of self-denial I had built with her, and I could have cried....

"Why come here and parade it in front of me?" I shouted. "Why don't you take your human bulldozer and cross a couple of horizons with him? Why come here and rub my nose in it?"

She stood up, pale, and lovelier than I had thought a human being could be—so beautiful that I had to close my eyes. "I came because I had to have something to compare him with," she said steadily. "You are everything I have ever dreamed about, Leo, and my dreams are ... very detailed...." At last she faltered, and her eyes were bright. "Arthur is—is—" She shook her head. Her voice left her; she had to whisper. "I know everything about you, Leo. I know how you think, and what you will say, and what you like, and it's wonderful, wonderful ... but Leo, Arthur is something outside of me. Don't you see? Can't you see? I don't always like what Arthur does. *But I can't tell what he's going to do!* You—you share everything, Leo, Leo darling, but you don't—*take* anything!"

"Oh," I said hoarsely. My scalp was tight. I got up and started across the room toward her. My jaws hurt.

"Stop, Leo," she gasped. "Stop it, now. You can do it, but you'll be acting. You've never acted before. It would be wrong. Don't spoil what's left. No, Leo—no ... no ..."

She was right. She was so right. She was always right about me; she knew me so well. This kind of melodrama was away out of character for me. I reached her. I took her arm and she closed her eyes. It hurt when my fingers closed on her arm. She trembled but she did not try to pull away. I got her wrist and lifted it. I turned her hand over and put a kiss on the palm, closing her fingers on it. "Keep that," I said. "You might like to have it some time." Then I let her go.

"Oh Leo, darling," she said. "Darling," she said, with a curl to her lip . . .

She turned to go. And then—

"Arhgh!" She uttered a piercing scream and turned back to me, all but bowling me over in her haste to get away from Abernathy. I stood there holding her tight while she pressed, crouched, squeezed against me, and I burst into laughter. Maybe it was reaction—I don't know. But I roared.

Abernathy is my mouse.

Our acquaintance began shortly after I took the apartment. I knew the little son-of-a-gun was there because I found evidences of his depredations under the sink where I stored my potatoes and vegetables. So I went out and got a trap. In those days the kind of trap I wanted was hard to find; it took me four days and a young fortune in carfare to run one of them down. You see, I can't abide the kind of trap that hurls a wire bar down on whatever part of the mouse happens to be available, so that the poor shrieking thing dies in agony. I wanted—and by heaven I got—one of those wirebasket effects made so that a touch on the bait trips a spring which slams a door on the occupant.

I caught Abernathy in the contraption the very first night. He was a small gray mouse with very round ears. They were like the finest tissue, and covered with the softest fuzz in the world. They were translucent, and if you looked very closely you could see the most meticulous arrangement of hairline blood vessels in them. I shall always maintain that Abernathy owed his success in life to the beauty of his ears. No one with pretensions to a soul could destroy such divine tracery.

Well, I let him alone until he got over being frightened and frantic, until he got hungry and ate all the bait, and a few hours over. When I thought he was good and ready to listen to reason, I put the trap on my desk and gave him a really good talking-to.

I explained very carefully (in simple language, of course) that for him to gnaw and befoul in his haphazard fashion was downright antisocial. I explained to him that when I was a child I was trained to finish whatever I started to eat, and that I did it to this day, and

I was a human being and much bigger and stronger and smarter than he was. And whatever was good enough for me was at least good enough for him to take a crack at. I really laid down the law to that mouse. I let him mull over it for a while and then I pushed cheese through the bars until his tummy was round like a ping-pong ball. Then I let him go.

There was no sign of Abernathy for a couple of days after that. Then I caught him again; but since he had stolen nothing I let him off with a word of warning—very friendly this time; I had been quite stern at first, of course—and some more cheese. Inside of a week I was catching him every other night, and the only trouble I ever had with him was one time when I baited the trap and left it closed. He couldn't get in to the cheese and he just raised Cain until I woke up and let him in. After that I knew good relations had been established and I did without the trap and just left cheese out for him. At first he wouldn't take the cheese unless it was in the trap, but he got so he trusted me and would take it lying out on the floor. I had long since warned him about the poisoned food that the neighbors might leave out for him, and I think he was properly scared. Anyhow, we got along famously.

So here was Gloria, absolutely petrified, and in the middle of the floor in the front room was Abernathy, twinkling his nose and rubbing his hands together. In the middle of my bellow of laughter, I had a severe qualm of conscience. Abernathy had had no cheese since the day before yesterday! *Sic semper amoris*. I had been fretting so much over Gloria that I had overlooked my responsibilities.

"Darling, I'll take care of him," I said reassuringly to Gloria. I led her to an easy-chair and went after Abernathy. I have a noise I make by pressing my tongue against my front teeth—a sort of a squishy-squeaky noise, which I always made when I gave cheese to Abernathy. He ran right over toward me, saw Gloria, hesitated, gave a "the hell with it" flirt with his tail, turned to me and ran up my pants-leg.

The outside, fortunately.

Then he hugged himself tight into my palm while I rummaged in the icebox with my other hand for his cheese. He didn't snatch at it, either, until he let me look at his ears again. You never saw such beautiful ears in your life. I gave him the cheese, and broke off another piece for his dessert, and set him in the corner by the sink. Then I went back to Gloria, who had been watching me, big-eyed and trembling.

"Leo—how can you *touch* it?"

"Makes nice touching. Didn't you ever touch a mouse?"

She shuddered, looking at me as if I were Horatio just back from the bridge. "I can't stand them."

"Mice? Don't tell me that you, of all people, really and truly have the traditional Victorian mouse phobia!"

"Don't laugh at me," she said weakly. "It isn't only mice. It's any little animal—frogs and lizards and even kittens and puppies. I like big dogs and cats and horses. But somehow—" She trembled again. "If I hear anything like little claws running across the floor, or see small things scuttling around the walls, it drives me crazy."

I goggled. "If you hear—hey; it's a good thing you didn't stay another hour last night, then."

"Last night?" Then, "Last night . . ." she said, in a totally different voice, with her eyes looking inward and happy. She chuckled. "I was telling—Arthur about that little phobia of mine last night."

If I had thought my masterful handling of the mouse was going to do any good, apparently I was mistaken. "You better shove off," I said bitterly. "Arthur might be waiting."

"Yes," she said, without any particular annoyance, "he might. Goodbye, Leo."

"Goodbye."

Nobody said anything for a time.

"Well," she said, "goodbye."

"Yes," I said, "I'll call you."

"Do that," she said, and went out.

I sat still on the couch for a long time, trying to get used to it. Wishful thinking was no good; I knew that. Something had happened between us. Mostly, its name was Arthur. The thing I couldn't understand was how he ever got a show, the way things were between Gloria and me. In all my life, in all my reading, I had never heard of such a complete fusion of individuals. We both felt it when we met; it had had no chance to get old. Arthur was up against some phenomenal competition; for one thing that was certain was that Gloria reciprocated my feelings perfectly, and one of my feelings was faith. I could understand—if I tried hard—how another man might overcome this hold, or that hold, which I had on her. There are smarter men than I, better-looking ones, stronger ones. Any of several of those items could go by the board, and leave us untouched.

But not faith! Not that! It was too big; nothing else we had was important enough to compensate for a loss of faith.

I got up to turn on the light, and slipped. The floor was wet. Not only was it wet; it was soft. I floundered to the seven-way lamp and cranked both switches all the way around.

The room was covered with tapioca. Ankle-deep on the floor, inches deep on the chairs and the couch.

"She's thinking about it now," said the head. Only it wasn't a head this time. It was a flaccid mass of folded tissue. In it I could see pulsing blood vessels. My stomach squirmed.

"Sorry. I'm out of focus." The disgusting thing—a sectioned brain, apparently—moved closer to me and became a face.

I lifted a foot out of the gummy mass, shook it, and put it back in again. "I'm glad she's gone," I said hoarsely.

"Are you afraid of the stuff?"

"No!" I said. "Of course not!"

"It will go away," said the head. "Listen; I'm sorry to tell you; it isn't syzygy. You're done, son."

"What isn't syzygy?" I demanded. "And what is syzygy?"

"Arthur. The whole business with Arthur."

"Go away," I gritted. "Talk sense, or go away. Preferably—go away."

The head shook from side to side, and its expression was gentle. "Give up," it said. "Call it quits. Remember what was good, and fade out."

"You're no good to me,"' I muttered, and waded over to the book case. I got out a dictionary, glowering at the head, which now was registering a mixture of pity and amusement

Abruptly, the tapioca disappeared.

I leafed through the book. Sizable, sizar, size, sizzle—"Try S-Y," prompted the head.

I glared at it and went over to the S-Y's. Systemize, systole—

"Here it is," I said, triumphantly. "The last word in the S section." I read from the book. " 'Syzygy—either of the points at which the moon is most nearly in line with the earth and the sun, as when it is new or full.' What are you trying to tell me—that I'm caught in the middle of some astrological mumbo-jumbo?"

"Certainly not," it snapped. "I will tell you, however, that if that's all your dictionary says, it's not a very good one." It vanished.

"But—" I said vaguely. I went back to the dictionary. That's all it had to say about syzygy. Shaking, I replaced it.

Something cat-sized and furry hurtled through the air, clawed at my shoulder. I startled, backed into my record cabinet and landed with a crash on the middle of my back in the doorway. The thing leaped from me to the couch and sat up, curling a long wide tail against its back and regarding me with its jewelled eyes. A squirrel.

"Well, hello!" I said, getting to my knees and then to my feet. "Where on earth did you come from?"

The squirrel, with the instantaneous motion of its kind, dived to the edge of the couch and froze with its four legs wide apart, head up, tail describing exactly its recent trajectory, and ready to take off instantly in any direction including up. I looked at it with some puzzlement. "I'll go see if I have any walnuts," I told it. I moved toward the archway, and as I did so the squirrel leaped at me. I threw up a hand to protect my face. The squirrel struck my shoulder again and leaped from it—

And as far as I know it leaped into the fourth dimension or somewhere. For I searched under and into every bed, chair, closet, cupboard, and shelf in the house, and could find no sign of anything that even looked like a squirrel. It was gone as completely as the masses of tapioca....

Tapioca! What had the head said about the tapioca? "She's thinking about it now." *She*—Gloria, of course. This whole insane business was tied up with Gloria in some way.

Gloria not only disliked tapioca—she was afraid of it.

I chewed on that for a while, and then looked at the clock. Gloria had had time enough to get to the hotel. I ran to the phone, dialed.

"Hotel San Dragon," said a chewing-gum voice.

"748, please," I said urgently.

A couple of clicks. Then, "Hello?"

"Gloria," I said. "Listen; I—"

"Oh, you. Listen—can you call me back later? I'm very busy."

"I can and I will, but tell me something quickly: Are you afraid of squirrels?"

Don't tell me a shudder can't be transmitted over a telephone wire. One was that time, "I hate them. Call me back in about—"

"Why do you hate them?"

With exaggerated patience, she said carefully, "When I was a little girl, I was feeding some pigeons and a squirrel jumped right up on my shoulder and scared me half to death. Now, *please*—"

"Okay, okay," I said. "I'll speak to you later." I hung up. She shouldn't talk to me that way. She had no right—

What was she doing in that hotel room, anyway?

I pushed the ugly thought down out of sight, and went and poured myself a beer. Gloria is afraid of tapioca, I thought, and tapioca shows up here. She is afraid of the sound of small animals' feet, and I hear them here. She is afraid of squirrels that jump on people, and I get a squirrel that jumps on people.

That must all make some sense. Of course, I could take the easy way out, and admit that I was crazy. But somehow, I was no longer so ready to admit anything like that. Down deep inside, I made an agreement with myself not to admit that until I had exhausted every other possibility.

A very foolish piece of business. See to it that you don't do likewise. It's probably much smarter not to try to figure things out.

There was only one person who could straighten this whole crazy mess out—since the head wouldn't—and that was Gloria, I thought suddenly. I realized, then, why I had not called all bets before now. I had been afraid to jeopardize the thing that Gloria and I shared. Well, let's face it. We didn't share it any longer. That admission helped.

I strode to the telephone, and dialed the hotel.

"Hotel San Dragon."

"748, please."

A moment's silence. Then, "I'm sorry, sir. The party does not wish to be disturbed."

I stood there looking blankly at the phone, while pain swirled and spiralled up inside me. I think that up to this moment I had treated the whole thing as part sickness, part dream; this, somehow, brought it to a sharp and agonizing focus. Nothing that she could have done could have been so calculated and so cruel.

I cradled the receiver and headed for the door. Before I could reach it, gray mists closed about me. For a moment I seemed to be on some sort of a treadmill; I was walking, but I could not reach anything. Swiftly, then, everything was normal.

"I must be in a pretty bad way," I muttered. I shook my head. It was incredible. I felt all right, though a little dizzy. I went to the door and out.

The trip to the hotel was the worst kind of a nightmare. I could only conclude that there was something strange and serious wrong with me, completely aside from my fury and my hurt at Gloria. I kept running into these blind spells, when everything about me took on an unreal aspect. The light didn't seem right. I passed people on the street who weren't there when I turned to look at them. I heard voices where there were no people, and I saw people talking but couldn't hear them. I overcame a powerful impulse to go back home. I couldn't go back; I knew it; I knew I had to face whatever crazy thing was happening, and that Gloria had something to do with it.

I caught a cab at last, though I'll swear one of them disappeared just as I was about to step into it. Must have been another of those blind spells. After that it was easier. I slouched quivering in a corner of the seat with my eyes closed.

I paid off the driver at the hotel and stumbled in through the revolving doors. The hotel seemed much more solid than anything else since this horrible business had started to happen to me. I started over to the desk, determined to give some mad life-and-death message to the clerk to break that torturing "do not disturb" order. I glanced into the coffee room as I passed it and stopped dead.

She was in there, in a booth, with—with someone else. I couldn't see anything of the man but a glossy black head of hair and a thick, ruddy neck. She was smiling at him, the smile that I thought had been born and raised for me.

I stalked over to them, trembling. As I reached them, he half-rose, leaned across the table, and kissed her.

"Arthur . . ." she breathed.

"That," I said firmly, "will do."

They did not move.

"Stop it!" I screamed. They did not move. Nothing moved, anywhere. It was a tableau, a picture, a hellish frozen thing put there to tear me apart.

"That's all," said a now-familiar voice, gently. "That kiss did it, son. You're through." It was the head, but now he was a whole man. An ordinary-looking, middle-sized creature he was, with a scrawny frame to match his unimpressive middle-aged face. He perched on the edge of the table, mercifully between me and that torturing kiss.

I ran to him, grasped his thin shoulders. "Tell me what it is," I begged him. "Tell me, if you know—and I think you know. Tell me!" I roared, sinking my fingers into his flesh.

He put his hands up and laid them gently on my wrists, holding them there until I quieted down a little. I let him go. "I *am* sorry, son," he said. "I hoped you would figure it all out by yourself."

"I tried," I said. I looked around me. The grayness was closing in again, and through it I could see the still figures of the people in the coffee shop, all stopped in mid-action. It was one three-dimensional frame of some unthinkable movie-film. I felt cold sweat all but squirt from the pores of my face. "Where am I?" I shrieked.

"Please," he soothed. "Take it easy, and I'll tell you. Come over here and sit down and relax. Close your eyes and don't try to think. Just listen."

I did as he asked, and gradually I stopped shaking. He waited until he felt that I was calm, and then began talking.

"There is a world of psychic things—call them living thought, call them dreams if you like. Now, you know that of all animals, only human beings can reach these psychic things. It was a biological accident. There is something about humans which is tangent to this psychic world. Humans have the power to open a gate between the two worlds. They can seldom control the power; often they're not aware of it. But when that gate is opened, something materializes in the world of the humans. Imagination itself is enough to do it. If you are hungry, down deep inside, for a certain kind of woman, and if you picture her to yourself vividly enough, such a gate might open, and there she'll be. You can see her and touch her; she'll be little different from a real one."

"But—there is a difference?"

"Yes, there is. She is not a separate thing from you. She is a part of you. She is your product. That's what I was driving at when I mentioned parthenogenesis. It works like that."

"Parthenogenesis—let's see. That's the process of reproducing without fertilization, isn't it?"

"That's right. This 'materialization' of yours is a perfect parallel to that. As I told you before, however, it is not a process with high survival value. For one thing, it affords no chance to cross strains. Unless a living creature can bring into itself other characteristics, it must die out."

"Then why don't all parthenogenetic creatures die out?"

"There is a process used by which the very simple, one-celled forms of life take care of that. Mind you," he broke off suddenly, "I'm just using all of this biological talk as symbolism. There are basic laws that work in both worlds, that work equally on the high forms of life and the low. Do you see?"

"I see. These are just examples. But go on about this process that the parthenogenetic creatures use to mix their strains."

"It's very simple. Two of these organisms let their nuclei flow together for a time. Then they separate and go their ways again. It isn't a reproductive process at all. It's merely a way in which each may gain a part of the other. It's called—syzygy."

"Oh," I said. "That. But I still don't—let me see. You mentioned it first when that—that—"

"When Gloria met Arthur," the man finished smoothly. "I said that if it were syzygy, you'd be all right. Well, it wasn't, as you saw for yourself. The outside strain, even though it didn't suit her as well as you did, was too strong. You got hurt. Well, in the workings of really basic laws, something always gets hurt."

"What about you? Who are you?"

"I am somebody who has been through it, that's all. You must understand that my world is different from the one you remember. Time itself is different. Though I started from a time perhaps thirty years away, I was able to open a gate near you. Just a little one, of course. I did it so that I could try to make you think this thing out in time. I believe that if you could, you would have been spared all this. You might even have been able to keep Gloria."

"What's it to you?"

"You don't know, do you? You really don't know?"

I opened my eyes and looked at him, and shook my head. "No, I don't. I—like you, old man."

He chuckled. "That's odd, you know. I don't like me."

I craned around and looked over at Gloria and her man, still frozen in that strange kiss. "Will those dream people stay like that forever?"

"Dream people?"

"I suppose that's what they are. You know, I'm a little proud of Gloria. How I managed to dream up anything so—so lovely, I'll never know. I—hey—what's the matter?"

"Didn't you understand what I was telling you? Gloria is real. Gloria goes on living. What you see over there is the thing that happened when you were no longer a part of her. Leo: she dreamed *you!*"

I rose to my feet and put my fists on the table between us. "That's a lie," I choked. "I'm—I'm me, damn you!"

"You're a detailed dream, Leo, and a splendid job. You're a piece of sentient psyche from another world injection-molded into an ideal that Gloria dreamed. Don't try to be anything else. There aren't many real humans, Leo. Most of the world is populated by the dreams of a few of them; didn't you know, Leo? Why do you suppose that so few people you met knew anything about the world as a whole? Why do you suppose that humans keep their interests confined and their environments small? Most of them aren't humans at all, Leo!"

"I'm *me,*" I said stubbornly. "Gloria *couldn't* have thought of all of me! Gloria can't run a power shovel! Gloria can't play a guitar! Gloria doesn't know anything about the circus foreman who sang, or the Finn dynamite boss who was killed!"

"Of course not. Gloria only dreamed a kind of man who was the product of those things, or things like them. Have you run a shovel since you met her? You'd find that you couldn't, if you really tried. You've played guitar for no one but her since you met her. You've spent all your time arranging music that no one will ever see or play!"

"I'm *not* anybody's dream!" I shouted. "I'm not. If I was an ideal of hers, we would have stayed together. I failed with her, old man; don't you know that? She wanted me to be aggressive, and I wasn't."

He looked at me so sadly that I thought he was going to cry. "She wanted you to *take.* You were a part of her, no human can take from himself."

"She was deathly afraid of some things that didn't bother me at all. What about that?"

"The squirrels, and the sound of all the little feet? No, Leo; they were baseless phobias, and she had the power to overcome any of them. She never tried, but it was not difficult to create you without them."

I stared at him. "Do you mean to— Old man, are there more like me, really?"

"Many, many," he sighed. "But few who cling to their nonexistent, ghostly egos as you are doing."

"Do the real people know what they are doing?"

"Very few of them. Very few. The world is full of people who feel incomplete, people who have everything they can possibly want and yet are unhappy, people who feel alone in a crowd. The world is mostly peopled by ghosts."

"But—the war! Roman history! The new car models! What about them?"

He shook his head again. "Some of it's real, some not. It depends on what the real humans want from moment to moment."

I thought a minute, bitterly. Then I asked him, "What was that you said about coming back in world-time, and looking through a little gateway at things that had happened?"

He sighed. "If you *must* hang on to the ego she gave you," he said wearily, "you'll stay the way you are now. But you'll age. It will take you the equivalent of thirty or so years to find your way around in that strange psychic world, for you will have to move and think like a human. Why do you want to do that?"

I said, with determination, "I am going back, then, if it takes me a century. I'm going to find me right after I met Gloria, and I'm going to warn me in such a way that I'll figure out a way to be with Gloria for the rest of her life."

He put his hands on my shoulders, and now there really were tears in his eyes. "Oh, you poor kid," he said.

I stared at him. Then, "What's—your name, old man?"

"My name is Leo."

"Oh," I said. "Oh."

The Blue Letter

THEY SAT A dance out, finally, because her hair was sending dark tendrils over the nape of her neck. They sat together in a wing chair under the balcony, a chair just too big for one; and she pulled pins out of her hair.

"Lovely," he said. He touched it. "Lovely. I didn't know it was so long."

She smiled, arching her body to see into the wall mirror around the tall wing of the chair, and combed deftly.

"I have always— I've never—" he faltered. "I mean, women shouldn't be allowed to cut their hair."

"Didn't you say your wife has long hair?"

"Yes, she has, but not like that. She hasn't cut it since I married her, but it isn't like that."

The comb stopped, its teeth streaming little wakes like stones in a painted waterfall. He looked into the mirror and saw her face there, watching him gravely. She said, "Are you happy?"

He hesitated. None of his friends who had ever seen him with his wife had ever asked that. It would be silly to ask that.

Before he could speak, the comb finished its stroke and she half-whispered, "You said you were happy, while we were dancing."

"Yes, I did. I was. I never danced with anyone like you. I never danced as well."

She bent her head, making a part, looking at the mirror upward through her brows. "Your wife must be very good, judging by the way you dance."

He almost shook his head. "She's— She doesn't enjoy it very much."

She turned to him suddenly, with her eyes wide. They were green, and ever so slightly slanted. The planes of her ivory face were subtly distinct from one another. She spoke urgently, "She'll be back soon, won't she? And then you and I will— Well, I'll drop out, that's all. She's two thousand miles away from here, because you had to come back and make a new start alone. Well, you've made your new start, and it's not *right* for you to be alone. Why can't you—why can't we take what we want until she comes back?"

He didn't know which of them moved, but suddenly their lips were together, just barely touching. She closed her eyes, and her hair was softly around his face. She turned her head slightly, stroking his lips with hers, a kitten-paw touch and a high little sound spelled with m's escaped her. His shoulders and arms were rock-hard. His eyes closed too, and then she twisted away from him and to her feet, laughing. She stood before the mirror, rapidly twisting her hair up in two great swept-back wings. She was on tiptoe as she worked, stretching tautly, and he knew he would never forget her as long as he lived.

Later, he was in his room alone, wondering why he had given the taxi-driver her address first, wondering why he had refused the night-cap she offered, and knowing that it was because ultimately he would tell his wife about it, and that would be good as long as it was not unbeautiful in the telling.

There was a blue envelope on the floor under the maildrop. He picked it up, smiled at his wife's rounded handwriting, opened it and stood there until he had read it all. It was a very short letter, completely screened of any emotion whatsoever, and it said "I want a divorce." It went on about not wanting any money from him, and that she was genuinely sorry, but he certainly realized that the separation consisted of more than eight months and two thousand miles. It said that they both had known for a long time that he would go farther and faster alone, and it thanked him for those good years. It was utterly sincere and irrevocable, or she wouldn't have written it.

He laid the letter carefully on the table and removed his overcoat and hung it up. Then he went to the telephone and dialed.

"Yes?"

"I hope I didn't wake you. I just got a letter from my wife. Listen."

He read it to her. There was such a long silence that he thought she had hung up. "Hello?"

Surprisingly, she said, "I can't see your face. I have my eyes closed tight and I am listening to your voice, but I've never seen your face like that." She stopped, and he could hear her breathing. She said, "Are you glad?'

"Well, of course."

"I'm coming over."

"But you c—"

"Shush," she said, and hung up.

He cradled the telephone, picked up the letter and read it again. At last he smiled.

It was all right. It was all perfectly all right. Obviously a change-partners deal was indicated. Nobody need be hurt. A pity, possibly—funny little words he and his wife had made up together, little tricks they used to play on each other, a way they had of saying good night. Pawing the air and gnashings of the teeth could be left to the uncivilized. He'd be all right. Nice of her to make the break so quick and clean. Change partners. All right; make it a double ceremony. The whole thing was beautifully timed.

He was suddenly conscious of perfume, for a little clung to his cheek. He thought carefully of his wife, and then of the girl, and the comparison pleased him. He moved about, emptying an ashtray, straightening the cover of the studio couch, learning as he moved how to turn his head to catch the elusive fragrance of the perfume. He was still smiling when the padded knock sounded.

"Come in."

She was inside the room immediately, and the door was closed, with her hands behind her on the knob. "You poor darling," she said softly, and came toward him.

Puzzlement swirled in him. Sorry. She was *sorry* for him, as if something bad had happened.

She looked up into his face, and put her hands on his chest.

She said, "Didn't you know?"

"Not consciously. Not until tonight." He waved at the letter. "But it's all right. It's all perfectly all right."

"And she just let you have it . . . Just like that. What a rotten, bitchy thing to do!"

He watched her face, full of pity and passion, and he saw it go questioning. Slowly, fear crept into her eyes. She backed away from him. She opened her mouth but he said "Get out." "Get out," he said again, and began to move. She turned and ran, and when the door closed, he sighed. He was all twisted inside the way her face was twisted.

He slumped to the couch. He sat that way all night without moving.

Wham Bop!

IT'S THE KIND of thing you wonder about, so I went and asked him at the end of the number.

"How do you get to whip the skins in the big time?" he repeated, and grinned at his sweating combo. He racked his sticks. "Take ten," he called to the boys, and then turned back to me. "Lead me to a cola with the emphasis on ice, and I'll tell you."

He was a big fellow, red-headed, with wide shoulders and a good grin. We got off the stand and around to the tables. He buried his mouth amongst the ice cubes for a long moment and came up out of it with a sigh. It was hot that night.

"Saw you stompin'," he said. "You're a cat."

"You and your drums got me to jumping," I smiled back.

"Thanks," he said, and I could see he meant it. "Now I'll tell you how a guy can beat his way to the top." He leaned back and, as he spoke, looked at something over my head and quite a while ago.

"The very first combo I had," he said, "was a five-man group—clarinet, alto, trumpet, guitar, and me. No piano—we were strictly portable. We were all in school and playing this river resort, partly for peanuts, mostly for kicks. After the first couple of weeks, we began to drag a pretty faithful public. Word got around the way it does, and pretty soon the lot began to fill up with out-of-town license plates. I can't say that any one of us was really terrific. Thing was, we meshed. When we rode it, we rode it together. It was fine.

"Things went on that way for a while, and we were in pretty solid. There was no talk of bringing in any pro outfit, anyhow.... Oh, I might as well come out with it. This river place I'm talking about, it was my uncle's. See what I mean? But don't get me wrong. We delivered. At first, anyhow.

"Maybe I got a little cocky, after a while. I began to circulate among the customers a little. Nothing wrong with that. Joey Harris was on guitar. Very solid. That was rhythm enough for some numbers, and the cats liked the drums all the better after I'd given 'em a miss for a while. Anyhow, I planned to go places in the music business, and I figured one good way to do it was to play the customers person-to-person as well as from the stand. Dig me?

"Well, you can go too far with that kind of horseplay. It had to rain sometime, and when it did, and we drew a small crowd, I couldn't see the sense in knocking myself out. You might remember that—too much glad-handing is slow poison.

"One night it was like that—ten or a dozen couples and the band with or without me was strictly so-what. I was down in the far corner telling somebody about myself when I heard the drums.

"It was a kid called Manuel. Black-haired sleepy-looking guy, sort of round-shouldered and slow. He was crouching in my saddle up there over the suitcases, running over the trap with the brushes. Nothing loud, you know. Easy. Easy like breathing. I just relaxed. I knew the kid. His old man had a motor-launch downstream on charter. They fished some. Manuel used to hang around a lot, watching me on the drums. He knew what he'd get if he tore a head on me. He was careful. And besides, there was nothing going on.

"He got his foot on the bass pedal and filled out his beat some. Before I knew it the cats were out on the floor, letting the chairs get cold for the first time that evening. Well, that was all right with me too. I like to see people enjoying themselves. All hands were cutting it, and my trumpet man, Stompy Pearle, was sitting up straight for the first time that night.

"There was a change in the tone of the drums, but not the beat. Manuel had dropped the brushes and grabbed the sticks. And without seeming to make a move, he brought a lick out of those drums that was like a bucket of gas on a coal fire. It brought me right up on my feet, and Brot Hoffman—well, you could see him shiver from the far end of the floor. He pointed his clarinet at the roof and blew out a climbing riff that'd make your hair curl. It got Stompy too; he stood up on his chair and caught the riff at the very top and brought it back down again with the trumpet. Joey began stroking all the upbeats—something he only did when he was really sent. Every gate in the place said 'Ah-h-h' at the same time and stopped dancing.

"They stopped dancing! What was going on on the stand was just frantic, but nobody moved. They just stood there and soaked it in, with their mouths and nostrils open. Something went *pop!* inside my head. I was wild. I'd had 'em driving before, but I'd never seen the lid blow off like that.

"I went up to the stand and back to the drums. I nudged Manuel. He was adrift. I nudged him again. He looked up, still working, waking slowly. I said, 'I'll take it.' He slid out, and I slid in. I got the sticks from him without missing a beat."

Red brought his gaze down to me and shook his head slowly. "You're a cat. You know. You're playing along, all of a sudden something happens, the whole place is twenty-two thousand feet altitude—and all of a sudden you're back to earth. You don't know when or why it starts or stops, but there it is." He shrugged. "That's what happened when I took over." He turned a thumb down. "Like that. The boys fumbled it for a measure and then slipped into our usual arrangement of 'Whispering.' But it was all gone. I wanted to take them out one by one and husk them. I didn't like it a bit. I was mad clear through.

"We finished it somehow. On the last beat I threw my sticks on the floor and beckoned to Manuel. When you want to tear into somebody, call them over. Don't go to them. I waited until he was standing by me. He looked very worried and anxious. I guess he could see I was mad. Joey Harris put down his guitar and came over too. I said to Manuel, 'Who told you to horn in?'

"Manuel just stood there licking his lips. Joey spoke up. 'I told him to sit in, Red,' he said. 'Somebody around here's got to play drums once in a while.'

"I told him I'd talk to him later. I said to Manuel, 'Look, bud, you know you're a little out of your element around here.' He just looked at me, sort of squinching up his face. He knew what I meant. Joey and Brot and Stompy and Fred—that was the guy playing alto—

and me, we were all from the resort. There were no tracks around there, but this Manuel, he was from the wrong side of them. Dig me? I said, 'Maybe you ought to go graze in your own pasture.'"

Red went back to his cola. I watched him. I didn't quite know what to think. I said, "I thought you were going to tell me how a drummer gets into the real big time."

He flashed that grin at me. "Stick around. I'll get to it. What it amounts to, a guy's got to be good. Then, he's got to be smart. He's got to be smarter than anyone who tries to crowd into his spot. Well ...

"Joey and Brot were still hanging around. They watched Manuel climb off the stand and amble across the floor and out. Then they looked back at me. They just stood there. Nobody said anything. Well, I guess they didn't like it. But a guy's got to look out for himself. Those skins were important to me, see?

"Those guys surprised me after that. They sort of ganged up on me. No kidding! Can you tie it? Wasn't much they could do. There was nowhere else to play around there, and they knew that a word from me would bring another outfit into the resort. I had 'em, but all the same they laid down some law. I was supposed to keep hands off Manuel. I was even supposed to let him sit in sometimes.

"I okayed that. Yeah. It wasn't backing down. It was just being smart. I told them that I had nothing against the kid, and he could sit in any time things were slow, like tonight. But not when we had a mob. That was all right with them. They wanted Manuel's kind of drums for themselves, not for the customers. We dropped it there. After that we played a lot of music, and if I didn't get much company from them, I got along all right without it. One of them—I don't know who—went down to see Manuel the next day and explained things to him. He showed up every once in a while after that, when he wasn't working the launch with his father. Sat in a few times, too. But never unless I told him he could, and that was only often enough to keep the boys happy. He was good. I had to admit that. Had the easiest attack I've ever seen. Strictly relaxed. A simple, shuffling stroke that left you cold—you thought—until you felt the goose-pimples.

"Couple weeks after that there was a picnic and dance down at the Island. It was two miles downstream and out toward the middle of the river. A nice place. Pavilion, tables—you know. Most of the customers would go down in their boats. The resort hired the old launch to take care of the overflow.

"I remember it struck me as peculiar that Fred came to me before rehearsal one afternoon and mentioned Manuel. Wanted to know if the kid could sit in at the picnic. I said sure. Why not? We wouldn't be drawing anything much but local people. He seemed happier about it than he let on. I forgot about it.

"It was Joey that gave me the first idea that there would be anything special about that picnic. As I said, Joey played very solid guitar. He could read, but mostly he ran his progressions by the seat of his pants. He broke into the middle of 'One O'clock Jump' and wanted to know about that modulation in the bridge section, and should he go through an augmented fifth instead of right from his tonal seventh to the dominant. Stop popping your eyes! Guitar players all talk like that. I said, 'Let's hear it.' He ran it off both ways: the new way was strictly from Roxy. I told him yes, if he liked it that way. I trusted him. Next thing I know Fred is up, blushing like he used to do. His mouth was almost useless to him without a saxophone in it, he was so shy. Seems he'd worked out some counterpoint with Stompy and Brot. Could they run it off ? Well, I didn't know they'd been rehearsing among themselves, but why should I kick? I put out an ear and they tore off into this thing.

"It was a sort of fugue. It was like braiding three colors of rope together, so that you get one strand but you can follow each color of each rope all through it. I'd never heard anything like it before. Not from a jive combo, anyhow. It killed me.

"When they were finished, nobody said much. Joey was sitting back with his eyes rolled up, making little noises with his tongue.

"'Fred.' I said when I got my breath back, 'you've been sneaking into dark corners, that's what you've been doing, and you've been listening to Bach. You're a Persian, Fred, a long-haired cat. It's beautiful. It's gorgeous. I'll buy it.'

"We ran it off again while I worked the drums in. At first I accented it hard, but the three of them looked as if I was cussing in

Sunday school, and Joey held his hands up in front of his face. I got the idea and dropped off to an easy brush, just a low-down walkaway behind all that precision stuff. It was fine. And I still didn't get the idea. Why should they take all that trouble for a picnic date?

"I got the idea the day before the picnic, though, but good—and I went up in a mushroom-shaped cloud. My uncle got hold of me and told me to play some really good music at the Island. I said we always played good music. He took out his toothpick and told me no, this was important, or it could be. Seems that one of the out-of-town guests was Phil Drago. The Marshalls were bringing him.

"Phil Drago! Can you imagine how I felt?" asked Red.

"No," I said. "Who is he?"

"One of the big wheels in the music business. The public knows all the name bands, but the real cats know who plays what instruments how well. Guys like Drago, though, they never get a spotlight. They're the arrangers and orchestra managers. They do the styling, making one orchestra sound different from another. And mostly, what they say goes. Drago, he was with the King of Swing himself that year."

It began to dawn on me. "And that was the year that the King's drummer got into that—"

He nodded. "That was the year the King was looking for a new drummer. And you know how he used to pick up players from the bush. Man, this was it!

"Well," he went on, "first of all, I wanted to tear into that gang of mine and rip 'em apart piece by each. That bunch of so-and-so's had probably known about this for days. Hence all that frantic arranging. Hence something else—I'd been caught unawares and made a promise to let Manuel sit in. I saw the whole pitch. If I laid down the law, they'd give me the big Or Else. They knew the spot I was on. If I was going to play the kind of drums Phil Drago would notice, I'd need a group to back me up, and if I didn't let Manuel get in a couple of licks, I wouldn't have a group.

"Now, you were asking me how a guy gets to the top in this business. Remember what I said? You've got to be good in your work.

And you've got to be smarter than anybody who has his eye on what you want."

"I'm making a list," I said. "What's the next item?"

"The next item," said Red, and made the grin again, "is to be quite sure of what it is you want, and then to use any material at hand to get it. And I mean *any.*"

"How low can you get?" I muttered. I was embarrassed when I realized he'd heard me. He just laughed.

"How ambitious can you get?" he said, and went on with his story.

"As I told you, this Manuel character helped his father with a launch. It was a busted-up old scow, long ago retired from harbor service, where it used to carry sailors out to ships at anchor and stuff like that. Maybe you won't blame me too much for what I did. Manuel was a darn good mechanic and knew his boats. I really believed that he'd be happier sticking with it. He might get a disappointment with the drum deal, but he'd get over it. As for me, I felt that the drums were my high talent. I could justify what I did—to myself, anyway. And it was easy to do. You see, Manuel and his father were the only ones in miles who held inland waterway licenses. The launch had to run that night. It was chartered by the resort, and they needed the dough. If Manuel's father couldn't run it, Manuel would have to. You don't take chances with the Steamboat Commission." He shrugged. "Manuel's father wasn't there to run the launch that night. He was out of town. He got a telegram from his sister. She was awful sick. Or at least that's what it said in the telegram—that I sent." He smiled.

I said, in a certain way, "Well."

Red gripped my arm. "Wait now. Let me tell you what happened. This is something you've got to hear all of, or not at all."

I settled back. "Go ahead."

"It couldn't have been timed better. Manuel's father worked the whole early part of the evening. He was at the wheel of the launch when it took the combo to the picnic. I even left Manuel to set out the drums and warm himself up while I circulated, and while the old man went back for another load. My guys warmed up with Manuel, and they were raring to go. It was on that trip that the old man found the telegram waiting for him. He came back to the Island, picked up Manuel, and turned the launch over to him. And Phil Drago hadn't showed yet!

"We played some great stuff. The boys were feeling good because they thought they'd put one over on me, and I felt good for reasons of my own.

"The Marshalls arrived and I had a good gander at the little guy with them. Mousy-looking fellow, with hair like an unmade bed and great big, intelligent-looking eyes. He didn't say much to anyone. Just listened. We swung into an oldie—'Sweet Sue,' I think it was—and gave it a treatment. It was fine. Afterward I told the boys to take fifteen. I didn't want to rush it. Slip it to him a little at a time. I circulated some, but had the sense to stay away from Drago. Playing sells these guys, not personality.

"In the meantime Fred went down to the dock to find out what was keeping Manuel. When he came back his, chin was dragging. He slouched up to the stand and broke the news that Manuel would have to work all evening.

"You could see the heart go out of those boys. It was as if something dropped out of them and rolled under the stand. The rest of that evening was a nightmare. Those guys played tall and green. Nobody fluffed anything, understand. But there was no jump. I did my best on the skins, and only succeeded in putting the drums front and center with nothing to back them up. I felt foolish, and I guess I looked it.

"I called a huddle in the second intermission. I said, 'What in time is the matter with you guys?'

"Joey said, 'Maybe we'd be better if you'd get that grin off your puss. What've you got to be so happy about?'

"Joey didn't usually talk like that. I was about to pin his ears back when I noticed the look on his face. I shrugged it off. Time enough to start trouble when we were back at the resort. I said, 'We're serving it up cream-style to that orchestra scout over there.' It was the first time we'd mentioned Drago right out, though I knew they'd all had their heads together. I said, 'What say we riff off that fugue-break of Fred's? That'll send the whole place airmail special.'

"Fred looked up from where he'd been diddling with the spit-valve on his alto horn. He didn't blush, either. He said, 'No.' Just like that.

"I looked around at the rest of them, and I could see that they'd go along with him. 'For Pete's sake, why not?'

"Brot Hoffman shrugged his shoulders. He said, 'It takes a special kind of drums.'

"I got my mouth open to say something and then closed it again. I suddenly knew what he meant. That low-down, easy walkaway wasn't my style at all. Fred had worked out that fugue for Manuel.

"I didn't say anything for a minute. This wasn't the way I'd planned it at all. On the other hand, I had half of what I wanted. Drago was not going to hear Manuel. I was sore, but not sore enough to stop being smart. I said, 'Let's get back to it. And try to sound at least like a cylinder phonograph, will you?'

"It was the longest evening I ever sat through. It was awful. The music was good enough to dance to. Period. Nobody ever got anywhere playing music just good enough to dance to. Once I noticed the Marshalls making get-up-and-go-home movements, and I saw Drago stop them. That was encouraging, but not very. We just played it out, and played-out was the way we sounded.

"At last, they were shutting the place down for the night and we were at the dock with our cases, waiting while Manuel warped in his old ark. I was so disgusted I almost forgot to be mad. The Marshalls and Drago came down the duckboards. I could hear Drago talking. He was saying something about being sorry to have kept them there so long. 'That redhead was playing very clean drums when we arrived. I was hoping to hear more of it. A fluke, I guess.' Oh, brother! Was it a fluke!

"Manuel tied up and we loaded aboard. I hated the looks of that launch and the smell of it and the whole idea of getting near it. If it wasn't for that Manuel, why I'd be—I dunno. I was fit to blow a fuse. When he came down the companion ladder—the seats were inside ranging around the crummy old engine—and spoke to me, I barked at him. He said there wasn't enough room forward for all the instruments. Would I mind storing the drums in the lock-up on the dock? He'd pick them up in the morning. I told him to do whatever he wanted. He went away again.

"Drago was sitting across from me, talking quietly with the Marshalls. It occurred to me to squeeze into the conversation and do myself some good, but I didn't have the heart for it.

"Manuel cast off and kicked the starter. The motor caught. Great grovelin' day, what a racket that was! Not loud. No. It sounded as if every rev would be its last. I never had trusted the old barge, but this trip it sounded really sick. Something the matter with the timing, it seemed like. The first cylinder to fire let go with a sharp *wham,* and the second barely popped, and the third and fourth just gasped. What with that series of torturous sounds, over and over and over again, and the intermittent *clip clop* as the wheel took up the slack in the steering lines, it was a fit finish to a dismal evening.

"The noise of that sick engine crawled in between my ears and curled up there with every intention of spending the night. I looked around for something—anything—to take my mind off it. All the guys were looking at Drago."

Red gulped down the last of his drink and spread his hands on the table. "Ever watch a drummer really sending? Most of 'em talk it, especially when they're doing a lot of shifting. Sometimes they do it right out loud while they work. Sounds crazy by itself, but it makes a pattern that you can follow with your sticks. *Skiddle-d'wee, skiddle d'wat, skwit-bap, skiddle-d'tat,*" he recited, tapping the table.

"Yes," I said. "A lot of them do it."

"Well," said Red, "that's what Drago was doing. His eyes were glazing over and he was talking along with that deathbed motor. I followed it on his lips. He had it just right:

"'*Wham-bop, shillu, shillop,*
Wham-bop, shillu, shillop.'

"I looked around again. Joey's hands were moving. Fred and Brot leaned forward suddenly as if they'd been pulled by the same string. Stompy just looked vacant. His three valve fingers trembled the way they do when he's clearing his horn for a high riff.

"Wham-bop, shillu, shillop,
Wham-bop, shillu, shillop . . .

"I tell you, it rocked part of you right to sleep and brought something else in you wide, wide awake.

"All of a sudden there was another noise in with it. The steering lines, whipping up slack as the wheel was twitched from side to side—not enough to turn the rudder, mind you; just sufficient to slap the lines against the inside of the guards—and mixed up in it was the very gentle tapping of feet on the deck overhead and a little aft, by the wheelpost. One toe, one heel. And all the while this motor noise backing it. Subtle? Hey! I'll try to talk it for you:

"Wham-bop, shillu, shillop,
Wham-bop, shillu, shillop . . .
(And with the feet and the ropes:)
Tickety wham-bop t'tick shillop,
T'tickety bop shillu, shillop,
Tack bop t'tock shillop . . .

"Drago sat there soaking it up. He put his palms together very carefully and began to squeeze, and began to smile a little too. Brot gasped something about 'That's for me!' and dove for the forepeak where the instruments were stowed. He tore his clarinet out of its case, just dropping the case where he stood—and Brot was usually a very careful character. He got the reed into his face and ripped out that incredible climbing gliss that had been torn out of him the first night Manuel played the drums. And all the while that motor was beating it out—

"Wham-bop, shillu, shillop . . .
(And Brot rode in:)
Hoodle-de-dop, bop, d'dewdy . . .

"Stompy and Joey beat their heads together on their way to the forepeak. The sound of it faded right in on an upbeat. It was beautiful. Brot carried that frantic solo until he saw Stompy with the brass on the side of his mouth, the trumpet bell turned upward like a nestling waiting for breakfast. Brot blew out that hand-over-rail wail and the trumpet went right up after it, caught it, brought it back down again and threw it to the motor like:

> "*Wham-bop, shillu, shillop . . .*
> (and then Stompy:)
> "*Reet! Bop, rootu shillop*
> *Wham-tareet shillu tareet . . .*

"And by that time Joey had undressed his guitar and was throwing a chord-circle around Stompy's theme. Minors, they were—A minor, D seventh, B flat minor, A again, like:

> "*Whum-bum, shillum, shillop . . .*

"It was heartbeat, Jack. It was murder. It was riff-marole, but brutal. *And me without my drums!*

"Aw, I had to admit it. Nobody there needed drums. Fred was in there now, with a quiet, bubbling sort of trill on the sax that took the clarinet and trumpet down to it, and the three of them stayed low that way, sort of tumbling over each other and getting fainter and fainter. And then it came.

"The wheelpost was behind us and over our heads—a bronze casting, kind of an inverted funnel. It had an opening at deck level, so that in effect it was an upside-down megaphone. Out of that hole came the shuffle:

> "*Sh-shuff-shop, shillil, sh'shuff,*
> *Shoosh! Shop, shill, shup . . .*

"The real walkaway. Fred opened a corner of his mouth away from the sax and came out with the oddest squeak I've ever heard from a human being. Then he set his lips around that alto horn and tumbled on into the first notes of his fugue in re-bop, with Stompy and Brot right in there. They played it in technicolor, but through a sepia filter, if you dig me. Low and easy, bright but quiet. Drago's eyes rolled right up out of sight. I had to see that shuffashuff done. That was backbone stuff, man.

"I ducked out of the cabin and looked up at the wheel. Manuel was up there, staring ahead at the channel lights, and scrubbing the wheelpost with two big wire brushes, the kind you use to dress rusty iron before you red-lead it. I could see the gleam of brass under the brushes where they'd taken the paint off. But his hands were light as—as—did you ever see a cat drink milk? You know how his whiskers twitch on the surface? It was like that. I went back below and sat down and pictured those hands while my eyes were closed. Oh, a handsome drive those hands had!"

They wound up that fugue and came out even, Joey coming in powerfully on a sixth chord that brought everything over, out and clear. After that everybody just sat, and there was only the motor left:

"*Wham bop, shillu, shillop . . .*

"Then it slowed and cut, and we bumped the dock gently. We still sat. I think we were waiting for Drago to say something. He finally whispered, 'Who *is* that?' as he thumbed the overhead.

"I called, 'Manuel!'

"He came down, looking as if he had stolen something. He said, 'What, Red?' I pointed at Drago. Drago looked at the kid as if he was afraid he'd disappear in a puff of smoke. He said, 'You come and see me tomorrow. Now—don't anybody say anything.' He turned to look at the engine, murmured, '*Wham-bop*' and went up the ladder like a sleepwalker, with the Marshalls behind him.

"I said, 'Beat it, you guys. I want to talk to Manuel.' Fred said, '*Oh,* no!'

"Everybody looked at me. 'What do you take me for?' I bellowed at them. 'I'm not going to do anything!' Joey came up and looked into my face. Joey always seemed to understand things. He said, 'Come on, fellows.' They packed their instruments and went ashore.

"Manuel said, 'I thought you'd be sore.'

"I punched him on the shoulder, but easy, easy. I said, 'Manny, whatever else I might be, I guess I'm a cat first. You're a genius.'

"He looked like he was going to cry. 'You're being real big about this,' he told me. 'I'm sorry, Red.'

"That flattened me. 'Sorry? What have you got to be sorry for?'

"He gulped. He beckoned me down below. He leaned over the engine and snapped off the distributor cap. 'When you ride an old barge like this as long as I have, that beat gets into your blood.' He lifted out a little crescent of gasket material. 'You see? When the rotor came around to here, this stuff lifted it enough to give bad contact to two cylinders and delay the third until it was half-flooded when it fired.' He looked at me. 'I even made you leave your drums at the Island. Aren't you sore, Red?'

"Well, I just sat down and laughed until I got lost. When I sobered up I grabbed his hand and shook it. Easy, though. You treat hands like that with respect. I said, 'Manny, you sit in every minute you can, hear? There are things I want to learn about drums.' "

Red was quiet a minute, grinning. "He never did, though. Drago took him to New York the next day. He played with the King only one season, and then went out with a band of his own. His name's Reskin."

"What?" I shouted. "Riff Reskin?"

Red nodded. "Manuel 'Riff' Reskin. Six hundred thousand phonograph records last year. That's the boy."

Somebody called from the stand. Red got up, swung back to me, while I was trying to ravel up my gaping jaw. "Hey," he said. "That list of yours. Remember it?"

"Huh? Oh. I think so." I ticked them off. "To get into the big time, you've got to be good at your spot; you've got to be smarter than anyone who's after what you want; and you've got to be able to use the materials at hand." And I laughed with him.

He went back to the stand. He had a drum break in the next number. He did it with a brush and a stick. It went,

Wham-bop, shillu, shillop . . .

And the joint rocked, really rocked—like a boat.

Well Spiced

TAMARISK JUST HAPPENED. Some forgotten Conestoga cap'n had chosen the Tamarisk hollow as a route down the valley, rather than the exactly similar hollow on the other side of the rise. The town's first building appeared when one Pericles Zapappas sold the oxen which hauled his chuck wagon. The old wagon, hub-deep in the sandy soil, was the nucleus. Because it was there, it was logical to set up a general supplies shack near it, and because of the shack and its increasing stock, settlers took to the nearby lush foothills, knowing they had a trading place. With the settlers came the helpers and the hangers-on, the blacksmiths and the gamblers, the assay office and the livery stable and the hotel.

Pericles Zapappas stuck with Tamarisk. He hadn't planned to; he hadn't planned not to. It was just that there were so many people to feed—and he liked feeding people. He liked to see the tin plates, and later, the thick china ones, mopped clean with great chunks of sourdough bread, or the muscular black loaves he baked himself. The old wagon soon sported a canvas awning which became a mess tent which gradually acquired wooden walls and a tin roof, and as the busy years and the busy wagon trains passed, there was a new building with a real kitchen, rows of iron skillets, three glass sugar bowls, and a spittoon.

Pericles was the only fixture that showed no change. He was a grizzled, tubby little man, with a complexion the color of a frankfurter and a skin like a silk pillow slip that has been slept on for three hot nights. His eyes were round, clear, and blue, giving the impression of red-hot portholes into an ice box. He smiled often, never laughed, and was always a little frightened—afraid that the meat wouldn't arrive, that the coffee would boil, that a customer wasn't getting enough to eat. He absorbed insults and compliments with the same gentle smile and the same shuffling backward retreat, as from royalty.

Tamarisk was good to live in, as such places go, when the wind was from the hills. But when it came panting up from the desert with fire and salt on its breath, the town shimmered and crackled and dried in it. It was on such a day that Fellows stamped into Pericles's place, and the youth's language was not one whit less blistering than the desert wind. His profanity swirled in, all but sweeping Pericles off his precarious perch on a serving table, where he was hanging mesh bags of garlic, strings of melon rind, and chains of herbs and barks to dry; for Pericles was a great hand in the spice department.

"Feed me!" roared Fellows. "By God, likker won't do fer this. Gimme some o' that slumgullion of yours, the kind that wallops you hot an' then smooths you off easy."

Pericles climbed down and framed the kid in his round blue stare. "Hey boy. Whatsa do—burn down you stable?"

"It's thet money-jinglin' Eastern toad, Barstow," spat the youngster. "Him an' his gunmen an' his 'fer th' good of th' country'!"

"Meest' Barstow is crazy," said Pericles mildly. 'Tamarisk is a plenty big town for the valley. Whats 'e wan' for to make a new one?"

Fellows folded himself into a creaky chair, knocking his holster clear so that it swung as he sat. "Jest why he's doin' it don't worry me right now. It's whut he's doin'. You know what he done? He started a livery stable over there. He ain't got but four hosses, an' nothing but a drunked-up ol' prospector to care for'm. But he's *givin'* 'em away! I can't charge a ranny prices like thet! Feed costs me, Peri, thet an' a hand to guard the place at night, what with hoss thieves an' fire an' all."

Pericles, well within earshot, stirred his spices into the witches' brew he called slumgullion. "Meest' Barstow dig a well," he called.

"Yeh. I heerd about thet. Whut's he aim to git from it—tamarisk roots?"

Pericles, tipping some of the precious fluid from a carboy mounted on a pivoted frame, grunted, "Water, Fellows. He got it, also."

"You mean to tell me he struck water over there?"

"He got town well. Cab Jenks, this man with piebal' gelding, he come tell me this morning."

"Oh," said Fellows, and it was an eloquent syllable. There was a recess for thinking, and then he said, "Peri, if he's got water, it ain't no good for Tamarisk."

"Yes," said Pericles. "No good."

"What's Tamarisk?" Fellows burst out after a troubled silence. "So many shacks, so many people—what the hell. Let it go. It might's well be a ghost town, like Harriston or DuMoulin's Gulch."

"Yes," said Pericles, coming around the partition with a deep, steaming bowl of stew. "But—we build Tamarisk. You, you stable. Me, my place. Gomez an' he saddles. Trask an' he cotton goods. Rogers an' Hark an' that ol' fella Mickey Mack. Hm?"

"Yeh, Peri—but a *well!* We ain't got no well. We dug for'm twice, an' you know what we got. Sweat, not water. We got to haul water a mile and a half from Feegan's Brook." He dug into the stew as if he hated it, which he did not. "How'd he know he'd strike water there?" he demanded with his mouth full. "Builds six shacks," he growled—quite an achievement through that much stew, "an' suddenly hits water in country where they ain't a water hole in ten miles, 'cept where the desert drinks up Feegan's Brook."

"What's about the spring, Fellows?"

"Spring? Oh—thet. Yeah. Four miles over the other way. Whyn't he build his town over by there, if he had to build a town?"

Pericles smiled—the smile he used instead of a laugh. "Spring in the cliff. What trade he get by there? Bighorns? Rock squirrels?"

"I see what you mean. His place and Tamarisk sit smack in the middle of the only two trade routes through here. Aw, mebbe you're right, Peri. Maybe he's jest crazy."

"Ask him," said Pericles, in a slightly awed voice.

"Huh?" Fellows's startled eyes swung from the Greek around to the door, which was being blocked at the moment by several cubic feet of flabby flesh, girdled by a too-new cartridge belt and topped with a city-made Stetson. "Barstow!"

"Good morning, good morning," said the heavy man, laughing

what had been described as a diddling laugh, "and how are the thriving burghers of Tamarisk today?"

Fellows put down his spoon and hooked his thumbs in his belt, the fingers of his left hand sliding down to check the gentle swinging of his holster. His eyes were like cracks in a board as he took the Easterner's measure.

Barstow looked him up and down and turned a broad and insulting back. "Mr. Zapappas," he said unctuously. "Ahh. You're looking well this morning. How's business?"

Pericles sidled behind a counter. He regarded Barstow without his smile. "Business always good."

"Splendid, splendid," said Barstow heartily. "Glad to hear it. Make the best of it while it lasts, I always say." Then there was that laugh again. Suddenly he turned to Fellows—so suddenly that the youngster dropped his spoon and cursed viciously. "And how is the livery business?"

"Good, no thanks to you," snarled Fellows.

"Hey, Fellows, make no trouble in my place, huh?"

Barstow tittered. "There won't be any trouble, Mr. Zapappas," he said. "Mr. Fellows is not familiar with—ah—modern business methods. Now, if he would like to take over my stable, perhaps—"

"I'd jest as soon go back to ridin' fence," said Fellows evenly.

"That's good! Ha ha! that's very good. Young man, by the time Tamarisk is a ghost city, I'll own all the fences hereabouts, and you'll have to travel many a dry mile before you can hire out without my permission. Ha ha! Better come in with me while you can. I could use a good—"

"Y' won't use me," snapped Fellows.

Barstow shrugged, as if the movement were sufficient to send Fellows into limbo and beyond, and turned back to the Greek. "It so happens, Mr. Zapappas, that there is no eating place in Well City at the moment."

"What's you say, Well City?"

"Ah, yes, yes indeed. Well City it is, and Well City it will be. Ha! The very name shows that it has a future. Tamarisk! That's all anyone could expect to find here—desert greens. Now, in Well City, there's water—good, pure water."

"I heard," said Fellows, looking out at the rolling desert and its clumps of tamarisk.

Barstow ignored him, to hang his belly on the edge of the counter. "Now, Mr. Zapappas—surely we can come to some agreement on a catering establishment in Well City."

Pericles shook his head with such timidity that the gesture was a mere quiver of wattles.

"Now, now," said Barstow heartily, "at least come over to look us over. Well City's going to be a great little place. I'm wrong. Well City *is* a great little place. A foresighted businessman—"

"Ef it's so nice yonder," drawled Fellows, "why don't you go on back to it?"

Pericles recognized the tone. It reminded him vividly of his dislike of the smell of gun smoke indoors and its attendant corpses. He opened his mouth, closed it, opened it again and said, "Sure. Sure, Meest' Barstow. Tomorrow."

Barstow brought his hands together with a meaty crash and scrubbed them happily against each other. "Splendid, Mr. Zapappas. Splendid. You shall have the—ha!—keys to the city. A good day to you, sir." He strode to the door, turned and stared coldly at Fellows. "As for you, young man, it will pay you to remember that the law is loaded heavier than that pop-gun of yours."

Fellows emitted a .45-caliber oath and sprang up, clawing at his hip. Pericles yelped as if burned, and by the time Fellows had looked at him and back to the door, Barstow was gone.

"Peri," said Fellows menacingly, "you are a traitor. You ain't really goin' to go over to thet—Well City tomorrow?"

"I think yes," said Pericles faintly but firmly, his eyes on Fellows's gun hand. "Hey, finish you stew."

"Thet Barstow walked out o' here with my appetite," grumbled the youngster. He threw a leg over his chair and sat down with an elbow on each side of his bowl. The spicy vapors of the stew curled into his angry nostrils, and he began to shovel tentatively, but shoveling, nevertheless. It took three spoonfuls to fill his mouth, whereupon he said, 'Whut's this law ol' frog-face is talkin' about?"

Pericles frowned worriedly. "Big talk."

"It's more'n thet," said Fellows grudgingly. "He's mighty cocky to be bluffin'. Y' reckon he's on to somethin' we don't know?"

At last Pericles smiled. "Soon we know," he said. "Tomorrow. Hm?"

Fellows glanced up as the light dawned in his brain. "Peri, you got somethin' up your sleeve, or stuck in your boot. I know you, you greasy ol' son-of-a-gun. Whut you aimin' to do over there tomorrow?"

"Spice a little, stir a lot," said Pericles happily, using his stock answer to questions about his cooking.

It was late the following afternoon that Pericles's flea-bitten mare plodded wearily up to the restaurant. Fellows was standing in the shade, leaning back and whittling. He stepped out and caught the bridle, holding it while the little man dismounted heavily.

"Hot," said Pericles unnecessarily.

"It is thet," said Fellows, throwing the reins over the rail. "Hey, Peri—whut's the idea o' them oversize saddlebags? Whut'd you tote over there—a month's grub?"

Pericles ignored the question, mopping his crinkled face. "Well City very busy," he said.

"Is, huh?"

They went inside. "Plenty fellas driving stakes," wheezed the Greek. "Marking streets. Meest' Barstow show me everyt'ing. Place for courthouse, place for smithy, place for hotel and dance hall."

"Holy smoke! What's he think he's doin'?"

Pericles knelt to kindle the stove. "Place for depot too."

"*Depot?* Depot for what? Pony Express?"

Pericles shook his head. "Meest' Barstow, he tells me the big secret. Railroad coming through the Valley."

Fellows, poised over a chair, said *"Ah-hah!"* sitting heavily with the second syllable. "So thet's whut th' horned toad is after. Finds out they're runnin' a railroad survey through here, buys up some desert from the Federal Gov'm'nt, stakes out a town, and sits in it ontil th' railroad goes through." He clapped his hand to his head and moaned, "An' he has to go and find hisself a well. Hey—Peri! How about thet? D'you see it?"

"I see it. Meest' Barstow, first thing gives me a drink water from it. Pull up the bucket himself. Pour it like he think it's beer. All morning, want me for drink more."

"So he's really got water in his town, huh? Oh, thet ain't good, Peri."

"Not good. Well right in the middle of town."

"Yeah. I c'n see whut's goin' to happen to us an' Tamarisk when Well City gits to be a rail town." He shook his head. "No wonder Barstow took a day showin' you around."

"No all day. I took a ride," said Pericles cryptically. He went to the door and looked out toward the rise and Well City. "Fellows."

"Huh?"

"You know what? I never learn to load six-gun like yours."

"Well, I'll be—I never knowed you was interested. You don't never carry a gun." His eyes narrowed. "You expectin' trouble, Peri?"

Pericles shrugged. He looked up at the rise again. There was a feather of dust at its lip. "Show me, Fellows."

"Why shore." Fellows slipped the plated hogleg out of its holster. "Ain't nothin' to it. You pull this back, break it like this, an' jest slip your cartridges in these here holes."

"Whats about this thing. What you call? Cylinder?"

"Thet? It spins a little each time you shoot. You know thet.

"If it jams? Why, thet's easy enough. With the gun broke like this, the cylinder lifts right out. See? Then you can rod the holes out."

Pericles reached for the cylinder, his bright eyes glinting as his hand closed on it. "I see. Fellows—*look!*"

The youngster followed Pericles's pudgy finger. Down over the rise swept a group of horsemen.

"Wh— Hey, they're from Well City! That's Barstow's crew!" He spun back to the Greek, who had moved behind the partition, where his concoctions were beginning to steam and simmer on the stove.

Fellows skidded around the counter and into the rear. "Peri! I don't know how much you know about this, but those guys are loaded for bear. What's goin' on?"

At Fellows's first shout, Pericles had started elaborately, and was now staring dismally into one of the pots. "Hey, boy. You shout too much with you mouth. Now look what happen, I drop you dirty cylinder into my stew."

"You what? Why, you galoot! Thet thing—"

The Well City posse swept past, thirty strong, whooping. There were one or two shots. Fellows cursed, scooped up his gun, and ran for the door. Pericles smiled radiantly, sounded the stew with a wooden spoon, and delicately fished out the cylinder. He carefully washed it and dried it, and put it in the cash drawer.

Twenty minutes later he was busily packing liquor bottles into a crate with straw. There was the rustling beat of hoofs on the hard-packed street, and the posse streamed past, bunched around two riders with dispatch cases.

Fellows pounded in, his face scarlet from the effort to exude profanity and take in air simultaneously. "Peri! Gimme my —— cylinder while I fill their ——s full o' —— lead!"

"Whatsa do?"

" 'Whatsa do?' " screamed Fellows, dancing as if his chaps were full of fire ants. "Don't ask me questions, damn yuh! I'm mad enough at your clumsiness. You done cass-trated my hawglaig. Now don't make me madder by actin' foolish."

Pericles glanced out at the rise, where the posse was dwindling out of gunshot. He moved to the cash drawer, set the cylinder on the counter, and scrambled in quivering panic away from Fellows's wild dive for it. The kid punched it into his gun, rammed home some shells, and bolted for the door. The sight of the posse pouring over the top of the hill and out of sight deflated him to the point where his shoulders seemed to dislocate. He went completely limp except for his jaw muscles. He made no sound.

Pericles smiled. "You cuss too much," he observed. "An' when you get real mad, you got not'ing left to say. Hm?"

Fellows turned slowly, slowly raised his fists to his cartridge belt, and treated Pericles to a glare that would have dried up an oat-fed cow with a three-day calf.

Pericles turned pale. "Want a cup coffee?" he murmured.

Fellows ignored the suggestion, while Pericles bustled himself pouring the coffee into a mug. "Peri, you are jest too good-hearted an' stupid to stay alive. Don't you know what them rannies jest did?"

"Whatsa do?"

"I'll tell you 'whatsa do,'" rasped the youngster. "Surrounded the marshal's office, that's what, where ol' Mickey Mack keeps all the town records. They got all them papers and rid off with 'em before anybody in town knew which way to jump." He tapered off to a trickling, inarticulate mumble which returned in another flood of unprintables.

When the noise had died down again, Pericles asked mildly, "Was it legal?"

"Legal? Whaddeya mean legal? It was kidnappin', that's what the hell! Oh, they poked some papers at Mickey Mack fust—"

"What kind papers?"

"I dunno. Mickey tol' us—me and Hark and some more that was there. Somepin' about Well City bein' a county seat, an' a seizure order fer th' county records f'm the marshal's office at Topeka. So what's that?" He snorted. "Them was our records, Tamarisk records—all the deeds an' claims an' transfer notes an' all. What's Well City want with 'em?"

"It was legal," said Pericles quietly. Fellows sat while that sank in. Pericles put coffee before him and said, "It was legal, even if it was no good, boy. Your gun makes big noise, big trouble. Barstow, he say the law is loaded heavier'n you are. Is right."

"Why, you interferin' ol' belly-stuffer!" bawled Fellows. "You spiked my gun thet a way a-purpose!"

"Please," Pericles whispered out of a dry throat. His face was puckered with terror, for Fellows was three degrees uglier than just formidable when his dander soared. "Fellows. Please, boy. Hey. No make trouble in my place. Drink you coffee. You right. Meest' Barstow tell me about this county seat business. Federal judge, he give charter because of well. No use to tell you—you get mad, all you sense run out you mouth, you shoot and then you hang. No good. Well City is county seat. Is legal."

"They cain't do this!" wailed Fellows. "All this country here was settled out o' Tamarisk! Then this Easterner walks off with the rail line an' th' county records and sits down on desert he bought fer nothin' and can sell fer a mint!"

"Is the business methods he talk about."

"It's the business, all right," gritted Fellows, and added something about Barstow that would have been shocking in Greek. Or even in Portuguese.

Fellows slurped broodingly at his coffee. Pericles went back to packing liquor bottles in the crate. At length Fellows said, "We c'n git up a bigger posse than Barstow."

Pericles froze, half bent over the crate, his shoulders hunched up and his head back as if his nape had been touched by a hot iron. He waited.

"Scoop up our own records, huh?" muttered Fellows inevitably. "Hell, we c'n shoot our way through those shacks of his'n and be gone with th' papers before they know what's up. And it'll take a damn sight more'n twenty armed men an' a coupla court orders to pry us loose, this time."

"Now, Fellows," said Pericles carefully. "Don' talk this kind stuff, you hear? You get troops from Topeka an' a rope for your neck."

"Not me," snarled the youngster. "I'll get lead in my blood, or I'll be over th' border afore that happens."

"Fellows," said Pericles pleadingly, "you can't fight everyt'ing with guns. Yes? Sometimes you got to use somet'ing else."

"Fer the likes o' Barstow? What you goin' to do? Use a skillet an' a han'ful o' cayenne? Maybe you want to feed Barstow an' his gunmen ontil they bust, huh?" He regarded the Greek with scorn, which changed to interest as he noticed what Pericles was doing. "What's the idea o' stashing all the firewater?"

"So it not break."

"Break how? You expectin' trouble here?" He leaped to his feet. "Someone pushin' you around, Peri? Who is it? Le's stop it afore it starts. Who do you want hawg-tied an' branded?"

"Shh, boy." Pericles almost laughed. "Don' you worry your head." He took down a hammer and battened the top of the crate. When he had finished he stood up, mopped his face and head, and came around the counter.

"Fellows, listen. You good feller, see? I don' wan' see you in bad trouble. Wait awhile, hun? Don' make this posse stuff. *Please,* Fellows, hun? This Meest' Barstow, he is a hard man. Well City got plenty guards, boy. Rifles. All night, until four o'clock in morning, it gets light a little, Barstow got guards out. You get posse, you get killed. Somebody get killed, anyway. Tamarisk men they get killed. Wait awhile, hun?"

"Wait, hell. Armed guards? This toad wants a war, does he? This one askin' fer it." Fellows scowled; then his head snapped up. "You say he pulls his guards an hour before sunup?"

"Sure. No need them. Men stirrin' about then anyway. But make to forget it, hun, Fellows? You a good boy. Don' get in bad trouble. Don' use you hosses for to make posse."

Having planted his seeds, Pericles bent to the task of sliding the heavy crate around behind the partition. That, oddly enough, placed it by the side door and its loading-stage, against which was backed his battered old buckboard.

Trask, the yard-goods merchant, an ex-sailor and a crack shot, reined in beside the glowering Fellows. Around them jogged the rest of the Tamarisk posse. A crescent moon showed the Well City trail vaguely, and pointed up the twin ruts of a wagon that had passed earlier.

"Hell of a note," grunted Trask. "Skedaddlin' around this time o' night. I tried to turn in after the meetin' an' didn't know whether I should stay up late or git up early. Turned in an' tried to sleep, still couldn't make up my mind, an' now"—he yawned hugely—"I don't rightly know if I'm awake or not. Way I feel, I wouldn't know silk f'm sailcloth."

"You damn well better be awake when we ride into Well City," said Fellows.

"Now, look, puppy," said the grizzled Trask. "Maybe you set this here forest fire, but just because we think you was right don't say you kin snap an' snarl at yer betters."

"Ah, it's that lousy Zapappas," said Fellows. " All this time claimin' he's a friend o' mine, an' then pullin' a thing like this," and he nodded at the wagon tracks. "What was it you tol' me about rats leavin' a founderin' ship?"

"Don't blame him too much," said Trask. "He's stuck with Tamarisk longer'n any of us an' he rates a break from it. You know what they say about little fat guys. They're all good-natured because they can't fight an' they can't run."

"Thet's all right s'far as it goes," said Fellows. "But he didn't have to tote all thet likker over to Well City to grease his way into their gold mine."

Trask gave a reluctant, affirmative snort. "That was sorta small."

They went through the draw and emerged on a shelf overlooking Well City. There were two guttering fires to be seen north and south of the town, which was dark and still under the bright stars and the weak moonlight. The posse milled together and drew up.

"What time is it?"

"Not four yet."

Whup-whup-whoo-oop!

"Whut'n blazes was that?"

"A drunken poke if ever I heerd one."

There was a blaze of light in the largest building as the door was flung open, apparently blown by a gust of loose laughter.

"Ev'vy man Jack in th' town must be in there gettin' fried," somebody said.

"Yeah, on Zapappas's likker, the skonk," said another.

"Thet's one feller we'll squar' with, whatever."

"I brung a rope."

Somebody cracked a bullwhip. "This is better."

Trask spoke up. "It won't get Tamarisk a thing to stampede that little coyote. Let'm alone. He don't know what he's doin'."

"Feelin' real friendly, ain'tcha?" said an anonymous voice from the rear ranks. "Why don't you go on down and have a drink o' whisky?"

"Stow that," barked Trask. "We git to pullin' an' haulin' amongst ourselves, we won't get no town records out o' Well City. Now settle down fer about forty minutes. Mickey, get that there phony seizure paper of yours ready to whip out. You sure it's got enough 'Whereas's' on it to keep 'em puzzled ontil we get clear with th' records?"

"That it has," said Mickey Mack. "*And* a gold seal. With ribbons."

"Good. Relax, boys. Talk quiet an' try to keep your hosses offen the rocks."

The posse dismounted and hobbled their mounts. Fellows lounged over to the Well City side of the draw and stood looking out at the half dozen shacks that were the county seat. A few feet down the slope from him were the shadowy masses of a large boulder and a small one. He felt the scalp muscles behind his ears contract at the faint hiss that suddenly reached him from the rocks. He froze, stared. Nothing. As he relaxed, the hiss was repeated.

Now, any other man there would have reported the matter and gotten cover for an investigation. But Fellows's approach was always a direct one. He tiptoed forward, gained the small boulder, waited tensely, then moved on to the larger one. Bracing himself with his hands, he peered carefully around it. Behind him, and between the two boulders, an extension of the black shadow reached out and lifted his gun from his holster, to jam it firmly into his spinal column, just below the shoulder blades.

"Walk," said a faint whisper.

The bruise-making solidity of the gunsight in his back was completely convincing. Without a sound he walked downgrade, without attempting to turn around or to make a sound, and the gun shifted only enough to steer him. His captor kept him to the blackest shadows, and turned him into the mouth of a dry gulch that opened on the draw a hundred yards away. *He won't shoot me if I don't make him,* he thought desperately. *The posse—*

The gun turned him to the wall. He stopped, his hands up. This was it, whatever "it" might be. "Well?" he said softly.

"Hey, boy. Don' be mad, hey."

"Zapappas!"

The gun muzzle rammed in agonizingly. "You be quiet with you mouth."

There was a tense silence, and then Fellows, breathing hard, whispered, "All right, Peri. You talk. I'll listen."

"At's good, boy," said Pericles in a low voice. 'Hey, you t'ink they goin' hang me?"

"Reckon they will, Peri."

"Oh no. No. This wrong. You tell 'em."

"Me? I'd help 'em ef you'd get that equalizer out'n my back."

Surprisingly, Pericles's voice was gentle, and the gun was removed as he said sadly, "Sit down, Fellows. Here. Tak you gun."

Fellows stayed, stunned, where he was, face to the rock wall, hands raised, until Pericles's hand on his shoulder turned him around. The little man, he could see dimly, was extending the gun to him. "Sit down, Fellows."

Then he talked. He talked for seven minutes, and it was not a gunshot, but a shout of laughter that brought the posse tumbling down the draw. There was no attack at four o'clock.

The bar of morning sunlight had crept so gradually onto Barstow's sodden face that it had not awakened him. He lay unbeautifully on his back, his collar and belt open, his Eastern clothes rumpled, and his chin higher than his nose.

When the sunlight was abruptly cut off, however, he twitched, turned his head from side to side, moaned, clasped his temples, and sat up. Keeping his eyes tight shut, he shifted his hands cautiously over them, and in the soothing shade, ventured to ease the lids up. A vast throbbing inside his big head nudged another moan through his dry lips. "What a shindig," he muttered, "for a county seat. Hate to think of the high-jinks when we get to be a state capital."

Then it was he realized that there was someone standing over him, blocking the sunlight. He looked up quickly, wincing from the effort.

"Git up, Barstow," said Trask. "You're done."

"What are you doing in my—"

"Move," said Trask, and in such a tone that Barstow, without a second thought nor another syllable of bluster, moved. Trask waited while he pulled on his boots, and then stood aside, nodding toward the door. Barstow's gun belt hung over a chair near the window.

Trask stood between it and the door. The belt stayed where it was as Barstow walked out.

The Easterner stopped dead as soon as he could see in the light. There was a clump of silent men around the well, watching him.

"H-How—what—" goggled Barstow. He turned, bellowed, "Smith! Oviedo!"

"They took off at daybreak," said Trask quietly. "The rest of your boys are with us, only maybe a little bit madder."

"I don't—I won't—" Barstow began, turning back toward his shack. Trask spun him around, placed his boot in the small of Barstow's back, and shoved. Barstow staggered a few steps, went to his knees, scrambled up again, and went toward the well, purely because the men there seemed less menacing than Trask, who followed close behind.

"Wh—what are you going to do?"

"Jest show you something," said Trask grimly. "Show him, boys."

Rough hands propelled Barstow through the crowd to the well. Fellows caught him there, put a hard young hand to the nape of the flabby neck, and shoved Barstow's head over the coping. "What do you see, Barstow?"

Barstow squirmed. "Nothing."

"Speak up, Barstow."

"The well is dry," said Barstow hoarsely.

"Why, Barstow?"

"Those drunken ——s!" swore Barstow. "They forgot to fill the well!"

"Filled it every night, didn't they, Barstow?"

"They—I—" He looked around at the men, some grinning, some glowering. He gulped and nodded his head.

Fellows guffawed. "That's it, boys. This swamp-frawg had men a-haulin' water from the spring, every night, when the rest o' his crew was sleepin'. Figgered to make this place the county seat, get the railroad through here, an' then sell his holdings an' clear out, leavin' someone else to worry about a dry well an' a useless town."

Barstow put his hands up to his face miserably, and slumped

against the well. "What are you—" He licked his lips. "What are you going to do?"

"With you?" said Trask. "Why, we talked it over some. At first most of the boys wanted to throw you into your hole in the ground and fill it in. But we figger we'll do better to tell you how we found out about this, and then turn you loose. We like to think of you rememberin' it."

"It was that little guy you were tryin' to buy into your county seat," grinned Fellows. "Pericles Zapappas, his name is. He got to figgering. He's been in this country a long time, longer'n any of us, an' he knew damn well that there ain't no water to be dug for hereabouts. So he took up your invite an' came over here to look at your well. He was so sure there was somethin' wrong with it that he loaded his mare with two cook pots full of some stuff he brewed. After he left you he circled back and headed for th' spring. He seen enough of a beaten track up there to make him think he was right. He dropped his pots into th' spring. They wuz covered with sheep parchment and th' stuff in 'em leaked through real slow and flavored up th' water jest fine." He laughed again.

Trask took over. "He loads up his buckboard with hard likker last night and comes over here to help you celebrate gettin' the county seat—*after* goadin' Fellows here to git up a posse to shoot you loose from the county seat records. So thanks to him, all your hands got drunked up. Once he has you all nice and wound up, he takes a drink of water from the well. It tastes just like he knowed it would—like the stuff he put in the spring. That clinches it. He leaves y'all to waller in his likker and goes up to the draw yonder to wait for us."

"We was goin' to hang him," said Fellows with awe in his voice.

"Tell'm what Zapappas put in the spring, Fellows," said Trask.

"Tamarisk," said Fellows solemnly. "He's a great hand with the spices, he is. Stripped the bark of tamarisk and biled it down. It's bitter as hell. He uses it in his stew."

"Let's go, boys," said Trask. "Zapappas is back in Tamarisk by now, fixin' up the damnedest celebration breakfast this country has seen yet."

"What about me?" asked Barstow.

"You could drop dead," said Fellows helpfully.

"Yer county water commission," said Trask, "seems to of stole your hosses. You should be glad. Gives you a chance to walk off some o' that blubber. They's a tradin'-post forty mile up the valley, and a fort thirty mile the other way."

The last they saw of Barstow was a deflated, dejected figure squatting on the sand by his dry well, in sole possession of a county seat—a ghost town.

Riding through the draw, Trask said thoughtfully to Fellows, "It's a wonderful thing how a man'll fight with his own tools. I seen many a sailor brain people with a fid, and I seen a seamstress run a hatpin into a drunk. Zapappas, he fights right out'n his kitchen."

"Yup," said Fellows. "Usin' only kitchen tools." And he swore to himself to keep his bare back out of sight until those ring-shaped bruises on it disappeared.

Hurricane Trio

YANCEY, WHO HAD once been killed, lay very still with his arm flung across the pillow, and watched the moonlight play with the color of Beverly's hair. Her hair was spilled over his shoulder and chest, and her body pressed against him, warm. He wondered if she was asleep. He wondered if she could sleep, with that moonswept riot of surf and wind going on outside the hotel. The waves blundered into the cliff below, hooting through the sea-carved boulders, frightening great silver ghosts of spray out and up into the torn and noisy air. He wondered if she could sleep with her round, gentle face so near his thumping heart. He wished the heart would quiet itself—subside at least to the level of the storm outside, so that she might mistake it for the same storm. He wished he could sleep. For two years he had been glad he did not sleep. Now he wished he could; it might quiet his heart.

Beverly, Beverly, he cried silently, you don't deserve this! He wished the bed were larger, so that he might ease away from her and be but a shriek among shrieks, melting into the hiss and smash and ugly grumble of the sea's insanity.

In the other bed, Lois shifted restlessly under the crisp sheet. Yancey looked at her without turning his head. She was a thing of long lines under the dim white, her face and hair two kinds of darkness on the pillow. She was lean and somber. Beverly was happy and open and moved about like the brightly colored bouncing ball which used to lead the singing at theaters, leaping along the lyrics. Lois walked as if she did not quite touch the floor, and the tones of her voice were like the tones of her skin and the clothes she favored—dark and smooth. Her eyes were long and secret and her face was a floe. Her nostrils, and the corners of her mouth, and sometimes the slightest concerted movement of a shoulder and an eyebrow, hinted at a heat submerged and a strength relaxed and aware, not asleep, not a sleep. Lois ... a synthesis of subtleties, of mysteries, of delicate scents and soft puzzling laughter.

Lois moved again. He knew that she too was staring tensely up into the mottled darkness. The spume-flecked moonlight was intolerant of detail, but Yancey had memorized her face. He knew of the compression of her lips, and that the corners of her mouth were softly turned despite the tension. He was deeply troubled by the sound of the sheet as she moved, for if he could hear that over the storm, how could Beverly miss the throb of his heart?

Then he all but smiled: of course Beverly did not hear as he did, nor see, nor feel, nor think with all her mind. Poor Beverly. Poor bright, sweet, faithful bird, more wife than woman, how can you compete with one who is more woman than ... anyone?

Better, this was better than the fearful joy that was like rage. His heart began to obey him, and he turned his cheek slightly to touch her hair. Pity, he thought, is a sharing sort of thing—you can feel the helplessness of the unarmed—whereas rage, like passion, stands apart from its object and is a lonesome thing.

He settled himself now, and without moving he went limp in the thundering night, giving himself up to the glimmer and shift of his thoughts. More than anyone else on earth, he was sure, he enjoyed being alive, and his perpetual delight was in being alive altogether, awake and aware, conscious of his body and how it lay, and where, and at the same time afloat like a gull on the wind of his thought, yielding, controlled. Perhaps he enjoyed the dark part of his unending day the most, camouflaged by a coverlet and the closing of eyes. In the day he lived with that which, if he wished, he could command; at night he lived with that which he *did* command. He could call a symphony to heel, and make a syllogism stand and wait. He could cut a stack of places, fan a hand of faces, choose his pleasure of them and discard the rest. His recall was pinpoint perfect back and back to the point where he had been dead; before that, only excellent. He used it now as a measure against his heart's rebellion, so that Beverly could sleep, and, sleeping, not know.

And because the idea of Lois, here, was unbearable, he let his mind take him back to Lois when she was only a secret. She had been an explosion within him, a pressure and a kind of guilt; but all the things she had been were things he could contain, and no one knew. So back he went, to his renascence; back through the time he had been dead, and still farther to Lois-first-seen, to a time when a man with a job and a wife and a settled gray life found this special astonishment.

There was a lake, and small cheap cabins crouched in a row to sip its shores. There was a "lodge" with its stilted forefeet in the water and its rump on a hillside. There were boats and a float, a splintery dance floor and a bar which purveyed beverages all the way up to beer.

Yancey, with little money and only two weeks' time, had rented a cottage here sight unseen. He expected little of it, being resigned to the truism that a change of surroundings constitutes a vacation all by itself. He expected little of anything in those days. His life had reached a plateau—a long, narrow, slightly downgraded plateau where the horizons were close and the going easy. His job was safe and, by the chemistry of paternalism, would increase in value as it aged, for all a large business requires of the bulk of its employees is that they stay just as they are.

He had been married for seven years to the blithe and patient Beverly, who was content with him. There had been a time when they interrupted one another in the rush to share themselves, and a longer time when there seemed very little to say, which made them both vaguely unhappy, and they lived with a mild and inexpressible sense of loss. And at last they had discovered that coded communication devised by most folk with their unexciting familiars: small talk, half-finished sentences, faint interrogative and exclamatory sounds, and present—as opposed to absent—silences. Life for Yancey and his wife was not dull—it was too unplanned for that—but its pulse beat between comfortable limits.

This unplanned quality (for why make plans when life is basically so certain?) was responsible for their late arrival at the lake. Last year's map did not include the dozens of roads closed by the

Thruway; somehow Yancey had never gotten around to having the spare fixed, so of course they had a flat; then they had to drive back for the checkbook Yancey had forgotten; and naturally it rained. It had rained all the previous night and all day, and when they turned into the lake road it was past eleven at night and still raining. They pulled up beside the lodge, where a glistening faded sign proclaimed OFFICE, and Yancey turned up his jacket collar and plunged out into the rain and floundered up the wooden steps. When there was no answer to his knock he noticed a soggy pasteboard stuck between the doorframe and a loose pane. He tried to read it and could not. He went to the head of the steps and called, "Bev! Turn the spotlight up here!"

Beverly, between the loose-valved clacking of the motor and the drumming of rain on the car roof, heard a voice but no words. She turned off the ignition and rolled the window down. "What?"

"The light. Spotlight. Shine it up here."

She did, whereupon Yancey went back to the door and crouched before the card. In a moment he came back to the car and slid in, dripping. "They're all in bed," he said, "in cabin 14."

"Which one is our cabin?"

"I don't know. They never said. Just confirmed the reservation. We'll have to wake them up." He pressed the starter.

And pressed it, and pressed it.

When the starter would deliver nothing but a click and a grunt, Yancey leaned back and blew sharply through his nostrils. "Wires wet, I guess."

"What are we going to do?"

"Walk. Or sit here."

She touched his sodden shoulder and shuddered. "It can't be too far ... we'll have to take a bag."

"Okay. Which one?"

She considered. "I guess the brown one. It has my robe in it, I remember ... I think."

He knelt on the seat and reached into the back, found and fumbled the brown suitcase out. "Better turn off the lights. Ignition, too."

"The ignition *is* off," Beverly said, trying it.

"What!"

"When you were on the porch. I couldn't hear you. I turned it off.

The advantage of that status between married folk which communicates by grunts and silences is that scorn, as well as contentment, can be expressed with little effort. Yancey was simply and completely silent, and she said, "Oh dear." Then, defensively, "How was I supposed to know you didn't turn it back on?"

Yancey merely snorted. Beverly huddled in the seat. "Now it's all my fault," she muttered. This was more than a statement of fact; it meant in addition that any discomfort from this point on would be laid to her, and that the day's previous delays and exasperations would also be attached to her, making her culpable in every way for everything. Yancey maintained his silence. Anything he might say would militate in her favor—to say one thing would forgive her, another would give her some ground for defense or counterattack. There was no real vindictiveness in his silence. He did not care whether or not she accepted the guilt as long as it was clear that guilt was not his. To put it another way, married familiars in this stage, though not necessarily enemies, are just not friends.

They left the car by their respective doors, and the rain immediately increased as if it had been cued from the wings. The sporadic wind died completely and suddenly and water seemed to displace air altogether. It ran down Yancey's spine, it bashed at his eyelids, it threw gouts of mud up to his knees. He felt his way along the fender and around the front of the car until he collided with Beverly. They clung together, gasping and waiting for some kind of light to penetrate the hissing deluge. Some did, at last, a sodden skyglow with a dimmer echo from the lake, and they began to wade up the shore along the line of cabins.

Visitors to the lake have been known to complain that the cabins were built too close together. It is clear that such plaintiffs never walked the row in the seething black of a summer rain. Each cabin boasted a wooden post with a number, cut from plywood with a jigsaw, perched on it. These could be read by water-wrinkled fingertips as they progressed, and they seemed to be fully half a mile apart.

Yancey and Beverly did not attempt to talk; the only speech between them was a muttered number when occasionally they investigated one of the posts to check their progress. It was enough to make exasperation itself turn numb, not to be reawakened until they found cabin 12, bypassed the next, and turned in at what should therefore be 14, only to find it called 15.

"Fifteen, fifteen!" Beverly wailed wetly. "Where's fourteen? It's gone!"

"Gone, hell," growled Yancey, uselessly wiping at the water streaming over his mouth. "That'll be it there, that we just passed. Afraid to number a cabin thirteen. Superstition. Well, you know a woman runs this place," he added.

Beverly inhaled, a sharp gasp at this injustice, but took in as much water as air and could only cough weakly. They backtracked and fumbled their way up to the dark bulk of cabin 14. Yancey dropped the suitcase noisily on the small porch.

"Yance! You'll wake everybody up!"

He looked at her and sighed. The sigh transmitted, "What did we come here for?"

He pounded on the door and they pressed close to it, trying to get some shelter from the decorative gable over the door. A light showed, the doorknob moved, and they stepped back into the rain. And nothing, nothing at all told Yancey that in this second a line fell across his life, so that forever his biography would consist of the parts life-before-Lois and life-since-Lois, with nothing between them but a sheet of rain and the opening of a door.

It opened altogether, fearlessly. He said, "I'm Yance Bowman, this is my wife, and we—" and then he saw her face, and his voice failed him. Quickly, effortlessly, Lois spoke into his sudden silence and made it unnoticeable. "Come in, come in!" With one swift balanced movement she took the suitcase from his hand, whirled around them to reach out in the rain for the doorknob, and, closing the door, swept them in.

They stood panting and dripping, looking at her. She wore a maroon hostess robe with a collar that stood up like an Elizabethan ruff; the material fell away and draped from her wide flat shoulders with the static fluidity of a waterfall, all movement even while she was still. Her slight turn and bend as she set down the suitcase told him that those wide shoulders were indeed shoulders and not padding, and the flash of a bare foot declared that here was a woman who would stand and look straight into his eyes.

Beverly spoke, or began to; he turned to her and saw that she was, by comparison, dumpy and wet and exceedingly familiar. "We didn't know which cabin to—"

"Never mind that," said Lois, "we'll have two weeks to explain ourselves to each other. First of all you've just got to get out of those wet things, both of you. I'll heat some coffee."

"But-but-but we can't—"

"But you can," said Lois. "Not another word. Go on," she said, crowding them into the hall which led away to the left. "There's the bath. Take a shower. A hot shower." Without pausing she scooped thick towels from a shelf and dropped them into Beverly's astonished hands. She reached past them and turned on the bathroom light. "I'll get your bag."

She was gone and back before Beverly could get her mouth around another syllable. "Hurry now, before the muffins get cold."

"Muffins?" Beverly squeaked. "Oh now, please don't go to that tr—" but she was in the bathroom with Yancey, with the door closed, and Lois's swift light footsteps answering her like a laugh as they ran away down the hall.

"Well I—" said Beverly. "Yancey, what can we do?"

"Like the lady says, I guess." He gestured. "You first."

"A shower? Oh, I *couldn't!*"

He pulled her over in front of the basin and aimed her face at the mirror. "Wouldn't hurt."

"Oh . . . oh dear, I'm a sight." She had one more second of hesitation, murmured, "Well . . ." and then pulled her soaking dress off over her head.

Yancey undressed slowly while Beverly splashed under the shower. About the time the mirror was thoroughly steamed up she began to hum, high and happy. Yancey's numbed brain kept re-creating the vision of Lois as he had first seen her, framed in lamplight which was in turn framed by a hurtling silver halo of rain. His mind formed it and bounced away, formed it again and again retreated. It would only look and look back; it would not evaluate. His world contained nothing like this; he doubted, at the moment, that it could. His only analytical thought came as an academic question, not to be answered by any process he then knew: how could a woman be so decisive, so swift, yet so extraordinarily quiet? Her voice had come to him as through earphones, direct and with fullest quality, yet seeming not to reach the walls. Anyone else in the world, taking charge like that, would certainly have roared like a drill sergeant. "Don't turn it off," he said to Beverly.

"All right." She put a parboiled arm through the curtains and he dropped a towel across it. "Mmm, good," she said, rubbing briskly as she emerged. "I feel as if we'd been kidnapped, but I'm glad."

He stepped into the shower and soaped up. The scalding water was good on his chilled skin; he felt muscles relax which he hadn't known were taut. It was far and away the best shower he had ever taken up to the point when Beverly uttered a soft and tragic wail. He knew the sound, and sighed. "What have you done *now?*" he inquired, his voice carrying a labored patience. He turned off the shower and peered through the mists at his wife. She had a towel round her head like a turban, and her pale blue chenille beach robe hung from her shoulders. "The black one," she said.

"Give me a towel. What black what?"

"Suitcase. This is all the beach things. There isn't a thing of yours here but your bathing trunks."

"This," he said after a suitable silence, "is just your night."

"Oh, Yance, I'm sorry."

"I'm sorry too." He stared fixedly at her until she wilted. "I'll just get back into those wet clothes."

"You can't!"

"Got a better idea? I'm not going out there in bathing trunks."

There was a knock on the door. "Soup's on!"

Before he could stop her, Beverly called out with a distressed bleat, "Know what I did, I brought the wrong suitcase, there's nothing here for my husband to wear but his *bathing* suit!"

"Good!" said the soft voice on the other side of the door. "Put it on and come on out. The coffee's poured." When they did not respond, Lois laughed gently. "Did you people come to the lake to be formal? Didn't you expect to be seen in bathing suits? Come on," she added, with such warmth that in spite of themselves they found some sheepish smiles and put them on. "Coming," said Yancey. He took the trunks out of the open suitcase.

In the living-room a fire had been lit and was just beginning to gnaw on the kindling and warm a log. A table was set, simply and most attractively—gray place mats, black cups, wrought-iron candlesticks with black candles. There was a steaming glass urn and an electric toaster which clucked once and popped up two halves of an English muffin just as they sat down. Lois came out of the kitchen carrying a black sugar bowl. She glided up behind them as they sat at the table, leaning over them. One long arm put the bowl down; her other hand touched Yancey's bare shoulder. Something—

Something *happened.*

In the other bed, Lois abruptly turned on her side, facing him. She reached over to the night table between the beds, found a cigarette. The wind died just then, taking a deep quiet breath for the next shriek; and in the jolting silence a great sea smashed the cliff below. Lois struck her match, and the light and the explosion of water together plucked Yancey's nerves in a single shattering chord. He steeled himself and did not start. In the blinding flare of the match, Lois's face seemed to leap at him—a partial mask, centered on the arch of an eyebrow, the smooth forehead over it, the forehead's miniature counterpart in the smooth lowered lid beneath. The arches were stable, flawless; things on which could be built a strong and lovely structure if one could only . . . only . . .

He lost the thought in the ballooning glow of her cigarette as she lay back and puffed quickly, too quickly for her to enjoy it, surely. She drew the glow into a ruddy yellow sharp-tipped cone, and the smoke must have been hot and harsh to taste. Hot and harsh. He moistened his lips.

A surge of anger began to rise within him, matching again the sea outside. With an approaching breaker, the anger mounted and swelled and exploded. But the breaker could turn to foam and mist, and disperse, and he could do nothing but clench his teeth and press his head back into the pillow, for he must not wake Beverly.

This thing was so ... *unjust!* Beverly gave him everything he wanted. She always had, especially since that time at the lake. Especially since ... Her capacity for giving amazed him, almost awed him. She gave with everything she did. Her singing was an outpouring. She laughed with all her heart. Her sympathy was quick and complete. She gave constantly, to him more than to anyone or anything else on earth. They had—now—a marriage that was as good as a marriage could be. How, then, could there be room in him for this—this *thing,* this acute, compelling awareness of Lois? Why must there be this terrible difference between "want" and "need"? He didn't *need* Lois!

The anger subsided. He bent his arm and touched Beverly's hair. She moved, turning her head from side to side, burrowing closer in to his shoulder. This won't do, he thought desperately. Aren't I the boy with the Brain? The man who can't be pushed around, who is never puzzled by anything?

Go back, Yancey. Go back again to where your world was full of Lois and you could control it. If you could do it then, with a tenth of the mind you have now, then why ... why can't you ... why is your heart trying to break your ribs?

He closed his eyes against the shouting silver of the night and the bloom of Lois's cigarette. Back, he demanded, go back again. Not to the hand on the shoulder. Afterwards. The rain's letting up, and scurrying through the puddles and the sky-drip to their own cabin, the one next door. Hold it. Hold it right there ... ah. He had it again; he was back two years, feeling again what it was like to be able to keep Lois to himself, and his heartbeat normal.

Impossible! But he had done it for almost two whole weeks. Lois on the diving platform, then painted on the sky, forever airborne—forever because awareness such as his photographed and filed the vision; in his memory she hung there still against a cloud. And the square dance, with the fiddle scratching away into an overloaded p.a. system and feet clumping against the boards, and the hoarse, happy shouter: "Alamen *lef* an' around we go, swing yore potner do-si-do ... now swing somebody else ... an' somebody *else* ... an' somebody ELSE ..." and ELSE had been Lois, turning exactly with him, light and mobile in his arms, here and gone before he knew completely that she was there, leaving him with a clot in his throat and a strange feeling in his right hand, where it had taken the small of her back; it seemed not to belong completely to him any more, as if her molecules and his had interpenetrated.

Oh, and Lois breaking up a fight between one of the summer people and a town man, drifting close, ruffling the hair of one and laughing, being a presence around whom no violence could take place; Lois backing the station wagon skilfully among the twisting colonnades of a birch grove... And Lois doing unremarkable things unforgettably—a way of holding her fork, lifting her head, ceasing to breathe while she listened for something. Lois glimpsed through the office window, smiling to herself. Lois reading the announcements at lunch, her voice just loud enough for someone else on, say, a porch swing, yet audible to eighty people.

Lois walking, for that matter, standing, writing, making a phone call ... Lois alive, that was enough to remember.

Nearly two weeks of this, waking with Beverly, breakfasting, swimming, boating, hiking with Beverly, and his preoccupation cloaked in the phlegmatic communications of familiarity. What difference did it make if his silence was a rereading of Lois's face instead of a reconsideration of the sports page? He would not have attempted to share either one with Beverly; then what was the difference? Earlier in their marriage she might have complained that it was useless to have a vacation if he acted just the same during it as he did at home; at this stage, however, he was completely—one might say invisibly—Yancey. Just Yancey, like always.

But there was a line between possible and not-possible in Yancey's ability to contain his feelings about Lois. He did not know just where it was or what would make him cross it; but cross it he did, and there was no mistaking it once it happened.

It was a Thursday (they were to leave on Sunday), and in the afternoon Yancey had asked Lois to come to their cabin that evening. He blurted it out; the words hung between them and he stared at them, amazed. Perhaps, he thought, he was being facetious ... and then Lois gravely accepted, and he fled.

He had to tell Beverly, of course, and he didn't know how, and he made up, in advance, seven different ways to handle her in anticipation of the seven ways in which she might react. Each, of course, would result in Lois's coming. Exactly what the evening would be like he could not predict, which was strange in a man who was so ready with alternatives when it came to making a hostess out of Beverly.

"Bev," he said abruptly when he found her pitching horseshoes back of the lodge, "Lois is coming for a drink after dinner."

Beverly tossed a horseshoe, watched it land, skip, and fall, then turned to him. Her eyes were wide—well, they always were—and their shining surfaces reminded him at that moment of the reflecting side of a one-way mirror. What would she say? And which of the seven ripostes must he use to overcome her resistance ? Or would he have to make up an eighth on the spur of the moment?

She dropped her eyes and picked up another horseshoe, and said, "What time?"

So Lois came; her light, firm knock might just as well have been on the base of his tongue, so immediately did he feel it. If, later on, his will failed him a little, it was because now he sat still using it up, and let Beverly go to the door.

Beverly, he thought, for Beverly's sake, should not permit herself in the same room with Lois. Lois came in and filled the room, but without crowding; Lois went back and down into an easy chair as if carried by flying things; Lois's body grew up out of the cushions supported by what she breathed like an underwater plant. And Beverly bounced about with glasses and ice and talked ... *talked*. What Lois did was something different; Lois conversed. He sat dully, contributing little, watching and thinking his own thoughts. He was achingly aware of many things, but foremost was the realization that Lois was making an effort—a completely successful one, as far as he could judge—to put Beverly at her ease. She made no such effort for him, and he told himself with pride that this was because she had no need to; they understood one another, and must make things easy for poor Beverly.

He lay back almost drowsily, soaking in Lois's presence as if she were the sun and from her he were gradually acquiring a sort of tan.

Then they were alone in the room, when Beverly went to the kitchen, and then Beverly was wailing something about ice, oh dear, but the Johnsons in nine will have some, no don't bother I'll be right back; the screen door in the kitchen slammed and Beverly's quick feet went bam bam bam down the back steps, and ceased to exist as they encountered pine needles; all this in a brace of moments, and he was alone with Lois.

He rose and went to the couch and sat where its corner touched the arm of the easy chair. It seemed to take all the energy he had; he wanted a cigarette, he wanted to speak. He could do nothing.

After a silent time he felt Lois's gaze on him. He turned to her quickly and she dropped her eyes. He was glad, because their heads were so close, and he had never examined her this way, slowly. He wet his lips. He said, "Only ten days."

She made an interrogative syllable.

"Knowing you," he said. He rose suddenly and crossed in front of her. He put one knee on the broad arm of her chair so that his foot was by the back. He sat back on his heel, his other foot steadying him on the floor. She stayed just as she was, looking down at her long brown hands. "I want to tell you something, Lois."

A small frown appeared and disappeared on her smooth forehead. She did not raise her eyes.

"It's something I've never told even to ... never told anyone."

Lois moved a little. She did not raise her face, but now he had a three-quarter view of her profile. She waited, still as a dewdrop.

"The night when we arrived. You made coffee and I sat at the table. You came up behind me to put something down.

"You touched me."

He closed his eyes, and put his arm across his chest and his hand high on his own shoulder. "Something ... *happened,*" he said, with an unaccountable difficulty.

Yancey was, in a small way, an engineer. He began abruptly to explain, in didactic tones, "It wasn't static electricity. It couldn't have been. It was pouring rain outside and the air was humid, not dry. You were on the bare floor in your bare feet; it wasn't one of those deep-pile-rug phenomena. So it wasn't anything . . ." He opened his eyes, swallowed. "Static, or anything like that," he managed. Then he was quiet, watching her.

Her face, the flexible mask, was breaking up like an ice floe in a sudden warm strong current. Her brow was like a snowbank with the marks of a kitten's claws on it. There was a tear drop on her left cheek, and the streak of a tear on her right, and her teeth were driving into her lower lip. The corners of her mouth were turned upward, precisely as they would be in a smile, and there was a delicate pucker in the flesh of her chin. She made not a sound. She rose, her eyes seizing his and holding them as she backed to the door. There she turned and ran out into the dark.

When Beverly came back he was still half-crouched, balancing on the arm of the chair. "Why—where's Lois?"

"She left," he said heavily.

Beverly looked at him. She looked at his eyes, quickly at his hairline, his mouth, and again at his eyes. Then she went into the kitchen and he heard the ice she was carrying fall explosively into the sink. She called out, "Is anything the matter, Yancey?"

"Nothing's the matter," he said, getting up.

She said, "Oh." They cleared up the glasses and ashtrays and went to bed. Lois was not mentioned. Nothing was mentioned. They went about the ritual of retiring in silence. When the lights were out he said, "I've had enough of this place. Let's go home in the morning. Early."

She was quiet for a long time. Then she said, "If you want to."

He thought she slept badly. He did not sleep at all.

In the morning he drove furiously. For the first twenty miles he could not understand what he felt; then he began to understand that it was anger. For another fifty miles he could find no direction for the anger; none of the people involved had, after all, done anything, so how could there be anger?

Occasionally he glanced at Beverly. Ordinarily she sat back, looking forward at the sky, sideways to scenery, or inward to whatever it was she communed with during those silent times they spent together. This morning, however, she sat straight and kept her eyes on the road ahead, which made him aware that he was driving too fast and which annoyed him beyond description. Childishly, he increased both his speed and his anger.

And at last, with a feeling that approached relief, he found something to be angry at.

Beverly.

Why wouldn't she say, "Slow down!" Why had she agreed to let Lois come to their cabin? Why had she gone on blandly being herself this whole time, while he was tearing himself apart inside? Why hadn't she even questioned him when he decided so abruptly to leave? "If you want to," she'd said. "If you want to." What kind of self-respect is that?

Or—maybe she just didn't care.

If you want to ... for the first time he realized that this was her code, her basic philosophy of life. They had red curtains in the living-room. They had always had red curtains in the living-room. Well, he liked red curtains. He'd said so. She had put up red curtains.

He glanced at her. She was watching the road tautly. He squeezed down a bit more on the accelerator.

The place they lived in, the job he kept; the food they ate and probably the clothes she wore; were they really chosen because they were what he wanted?

Were they what he wanted?

Should he have what he wanted?

Why not? Beverly had.

He laughed, making Beverly start violently. He shook his head at her, which meant either "I won't tell you" or "Mind your own business." He had disqualified himself from finding any flaw in this new and breath-taking conclusion and it made him exultant. He enjoyed speed in his exultation, and control. He sent the car howling through a deep cut in the crest of a hill, and around the blind turn on the other side, which is where he collided with the space ship and was killed.

As it will at times in the wake of a hurricane, the wind died. Less tractable, the sea punished the cliff unabated. The night was as noisy, but the noise was so different it was as shocking as sudden silence. In it, Lois twisted and angrily rammed her cigarette into the ashtray on the night table. With a crisp angry rustle of sheets, she turned her back and then sighed. The sound was only half vocalized, but such a voice propagates more like light than like sound. Beverly came hurtling up out of slumber and flashed free like a leaping fish, only to fall back and swirl near the under surfaces of sleep. She raised her head, turning it as if seeking, but her eyes were closed. "Hm?" she said sleepily. Then her face dropped to Yancey's chest again and she was still.

What I should do, thought Yancey wildly, is to sit her up and slap her awake and say, "Look, Bev, you know what? I got killed that morning when we had the accident, I was dead altogether, the late Yancey Bowman, r. i. p., and when they put me back together I was different. For two years now you've been living with a man with a mind that never sleeps and never makes mistakes and does ... can do ... anything it wants. So you can't expect ordinary conduct from me, Bev, or rational behavior based on any reason you can understand. So if I do anything that ... that hurts you, you mustn't be hurt. Can't you understand that?"

Of course she wouldn't understand.

Why, he thought desperately, when they put me back together, didn't they iron out that little human wrinkle which made it possible for Pascal to make that remark about the heart having "reasons which reason does not know"?

He snorted softly. Heart. Heck of a name for it.

He lay on his back and watched the motion of surf-scattered moon on the ceiling. He let his mind float into the vague shadows, be one with them away from, above, beyond his insupportable, insoluble problem. And gradually he found himself back there again, two years ago—perhaps because of the momentum of his previous thinking, perhaps because, in reliving a time when there was Lois (and he could stand it) and a time when there was Lois (and he could not), it was a welcome thing to go into a time where Lois, and Beverly, and for that matter Yancey Bowman, had little significance.

As the space ship lifted, it retracted its berthing feet; it was one of these which Bowman's sedan struck. The car continued under the ship, and the edge of the flat berthing foot sliced it down to the belt line, leaving a carmine horror holding the wheel. The ship hovered momentarily, then drifted over to the side of the road where the mangled automobile had come to rest. Directly above the car, it stopped. An opening appeared in the bottom of the ship and dilated like a camera iris. There was a slight swirl of dust and leaves, and then what was left of the car rose from the ground and disappeared into the ship. The ship then slid away to the clearing in the woods where it had lain hidden during its stay on Earth. Here it settled. It camouflaged itself and lay outwardly silent.

Exactly what was done to him, Yancey could not know. He was made aware of the end results, of course. He knew that what had been injured had been repaired, and that in addition certain changes had been made to improve the original. For example, his jaw hinges had been redesigned to eliminate a tendency to dislocation, and a process was started which would, in time, eliminate the sebaceous cysts which had kept forming and occasionally inflaming ever since he was an adolescent. His vermiform appendix was gone—not excised, but removed in some way which would indicate, in the event of an autopsy, that it had never formed in the first place. His tonsils had been replaced for reasons which he could not understand except that they were good ones. On the other hand such anomalies as his left little toe, which since birth had been bent and lay diagonally across its neighbor, and a right eye which wandered slightly to the right when he was fatigued—these were left as they had originally been. The eye was one of the most interesting items, he thought later; the toe had simply not been improved, but the eye had been restored with its flaw. His teeth, too, were as irregular as before, and contained fillings in the same places, though he knew there had been little enough left of them. In sum, he had been altered only in ways which would not show.

He did know, however, *why* these things had been done. There was inside that ship an aura of sympathy mixed with remorse unlike anything he had ever felt. Another component was respect, an all-embracing respect for living things. Somewhere near where he lay in the ship's laboratory was a small covered shelf containing a cicada, two grasshoppers, four summer moths, and an earthworm, all casualties in his accident. Their cell structure, organic functions, and digestive and reproductive processes were under study as meticulous as that which was being lavished on him. For them restitution was to be made also, and they would be released in as good condition as this unthinkably advanced science could make them. The improvements seemed to be in the nature of a bonus, an implemented apology.

And, of course, there was no denying that as long as such repayment was made the alien footsteps on Earth were fairly obliterated. Yet Yancey was always certain that this was not a primary motive, and that the aliens, whoever they were, wherever they came from, would have sacrificed anything, themselves included, rather than interfere with terrestrial life.

He was to find out later that they had done the same things with his car as they had done with him. He had not the slightest doubt that if they had wished they could have rebuilt the old sedan into a gleaming miracle, capable of flight and operable forever on a teacupfull of fuel. He found it looking as it had always looked, even to rust spots and a crinkling around the windshield where moisture had penetrated the laminations of the safety glass. Yet there was a little more pickup, a little more economy; the brakes were no longer grabby in wet weather; and the cigarette lighter heated up in fewer seconds than before.

Who were they? Where had they come from? What were they doing here and what did they look like?

He was never to know. He knew precisely as much as they permitted. He even knew why he knew as much as he did. They could restore his crushed head and shoulder, and did. They could make slight improvements, and did. But even they could not predict every situation in which he might find himself in the future. It was deeply important to them, and it would be to him, to conceal the changes which had been made, or the reciprocal impacts between him and his society might greatly affect both. The best concealment would be his full knowledge of what had been done, and a solemn injunction to divulge nothing of it to anyone. That way he could never innocently perform public miracles and then be at a loss to explain.

What miracles?

Most miraculous, of course, was the lowered impulse-resistance of his nervous system, including the total brain. He need no longer run over and over a thought sequence, like a wheel making a rut, to establish a synapse and therefore retain knowledge. He had super-fast physical reactions. He had total recall (from the time of his release from the ship) and complete access to his previous memory banks.

Yet a prime directive among his "surgeons" seemed to have been a safeguarding of what his world called Yancey Bowman. Nothing—nothing at all—was done to change Yancey Bowman into something or someone else. He functioned a little better now, but he functioned as Yancey Bowman, just as the changes in his digestive system were basically improvements rather than replacements. He could get more energy out of less food, even as he could breathe higher concentrations of CO_2 than he could before. He could be, and was, Yancey Bowman more efficiently than ever before. Hence nothing was changed ... even (or especially) the turmoil which was uppermost in his mind when he died.

So it was that after death had struck one Friday morning, the same morning hour on Sunday revealed a strange sight (but only to some birds and a frightened chipmunk). Slipping out of earth itself, the ship spread topsoil where it had lain, covered it with a little snow of early-fallen leaves, and shouldered into the sky. It wheeled and for a moment paralleled the deserted highway below. The opening on its belly appeared, and down through the shining air swept an aging two-door sedan, its wheels spinning and its motor humming. When it touched the roadway there was not so much as a puff of dust, so perfectly were wheels and forward motion synchronized.

The car hurtled through a cut in a hilltop and around the blind turn on the other side, and continued on its way, with Yancey Bowman at the wheel, seething inwardly at the unreachable stupidities of his wife.

And was there a moment of shock when he found himself alive and on his way unharmed, in his undamaged automobile? Did he turn and crane to see the dwindling speck in which his life had ended and begun again? Did he pull over to the side, mop his brow, and in a cascade of words exult over his new powers? Did Beverly demand to know what had happened, and would she not go out of her mind when she found that Friday was Sunday now, and that for her there had been no Saturday this week?

No, and no, and no. There was no shock, because he was certain to his marrow that this was the way it would be; that he would say nothing and that he must not look back. As for Beverly, her silence on the matter was proof enough that her convictions would suit the situation as well.

So he drove too fast and was too quiet, and his anger bubbled away until at length it concentrated into something quieter and rather uglier. As it formed, he drove more sensibly, and Beverly relaxed and leaned back, turning now and again to inspect the shutters or the curtains in a house they passed, watching the sky up ahead while she thought her own thoughts.

If you could call them thoughts, he reflected.

The product of his anger was a cold projection, and took the form of an unspoken dictum to Beverly. He found that with his new reflexes he could give the matter his full attention, since now his hands seemed quite able to drive by themselves, and even, it appeared, to read route signs.

So, echoing noiselessly in his mind, this structure built: This is not the end, Beverly, because the end must have been long since. You are not a woman living her life; you are a half-person living mine. Your ambition could not push me ahead, your senses could not know when I was in torture, your taste is not your own, and your abilities are limited to a dull search for what might please me and a trial-and-error effort to get it for me. But aside from me you are nothing. You do not and you could not earn your own living. Cast out on your own resources you could not so much as fill a receptionist's chair, or even run a summer resort. If nothing whatever had happened to me during these three days, what we have could never be called "marriage" again, not by me. I have looked into the sun, Beverly; I have flown; I can never crawl the mud with you again. I was too much for you before; what then am I now?

So it ran, turning and elaborating itself but always returning to a silent scornful chant, buoyed up by glimpses of freedom and far horizons. After about an hour of this he sensed her gaze, and turned to look at her. She met his eyes and smiled her old smile. "It's going to be a lovely day, Yance."

He turned abruptly back to the road. Something in his throat demanded attention, and he found that he could not swallow it. His eyes stung. He sat, unwillingly examining his feelings, and slowly it came to him that among his other traits, that characteristic called empathy—the slipping on of other people's shoes, the world seen through the eyes of others—this quality too had suffered a sea-change and was heightened more than was comfortable. What, to Beverly, had happened? Numbly, perhaps, she had been aware that something was amiss at the lake. He seriously doubted if she had identified the something. She'd known it was important because she'd okayed their leaving so abruptly without asking any questions. But what was this "lovely day" business? Did she think that because their backs were turned to the unidentified threat, it had ceased to exist? Why, that must be exactly what she thought!

Oh Beverly, Beverly, are you going to get a kick in the teeth!

But a day went by and no such thing happened. It didn't happen the first week, either, or in a month. Part of this was because of his work. He went back to it with a new sense, an awareness. He became totally sensitive to a condition called "integration," himself with his job, his job with his office, his office to the firm, and the firm itself in the economic mosaic. He wasted no motion in his job, and found himself spending his working day in pondering the structure of his surroundings. His first new effort was expressed through the suggestion box. It was perfect of its kind. It was an idea simple enough to have been thought of by his pre-accident self, and unlikely to be advanced by anyone not in this particular job. It eliminated the job and Yancey was advanced two grades and given new work to do. So he was busy, immersed, engaged, even at home. That in itself was enough to submerge his feelings about Beverly.

But it was only a part of his procrastination. (He called it that at first: sooner or later, he thought, there would be changes made.) Largely, he delayed because of this accursed empathy. Beverly was so *happy.* She was happy and proud. If he became unaccountably silent, she tiptoed about the place, quite convinced that the great man was dreaming up something else for the suggestion box. If he was short-tempered, she forgave. If he bought her something, or approved something she had bought, she was grateful. Home was harmonious; Beverly was so happy she sang again. He realized that it had been a great while since she had sung.

And all the while he knew how she felt. He knew it surely and painfully, and was fully aware of the impact she would suffer if he broached to her his inner thinking. He'd do it; oh yes, he'd do it, some day. Meanwhile, it wouldn't hurt anything if she got that new winter coat she had eyed so wistfully in the Sunday paper. . . .

So a year went by and he did nothing about the matter. Actually, he thought less about it after a year, though there were moments. . . . But work was more engrossing than ever, and home was such a pleasure—though a quiet one—and Beverly was fairly blooming. If a man has the virtue or the curse of empathy, he has to be kind. He must, for the most selfish of reasons: any time he kicks out at another human, he will find bruises on his own shins.

Once, suddenly, he asked her, "Beverly, have I changed?"

She looked puzzled, so he enlarged it. "Since last year, I mean. Do I seem different?"

She thought about it. "I don't know. You're—nice. But you were always nice." She laughed suddenly. "You can catch flies," she teased. "Why, Yance?"

"No reason. The new job, and all." He passed the reference to flies. One had been bothering her last fall and he had absently reached out and caught it on the wing. It was the only time he had come near betraying some of his new talents. She had been astonished; in eight years he had never demonstrated coordination like that. She would have been more astonished if she had noticed that he caught the fly between his thumb and forefinger.

"The new job hasn't gone to your head," she said, "if that's what you mean."

He maneuvered a situation in the office which required attention in an out-of-town branch and arranged matters so that sending him out there was only logical. He was gone two weeks. He had seen to it that it was not the kind of task that required genius, just application and good detail work. He met two girls while he was there, one brilliant and high in the company, the other far better than anything the company would ever be able to hire. He left them alone, disliking himself not a little because he knew, in his heart of hearts, whom he was being faithful to.

And it was good, good to get home. Due to what he had done out of town, he was raised another notch but had to reorganize his new office, so there was no vacation that year. He could easily have analyzed this development, and determined for himself whether he had purposely avoided a vacation, but he did not. He'd rather not know.

There was a company picnic, and Beverly sang. People reacted so enthusiastically—especially to Yancey, as if he had invented her—that he coaxed and goaded her into auditioning for a television show. She won the audition and appeared. She lost the audience vote to an eight-year-old boy with an accordion, but she was incandescently happy because Yancey had cared, Yancey had helped.

In the matter of Beverly, Yancey began to like himself.

That, in Yancey's private code, was the Year of the Big Christmas. They took a week off and went to a ski lodge in New Hampshire. They did a number of things together, and nothing was wrong about any of it. And one night they sat before a Christmas-card kind of fireplace with a crowd of kindred souls, drinking *glögg* and roaring carols, until they were too sleepy to move. After everyone else had gone to bed, they sat holding hands silently and watching the fire go out. As it will at such moments, when one is living, not dying, his life whisked across his inner eye and stopped here at this hearth, and on it was superimposed the uneasy question *What am I doing here?* Over him came a flood of tenderness for Beverly, poor Beverly. For the first time it occurred to him that the fantastic thing that had happened to him might have a grim and horrible result. His metabolic efficiency, his apparent immunity to everything from the common cold up, his outright inability to get too little rest or too little food ... suppose he should live—well, not forever, but—

He glanced at his wife, and though she was young-looking for her age, his quick mind vividly supplied a wrinkle here and there, a little sag. He'd be able to conceal his feelings about it, of course, but would she? Empathetically, he went through a brief torture with her future, seeing her wither while he went on as he was.

He averted his face, and his eyes filled with tears.

Gently she disengaged her hand. He felt it stroking, stroking his wrist. And she had the wit, or the luck, to say absolutely nothing as she did it.

When he thought back on it, much later, he thought too that though there were many women who could do many things Beverly couldn't do, not one of them would have done just that, just that way.

In the spring he turned down a promotion, sensitive as he was to the feelings of his co-workers; this would benefit him far more in the long run. And again it was summer, and this time there would be a vacation.

Well—where? He would choose a place, and Beverly would say, "If that's what you want, darling," and off they'd go. He thought, and he thought about it. With his total recall, he recreated a great many scenes for himself. He all but decided, and then he hesitated; and then, sitting at his desk in the office, he said aloud, "No! No, not yet," and startled some people.

They went to New England, to a place new to them, craggy, rugged, sparkling, where sailboats notched the skyline and the wind smelled clean and new and quite unused by anyone else. For four days they fished and swam, danced, and dug littlenecks. On the fifth day they stayed snugly indoors while the sky pressed down like a giant's palm. At three o'clock the small-craft warnings went up. At four the Coast Guard called and warned them away from their rented shack; yes, it was a hurricane, a real hurricane and not just a storm.

They loaded the car haphazardly and tumbled into it, and already there was a blinding fog of spume blowing horizontally across the coast road. They ground up the hill to the town and pulled into the hotel yard.

The hotel, of course, was full, with a bed laid in the linen room and a cot set up behind the desk.

"What are we going to do?" Beverly wailed. It was not distress, not yet. This was exciting.

"We're going to have a drink. Then we're going to have some hot chowder. Then we're going to think about what we're going to do."

With their lungs full of ozone and their eyes full of sparks, they went to the dining-room.

There was a picture which, say, a year ago, Yancey used to call to mind so often that it was as familiar as his safety razor. A slim back, wide shoulders clad in rich brown moleskin: lamplight glancing from dark obedient hair, and a long brown hand resting lightly against an ivory cheek. When he saw it now, right before his eyes, he discounted it as an unwelcome phantom, a trick of the charged air. But Beverly squeezed his elbow and cried, "Yance—look!" and before he could draw a breath she sprang away from him to the table.

"Lois! Lois, whatever in the world are you doing here?"

This, Yancey told himself heavily, just had to happen. He went forward. "Hello, Lois."

"Well . . . !" It was a single syllable, but it contained warmth and welcome and . . . but how would you ever know, even when she smiled? A mask can smile. "Sit down, please sit down, Beverly. Yancey."

There was a rush of small talk. Oh, yes, she had sold the resort, last spring. Worked for a while in town. Resigned, looking for something better. Came up here to let the wind blow the smog out of her hair. "Now I'm afraid it'll take the hair too." Oh yes, Beverly was saying, so warmly, so proudly ... two promotions ... turned down another one too; he'll run the place in another year, just you watch ... and a good deal more, while Lois watched her hands and smiled a small smile. "What about you, Lois, are you married or anything?"

"No," said Lois huskily, "I'm not married"—and here Yancey dropped his eyes; he couldn't bear to meet hers while she said it—"or anything."

They had a drink, and another, and then some superlative New England chowder, and beer, and another drink. And then it was over, and Yancey, paying the check, was telling himself glumly, "You did fine, boy; so if you're a little on the silent side for a day or two, what's that? I'm glad it's over. But I wish ..."

Rising, Beverly said, "You're staying here?"

Lois smiled oddly. "There's nothing they can do about it."

Before he could stop himself Yancey said, "Now what exactly does that mean?"

Lois laughed quietly. "I just got in an hour and a half ago. I never dreamed I'd need a reservation—funny, isn't it, after my experience? Anyway, they're full up. I shall just sit here until they want to close the place. I will then be a problem, and it'll be up to them to solve it." She laughed again. "I've solved worse ones in my time."

"Oh, Lois, you can't! They'll make you sleep on the bar!"

She shrugged, really not caring.

"Yancey," said Beverly. She was flushed and urgent. "Do you remember a time when two wet strangers couldn't find their beds, and what happened to them?"

He did meet Lois's eyes this time. This was when his heart began hammering.

Beverly said, "It's our turn. We're going down the coast. We'll find a place. Come on. Come *on,* Lois!"

Yancey thought, listen to her, taking the bit in her teeth. Doesn't she usually find out first what I want? And he answered himself, no; most of the time she just does what I want without asking. And he told himself further, stop talking like a damn fool.

Ten miles south there was a town with a hotel. Full up. Four miles further, a motel. Packed to the eaves. The next stretch was twenty miles, and it was getting late. It was raining the kind of rain they had slogged through to Lois's cabin two years before, but this time they had a howling gale along with it.

And by the time they reached the next town, the warnings were in; the hurricane, true to its unpredictable breed, had swung east leaving rain and a maddened sea, but no further danger. So they drove into the slick shining streets of a city still quaking in its boots, but vastly relieved.

Here and there a store was open. There were three hotels, two of them full. They stopped at an all-night drugstore to ask directions to the third and Lois bought cigarettes and Beverly found a book-club edition of *Anna Karenina* and scooped it up with joy; she said she'd always wanted to read it.

The third hotel had one double with bath.

"Twin beds?"

The clerk nodded. Yancey looked at Lois but her eyes were cloaked. He looked at Beverly and she said, "Why not? We can fit in a twin bed. I'm not very big."

No, Bev, he thought, you're not.

Lois said, "Beverly—"

"Shh," said Beverly. "We'll take it," she said to the clerk.

Lois turned again. Now she was looking up at the ceiling with him. Think of that! he thought acidly, here we are sharing some antiseptic moonbeams.

His biting thought was protection for a very brief while. His heart began again. It shook him with each beat. It shook the bed, the walls, the building, the beaten cliff outside, making it hurl back the sea with even greater violence.

There was the softest butterfly-wing touch on his chest. Beverly had opened her eyes.

Yancey thought madly, it's like one of those meaningless conjugations they give you in first-year French. I stare up into the darkness, you stare up into the darkness, she stares up into the darkness....

Beverly moved. She wriggled up closer. She put her hand behind his head, pulling it toward her. She put her mouth on his ear. He felt her warm breath. Barely audible, her breath said, "Darling. What is it? What do you want?"

What did he want? Nothing, of course. Nothing he could have. Nothing, certainly, that he should have. He shook his head.

Beverly crept back until her head was on his shoulder again. She lay still. She slid one hand over his chest, to rest lightly on his hammering heart.

Lois sighed quietly and turned over, away from them. The wind laughed and laughed outside, and another breaker smashed and spouted. The room grew black, then silver again.

An hour-long five minutes passed.

Abruptly Beverly sat up. "I can't sleep," she said clearly.

Lois was silent. Yancey watched Beverly. The silver light made everything in the room look like an overexposed photograph, but Beverly's flesh seemed pink—the only thing in the whole mad, pulsing world that had any color but grey or black or silver.

Beverly swung her legs out, stood up, and stretched in the moonlight. She was small and firm and—pink? Was she really pink, or was that a memory too, like the reconstruction of the two kinds of darkness on Lois's pillow that to his mind looked like Lois's face and hair?

What a beautiful complementation, he thought hotly; how balanced an equation expresses this chaos! Beverly, small and fair; open, simple, direct. Lois, tall, slender, dark, devious, complex. And each so clearly lacking just what the other had.

Beverly said, "I have nineteen chapters of *Anna Karenina* to read. Take me about an hour." She knelt on Yancey's bed briefly, reached across to the night table, and scooped something up. Then she went to the highboy and got the book. She went into the bathroom. Yellow light appeared starkly under the closed door.

Yancey lay quite still, looking at the line of yellow light. He heard Lois's sheets.

At last he rolled over and looked at her. He could see the sliver of yellow again, across her eyes. She was half sitting, resting her weight on one slender arm. She was looking at him, or past him, to the closed door.

"What was it she picked up from the night table, Yancey?"

"Her watch."

Lois made a sound, perhaps "Oh." She sank down slowly, until she rested on her elbow. She *was* looking at him now. He would know that even if he closed his eyes.

He lay still, wondering if Lois could hear his heart. She probably could. Beverly probably could, through the door. He wondered, with shattering inconsequentiality, whether Beverly liked red curtains.

Lois made a slight motion with her chin toward the yellow gleam. She whispered, "I couldn't do that."

A great hungry yearning came over him, but at the moment, incredibly, it seemed to have no direction. It yawned somewhere beneath him, waiting to engulf him. A puzzlement plucked at him, and then, seeing the polished yellow lines in Lois's eyes, it came to him which of these women was simple and direct, and which was subtle and deep and complex.

"I couldn't do that," Lois had said. How many other things could Beverly do that Lois could not?

What kind of a woman was Beverly?

For the very first time Yancey Bowman asked himself what had happened to Beverly the day he was killed. He'd assumed she was simply in cold storage while they put him back together. He'd assumed ... how could he assume such a thing? He had never even asked about her. That was impossible! Unnatural!

But of course—he wasn't to ask. He would not have thought of it, and the chances were that he could not have asked her even if he'd thought to.

Why could he think of it now?

It must be time to think of it. Something had happened to him, permitting him to. Qualifying him to. But he hadn't changed; he couldn't change. He was built and rebuilt and designed and redesigned, to be Yancey-Plus. What change could ...

Supposing, he told himself, they had a very young thing to rebuild.

Wouldn't they build it so that it could go on growing? Then he could have grown. How? How?

Well, what would he have done in this same mad situation, two years ago, even after he left the space ship? He wouldn't have lain here these swift seconds, speculating; that was for sure.

"I couldn't do that," Lois had whispered. Supposing Beverly had been killed too, and changed as he had been changed. He had never told her what he knew; why would she have told him? Wasn't the prime purpose to improve a little, but to change nothing? He was Yancey-Plus, who went right ahead ruling the roost, accepting his wife's quiet variety of slave labor. Wouldn't she go right on being Beverly, giving him always what he wanted?

And suppose she hadn't been killed, hadn't been changed. What kind of a woman was she, who could do what Lois could not do, what—it painfully occurred to him—he himself, with all his powers, could never do? Was the original Beverly a bigger person than Yancey-Plus?

Then it was, with a surge of relief that made his head spin, that his heart eased and he smiled. He knew now how he had changed, how he had grown. He knew, all at once, what to do now and what to do for the rest of his life with Beverly. Up to now he had not been able to ask her if she was the same Beverly he had married. Now, by choice, he never would ask her. Their marriage would be spiced and underscored and made most beautiful by that one mystery between them, each held from the other.

All this in seconds, and he became aware again of the yellow lights in Lois's long eyes. Quite changing the subject, he used her exact words. "I couldn't do that," he whispered.

Lois nodded slowly. She sank back on the pillow and closed her eyes. He thought she trembled. He didn't know. He didn't much care. He turned over and filled his lungs, as he had not been able to do for more than an hour because of his leaping heart. "Beverly!" he bellowed.

The book fell on the tiles. There was silence for a moment, and then the door opened.

"Yes, Yance."

"Get back to bed, idiot. You can read that some other time. You need your sleep."

"I just—all right, Yance, if you want."

She switched off the light and came in. A moonbeam swept across her face as she approached. She was looking across him at Lois, her lips trembling. She got into bed. He put his arms around her, gently, humbly. She turned to him and suddenly held him so tight that he almost cried out.

That Low

There was a "psychic" operating on Vince Street. Fowler went to see her. Not that he had any faith in mumbo-jumbo: far from it. He had been told that this Mrs. Hallowell worked along strictly logical lines. That's why he went. He liked the sound of that, being what he was. He went to her and asked her about killing himself. She said he couldn't do it. Not "You won't," or "shouldn't." She said, "You can't."

This Fowler was a failure specialist, in the sense that a man is a carburetor specialist or a drainage specialist or a nerve specialist. You don't get to be that kind of specialist without spending a lot of time with carburetors or sewers or nerves. You don't stay nice and objective about it either. You get in it up to the elbows, up to the eyeballs. Fowler was a man who knew all that one man could know about failure. He knew all of the techniques, from the small social failure of letting his language forget what room of the house his mouth was in, through his declaration of war on the clock and the calendar (in all but style he was the latest), to the crowning stupidity of regarding his opinions as right purely because they were his opinions. So he had fallen and floundered through life, never following through, jumping when he should have crept, and lying down at sprintingtime. He could have written a book on the subject of failure, except for the fact that if he had, it might have been a success . . . and he hated failure. Well, you don't have to love your specialty to be a specialist. You just have to live with it.

It was understandable, therefore, that he should be impressed by Mrs. Hallowell's reputation for clarity and logic, for he truly believed that here was a kindred spirit. He brought his large features and his flaccid handshake to her and her office, which were cool. The office was Swedish modern and blond. Mrs. Hallowell was dark, and said, "Sit down."

"Your name?"

"Maxwell Fowler."

"Occupation?"

"Engineer."

She glanced up. She had aluminum eyes. "Not a graduate engineer." It was not a question.

"I would of been," said Fowler, "except for a penny-ante political situation in the school. There was a fellow—"

"Yes," she said. "Married?"

"I was. You know, the kind that'll kick a man when he's down. She was a—"

"Now, Mr. Fowler. What was it you wanted here?"

"I hear you can foretell the future."

"I'm not interested in gossip," she said, and it was the only cautionary thing she said in the entire interview. "I know about people, that's all."

He said, "Ever since I could walk and talk, people have been against me. I can whip one or two or sometimes half a dozen or more, but by and large I'm outnumbered. I'm tired. Sometimes I think I'll check out."

"Are you going to ask me if you should?"

"No. If I will. You see, I think about it all the time. Sometimes I—"

"All right," she said. "As long as you understand that I don't give advice. I just tell about what's going to happen."

"What's going to happen?"

"Give me a check."

"What?"

"Give me a check. No—don't write on it. Just give it to me."

"But—"

"You wouldn't pay me afterward."

"Now look, my word's as good as—" and then he looked into the eyes. He got out his checkbook. She took a pen and wrote on the check.

She gave it back to him and he looked at it and said, "That's foolish."

"You have it, though."

"Yes, I have, but—"

"Sign it, then," she said casually, "or go away."

He signed it. "Well?"

She hesitated. There was something—

"Well?" he rapped again. "What'll I do? I'm tired of all this persecution."

"I take it you're asking me what you *shall* do—not what you should or will do."

"Lawyer's talk, huh."

"Laws," she said. "Yes." She wet her lips. "You shall live a long and unhappy life." Then she put away the check.

Maxwell looked after it, longingly. "It can't be unhappier than it is."

"That may well be."

"Then I don't want to live a long life."

"But you shall."

"Not if I don't want to," he said grimly. "I tell you, I'm tired."

She shook her head. "It's gone too far," she said, not unkindly. "You can't change it."

He got up. "I can. Anytime, I can. Then you'll be wrong, won't you?"

"I'm not wrong," said Mrs. Hallowell.

"I'll kill myself," said Maxwell, and that was when she told him he couldn't. He was very angry, but she did not give him back his check. By the time he thought of stopping payment on it, it had cleared the bank. He went on living his life.

The amount of money he had paid Mrs. Hallowell dug quite a hole, but for a surprisingly long time he was able to walk around it. However, he did nothing to fill it up, and inevitably, he had the choice of facing his creditors or killing himself. So he got a piece of rope and made a noose and put it around his neck. He tied the other end to the leg of the radiator and jumped out of the window. He was a big man, but the rope held all right. However, the leg broke off the radiator, and he fell six stories. He hit a canvas marquee, tore through it, and fell heavily to the sidewalk. There was quite a crowd there, after a while, to listen to the noises he made because of what was broken.

Fowler took a while to mend, and spent it in careful thought. He took no comfort from his thoughts, for they were honest ones, and he did not care at all for his conclusions, which drafted a portrait no one would admire and an insight no one would want as a bedfellow. He got through it, though, and put a list of his obligations down on paper and drew up a plan for taking care of things. It was a plan that was within his capabilities and meant chip, chip, chip for a long, long time before he could ever call himself honestly broke again. The first person he tried it out on was the business manager of the hospital, and to his immense surprise it worked: that is, he wouldn't get sued for the bill, and the hospital would go along with him until it was all straightened out. Nobody had ever given him that much of a break before; but then, he had never tackled a problem this way before.

He got out of the hospital and began chipping.

Mrs. Hallowell had a bad moment over Fowler. She started up out of her sleep one night, thinking about him.

"Oh, how awful," she said. "I made a mistake!"

She phoned in the morning. Fowler was not there. Mrs Hallowell phoned and phoned around until she got someone who could tell her about Fowler. The tenant in the apartment next to Fowler's had made a mistake about a gas heater, and had a bad cold, and lit a match, and blew the end of the building out. Fowler had been picked up from the wreckage, bleeding. The someone said, "Is there any message I could send to him?"

"No," said Mrs. Hallowell. "No. Not . . . now."

They saved Fowler that time, too. It was a lot of trouble. They had to take this and that off, and the other out. He was put, finally, in a very short bed with a mass of equipment beside him, humming and clicking. It circulated fluids, and another part of it dripped into a tube, and there was a thing that got emptied a couple of times a day without Fowler's worrying about it.

That was the trouble with Mrs. Hallowell's talent. It lay in such broad lines. A mistake could cover a lot of territory. Fowler gradually became aware of her mistake. It took him about two months.

People came by and clucked their tongues when they saw him. There was a bright-eyed, dry-faced old lady who put flowers near him every week or so. He didn't have to go on with that chip, chip, pay, pay any more. Everybody was sorry for him, and everybody always would be, as long as he lived, which would be very nearly as long as the equipment could be kept running. A long time. A long life. Mrs. Hallowell had been right, dead right, about the long life.

Where she made her mistake was in thinking that he would be unhappy.

Memory

JEREMIAH JEDD STOOD in the igneous dust of the spaceport margin, staring into the sky and shading his eyes with his arm. Occasionally he checked the time by his ristkron, shaking it to make sure it was wound, craning back toward the hunched Customs House and the great clock. The sign there announced placidly that the *Pinnacle* had reported, was overdue and would discharge passengers at Gate Three.

Jeremy shook his head and took the letter from Mars out of his pocket again. Slowly he unfolded it and read, in the manner of a man checking his mnemonics. He was certainly familiar enough with it after so much re-reading. The letter said:

> *You must have heard by this time that General Export has installed a fabricating plant here, just outside Fort Wargod. It cost them plenty in time and money to get it set up—actually most of it was shipped as hand luggage because of the shipping space situation.*
>
> *Like a lot of other people, I thought it was a foolish move, because the finished piping they could have shipped in the space is at such a premium on Mars, and because their plant is going to require power—a hard thing to get here. I didn't worry too much, though. Why should we care what our competitors do with their money?*
>
> *But here's the joker. In spite of the fact that the plant is small and comparatively crude, it will fabricate pipe. And the material is plastic, chum, and they can now ship it in sheets! I don't have to tell you what that means to us. We only got our cargo-space contracts from General Export because the Government okayed our shipping system—nesting the smaller diameters of pipe inside the larger ones. Genex's own pipe is shipped that way now, too. The idea isn't patentable.*

So unless we find a patentable way to ship pipe in less space, finished, than Genex is taking for their sheet-stock, we're done, brother—wiped out. Genex means to get everything in the Colonial System—you know that. They have all the ships now, and most of the goods and services. I'm afraid we're going on the long list of small operators who have tried to buck them.

Jeremy lowered the letter and rubbed his eyes again. They ached. Since he had received it a week ago, he hadn't slept much. Supplying pipe for the Mars project was work enough without these long nights in the laboratory trying to figure a way out of this spot. Everything he and Hal had in the world was in this deal. They had worked together ever since they left school, right up until the time Hal went up to handle the Mars end.

Fervently he wished it were the other way around. If Hal were here, he'd dope out something. He had always been the real brains of Jedd & Jedd. And as a matter of fact, Hal already had doped out something. What an irony! Whatever his process or system was, he couldn't write it or wire it. General Export carried the mails too, and if they wanted to find something out, it would be only too easy.

Jeremy looked up again. There was a growing, gleaming dot in the sky. He glanced at the building. Near it, men were manning the heatproof launch. He turned back to the letter, to read the cryptic part about Phyllis Exeter:

I know a way to ship this, bud. I'm not telling you about it in a letter—you know why. I'm hoping and praying that you'll figure it out yourself. The new hauling contracts are coming up, and priorities for shipping space go to the pipe company that can pack the most in. My process is very simple, really. It's nothing that Budgie couldn't have told you. You have three weeks to figure it out after you get this note, and don't forget it takes ten days to file a patent application.

And in connection with this idea, Phyllis Exeter is due to arrive on the Pinnacle. *I'd like you to meet her when the rocket-ship docks. She really has what it takes. I got quite chummy with her while she was out here in Thor City. She'll probably have a lot to say about it. She'll have a lot to say, period. She talks more than Budgie. Be good, little man.*

Jeremy's brows matted together as he folded the note and put it away. There was more than met the eye in those last two paragraphs—much more. He got some of it. "Be good, little man." And the references to Budgie—he wasn't too sure, but he had the idea they weren't in there for the purpose of using up ink. And the specific mention of Phyllis Exeter and her arrival. Now *that* was something.

If Hal wanted to be absolutely positive Phyllis Exeter would see him, he'd sure picked the right way. Just that line in the letter would be enough to have Phyllis hunt him up anywhere on Earth, even if he hid. General Export carried the mails. But why Phyllis? After all, Hal and Phyllis had been— He shrugged. If Hal wanted to throw them together again, all right. He began to get the old, familiar feeling, just thinking about it.

From overhead came the blowtorch susurrus of the *Pinnacle*'s braking and hovering jets. Down she came on her bed of fire, until she hesitated at five thousand feet. He distinctly heard the sudden shift to cold-jets, and in another minute the dust-cloud was piled up to receive her.

Jeremy stepped into the waiting room of Number Three Gate, just avoiding the sudden angry gusts of dust-laden air. He shouldered past the chattering crowd inside and got to a port, which was covered with a disc of transparent plastic whirling at high speed to afford clear vision through the mucky dust which hurtled so violently about the building. From the spaceport central, the little heatproof drifted toward the grounding liner, waiting its chance to settle on the huge hull and sink its extensible airlock into the monster like an ovipositor.

Fifteen minutes later the heatproof whickered slowly down to the roof of the gate building. The crowd pressed toward the elevators and was shunted back by the pageboys and officials. Jeremy stood on the fringes, trying to look indifferent and doing a very poor job of it.

The first load came down. A heavy-set man with a dark, rocky face. A quick, slender, cold-eyed man. These two stood aside and let a woman with two children and an aged couple pass them. And then Phyllis stepped out.

He wondered again, looking at her, what a man would have to do to ruffle that sleekness, to crumple the brilliant mask she seemed to wear. Throw a kiss or a fist in that face, and there would be little difference. Her hair was soft, and iridescent green, now. She smoked with a long holder and the smoke matched her hair. Her voice was as lustrous, as colorful as ever, when she saw him.

"Jeremy!" she said. "Jeremy Jedd! How are you, darling?"

"Don't call me darling," he said.

"Oh, these people won't think anything of me that they don't think already," she said.

"They might think it of me," he said grimly. He took her arm, while she laughed as if trying to find out whether she could. She could.

"Come on," he said. "I need a drink. Before, I just wanted one."

She hung back and pouted. "You seem quite sure I'll come."

"You've been reading my mail!" he quipped grimly. She stopped hanging back. They moved toward the door and down the short path to the Customs House. Jeremy glanced back. The two men he had noticed at the elevators were following them. He gestured slightly with his head. "Yours?" She shrugged. "Oh, you know how it is."

"No," he said, "I don't. Not altogether. But I'll learn the rest of it."

She laughed again, and hugged his elbow close to her body. "Jeremy," she said cozily, "do you still feel the same way about me?"

He glanced down into her wide gray-green eyes. "Yup. Always will, I guess. Worse luck."

"Worse luck?"

"It gets in my hair," he grumbled."When I think of all the time I've spent thinking about you when I could've been making pipe—"

"That's what I like about you," she flashed. "You make a person feel so—welcome." She released his arm. "What makes you think you can treat me like that?"

"Several things. They all add up to the fact that you won't walk away from me until you find out what you think I know about stowing pipe. No matter what I say or do to you, you'll tag right along."

"All right," she said, in quite a new, matter-of-fact voice. "I'd just as soon play that way then. All the cards face up, and such sordidness. It could have been pleasant, too."

"Not with me. Not with you and me."

"That's what I meant."

Inside the building they turned to the right elevator bank and dropped to the cafeteria two levels below. There was no conversation in the elevator due to the silent presence of the two men who had followed them from the gatehouse. Jeremy glared at them, but the younger man refused to catch his eye and stared at the ceiling, whistling softly. The other man gazed at Phyllis's feet.

"I think," Jeremy said, as they emerged, "that you have hired these pugs just to bolster your ego. You'll have men following you whatever you have to do."

"It isn't necessary to hire them for that," she said coldly. "I'm sorry you find this unpleasant, Jeremy. But please don't make it any more so than you have to. Strangely enough, there are lots of places I'd rather be than with you. Alone, for example."

"You know," he said, as he politely pulled out a chair for her, "I like you like this. I mean, I could if I tried. This is the first time I have ever seen you when you weren't swinging the figurative female lasso round and round."

"Compliments from you are more unpleasant than anything else could be. Light the menu, will you?"

He touched the stud that illuminated the menu screen. She studied it for a moment, and then dialed the code numbers of the items she wanted. Jeremy studied her as she did so.

She was an amazing girl, he admitted grudgingly. How she looked, what she was—amazing. Her smooth brow was crinkled a bit now, between the eyes. She used to look like that in college once in a while. It generally signified she was out of her depth, and it also meant that she was about to do something about it, like flapping her eyelids at a vulnerable professor, or cribbing from someone else's paper.

Frowning, Jeremy studied Phyllis for several minutes more. Then he spoke.

"Tell me something," he said. "Exactly how was this thing supposed to go?"

"I don't know what you mean."

His voice tuned itself to his strained patience. "I mean, what was supposed to happen here? You would meet me at the gate, or you would hunt me up, and then what?"

"You seem to know everything. Answer your own questions."

"All right. You were going to overcome my time-honored distaste of you and give me the business—most likely the remorse angle. The time you pulled that factory-lease out from under us for the benefit of a cosmetic factory—and General Export, who were starting in the pipe business—you are sorry about that. The time Hal fell for Dolly Holleson and you told her so many lies about him that she up and married somebody else—you're sorry about that too. The time you—" His voice got thick "—accepted my ring, all of my grand old 'forgive and forget' attitude, and a third of our company stock, only to turn the stock over to Genex and tell me to go fly it—that was an awful misunderstanding!

"You know, Phyl, if I had known when I gave you the stock that Hal had phonied up the stock certificate, I'd have killed him, I think. He took the chance. Felt that if you were on the up-and-up he could straighten out the stock later. If you weren't—well, nothing would be lost but a little of mind. Mine." He breathed very deeply, once. "Anyhow, Hal thinks you're poison, and I think you're poison, and I don't know what in the universe you think you are, but certainly it isn't anything that will get a new pipe-stowage process out of me."

"You really slug when you start, don't you?" she whispered. He had never seen her eyes so big, nor her face so white. "And you don't mind lowering your sights, to mix a metaphor."

"I adjust to the most obvious target," he said bluntly. "Why don't you get sore? Why don't you leave?"

Slowly, with a small, tragic smile, she rose. "Watch," she said.

She turned toward the door. At a far table, a man rose and sauntered toward the exit. Behind Jeremy, there was a scraping of chairs on the glossy flooring, and the two men who had followed her from the ship went past.

The man at the door, a suave-looking individual, lean and white-templed, folded his arms and leaned against the wall just out of range of the photocell which opened the door. When Phyllis drew abreast he spoke softly to her. She stopped and shook her head. He smiled then, and shook his. She bit her lip, lowered her head a little and moved toward the door again. So smoothly that it did not seem swift at all, he blocked her.

The other two men reached them, greeted her effusively, took an arm each and led her back toward their table, talking and laughing. When they neared Jeremy's place, they released her and went back to their own table, leaving her standing alone, staring at Jeremy with angry and terrified eyes. The whole thing was done so smoothly that no occupant of the restaurant seemed to notice.

"I have just seen something very lovely," said Jeremy happily. "A pushing-around with you involved, where you are getting pushed for a change. Now come and sit down and tell me all about it in a sisterly fashion."

She came. Again he was struck with the difference in her, the air of being out of her depth. She sank into her chair, her eyes averted from his. She put her hands tight together on the table, but they would not stop shaking. She volunteered nothing.

He reached over the centerpiece of the table and opened the cold-chamber on her side, removing the drink she had ordered. Pushing it across to her, he said gently:

"Gulp some of that and for once in your life give me a straight story. Whose side are you on besides your own? How did it happen? And why do these dawn-men take such an interest in leaving you alone, providing it's with me?"

"Everything's gone wrong. You—you know too much, Jeremy. And you don't know enough. All right, I'll tell you. Telling you won't help me—I mean, you won't help me, no matter what. I thought I could get what I wanted out of you without your ever knowing that they—that I—"

"That they have the heat on you," supplemented Jeremy. "Source, Genex. Temperature, high." He shook his head wonderingly. "That's always been the trouble with you, Phyl. So self-sufficient. Never asked anyone for help in your life. There was always a way out, generally paved with somebody's face. I gather that Genex is as wise to you as I am."

She nodded, with a submissiveness which wrung something within him. His hand went out toward her. He drew it back without touching her.

He said, "Talk, now."

"I was doing all right," she said in a low voice. "I pulled lots of—of deals for General Export. They want everything. They want the entire Colonial trade—ships, supplies, personnel, everything. They're getting it, too, any and every way they can. They'll have Mars when they're through."

"Then what? They're still under government authority."

"Oh, it's long-range, Jeremy. You remember your history. There's a colonial phase, after discovery and exploration. Colonizing is a job in itself—development doesn't really set in for quite a while. Nowadays, of course, the whole process is enormously speeded up. You know the potentialities of Mars. Uranium, iron, diamond-coal and drugs. Why, it's an unlimited opportunity for whoever controls it. For perhaps two generations, Mars will look to Earth for government and guidance. But then there will be patriots, Jeremy. Earth will find herself with a competitor instead of a dominion. And the way that competitor will be run will gradually swing the direction of control the other way—or else. Genex isn't out after a world. Genex wants two worlds—the system—the galaxy, if you like. But it will be for Genex and its heirs; it won't be for the little guy."

Jeremy sat back and stared at her amazed. "You figured all that out yourself? I can't believe it. No, by heaven, I don't believe it. Whom are you quoting?"

"Hal Jedd," she said with an effort.

"Well, well, well!" He took out Hal's letter and opened it. Her eyes darted to it, to his face, and down again. "Don't play," Jeremy said grimly. "I know you've seen this. You and every stooge Genex could put on it." He glanced through the letter, speared a sentence with his finger, and read aloud: "'Phyllis Exeter due. I got quite chummy with her while she was out here in Thor City.'"

"That's what put me in this spot," she said with sudden bitterness. "Yes, I saw him. Lots. The word got around that he had developed something radical in the line of pipe stowage. He has a suitcase-size lab back of his office, you know. Well, I was put on it."

"You volunteered—isn't that more like it? You said, 'Let me at the sucker. I've been able to wind him and his dopey brother around my finger since we were kids; and besides, I have a little score to settle. They're one up on me.' That right?"

She almost laughed. "I didn't call him a sucker," she said faintly. She took a swallow of her drink. "Take care of the steak, will you, Jeremy? I'm hungry."

Jeremy took the raw steak out of the cold compartment. It was tenderized and seasoned. He slid it into the induction-heater.

"How do you like it?" he asked.

"Seared and rare," she answered.

He adjusted the controls and closed the drawer, while she continued.

"I saw a lot of Hal. He got under my skin, Jeremy. Not anything about him personally—I don't go for his type. These scholarly boys leave me cold. I like big men with blond hair, strong enough to smack a gal down when she deserves it, or even to keep their hands off her. And maybe with a little cleft in a square jaw—"

Unconsciously fingering just such a concavity on his chin, Jeremy threw back his blond head and snapped, "Baloney to you and your shopping lists! Go on with the yarn. What did get under your skin?"

"What he had to say about Genex. I don't know—maybe I never bothered to take it apart before. Maybe my paychecks and bonuses kept me from thinking. Whatever it was that happened, it happened so gradually that I didn't notice it. But the things he said about long-range thinking—well, here I was on the inside and knowing even more about what went on with Genex than he did. The more I looked at it, the less I liked it. Maybe I should have left Hal alone. Maybe I should have tuned him out while he talked. But, as I said before, he had me before I knew what was happening."

Jeremy smiled "Hal's like that. He has a theory that a quiet voice in a noisy room is louder than a shout. He thinks quietly and loud that way too," The centerpiece chimed softly and the drawer slid out. Jeremy took the plate-tongs from the rack and lifted the steak and its perfectly cooked side-dishes over to Phyllis.

"Thanks. Well, I met a boy at Fort Wargod. A blue-eyed innocent of a cadet. Maybe it was moonlight. Moonlight's twice as tricky on Mars, you know. Maybe it's because I'm a little crazy, and can't resist trying things out on people. Well, this kid needed to be impressed worse than anyone I ever met. Before I knew it we were on the parapet looking at Earth, hanging out there so bright and blue, and I was spilling all this stuff about colonies, dominions, and the patriotism of the second-generation Martian. Loose talk. Really, I don't know how much of it I believed myself."

She shook herself suddenly, all over, as if trying to wriggle out of something tight and hot. Pulling herself together with an effort, she cut into her steak busily.

"Well," she said after she had swallowed the first bite, "my blue-eyed babe in the woods turned out to be a Genex man, put there for the specific purpose of finding out where my indoctrination stood."

Jeremy roared with laughter, a great cruel burst of it. He cut it off instantly and leaned forward. "So it happened to you," he said viciously. "I'm mighty glad to hear it. Some sweet and gentle character made you open up your heart, did he? Tell me something, slicker—did you try to give him some of your company's stock?"

This hit home. In sudden anger she stopped eating and cursed Jeremy. Then all at once, she smiled and shrugged. It was an odd little gesture and the resignation in it made that something within him flinch again. Phyllis had tried so hard, for so long, to cover up that soft, lost part of her. She had succeeded so well, until now. She was such a magnificent product of her own determinations, and it hurt him to see such a product spoiled, even though he hated everything it represented. So he said, "I'm sorry," and to his surprise, the words tasted good in his mouth.

"So here I am," she said in a low voice. "I failed with Hal, as I should have expected. I got quite a carpeting for it, and for that business with the cadet. And then Hal wrote that letter. Genex carries the mails. Every big brain in the place, and a lot of little ones, has been racking over it ever since. And they put me on to you. This is supposed to be my last chance—my double or nothing play. If I get that process from you, I get back where I was. On probation, of course, but I'll string along with Genex. If I fail, I'm done. Outside of Genex there isn't much doing, and I don't doubt that I'm pretty thoroughly blacklisted."

"You are," he said flatly. "I get the score now. These plugs around here are supposed to keep you with me until you get the info. *Hmm.* Suppose I leave?"

"I go with you. I keep after you, I catch up with you some way, I keep trying.

"How long is this supposed to go on?"

"Until I get the process. Or until Genex gets the pipe hauling contract from the Government. In which case I'm automatically out."

"Suppose you quit trying?"

"Then I'm out, as of that moment."

"In other words, your fate is in my hands, to corn a phrase."

"I guess it is, Jeremy." And to his utter astonishment, she began to cry with her mouth open. For such an accomplished actress, she did it very badly indeed. Her heart was in it.

Jeremy sat back and watched her, his brain racing. Hal's letter had taken on a few new meanings, but not enough. "Be good, little man." The rest of that old routine was "And if you can't be good, be careful." Well, maybe he could have been more careful, but Phyllis seemed to have responded well enough to the bulldozer treatment. Jeremy knew what was the matter with her. She was scared. She had lived by her not inconsiderable wits for a long time, and the clear picture of the end of the line she was facing was a frightening one.

But what about the process? Now it was up to Jeremy to figure it out!

Hal had done his astute best to explain the process to Jeremy Jedd in that letter. Somewhere in that letter, somewhere in the odd fact of Phyllis's being here—in these three places were components of the process.

She was quieter now.

"Sorry," she sniffled. "I'm in a bad way, I guess. Do you know why I was crying? It was because you didn't get up and leave when I told you all this. You will help me, Jeremy? You will?"

"Help you? How can I?"

"Tell me the process." She leaned closer, excitedly. "Or tell me something almost as good as your process, but better than what Genex has.

"You're very flattering." She really thought he had the process, then. Be good, little man. He'd have to be. But *good.* "I gather Genex has set up a welding plant on Mars. Why are they worried?"

"Power," she answered. "There are only two power-piles on Mars, and they're worked to the limit. They're so heavy, with the shielding and all. Shipping space is so scarce, with foodstuffs, development equipment and so on, that piles aren't set up until they are absolutely essential. Power is rationed, and it is costing Genex a fortune for the piddling amount they need to process sheet stock into pipe. Their advantage, of course, is to procure the space for themselves and get rid of one more independent outfit."

"Uh-huh. The fight is really over a much bigger thing than pipe. *Hmm.* And the outfit that finds a way to ship pipe in less space than sheet stock, gets the contract and for once has a solid footing against the corporation's expansion."

"But how can you do it, Jeremy? How can you possibly ship pipe in less space than stacks of plastic sheet?"

He smiled. "You really think I'll tell you, don't you? I have no reason to trust you. You have thrown yourself on my mercy, more or less, and given me the choice of saving your skin—your career, anyway—I suppose you call it that—at the risk of having you hand the process to Genex and not only kill off Jedd & Jedd but also kill the brightest chance in fifty years of checking the monopoly. Nope. I'm telling you nothing." I wish someone would tell me, he added to himself.

"But you still stick around," she said thoughtfully. "You met me at the spaceport, you don't throw me to the wolves when you have a chance, you—why, you don't know the process yourself!"

"On the contrary. I'm just sitting here cruelly amusing myself. I've waited years to see you crawl."

"I'm not going to listen to you," she said tightly. "I think I'm right. The only thing I can do is to help you to figure it out. That letter. You. Me. The process is right here at this table, if we can only find out how to put it together."

"This is going to be very entertaining," said Jeremy, far more jovially than he felt. How could this girl, who in the long run operated so stupidly, be so incredibly sharp in detail? "Where would you start?"

"With the letter," she said promptly. She closed her eyes and her lips moved. It dawned on him that she had thoroughly memorized the letter. She opened her eyes wide and asked, "Who is Budgie?"

"A childhood companion," he said, a little taken aback.

"That's a lie. Every fairly close associate you have ever had in your life has been checked."

Jeremy's mouth slowly opened. Then he brought a hand crashing down on the table and bellowed with laughter.

"Do you mean to tell me," he gasped, "that Genex's investigators have been gravely looking through lists of my schoolmates, cousins, bartenders and dates looking for *Budgie?*"

"We—they tried everything," she said, and added, "Stop that silly cackling. Who was it?"

He held up an irritating forefinger. "Ah-ah! Manners, now. Let us act like ladies and gentlemen, chicken, or I send you to the salt mines."

"I'm sorry," she said angrily. He set his mouth. "I'm sorry," she said with a great deal more sincerity.

"Better," he said. "Now then, I don't think it'll hurt to tell you. Budgie was a parakeet we used to have. He was around very nearly twenty years. We gave him a fine funeral."

The girl stared at him, her eyes glittering with disbelief.

"And yet, according to that letter, the process is nothing Budgie couldn't have told you. Jeremy, I don't believe you. Who was Budgie?"

"So help me, the only Budgie I ever knew was that bird. He swore like a soybean farmer in a urea factory, he did. We called him Budgie because he was a budgerigar, or, to you, a Zebra Parakeet. A budgerigar is the talkingest bird that ever lived."

"What?" she said in disgust. "A creature with memory and no brains could tell you what the process is?" Jeremy started, and she asked, "What's the matter? Have a rush of brains to the head?"

While he fumbled for an answer, she leaned back with narrowed eyes. "I came awfully close to it that time, didn't I? Come clean, Jeremy. You've known about the process ever since you were a kid, now, haven't you?"

"You've got it," he mumbled. She's got it? Who's got what? He clapped his hand to his head. "Memory without brains. That's me."

They stared at each other. "If only I knew a little more about plastics," she breathed. "Or even about your brother. I'll bet if I knew as much about the way Hal's mind works as you do, I could sit right down and write that process out."

Jeremy stared at her and knew she told the truth. His was a quick mind as well as an encyclopedic one, but she was his master at quick intuitive reasoning. A wild plan flitted through his mind—to leap up and rush out, to draw an attack from one of the Genex men who waited patiently for Phyllis to do her work; to prefer charges against the corporation, perhaps. But he rejected it instantly.

They were too clever for that. They would let him go. One of their plastics engineers would work with Phyllis until some hunch she had gotten made sense to him. Then what? Well, either he would figure it out in time or he wouldn't. If not, he was sunk. If so, Genex would so radically underbid his pipe to drive him out that he would be sunk anyway.

"Hal!" The name slipped from his lips, so profound was his sudden wish for his brother. Hal could set him straight with a word, if only he could send the word.

"Me too," whispered Phyllis. "If only I could see Hal once, only for a minute, I'll bet I could—" Suddenly she dived into her handbag, clawing out a potpourri of feminine conglomerata. "Where is it? Where is—oh—here." She held a rectangular piece of plastic in her hand. It was blue, smooth, heavy.

"What's that?"

"Just a compact. A lighter. A torch. One of those things. But Hal gave it to me. And I'm just mystic enough to think it'll help me think. He had his hands on it. Didn't you know that all women—even modern women—are witches?" She closed her eyes, clutching the compact, frowning in concentration.

Staring at her, Jeremy frowned too, and thought harder than ever in his life before. Something about memory without brains. Something—and then a line in the letter swam before his mind's eye.

I'd like you to meet her when the rocketship docks. She really has what it takes.

"Give me that," he spat, and snatched it roughly out of her grasp. Instinctively, she reached for it. He batted her hand out of the way, hard. She sat on the edge of her chair, her nostrils dilated, rubbing her hand and watching him like a cat.

He turned it over and over, shook it, smelled it, felt it. He opened it, shook out the tinted powders, cracked the mirror retainer with his thumb and slid the glass out. There was nothing unusual about the compact. A little expensive, perhaps, but not unique at all. There was no trademark.

"Where did Hal get this?"

"He didn't say. Bought it, perhaps. Maybe he made it. He has a little outfit. Give it back to me!"

"I will not." Jeremy fell to studying it again.

"Jereee," she said sweetly.

He looked up. She was her old self. She was erect and beautiful and the color was back in her cheeks. Somewhere in a side corner of his mind, he deeply regretted the fact that he admired her so much. She put out her hand. "Give."

"Nope."

She glanced around. "It's evidence. I've been robbed. The property was forcibly taken from me by that man, officer," she said, mimicking a sweet, wronged young thing. "There we were sitting peacefully over a drink and a snack, when he went berserk and took it away from me and began tearing it apart." Her face went cold and direct again. "Would you tell the nice policeman exactly *why* you wanted to keep it, Jeremy?"

"Not while Genex and the police get along so nicely," he said grudgingly. "Okay. I'm open to compromise. You don't know the significance of this piece of plastic. You just might be wrong. If Genex's plastics division can't find out anything about it, you're away out of luck."

"Oh," she said. She glanced around at the Genex watchdogs and shivered. "What's your proposition?"

"I have to find out something more. Just what, I'm not sure. Now think carefully. Exactly what do you remember Hal's saying about this compact?"

"Why, he never said anything, much. Just some philosophical quip about women, about me and plastics. I don't remember it exactly."

"Try."

"It was—it was something like this." She paused, and he knew she was running over and over it in her mind, poking and prodding at it for hidden meanings. Finally she shrugged, and quoted, " 'I like giving you plastics, Phyl. Plastics are an analogical approach to women, and some of 'em come pretty close. Some day maybe we'll all be familiar with a plastic that will react differently under the same stimulus, the way you do. Laughter this time, tears the next, whichever seems to be expected.' I didn't think it was very flattering."

Jeremy stared at her, comprehension sparking, flaming, coruscating in his brain. He said hoarsely:

"Give me the compact. I've got to get it to a lab."

"No," she said firmly. She took it out of his unwilling hands. "Frankly, I don't know what you've figured out. But I will, if I kick it around long enough. If I can't, I know those who can. Well," she purred, arching her body, "I'd better run along, Jerry darling. Thank you *so* much for everything."

The hand that closed on her wrist seemed to be made of beryl steel. "Don't you move," Jeremy said. He said it in a way which kept her from moving. "You can't take that chance. You don't know enough. If you take that away, I'll never know either, and I'd see both of us dead first. I'll make a bargain. Once more. I must make a test on that compact. I can do it right here. Let me do it. You can watch. Whatever happens, your description will be enough for a plastics engineer. It will give us both a break. And if there really is a secret there, you'll have a chance of getting what you want. You'll *know.* You don't know now—you only guess."

It was a long time before she nodded her head.

When she did, he took the compact and, with his knife, scraped off a shaving and dropped it into the ash tray. He took a platehandler from the warm rack and touched the shaving. Then he put his cigarette to it. Then he held it with the platehandler and held it in the flame of his cigarette lighter. Part of it burned. He sniffed the smoke, nodded, and set the temperature regulator on the induction heater.

He dropped the compact in and closed the drawer.

"No!" she shouted. "You're burning it! You've got the process, and you're destroying it so I won't have a chance!" She lunged for the drawer. He caught her wrists, transferred them both to one of his powerful hands, and shook his head.

"Sit tight," he snapped.

The centerpiece chimed, and the drawer popped open. Their heads cracked together painfully as they bent to look inside. Neither noticed the pain.

In the bottom of the pan lay a twisted piece of blue plastic. It spread almost all the way across the roomy drawer. It was flat, and followed a series of regular convolutions. It dawned on both of them at the same moment what it was.

Script.

As if the plastic itself were the track of a writing-brush, it spelled the two words:

I REMEMBER

"That's for me," breathed Phyllis. "And I'm a dope. The memory without brains—even I know about that phenomenon. Now that I see it done, I remember a demonstration in school, where a cube was compression-molded into a spool-shape. When it was heated again, it slumped together and formed the original cube. A little sloppy, but a cube nevertheless. With a little refinement, I don't see why extruded pipe shouldn't be compression-molded into rods, bricks, or bookends and still come out pipe when it's heated. Beats sheet-stock welding a mile. Jeremy, my boy, you may have my melted-up old compact with my blessings. You may frame it and hang it over your lab bench when you come to work for Genex, as you must or starve. 'I remember.' I like that."

"You don't remember how badly you needed help, Phyllis," he said hoarsely. "My help."

"Plastics and women, my boy. Remember?" She rose like a queen, gathered up her belongings and drifted doorward, beckoning imperiously to the watchdogs. Ignoring Jeremy Jedd completely, they followed her out.

Abruptly Jeremy came to his senses with an inarticulate, animal noise and raced to the door. The lithe man with white hair at his temples stepped in front of him.

"Want something, chum?" he asked softly.

Jeremy raised a hand to sweep the man aside but his eye fell on what the man was holding in his hand. It was a rectangular leatherette needle case. Jeremy had seen them before. A touch of the case, a little pressure on a stud, and you were needled. And the variety of hypos used was peculiarly horrible.

They stood there, frozen, for a long instant. Then someone passed. A spaceport guard.

"Guard!" Jeremy rapped, leaping backward. "This man's threatening me. Needle!"

The guard bobbled a remarkable Adam's apple at them and then strode toward the white-templed man.

"Give it here, bud."

The man smiled, raised the case, snapped it open and extracted a cigarette. "A joke, guard. Perfectly harmless."

"Ha-ha!" said the guard with his mouth only. He clicked his lips shut and looked at Jeremy with one eyebrow raised. "You sure are jumpy, Blondy," he remarked, and strode off.

Jeremy controlled himself with a prodigious effort,.and swung on the older man. "Listen, you—"

The man blew smoke at Jeremy. "Better cool down, son," he said kindly. "We joke often, but not always. *Hold it!*" he snapped, watching Jeremy's darkening face. "You can butter me up and down these walls, but I'm only one of a couple of thousand that you'd have to whip afterward. Better go on back now and have another drink." And before Jeremy could move so much as a lip, the man was striding up the corridor in that way which did not seem to be swift.

Balked, frustrated, furious, Jeremy stood for a while and then turned back into the restaurant. He slouched back to his table, kicked the chair out and dropped into it. He could use that plastic memory stunt to stow pipe. Sure. And when he thought of the low bid that Genex would put up against him, his stomach turned over.

He glowered into the heater drawer where the blue plastic script told him placidly what he would never forget:

I REMEMBER

And then he thought of Hal's words to Phyllis.

The demonstrations supporting registered bids were made in a public hearing, in the vast offices of the Shipping Space Priority Board. The Space Commissioner, an oldster with a snowy lion's mane and the eyes of an eight-year-old child, had his wattles in his palm and his elbows on his desk. He was flanked by the featureless protocolloids of his well-peopled bureau.

In the wide area before him were three groups of people each hovering over a tangle of apparatus. Behind them were the rows of seats, for the interested public, one third of the seats occupied. The second demonstration was in progress. The first demonstrator and his helpers were dismantling their bulky machine—part brake, part automatic welder, it had produced several hundred feet of inch-and-a-half pipe out of a long and compact bale of sheet stock.

The galleries had regarded the performance as quite impressive, whether or not they knew that Winfield and Shock, who presented the process, was a General Export affiliate, brought in to establish a figment of competition.

General Export's management had shrewdly chosen a presentable demonstration by a more than presentable demonstrator. She was slender, poised, clear-eyed, clear-voiced, and her hair was green. She was saying:

"—and in spite of the question of simultaneous patent application, General Export will offer this pipe at a lower price per unit shipped than any competitor could conceivably meet, due to a secret treatment of the original plastic."

"Due to the secret mistreatment of competition," growled a man in the gallery, who had once owned a space-line.

The demonstrator walked gracefully to a stack of long, slender plastic rods beside her machine and lifted one. "Mr. Commissioner, this rod is twelve feet long and one sixteenth of an inch square. As you will observe, the rod is extremely flexible. Stowage of these rods will therefore be compact and economical, since rectangular holds are not necessary. Bundles of these rods will follow the curves, if any, of the retaining bulkheads, and therefore use every cubic inch of space economically. I shall now demonstrate the creation of usable seamless pipe from these rods."

She stepped over to her machine, slid the rod in at one end, and threw a lever. "This is a very simple heater. On Earth or Mars, particularly on Mars, it may be adequately operated by sun-mirrors, thereby tapping no local power-source."

There was a faint hiss. A small motor whined, and a twelve-foot length of pipe shot out with a dry clatter. She repeated the performance twice more and then bowed respectfully to the Commissioner, who said:

"Thank you very much, Miss Exeter. Next!"

A clerk sang, "Mr. Jeremy Jedd, of Jedd & Jedd! Process, pipe stowage, interplanetary!"

Jeremy stood up, ran off the customary courtesies of the applicant, and then said:

"I am deeply grateful to Miss Exeter for many things. One of these is her concise and well-presented description of the advantages of General Export's plastic-memory process. She has saved me much explanation, for my process is precisely the same. The difference lies in the plastic treatment before and after the processing you see here. I will say at the start that as regards price of the rods I am demonstrating, they cost at least five times as much as those shown by Miss Exeter. I am, apparently, drastically underbid."

Jeremy had to pause then to duck under the wave of comment that swept over the huge room. The Commissioner cleared his throat and raised a forefinger without moving his hand from his chin. A clerk raised a gavel without moving anything but his arm, and brought it down with a crash.

"Get on with it," growled the Commissioner. His tone said, If you can't compete with the other bids, you idiot, why waste my time, or even that of these thousand other people?

Jeremy stepped to his machine, which was almost a duplicate of the one Phyllis Exeter had used, and lifted an end of one of his rods. He did not attempt to lift it all at once; apparently it was quite heavy.

What followed was the same as the previous showing, with one noticeable exception; the pipe came out in a twenty-foot length. Again the room buzzed. This time Jeremy held up his hand. "The greater length of the pipe is an advantage over these other methods, but not the greatest," he said calmly. He threw the heater-control over again—

Without loading in another rod!

A twenty-foot length of pipe joined its predecessor.

Again he pulled the control, and again. Each time a twenty-foot pipe was produced, until six of them lay side by side on the floor. The air above them shimmered very slightly. They were uniform and perfect.

"Mr. Commissioner, I ask that space for shipment of pipe to Mars be allotted to my company because the stowage is as compact as any product on the market, because I can ship approximately nine point three times as much pipe per cube unit as my nearest competitor, and because I can deliver pipe per unit length at eleven per cent cheaper than anyone else on earth! And that in spite of the apparently prohibitively low bid of Miss Exeter's most altruistic firm. Thank you, gentlemen."

"Just a minute, young man!" said the Commissioner. "You have a most remarkable process. I—ah—hear comments to the effect that the pipe was concealed in the machine. Can you give some layman's explanation of this extraordinary effect?"

Jeremy smiled as he glanced at the machine in front of him.

"Certainly, sir. My company, you may remember, secured a portion of the space allotted to pipe shipments during your last session, by devising the present method of nesting the smaller diameters of pipe inside the larger ones—a method which was not patentable, which my competitors were slow to discover, but quick to copy.

"In the present case, I very much fear that they have repeated their lack of—if I may say it—logical thoroughness. You see, my pipe is still nested, one inside the other, six taking the space of one, and the whole compressed into the rods you see here."

"You nest pipe of the same diameter?" said the Commissioner incredulously; and that odd, mad, detached part of Jeremy's mind noticed hilariously that the oldster's bright eyes blinked with repressed anger.

"Yes sir, I do, in effect. But it is a question of density. The inner pipe is a condensed plastic—a patented process, by the way. This plastic, while undergoing the "memorizing" phenomenon so beautifully explained by Miss Exeter, restores its original density as well as its original form. The inner pipe, then, is simply condensed more than the one which surrounds it, and so on until the six are nested. Then the whole is compressed, molded into rods of precisely the dimensions of those admirably compact ones produced by General Export.

"Now, when heat treated, the outer pipe returns to its original form and is automatically ejected from the machine. It has, of course, pre-heated the next pipe, which pre-heats the one after. It takes, actually, far less heat per unit length to restore my pipe than it does to restore the pipe of—ah—any of my competitors. A small advantage, however, and merely hair-splitting under the circumstances."

"I feel you deserve many congratulations, Mr. Jedd. Purely as a matter of personal interest, might I ask how you came to discover such a remarkable effect?"

"Indeed you may, Mr. Commissioner. The process was developed by my brother on Mars. He enlisted the courtesy and kindness of a messenger to send me a sample. It was in the form of a compact—a lady's compact—and when heat treated it separated into a plastic sheet which formed in script the words 'I remember.'"

Jeremy grinned broadly. "It was some time before I realized that there was anything more to be learned from the sample, for the words covered the rest of it. When I put this—this message into my pocket, I saw the rest of the plastic and, guided by a hint in a rather cryptic verbal message concerning women and plastics, I again treated the sample. I got more script. It read, 'Density Two.' Then I knew what he was driving at. I treated it again and got 'Density Three' and still again and got"—he smiled—"a length of pipe. After that it was little trouble for me to analyze the plastic and develop the condensing treatment—I beg your pardon. I think somebody had better get Miss Exeter a glass of water. . . ."

They met that evening, and perhaps it was by accident. She was standing in the shadow near his apartment building when he came home from the lab,

"Jerry?"

"Phyllis! I—I'm sorry."

"Sorry? That's what you say when you realize you did a wrong. I don't think you mean that. Isn't it more of a kind of—pity?"

He did not deny it. He said, "What can I do for you?"

"I—I need a job now."

He took her hand and drew her into the pale light. Her hand lay in his like something asleep. "I couldn't give you a job, Phyl."

"Yes, I know, I know. I have never been—faithful. Jerry, I haven't been faithful to myself."

"I don't understand. You've always—"

"Always thought I could take 'em or leave 'em alone. Not so, Jeremy."

"Oh," he said. "Oh, that." He squeezed her hand a little. "Your hands are soft. Maybe that's part of the trouble, Phyl."

"I think I know what you mean. There are jobs for me, but—"

"—not jobs for your wit or your wits."

"I see. I think I can—get there, Jerry."

"I know you can. Goodbye, Phyllis."

"Goodbye, Jeremy."

There is one job which centuries of human progress has not done away with. No one has developed a self-washing window. When one of mankind's monuments to himself reaches a thousand feet into the air, and its windows must be washed, that washing is a job for a rare type of human. He must be strong, steady, and brave. He must live, away from his job, in ways which do not unfit him for it.

Jeremy was glad when he heard Phyllis was doing this work. He knew then what he had always guessed—that some day she would "get there." He knew it in his heart.

There Is No Defense

Cursing formality, Belter loosened his tunic and slouched back in his chair. He gazed at each of the members of the Joint Solar Military Council in turn, and rasped: "You might as well be comfortable, because, so help me, if I have to chain you to this table from now until the sun freezes, I'll run off this record over and over again until someone figures an angle. I never heard of anything yet, besides The Death, that couldn't be whipped one way or another. There's a weakness somewhere in this thing. It's got to be on the record. So we'll just keep at the record until we find it. Keep your eyes peeled and the hair out of your eyes. That goes for you too, Leess."

The bottled Jovian shrugged hugely. The infrared sensory organ on its cephalothorax flushed as Belter's words crackled through the translator. Glowering at the creature, Belter quenched a flash of sympathy. The Jovian was a prisoner in other things besides the bottle which supplied its atmosphere and gravity. Leess represented a disgraced and defeated race, and its position at the conference table was a hollow honor—a courtesy backed by heat and steel and The Death. But Belter's glower did not change. There was no time, now, to sympathize with those whose fortunes of war were all bad ones.

Belter turned to the orderly and nodded. A sigh, compounded of worry and weariness, escaped the council as one man. The lights dimmed, and again the record appeared on the only flat wall of the vast chamber.

First the astronomical data from the Plutonian Dome, showing the first traces of the Invader approaching from the direction of the Lyran Ring— Equations, calculations, a sketch, photographs. These were dated three years back, during the closing phases of the Jovian War. The Plutonian Dome was not serviced at the time, due to the emergency. It was a completely automatic observatory, and its information was not needed during the interplanetary trouble. Therefore it was not equipped with instantaneous transmissions, but neatly reeled up its information until it could be visited after the war. There was a perfectly good military observation base on Outpost, the retrograde moon of Neptune, which was regarded as quite adequate to watch the Solar System area. That is, there *had* been a base there—

But, of course the Invader was well into the System before anyone saw the Pluto records, and by that time—

The wall scene faded into the transcript of the instantaneous message received by Terran HQ, which was rigged to accept any alarm from all of the watch posts.

The transcript showed the interior of the Neptunian military observatory, and cut in apparently just before the Sigmen heard the alarm. One was sprawled in a chair in front of the finder controls; the other, a rangy lieutenant with the burned skin of his Martian Colonial stock, stiffened, looked up at the blinking "General Alarm" light as the muted, insistent note of the "Stations" bell began to thrum from the screen. The sound transmission was very good; the councilmen could distinctly hear the lieutenant's sharp intake of breath, and his voice was quite clear as he rapped:

"Colin! Alarm. Fix!"

"Fix, sir," said the enlisted man, his fingers flying over the segmented controls. "It's deep space, sir," he reported as he worked. "A Jovian, maybe—flanking us."

"I don't think so. If what's left of their navy could make any long passes at all, you can bet it would be at Earth. How big is it?"

"I haven't got . . . oh, here it is, sir," said the e.m. "An object about the size of a Class III-A Heavy."

"Ship?"

"Don't know, sir. No heat radiation from any kind of jets. And the magnetoscope is zero."

"Get a chaser on him."

Belter's hands tightened on the table edge. Every time he saw this part of the record he wanted to get up and yell, *"No, you idiot! It'll walk down your beam!"* The chaserscope would follow anything it was trained on, and bring in a magnified image. But it took a mess of traceable vhf to do it.

Relaxing was a conscious effort. *Must be slipping,* he thought glumly, *wanting to yell at those guys. Those guys are dead.*

In the picture recording, a projection of the chaserscope's screen was flashed on the observatory screen. Staring fearfully at this shadow picture of a shadow picture, the council saw again the familiar terrible lines of the Invader—squat, unlovely, obviously not designed for atmospheric work; slab-sided, smug behind what must have been foolproof meteor screens, for the ship boldly presented flat side and bottom plates to anything which might be thrown at her.

"It's a ship, sir!" said the e.m. unnecessarily. "Seems to be turning on its short axis. Still no drive emanations."

"Range!" said the lieutenant into a wall mike. Three lights over it winked on, indicating the batteries were manned and ready for ranging information. The lieutenant, his eyes fixed on the large indicators over the enlisted man's head, hesitated a moment, then said, "Automatics! Throw your ranging gear to our chaser."

The three lights blinked, once each. The battery reporters lit up, showing automatic control as the medium and heavy launching tubes bore round to the stranger.

The ship was still on the screen, turning slowly. Now a dark patch on her flank could be seen—an open port. There was a puff of escaping gas, and *something* appeared whirling briefly away from the ship, toward the scanner. They almost saw it clearly—and then it was gone.

"They threw something at us, sir!"

"Track it!"

"Can't sir!"

"You saw the beginning of that trajectory! It was coming this way."

"Yes sir. But the radar doesn't register it. I don't see it on the screen either. Maybe it's a warper?"

"Warpers are all theory, Colin. You don't bend radar impulses around an object and then restore them to their original direction. If this thing is warping at all, it's warping light. It—"

And then all but the Jovian closed their eyes as the screen repeated that horror—the bursting inward of the observatory's bulkhead, the great jagged blade of metal that flicked the lieutenant's head straight into the transmission camera.

The scene faded, and the lights went up.

"Slap in the next re— Hold it!" Belter said. "What's the matter with Hereford?"

The Peace delegate was slumped in his chair, his head on his arms, his arms on the table. The Martian Colonial representative touched him, and Hereford raised his seamed, saintly face:

"Sorry."

"You sick?"

Hereford sat back tiredly. "Sick?" he repeated vaguely. He was not a young man. Next to that of the Jovian, his position was the strangest of all. He represented a group, as did each of the others. But not a planetary group. He represented the amalgamation of all organized pacifistic thought in the System. His chair on the Joint Solar Military Council was a compromise measure, the tentative answer to an apparently unanswerable question—can a people do without the military? Many thought people could. Some thought not. To avoid extremism either way, the head of an unprecedented amalgamation of peace organizations was given a chair on the JSMC. He had the same vote as a planetary representative. "Sick?" he repeated in a whispering baritone. "Yes, I rather think so." He waved a hand at the blank wall. "Why did the Invader do it? So pointless ... so stupid." He raised puzzled eyes, and Belter felt a new kind of sympathy. Hereford's hollow-ground intelligence was famous in four worlds. He was crackling, decisive; but now he could only ask the simplest of questions, like a child too tired to be badly frightened.

"Yeah—why?" asked Belter. "Oh ... never mind the rest of the record," he added suddenly. "I don't know how the rest of you feel, but at the moment I'm hypnotized by the jet-blasted thing.

"*Why,* Hereford wants to know. If we knew that, maybe we could plan something. Defenses, anyway."

Somebody murmured: "It's not a campaign. It's murder."

"That's it. The Invader reaches out with some sort of a short-range disrupting bomb and wipes out the base on Outpost. Then it wanders into the System, washes out an uninhabited asteroid beacon, drifts down through the shield screening of Titan and kills off half the population with a cyanogen-synthesizing catalyst. It captures three different scanner-scouts, holding them with some sort of a tractor beam, whirling them around like a stone on a string, and letting them go straight at the nearest planet. Earth ships, Martian, Jovian—doesn't matter. It can outfly and outfight anything we have so far, except—"

"Except The Death," whispered Hereford. "Go on, Belter. I knew it was coming to this."

"Well, it's true! And then the cities. If it ever drops a disrupter like that"—he waved at the wall, indicating the portion of the record they had just seen—"on a large city, there wouldn't be any point in even looking for it, let alone rebuilding it. We can't communicate with the Invader—if we send out a general signal it ignores us, and if we send out a beam it charges us or sends one of those warping disrupter bombs. We can't even surrender to it! It just wanders through the System, changing course and speed from moment to moment, and every once in a while taking a crack at something."

The Martian member glanced at Hereford, and then away. "I don't see why we've waited so long. I saw Titan, Belter. In another century it'll be dead as Luna." He shook his head. "No pre-Peace agreement can stand in the way of the defense of the System no matter how solemn the agreement was. I voted to outlaw The Death, too. I don't like the idea of it any more than . . . than Hereford there. But circumstances alter cases. Are we going to sacrifice everything the race has built just for an outdated principle? Are we going to sit smugly behind an idealistic scrap of paper while some secret weapon chops us down bit by bit?"

"Scrap of paper," said Hereford. "Son, have you read your ancient history?"

The translator hissed. Through it, Leess spoke. The flat, unaccented words were the barest framework for the anger which those who knew Jovians could detect by the sudden paling of the creature's sensory organ. "Leess object phrase secret weapon. Man from Mars suggest Invader Jovian work."

"Cool down, Leess," Belter said, reaching over and firmly putting the Martian back in his seat. "Hey you—watch your language or you'll go back to the canals to blow the rust off supersoy. Now, Leess; I rather think the delegate from Mars let his emotions get the better of him. No one thinks that the Invader is Jovian. It's from deep space somewhere. It has a drive far superior to anything we've got, and the armament . . . well, if Jupiter had anything like that, you wouldn't have lost the war. And then there was Titan. I don't think Jovians would kill off so many of their own just to camouflage a new secret weapon."

The Martian's eyebrows lifted a trifle. Belter frowned, and the Martian's face went forcibly blank. The Jovian relaxed.

Addressing the Council generally, but looking at the Martian, Belter gritted: "The war is over. We're all Solarians and the Invader is a menace to our System. After we get rid of the Invader we'll have time to tangle with each other. Not before. Is that clear?"

"No human trust Jupiter. No man trust Leess," sulked the Jovian. "Leess no think. Leess no help. Jupiter better off dead than not trusted."

Belter threw up his hands in disgust. The sensitivity and stubbornness of the Jovian were well known. "If there's a clumsy, flatfooted way of doing things, a Martian'll find it," he growled. "Here we need every convolution of every brain here. The Jovian has a way of thinking different enough so he might help us crack this thing, and you have to go and run him out on strike."

The Martian bit his lips. Belter turned to the Jovian. "Leess, please—come off your high horse. Maybe the Solar System is a little crowded these days, but we all have to live in it. Are you going to cooperate?"

"No. Martian man no trust Jupiter. Mars die, Jupiter die, Earth die. Good. Nobody not trust Jupiter." The creature creased inward upon itself, a movement as indicative as the thrusting out of a lower lip.

"Leess is in this with the rest of us," said the Martian. "We ought to—"

"That'll do!" barked Belter. "You've said enough, chum. Concentrate on the Invader and leave Leess alone. He has a vote on this council and by the same token, he has the right to refrain from voting."

"Whose side are you on?" flashed the Martian, rising.

Belter came up with him, but Hereford's soft, deep voice came between them like a barrier. The Peace delegate said: "He's on the side of the System. All of us must be. We have no choice. You Martians are fighting men. Do you think you can separate yourselves from the rest of us and stop the Invader?"

Flushed, the Martian opened his mouth, closed it again, sat down. Hereford looked at Belter, and he sat down, too. The tension in the chamber lessened, but the matter obviously relegated itself to the "For Further Action" files in at least two men's minds.

Belter gazed at his fingers until they would be still without effort, and then said quietly: "Well, gentlemen, we've tried everything. There is no defense. We've lost ships, and men, and bases. We will lose more. If the Invader can be destroyed, we can be sure of a little time, at least, for preparation."

"Preparation?" asked Hereford.

"Certainly! You don't think for a minute that that ship isn't, or won't soon be, in communication with its own kind? Suppose we can't destroy it. It will be able to go back where it came from, with the news that there's a culture here for the taking, with no weapon powerful enough to touch them. You can't be so naive as to believe that this one ship is the only one they have, or the only one we'll ever see! Our only course is to wipe out this ship and then prepare for a full-scale invasion. If it doesn't come before we're prepared, our only safe course will be to carry the invasion to them, wherever they may be!"

Hereford shook his head sadly. "The old story."

Belter's fist came down with a crash. "Hereford. I *know* that Peace Amalgamated is a great cultural stride forward. I *know* that to de-condition the public on three planets and a hundred colonies from the peaceful way of life is a destructive move. But—can you suggest a way of keeping the peaceful way and saving our System? Can you?"

"Yes ... if ... if the Invaders can be persuaded to follow the peaceful way."

"When they won't communicate? When they commit warlike acts for nothing—without plan, without conquest, apparently for the sheer joy of destruction? Hereford—we're not dealing with anything Solarian. This is some life-form that is so different in its aims and its logic that the only thing we can do is reciprocate. Fire with fire! You talk of your ancient history. Wasn't fascism conquered when the democratic nations went all but fascist to fight them?"

"No," said Hereford firmly. "The fruits of fascism were conquered. Fascism itself was conquered only by democracy."

Belter shook his head in puzzlement. "That's irrelevant. I ... think," he added, because he was an honest man. "To get back to the Invader: we have a weapon with which we can destroy him. We can't use it now because of Peace Amalgamated; because the Solarian peoples have determined to outlaw it forever. The law is specific: The Death is not to be used for any purposes, under any circumstances. We, the military, can say we want it until our arteries harden, but our chances of getting it are negligible unless we have public support in repealing the law. The Invader has been with us for eighteen months or more, and in spite of his depredations, there is no sign that the public would support repeal. Why?" He stabbed out a stumpy forefinger. "Because they follow *you*, Hereford. They have completely absorbed your quasi-religious attitude of ... what was your phrase?"

"'Moral Assay.'"

"Yeah—Moral Assay. The test of cultural stamina. The will power to stand up for a principle in spite of emergencies, in spite of drastic changes in circumstances. A good line, Hereford, but unless you retract it, the public won't. We could bulldoze 'em into it, maybe; and maybe we'd have a revolution on our hands, get a lot of people killed, and wind up with a bunch of dewy-eyed idealists coming out on top, ready to defend the principles of peace with guns if they have to draft every able-bodied Solarian in the System. Meanwhile the Invader—and perhaps, by that time, his pals—will continue to circulate around, taking a crack at any target he happens to admire. Already the crackpots are beginning to yell about the Invader being sent to test their love of peace, and calling this the second year of the Moral Assay."

"He won't back down," said the Martian suddenly. "Why should he? The way he is, he's set for life."

"You have a lousy way of putting things!" snapped Belter, wondering *How much does personal power mean to the old saint?*

"Why this pressure?" asked Hereford gently. "You, Belter, with your martial rationalizing, and our Martian colleague here, with his personal insults—why not put it to a vote?"

Belter studied him. Was there a chance that the old man would accept the wishes of the majority here? The majority opinion of the Council was not necessarily the majority opinion of the System. And besides—how many of the Council would go along with Hereford if he chose to vote against it?

He took a deep breath. "We've got to know where we stand," he said. "Informally, now—shall we use The Death on the Invader? Let's have a show of hands."

There was a shuffling of feet. All the men looked at Hereford, who sat still with his eyes downcast. The Martian raised his hand defiantly. The Phoebe-Titan Colonial delegate followed suit. Earth. The Belt. Five, six—eight. Nine.

"Nine," said Belter. He looked at the Jovian, who looked back, unblinking. Not voting. Hereford's hands were on the table.

"That's three-quarters," Belter said.

"Not enough," answered Hereford. "The law stipulates *over* three-quarters."

"You know what my vote is."

"Sorry, Belter. You can't vote. As chairman, you are powerless unless all members vote, and then all you can do is establish a tie so that the matter can be referred for further discussion. The regulations purposely keep a deciding vote out of the Chair, and with the membership. I . . . frankly, Belter, I can't be expected to go further than this. I have refrained from voting. I have kept you from voting. If that keeps The Death from being used—"

Belter's knuckles cracked. He thought of the horror at Outpost, and the choking death on Titan, and what had happened to their asteroid. It and its abandoned mine workings had flared up like a baby nova, and what was left wouldn't dirty a handkerchief. It was a fine thing for every Solarian that at long last a terrible instrument of war had been outlawed, this time by the unquestionable wish of the people. It would be a bad thing for civilization if an exception should be made to this great rule. It was conceivable that, once the precedent was established, the long-run effects on civilization would be worse than anything the Invader could do. And yet—all his life Belter had operated under a philosophy which dictated action. Do something. It may be wrong, but—*do* something.

"May I speak with you alone?" he asked Hereford.

"If it is a matter which concerns the Council—"

"It concerns you only. A matter of ideology."

Hereford inclined his head and rose. "This won't take long," said Belter over his shoulder, as he let the peace delegate precede him into an antechamber.

"Beat it, Jerry," he said to the guard. The man saluted and left.

Belter leaned back against a desk, folded his arms and said: "Hereford, I'm going to tear this thing right down to essentials. If I don't, we can spend the rest of our lives in arguing about social necessities and cultural evolution and the laws of probability as applied to the intentions of the Invader. I am going to ask you some questions. Simple ones. Please try to keep the answers simple."

"You know I prefer that."

"You do. All right—the whole basis of the Peace movement is to prevent fighting . . . on the grounds that there is always a better way. Right?"

"That is right."

"And the Peace movement recognizes no need for violence in any form, and no conceivable exception to that idea."

"That is right."

"Hereford—pay close attention. You and I are in here because of the Invader, and because of the refusal of Peace Amalgamated to allow the use of the only known counter-measure."

"Obviously."

"Good. Just one more thing. I hold you in higher regard than any other man I know. And the same goes for the work you have done. Do you believe that?

Hereford smiled slowly and nodded. "I believe it."

"Well, it's true," said Belter, and with all his strength brought his open hand across Hereford's mouth.

The older man staggered back and stood, his fingers straying up to his face. In his eyes was utter disbelief as he stared at Belter, who stood again with his arms folded, his face impassive. The disbelief was slowly clouded over by puzzlement, and then hurt began to show. "Why—"

But before he could say another word, Belter was on him again. He crossed to Hereford's chest, and when the Peace delegate's hands came down, he struck him twice more on the mouth. Hereford made an inarticulate sound and covered his face. Belter hit him in the stomach.

Hereford moaned, turned, and made for the door. Belter dove, tackled him. They slid into a thrashing heap on the soft carpeting. Belter rolled clear, pulled the other to his feet and hit him again. Hereford shook his head and began to sink down, his arms over his head. Belter lifted him again, waited for just the right opening, and his hand flashed through for still another stinging slap across the mouth. Hereford grunted, and before Belter quite knew what was happening, he came up with one great blasting right that landed half on Belter's dropped chin, half on his collar bone. Belter came up off the floor in a cloud of sparks and fell heavily six feet away. He looked up to see Hereford standing over him, big fists bunched.

"Get up," said the Peace delegate hoarsely.

Belter lay back, put his hands under his head, spat out some blood, and began to laugh.

"Get up!"

Belter rolled over and got slowly to his feet. "It's all over, Hereford. No more rough stuff, I promise you."

Hereford backed off, his face working. "Did you think," he spat, "that you could resort to such childish, insane measures to force me into condoning murder?"

"Yup," said Belter.

"You're mad," said Hereford, and went to the door.

"Stop!"

There was a note of complete command in Belter's voice. It was that note, and the man behind it, which had put Belter where he was. Equally startling was the softness of his voice as he said: "Please come here, Hereford. It isn't like you to leave a thing half understood."

If he had said "Half finished," he would have lost the play. Hereford came slowly back, saying ruefully: "I know you, Belter. I know there's a reason for this. But it better be good."

Belter stood where he had been, leaning against the desk, and he folded his arms. "Hereford," he said, "one more simple question. The Peace movement recognizes no need for violence in any form, and no conceivable exception to that idea." It sounded like a recording of the same words, said a few minutes before, except for his carefully controlled breathing.

Hereford touched his bruised mouth. "Yes."

"Then," Belter grinned, "why did you hit me?"

"Why? Why did you hit *me?*"

"I didn't ask you that. Please keep it simple. Why did you hit me?"

"It was . . . I don't know. It happened. It was the only way to make you stop."

Belter grinned. Hereford stumbled on. "I see what you're doing. You're trying to make some parallel between the Invader and your attack on me. But you attacked me unexpectedly, apparently without reason—"

Belter grinned more widely.

Hereford was frankly floundering now. "But I . . . I had to strike you, or I . . . I—"

"Hereford," said Belter gently, "shall we go back now, and vote before that eye of yours blackens?"

The three Death ships, each with its cover of destroyer escorts, slipped into the Asteroid Belt. *Delta,* the keying unit, was flanked on each side by the opposed twins *Epsilon* and *Sigma,* which maintained a rough thousand-mile separation from the key. Behind them, on Earth, they had left a froth of controversy. Editorial comment on the air and in print, both on facsimile and the distributed press, was pulling and hauling on the age-old question of the actions of duly elected administrators. We are the people. We choose these men to represent us. What must we do when their actions run contrary to our interest?

And—do they run contrary? How much change can there be in a man's attitude, and in the man himself, between the time he is elected and the time he votes on a vital measure? Can we hark back to our original judgment of the man and trust his action as we trusted him at election time?

And again—the old bugaboo of security. When a legislative body makes a decision on a military matter, there must be news restrictions. The Death was the supreme weapon. Despite the will of the majority, there were still those who wanted it for their own purposes; people who felt it had not been used enough in the war; others who felt it should be kept assembled and ready, as the teeth in a dictatorial peace. As of old, the mass of the people had to curb its speech, and sometimes its thought, to protect itself against the megalomaniac minorities.

But there was one man who suffered. Elsewhere was anger and intellectual discourse, ethical delvings and even fear. But in one man, supremely, existed the struggle between ethics and expediency. Hereford alone had the power to undo his own work. His following would believe and accept when he asked them to make this exception. Having made it, they would follow no more, and there was no place for him on Earth.

His speech had been simple, delivered without a single flickering of his torture on the fine old face. Once the thing was done, he left Earth in a way foreign to everything he had ever believed, or spoken, or recommended. He, the leader of Peace Amalgamated, who regarded with insistent disfavor the very existence of weapons, left Earth with Belter, and shared the officer's quarters of a warship. Not only was it a warship, but it was the keying unit *Delta,* under the command of "Butcher" Osgood, trigger man of The Death.

For months they tracked the Invader, using their own instruments and information relayed to them by various outposts. Under no circumstances did they use tracers. One observation post and seven warships had been crushed because of that. The Invader's reaction to a tight beam was instant and terrible. Therefore, they were limited to light reflection—what there was of it, even from the bold, bright flanks of the marauder—and the detection of the four types of drive radiations used by the ship at different accelerations.

The body of descriptive matter on the invader increased, and there were certain irrefutable conclusions. The crew of the Invader were colloidal life, like all known life, and would be subject to The Death. This was deduced by the fact that the ship was enclosed, pressurized, and contained an atmosphere of some sort, which precluded the theoretically suggested "energy" and "crystalline" life-forms. The random nature of the enemy's vicious and casual attacks caused more controversy than almost any other factor; but as time went on, it became obvious that what the ship was doing was calling forth any attack of which the System might be capable. It had been bombed, rayed, and attempts had been made to ram. It was impervious. How long would it stay? When would its commanders conclude that they had seen the worst and, laughing, go back into the depths to bring reinforcements? And was there anything—anything at all—besides The Death that could reach the Invader, or stop him, or destroy him, or even let him know fear?

Right up until D-day—Death-day—the billions who had followed Hereford hoped that some alternative could be found, so that at least their earlier resolutions would be followed in letter if not in spirit. Many of them worked like slaves to this end, and that was the greatest anomaly of all, for all the forces of Peace were engaged in devising deadly methods and engines for use as alternative to The Death. They failed. Of course they failed.

There came a day when they had to strike. The Invader had all but vanished into the celestial north, only to come hurtling back in a great curve which would pass through the plane of the ecliptic just beyond the orbit of Jupiter. The Invader's trajectory was predictable despite his almost unbelievable maneuverability—even for him there were limits of checking and turning, which was another fact indicating colloidal life. There was no way of knowing whether he was coming back to harass the planets, or whether he was making one last observation before swinging through the System and away from Sol, back to the unknown hell which had spawned him. But whether it was attack or withdrawal he had to be smashed. There might never be another chance.

The three Death ships moved out from the Belt, where they had lain quiet amongst the other masses floating in that great ring of detritus. Still keeping their formation, they blasted away with crushing acceleration, their crews dopey with *momentomine.* Their courses were set to intersect that of the Invader, or close enough to bring them well within range of The Death—twelve to twenty thousand miles. Delicate, beamless scanners checked the enemy's course moment by moment, making automatic corrections and maintaining the formation of the three ships.

Delta was Earth-manned, *Epsilon* a Martian ship, and *Sigma* belonged to the Colonials. Originally, the plan had been to scatter Colonials through the three ships, and use a Jovian craft. But Leess, as the Jovian representative, had vetoed any Jovian participation, an action which had brought about a violent reawakening of antipathies toward the major planet. Public feeling was so loaded against the use of The Death that the responsibility must be shared. Jupiter's stubborn and suicidal refusal to share it was inflexible; the Jovian solidarity was as thorough as ever.

Four days out, the master controls dropped the acceleration to 1G, and the air conditioners blasted out enough superoxygen to counteract the acceleration drug. Personnel came to full life again, and the command gathered on the bridge of *Delta.* Hereford was there too, standing well back, his face misleadingly calm, his eyes flicking from the forward screen to the tactical chart, from Belter's absorbed face to the undershot countenance of Commander Osgood.

Osgood looked over his shoulder at the Peace leader. His voice was gravel in a wire sieve as he said: "I still don't like that guy hanging around here. You sure he won't be better off in his quarters?"

"We've been over that," said Belter tiredly. "Commander, maybe I'm out of order, but would it be too much trouble for you to speak directly to him once in a while?"

"I am satisfied," smiled Hereford. "I quite understand his attitude.

I have little to say to him, and much to say about him, which is essentially his position as far as I am concerned. It is no more remarkable that he is unfamiliar with politeness than that I should be ignorant of spatial ballistics."

Belter grinned. "O.K., O.K.—don't mind me, I'm just a poor military man trying to make peace. I'll shut up and let you and the Butcher have your inimical *status quo.*"

"I'll need a little quiet here for a while, if it's all the same to you, Councilman," said Osgood. He was watching the tactical chart. The red spot representing *Epsilon* was at the far right, the blur of *Sigma* at the left, and down at the bottom was *Delta*'s green spark. A golden bar in the center of the chart showed the area on the ecliptical plane at which the Invader could be expected to pass through, and just above it was a white spot showing the Invader himself.

Osgood touched a toggle which added a diagram to the chart—a positioning diagram showing the placement of the three Death ships in relation to the target. *Sigma* and *Epsilon* were exactly in the centers of their white positioning circles; *Delta* was at the lower edge of the third circle. Osgood made a slight adjustment in the drive circuit.

"Positioning is everything," Belter explained to Hereford. "The Death field is a resultant—a violent node of vibrations centering on the contiguous focal points of the opposed fields from *Sigma* and *Epsilon.* The beam from *Delta*—that's us—kicks it off. There's an enormous stress set up at that focal point, and our beam tears into it. The vibration changes frequency at random and with violence. It has been said that the fabric of space itself vibrates. That's learned nonsense. But fluids do, and gases, of course, and colloids worst of all."

"What would happen if the positions were not taken exactly?"

"Nothing. The two focal points of the concentrated fields from *Epsilon* and *Sigma* would not coincide, and *Delta*'s beam would be useless. And it *might* have the unhappy result of calling the Invader down on us. Not right away—he's going too fast at right angles to our course—but I'm not crazy about the idea of being hunted down by that executioner."

Hereford listened gravely, watching Osgood, watching the chart. "Just how great is the danger of The Death's spreading like ripples in a pool—out in every direction from the node?"

"Very little, the way it's set up. The node moves outward away from our three ships—again a resultant, strictly according to the parallelogram of force. How long it lasts, how intense it gets, how far it will go—we never know. It changes with what it encounters. Mass intensifies it and slows it down. Energy of almost any kind accelerates and gradually seems to dissipate it. And it varies for other reasons we don't understand yet. Setting it up is a very complicated business, as you have seen. We don't dare kick it off in such a way that it might encounter any of the planets, if it should happen to last long enough. We have to clear space between us and Outside of all shipping."

Hereford shook his head slowly. "The final separation between death and destruction," he mused. "In ancient times, armies met on battlefields and used death alone to determine the winner. Then, gradually, destruction became the most important factor—how much of the enemy's material could you destroy? And then, with the Atomic Wars, and the Dust, death alone became the end of combat again. Now it has come full circle, and we have found a way to kill, to punish and torture, to dissolve, slowly and insistently, colloidal cells, and still leave machines unharmed. This surpasses the barbarism of jellied gasoline. It takes longer, and—"

"It's complete," Belter finished.

"Stations!"

Osgood's voice sliced raggedly through the quiet bridge. The screen-studded bulkhead beside him winked and flickered with acknowledgments, as tacticians, technicians, astrogators, ballistics men, and crewmen reported in. All three ships were represented, and a master screen collected and summarized the information, automatically framing the laggards' screen with luminous red. There was little of the red showing, and in seconds it disappeared. Osgood stepped back, glanced at the master screen and then at the chart. On it, the ship symbols were centered in their tactical circles.

The commander turned away and for the first time in these weary months he spoke directly to Hereford: "Would you like the honor of triggering?"

Hereford's nostrils dilated, but his voice was controlled. He put his hands behind his back. "Thank you, no."

"I thought not," said the Butcher, and there was a world of insult in his scraping voice.

Before him was a triangular housing from which projected three small levers with round grips. One was red, one blue. The third was set between and in front of the others, and was green. He pulled the two nearest him. Immediately a red line appeared on the chart, running from *Epsilon*'s symbol to the golden patch, and a blue line raced out from *Sigma* to meet it. Just above the gold hovered the white spot representing the Invader. Osgood watched it narrowly as it dipped toward the gold and the junction of the red and blue lines. He rested his hand on the green lever, made one last check of the screens, and snatched it back. Obediently, a thin, bright green line appeared on the chart. A purple haze clouded the gold.

"That's it!" breathed Belter. "The purple, there—The Death!"

Hereford, shaking, leaned back against the bulkhead. He folded his arms, holding tightly to his elbows, obviously trying to get a grip on much more.

"Scan him!" spat Osgood. "This I've got to see!"

Belter leapt forward. "Commander! You don't . . . you *can't* beam him! Remember what happened at Outpost?"

Osgood swore. "We've got so much stuff between here and there already that a scanning beam isn't going to make that much difference. He's done, anyway!" he added exultantly.

The large scanning screen flicked into colors which swirled and fused into the sharp image of the Invader. Since the beam tracked him exactly, there was no sign of motion. "Get me a diagrammatic!" bellowed Osgood. His small eyes were wide, his cheeks puffed out, his lips wet.

The lower quarter of the screen faded, went black, then suddenly bore a reduced image of the Invader. Apparently creeping toward him was a faint, ever-brightening purple mist.

"Right on the nose!" gritted Belter. "He's sailing right into it!"

Startlingly, the large actual image showed signs of life. A stream of blue-white fire poured out of the ship side.

"What do you know!" whistled Osgood. "He's got jets after all! He knows there's something ahead of him, doesn't know what it is, and is going to duck it if he has to smear his crew all up and down the bulkheads!"

"Look!" cried Belter, pointing at the chart. "Why, he's pulling into a curve that . . . that— Man, oh man, he's killing off all hands! He can't turn like that!"

"Maybe he wants to get it over with quickly. Maybe he's run into The Death somewhere before," crowed Osgood. "Afraid to face it. Hey, Belter, the inside of that ship's going to be a pretty sight. The Death'll make jelly of 'em, and that high-G turn'll lay the jelly like paint out of an airbrush!"

"Ex . . . ex—" was as much as Hereford could say as he turned and tottered out. Belter took a step after him, hesitated, and then went back to stand before the chart.

Purple and gold and white, red and green and blue coruscated together. Slowly, then, the white spot moved toward the edge of the puddle of color.

"Commander! He's still side-jetting!"

"Why not?" said the Butcher gleefully. "That's the way his controls were set when his command got emulsified. He'll blow off his fuel in a while, and we can board him."

There was a soft click from the master communications screen and a face appeared on it. *"Epsilon,"* the man said.

"Good work, Hoster," said Osgood, rubbing his hands.

"Thank you, sir," said the captain of the Martian vessel. "Commander, my astrogators report an extrapolation of the derelict's change of course. If he keeps jetting, he's going to come mighty close."

"Watch him then," said Osgood. "If he comes too close, get out of his way. I'll stake my shoulder boards on your safety." He laughed. "He's a dead duck. You'll be able to clear him. I don't care if it's only by fifty meters."

The Martian saluted. Osgood checked him before he could fade. "Hoster!"

"Yes sir."

"I know you Martians. Trigger happy. Whatever happens, Hoster, you are not to bomb or ray that derelict. Understand?"

"Roger, sir," said the Martian stiffly, and faded.

"Those Martians," said Osgood. "Bloodthirsty bunch."

Belter said: "Commander, sometimes I understand how Hereford feels about you."

"I'll take that as a compliment," said the Butcher.

They spent the next two hours watching the tactical chart. The Death generators had long ago been cut out, and The Death itself showed on the chart as a dwindling purple stain, headed straight Outside and already fading. But the derelict was still blasting from its side jets, and coming about in an impossible curve. The Martian astrogators had been uncomfortably right, and Captain Hoster had been instructed to take evasive action.

Closer and closer came the white spot to the red one that was *Epsilon.* Viewers were clamped on both ships: the Martian had begun to decelerate powerfully to get out of that ratiocinated curve.

"Doesn't look so good," said Belter, after a careful study of the derelict's trajectory.

"Nonsense," said Osgood worriedly. "But it'd be more than a little silly to lose a ship after we've whipped the enemy." He turned to the control bulkhead. "Get me *Epsilon.*"

He had started his famous monotone of profanity before the screen finally lit up. Hoster's face was flushed—blotched, really. "What's the matter?" snapped Osgood. "You take your own sweet time answering. Why haven't you taken any *momentomine?*"

Captain Hoster clutched the rim of his communicator. "Lissen," he said thickly. "'Nvader out t' get us, see. Nobody push Martian around. 'S dirty Jovian trick."

"Acceleration disease," said Belter quietly. "He must've had some crazy idea of keeping away from the drug so he'd be able to keep on the alert."

"Hoster! You're hopped up. You can't take *momentomine* for as many years as you have and stay sober under deceleration without it. You're relieved. Take a dose and turn in. Put your second on."

"Lissen, Butch, ol' horse," mouthed the Martian. "I know what I'm doin', see? I don't want trouble with *you.* Busy, see? Now, you jus' handle your boat an' I'll handle mine. I'm gonna give that Jovian a case of Titanitis 'f 'e gets wise with me." And the screen went blank.

"Hoster!" the commander roared. "Sparks! Put that maniac on again!"

A speaker answered promptly: "Sorry, sir. Can't raise him."

In helpless fury Osgood turned to Belter. "If he so much as throws a dirty look at that derelict, I'll break him to an ammo passer and put him on the sun side of Mercury. We *need* that derelict!"

"What for?" asked Belter, and then wondered why he had asked, for he knew the answer. Hereford's influence, probably. It would be Hereford's question, if he were still here.

"Four drives we don't know anything about. A warp-camouflaged disrupter bomb. A chain-instigating ray, that blew up the asteroid last year. And probably lots more. Man, that's a *war*ship!"

"It sure is," said Belter. "It certainly is." *Peace Amalgamated,* he thought. *A great step forward.*

"Get 'em both on a screen," Osgood rapped. "They're close enough— Hey, Belter, look at the way that ship is designed. See how it can check and turn that way?"

"No, I— Oh! I see what you mean. Uses lateral jets—but what laterals!"

"Functional stuff," said Osgood. "We could've had that a hundred years ago, but for naval tradition. We put all our drive back aft. We get a good in-line thrust, sure. But look what he's got! The equivalent of ten or twelve of our stern-tube assemblies. What kind of people were they, that could stand that kind of thing?"

Belter shook his head. "If they built it that way, they could stand it." He looked thoughtfully up at the derelict's trajectory. "Commander, you don't suppose—"

Apparently struck by the same awful thought, Osgood said uneasily, "Certainly not. The Death. They went through The Death."

"Yes," said Belter. He sounded relieved, but he did not feel relieved. He watched the screen, and then clutched Osgood's arm.

Osgood swore and sprang to the control bulkhead. "Get *Epsilon!*

Tell him to cease fire and then report to me! Blast the hub-forted fun of a plistener! I'll pry him loose from his—"

Belter grunted and threw his arm over his eyes as the screen blazed. The automatic shields went up, and when he could see again, the screen showed him the Invader. *Epsilon* wasn't there at all.

After the excitement had died down a little, Osgood slumped into a chair. "I wish we'd had a Jovian ship out there instead," he rasped. "I don't care what they did to us during the war, or anything else. They could obey orders. When they say they'll do a thing, you can bet on it. What's the score on that business of the Jovians' electing themselves out, anyhow?"

Belter told him how the Jovian delegate had been insulted at the Council.

"Those hot-headed, irresponsible Martians!" said the Butcher. "Why in time did that drunken cretin have to fire on the derelict?"

"What derelict?" Belter asked dryly.

Osgood stared at him. Belter pointed at the chart. The white spot was slowly swinging toward the green—toward *Delta*. On the screen, the Invader still gleamed. It was not blasting any more.

One of the technician's screens flashed. "Detection reporting, sir."

"Report."

"Invader's Type Two drive radiation showing strong, sir."

"R-Roger."

The screen winked out. Commander Osgood opened his mouth, held it open silently for an unbearably long moment, and then carefully closed it again. Belter bit the insides of his cheeks to keep from roaring with hysterical laughter. He knew that the Butcher was trying to swear, and that he had met a situation for which no swearing would he adequate. He had shot his vituperative bolt. Finally, weakly, he said the worst thing he could think of—a thing that until then had been unthinkable.

He said: "They're not dead."

Belter did not feel like laughing any more. He said: "They went through The Death, and they're not dead."

"There is no defense against The Death," said the commander authoritatively. Belter nodded.

One of the screens flashed, and a voice said impersonally: "Mathematics."

"Go on," said the Butcher.

"The derelict's course will intersect ours, sir, unless—"

"Don't say 'derelict,'" whispered Osgood. "Say 'Invader.'" He lay back and, closing his eyes, swabbed his face with a tissue. Then the muscles in his jaw clenched and he rose and stood erect before the control bulkhead, pulling the wrinkles out of his tunic. "Batteries. Train around to the Invader. Tech! Put the batteries on auto. Everything—torpedoes, rays, artillery. Now give me all hands. All hands! Prepare to abandon ship. *Delta* will engage the enemy on automatics. Life craft to scatter. Take your direction from your launching port and maintain it until you observe some decisive action between *Delta* and the Invader. Fill up with *momentomine* and give your craft everything they can take. Over." He swung to Belter.

"Councilman! Don't argue with me. What I want to do is stay here and fight. What I will do is abandon ship with the rest of you. My only reason is so I can have another chance to take a poke at a Martian. Of all the blundering, stupid, childish things for Hoster to do, taking a pot shot at that killer out there was the most—"

Belter very nearly reminded the commander that Hoster had been instructed to let the "derelict" pass within meters if necessary. He swallowed the comment. It didn't matter, anyway. Hoster and his crew had been good men, and *Epsilon* a good ship. All dead now, all smashed, all gone to lengthen the list that had started on Outpost.

"You know your abandon-ship station, don't you, Belter? Go to your quarters and haul out that white-livered old pantywaist and take him with you. I'll join you as soon as everyone else is off the ship. Jump!"

Belter jumped. Things were happening too fast for him, and he found it almost pleasant to use someone else's intelligence rather than hunt for his own.

Hereford was sitting on the edge of his bunk. "What's the matter, Belter?"

"Abandon ship!"

"I know that," said the older man patiently. When they have an 'all hands' call on one of these ships there's no mistaking it. I want to know what's the matter."

"We're under attack. Invader."

"Ah." Hereford was very calm. "It didn't work."

"No," said Belter. "It didn't."

"I'll stay here, I think."

"You'll *what?*"

Hereford shrugged. "What's the use? What do you think will happen to the peaceful philosophy when news gets out that there is a defense against The Death? Even if a thousand or a million Invader ships come, nothing will keep us from fighting each other. I'm—tired."

"Hereford." He waited until the old man lifted his head, met his eyes. "Remember that day in the anteroom? Do we have to go through that again?"

Hereford smiled slowly. "Don't bother, friend. You are going to have trouble enough after you leave. As for me—well, the most useful thing I can be now is a martyr."

Belter went to the bulkhead and pressed into his personal storage. He got his papers and a bottle of viski. "All right," he said, "let's have a quick one before I go." Hereford smiled and accepted. Belter put all the *momentomine* in Hereford's drink, so that when they left the ship he, Belter, passed out cold. From what he heard later he missed quite a show. *Delta* slugged it out with the Invader. She fought until there was nothing but a top turret left, and it kept spitting away at the enemy until a disrupter big enough for half a planet wiped it out. She was a good ship too. The Invader went screaming up into the celestial north again, leaving the terrified *Sigma* alone. Belter regained consciousness in the life craft along with the commander and Hereford. Hereford looked like an illustration in the Old Testament which Belter had seen when he was a child. It was captioned, "And Moses Threw Down and Broke the Two Tablets of Stone."

Sigma picked them up. She was a huge old Logistics vessel, twice reconverted—once from the Colonial Trade, once as the negative plant of The Death. She had a main hold in her like a convention hall, and a third of it was still empty in spite of the vast pile plant she carried. Her cargo port was open, and *Delta*'s life craft were being warped in and stacked inside, along with what wreckage could be salvaged for study.

The place was a hive. Spacesuited crews floated the boats in, handling them with telescoping rods equipped with a magnetic grapple at each end. One end would be placed on the hull of a boat, the other on the deck or bulkhead or on a stanchion; and then by contracting or expanding the rod by means of its self-contained power unit, the boat would be pushed or pulled to its stack.

The boats had completed their rendezvous after two days of signaling and careful jetting. All were accounted for but two, which had probably tangled with debris. The escape of so many was largely due to the fact that there was very little wreckage large enough to do any damage after the last explosion.

Osgood's boat hovered outside until the last, and by the time it was warped in all the others had unloaded and their crews were inboard, getting refreshment and treatment. By the time the little "Blister" had been racked, the cargo port was sealed and the compartment refilled with air. *Sigma*'s captain opened the boat's hatch with his own hands, and Osgood crawled out, followed by a dazed Belter and a sullen Hereford.

"Your ship, sir," said the captain of *Sigma,* formally, in the traditional presentation of a ship and its facilities to a superior.

"Yeah. I need one at the moment," said the Butcher wryly. He stretched, looked around. "Get any parts of the Martian?"

"No, sir," said the captain. He was a worried-looking, gangly specimen from the Venusian Dome. His name had so many syllables that only the first three were used. They were Holovik. "And little enough from *Delta,* I'm sorry to say. Wh . . . what happened?"

"You saw it, didn't you? What do you think?

"I'll say it, if you can't get it out," said Osgood bluntly. "He has a defense against The Death. Isn't that fine?"

"Yes sir." The horizontal lines across Captain Holovik's forehead deepened, and the corners of his mouth turned down. "Fine."

"Don't burst into tears!" snapped the commander. He looked around taking stock of the salvage. "Get all available techs on that scrap. Find out if any of it is radioactive, and if so how much of what type. What's that?"

"That" was a thirty-foot tapered cylinder with three short mast antennae projecting at right angles to the long axis, near each rounded end.

"I don't know for sure, sir," said Holovik. "I knew that there were . . . ah . . . weapons, new ones. We don't get information the way we used to during the war—"

"Stop mumbling, man! If that's a secret weapon, it isn't from *Delta.*"

Belter put in, "It isn't from *Epsilon* either. I went over the specs of everything aboard all of these vessels."

"Then where did— Oh!" His "Oh!" was echoed by Belter and two junior officers who had overheard the conversation. It was a most respectful sound. Also respectful was the unconscious retreat all hands took to the inboard bulkhead.

Hereford, who had not spoken a word for nearly a day, asked: "What's the matter? What is it?"

"Don't know," breathed Belter. "but I'd like to see it out of here. Way out. It's the Invader's."

"G—get it out of here. *Jump!*"

They piled into the inboard section and sealed the cargo inspection hatch behind them, leaving three spacesuited e.m. and an officer to worry the object tenderly out of the port.

"You're a cretin," Osgood told the captain. "You're a drooling incompetent. Whatever possessed you to bring in an unidentified object?"

"I . . . it was . . . I don't know," stammered Holovik. Belter marveled at the degree of worriment the man's face could register.

A junior officer with communication pips spoke up. "That was the object which didn't register on the detectors until it was within a mile, sir," he reminded. "I still can't understand it, commander. Our detectors—all of 'em—are sensitive to fifty thousand at the very least. I'm ready to swear our equipment was in order, and yet we had no sign of this thing until it was right on top of us."

"Somebody in Detection asleep," growled the Butcher.

"Wait, commander," Belter turned toward the young sigman. "How was this thing bearing?"

"Right on the ship, sir. An intersection course from down left forrad, as I remember. We deflected it and then brought it about with the short tractors."

"It just appeared out of nowhere, eh?" rasped Osgood. "And so you invited it in."

"There was a good deal of debris in that sector, commander," said Holovik faintly. "We were busy ... tracers sometimes give resultant indications when they pick up two separated objects simultaneously—"

"Yeah, and then they indicate something where nothing is. They *don't* indicate nothing where there is something. Why, I'll break you to—"

"It seems to me," said Belter, who had been pursuing his own line of reasoning, "that what we have here is mighty similar to what hit Outpost. Remember? They put a tracer on it as they saw it leave the Invader. It blanked out. They got no radiation or radar reflection at all. But it came in and wiped out the base."

"The nonexistent, hypothetical 'warper,' said Hereford, with a wisp of his old smile.

Osgood glanced at him coldly. "If you're trying to tell me that the Invader used a warper to protect himself from The Death, you're showing your ignorance. The Death is a vibration, *not* a radiation. It's a physical effect, not an energy phenomenon."

"Blast The Death!" spat Belter. "Don't you see what we've got here? It's one of their disrupters. Short range—always short range. Don't you see? It *is* a warper, and for some reason it can only carry a limited amount of power. The Invader started popping away at *Delta,* and when she fought back, he let loose with everything he had. This must've been one of his disrupters which was launched while *Delta* was in one piece and arrived after she'd been blasted. Then it went right on seeking, but ran out of fuel before it reached *Sigma*. That's why it suddenly appeared to the detectors."

"Now, that makes sense," said the Butcher, looking at Belter as if he were seeing him for the first time. He creased his lower lip sharply with his thumb and forefinger. "Warp camouflage, eh? H-m-m-m. I wonder if we could get a look at that unit Maybe we could build something like it and get close enough to that devil to do some good." He turned to the fretful Holovik. "Captain! See if you can get a couple of techs to volunteer to de-fuse that thing. If you can't get volunteers—"

"I'll get them, sir," said Holovik, for the first time looking a little happier. It made him appear wistful instead of mournful.

It was easier to count those not volunteering, once the proposition went out over the intercom. In a few minutes *Sigma* lay off a couple of hundred miles to stand by while a crack squad worked over the drifting bomb. They carried three viewers, and the control bridge of the Death ship was mobbed with experts. Every move was carefully discussed; every possibility was carefully explored before a move was made.

They did it. It was slow, and suspense reached an agonized pitch; but once it was done and could be reviewed, it was unbelievably simple. The warhead was clamped to the main hull of the bomb. The activators were in the head, controlled simply by a couple of rods. The seeking gear, proximity circuits, power source, drive, and what was apparently the camouflage unit were all packed into the hull.

A torch was clamped to the warhead, which was cast adrift. The precious hull was towed a few miles with reaction-pistols and picked up by the ship, which then got clear and rayed the virulent little warhead into shocking, flaring extinction.

In shops and laboratories throughout the System, feverish work was carried on over plans and mock-ups of the alien weapon. One of the first things discovered about it was that the highly theoretical and very popular term "warper" was a misnomer. The camouflage was an ingenious complexity of wiring in concentric "skins" in the hull. Each impinging radiation caused the dielectric constant of the hull to change so that it reradiated that exact frequency, at the same intensity as received, but a hundred and eighty degrees out of phase. The heart of the device was what might have been the thousandth generation descended from a TR tube. It hunted so constantly, and triggered radiations with so little lag, that the device could handle several frequencies almost simultaneously.

What used most of the power was the drive. It involved a magnetic generator and a coil which carried magnetic flux. Induced in this was an extremely intense gravitic field, self-canceling forward and on all sides. The intensified "reverse" gravity pressure was, therefore, at the stern. Maneuvering was accomplished by variations in field strength by inductance-coupling of the mag-flux coils.

The hull was a totally absorbent black, and the missile was made of an alloy which was transparent to hard radiation.

All information was pooled, and sub-projects were constantly assigned from Science Center. Etherfac transmission was full of last-minute reports on phases of the problem, interspersed with frequent communiqués on the last known position of the Invader. He had indulged in an apparently aimless series of convolutions for several weeks following D-Day, evidently to assess his damage. After that he had maintained a great circular course, parallel in plane to the solar ecliptic, and the assumption was that he was undergoing repairs and engaging in reconnaissance. Both were certainly indicated, for he must have undergone an incredible strain in that wild curve on D-Day. And as before, he was the symbol of terror. If he struck, where would he strike? If not, he would leave. Then, would he be back? Alone, or with a fleet?

Belter's life was a continuous flurry of detail, but he found time to wonder about several things. The Jovians, for example. They had been a great help in the duplication of the camouflage device, particularly in their modification of the fission power plant it carried. The Jovian improvement was a disruption motor using boron, an element which appeared nowhere in the original. It gave vastly more range to the Solarian device. And yet—there was something about the Jovian willingness that was not quite in harmony with their established behavior patterns. The slight which Leess had suffered from the Martian was not, after all, a large thing in itself, but the fact that Leess had led his planet into a policy of noncooperation made it large. The sudden reversal of this policy since D-Day was more than puzzling. A hundred times Belter shrugged the question off, grunting "Jovians are funny people," and a hundred times it returned to him.

There was another unprecedented worry. The Martian delegate called Belter aside one afternoon and presented it to him. "It's that Hereford," the man said, scratching his sunburned neck. "He's too quiet. I know he lost a mess of 'face' over his vote on The Death, but he still has a following. More than I like to think about."

"So?"

"Well, when the big day comes, when we send a formation of the new camouflaged boats out there, what's to keep him from opening his trap and making trouble for us?"

"Why should he?"

"You know what the pacifists are after. If we fitted out a bunch of these new gadgets with disrupters and wiped the Invader out, they'd have no kick. They don't want that Death-defense to get back to the System. You know that."

"Hm-m-m. And how would you handle this on Mars?"

The Martian grinned. "Why, I reckon Brother Hereford would have a little accident. Enough to keep him quiet, anyhow—maybe for a little while, maybe for—"

"I thought as much." Belter let himself burn for a luxurious second before replying. "Forget it. Supposing what you say is true—and I don't grant that it is—what else can you think of?"

"Well now, I think it would be a bright idea to send a camouflage force out without consulting the Council. That way, if Hereford is waiting for the psychological moment to blow his mouth off, we'll get what we're after before he knows what's happening. *If* we can keep the lid on it, that is."

Belter shook his head. "Sorry, friend. No can do. We can stretch a point of security and take a military action without informing the people, but there's no loophole in the charter which will let any of us take military action without the knowledge of the Council. Sorry. Anyway, thanks for the tip.

This, like the Jovian matter, was a thing he shrugged off and forgot—five or six times a day. He knew the case-hardened character which lived behind Hereford's dignified mien, and he respected it for what it was and for what it could do.

There was a solution to these problems. He laughed when it occurred to him, smiled when it recurred; but he frowned when he realized that he had already decided. He must have, for he found himself slipping Addison's report into a private drawer of his desk. Addison was the Tech in charge of the local camouflage project. It was top secret and had been delivered, sealed, by an orderly. It invited him to inspect a two-place craft which had been finished and tested, fueled and equipped. The report should have gone to the Agenda.

He called Hereford, and when they were alone he asked, without preliminary: "Are you interested in heading off a war?"

"A rhetorical question, certainly."

"Nope. Question two. Have you anything special to do the next few weeks?"

"Why I—nothing out of the ordinary," said Hereford, sadly. Since his historic "Exception" speech, he had had little enough to do.

"Well, clear your social calendar, then. No, I'm not kidding. This is hot. How soon can you be ready for a little trip?"

Hereford studied him. "In about thirty minutes. I can tell by the way you act that you'd want it that soon."

"You're psychic. Right here, then, in thirty minutes."

Within two hours they were in space, aboard a swift scoutship. Behind him Belter left a bewildered deputy-chairman with a brief authorization in his hands, and an equally astonished Master-Tech, both of whom were sworn to silence. In the scoutship were a sworn-in crew and the black hulk of the camouflaged lifeboat.

For the first two days out he left Hereford to twiddle his thumbs in the cramped recreation room of the ship, while he closeted himself with the skipper to work out an approach course. It took him half of the first day to convince the young man that he was in his right mind and that he wanted to board the Invader—two facts that had been regarded, during the past three years, as mutual incompatibilities.

The approach was plotted to permit the boat to overtake the Invader using a minimum of power. The little craft was to be launched from the scout at high speed on a course which would put it in an elliptical orbit in respect to the sun. This ellipse was at right angles to the plane of the circular course the Invader had been maintaining for the past few weeks. The ellipse intersected this circle in two places, and the launching time was set to synchronize these points of intersection with the predicted position of the Invader on its own course. The big *if,* naturally, was whether or not the Invader would maintain course and speed. He might. He had, twice before, once for nine months and once for over a year. If Belter watched his tables, and spent enough time with his tetrant and calculex, it would require only an occasional nudge of power to follow his course, or to correct it for any variations of the Invader's predicted position.

After the matter was settled, and he had slept, he rejoined Hereford. The old man was apparently staring right through the open book on his knee, for his eyes were wide and unmoving. Belter slumped down beside him and expelled an expressive breath. "What a way to make a living!"

Amusement quirked the corners of Hereford's mouth. "What?"

"Finding tough ways to die," grinned the chairman. "I'm ready to tell you about this thing, if you want me to."

Hereford closed his book and put it by.

"It's the Jovians, first of all," said Belter, without preliminary. "Those critters think so well, so fast, and so differently that it scares me. It's tough . . . no, it's downright foolish to try to judge their actions on a human basis. However, they pulled one stunt that was so very human that it completely escaped me. If Mars had tried it, I'd have been on to it instantly. It's taken a long time for it to percolate, since it concerns the Jovians. Do you remember how ready they were to help out after D-Day? Why do you suppose that was?"

"I would judge," said Hereford thoughtfully, "that they had awakened to their responsibility as members of the System. The Invader had a defense against the ultimate weapon, the emergency was intensified, and they pitched in to help for the common good."

"That's what I thought, too. Has it occurred to you at all what would probably happen if Jupiter—and only Jupiter—had a defense against The Death?"

"Why, I don't think they would—"

Belter broke in roughly. "Never mind what you would like to believe. What would happen?"

"I see what you mean," said Hereford. His face was white. "We came up from almost certain defeat and won the war when we developed The Death. If Jupiter had a defense, we would be no match for them!"

"That's way understated," said Belter.

"But . . . but they signed a peace treaty! They're disarming! They won't break their word!" cried Hereford.

"Of course they won't! If they get their hands on that defense, they'll calmly announce the fact, give us time to prepare, even, and then declare war and wipe us out. There's a great deal of pride involved, of course. I'll venture to say that they'd even help us arm if we'd let them, to make the struggle equal to begin with. They're bugs for that kind of fairness. But the whole System knows that machine for machine, unit for unit, Jovian for man, there is no equality. They're too much for us. It is only our crazy, ingrained ability to manufacture suicidal weapons which gives us the upper hand. The Jovians are too wise to try to conquer a race which insists on introducing murder-machines without any due regard for their future significance. Remember what Leess said when the Martian insulted him? 'Earth dead, Jupiter dead, Mars dead. Good.' They know that unless we as a race are let alone, we will certainly find a way to kill off our neighbors, because as a race we don't care if we get killed in the process."

Hereford shuddered. "I'd hate to think you were right. It makes Peace Amalgamated look so very useless, for all its billions of members."

Belter cracked his knuckles. "I'm not trying to tell you that humans are basically rotten, or that they are fated to be what they always have been. Humanity has come very close to extinction at least four times that I know of, through some such kind of mass suicide. But the existence of Peace Amalgamated does indicate that it believes there is a way out, although I can't help thinking that it'll be a long haul to get us 'cured.' "

"Thank you," said Hereford sincerely. "Sometimes I think you might be a more effective peace worker than I can ever hope to be. Tell me—what made you suspect that the Jovians might be after the defense device for themselves?"

"A very recent development. You must know that the one thing which makes our use of the camouflage unit practicable is the new power plant. With it we can run up to the Invader and get inside his detectors, starting from far out of his range. Now, that was a Jovian design. They built it, ergo they had it first.

"In other words, between the time of its invention and the time they turned it over to us, they had the edge on us. That being the case, there would be only one reason why, in their supreme self-confidence, they would turn it over to us; namely, they didn't need that edge any more!"

"It fits," said Hereford sorrowfully.

"Good. Now, knowing Jovians—and learning more every day, by the way—I conclude that they gave us the drive, not because they had something better, but because it had already served its purpose for them. I am convinced that Jovian camouflage boats are on the way to the Invader now—and perhaps they have even ... but I'd rather not think about that." He spread his arms, dropped them. "Hence our little jaunt. We've got to get there first. If we're not first, we have to do what we can when we get there."

The boat, lightless, undriven, drifted toward the Invader. At this arc of the chosen ellipse, its velocity was low, and suspense was as ubiquitous a thing as the susurrus of the camouflage unit which whispered away back aft. Hereford and Belter found themselves talking in whispers too, as if their tense voices could carry through those insulated bulkheads, across the dim void to the mysterious crew of the metal murderer which hung before them.

"We're well inside his meteor deflectors," gritted Belter. "I don't know what to think. Are we really going to be able to get to him, or is he playing with us?"

"He doesn't play," said Hereford grimly. "You will excuse the layman's question, but I don't understand how there can be a possibility of his having no detector for just this kind of approach. Since he uses bombs camouflaged the way we are, he must have some defense against them."

"His defense seems to be in the range of his deflectors," answered the chairman. "Those bombs were hunters. That is, they followed the target wherever it moved. The defense would be to stall off the bomb by maneuvering until it ran out of fuel, like the one we picked up. Then his meteor-repellers would take care of it."

"It was obviously the most effective weapon in his arsenal," said Hereford hopefully.

"As far as we know," said Belter from the other end of the emotional spectrum. Then, "I can't stand this. I'm going to try a little drive. I feel as if we'd been hanging here since nuclear power was discovered."

Hereford tensed, then nodded in the dark. The boat was hardly the last word in comfort. The two men could lie prone, or get up to a cramped all-four position. Sitting was possible if the cheekbones were kept between the knees and the occipital bones tight against the overhead. They had been in that prison for more days than they cared to recall.

Belter palmed the drive control and moved it forward. There was no additional sound from the power unit, but the slight accelerative surge was distinctly felt.

"I'm going to circle him. No point being too careful. If he hasn't taken a crack at us by this time, I don't think he's going to." He took the steering lever in his other hand and the boat's nose pulled "up" in relation to the Invader's keel-plane. There was no fear of momentum-damage; the controls would not respond to anything greater than a 5-G turn without a special adjustment.

Within four hours the craft was "over" the alien. The ugly, blind-looking shape, portless and jetless, was infuriating. It went its way completely unheeding, completely confident. Belter had a mad flashback to a childish romance. She hadn't been a very pretty girl, but to have her near him drove him nearly insane. It was because of her perfect poise, her mask. He did not want her. He wanted only to break that calm, to smash his way into the citadel of her *savoir faire.* He had felt like that, and she was not evil. This ship, now—it was completely so. There was something unalive, implacable, inescapable about this great murderous vessel.

Something clutched his arm. He started violently, bumped his head on the overhead, his hand closing on the velocity control. The craft checked itself and he bumped his head again on the forward port. He swore more violently than Hereford's grip on his arm called for, and said in irritation: "What?"

"A—hole. A hatch or something. Look."

It was a black shadow on the curve of the gray-shadowed hull. "Yes . . . yes. Shall we—" Belter swallowed and tried again. "Shall we walk into his parlor?"

"Yes. Ah . . . Belter—"

"Hm-m-m?"

"Before we do—you might as well tell me. Why did you want me to come?"

"Because you're a fighting man."

"That's an odd joke."

"It is not. You have had to fight every inch of the way, Hereford."

"Perhaps so. But don't tell me you brought me along for the potential use of my mislaid pugnacities."

"Not *for* them, friend. Because of them. You want the Invader destroyed, for the good of the System. I want it saved, for the good of the System, as I see it. You could achieve your end in one of two ways. You could do it through Peace Amalgamated, back at Central. It would only need a few words to obstruct this whole program. *Or,* you could achieve it yourself, here. I brought you to keep you from speaking to Peace Amalgamated. I think having you here where I can watch you is less of a risk to the procurement of the Death defense."

"You're a calculating devil," said Hereford, his voice registering something between anger and admiration. "And suppose I try to destroy the ship—given, of course, the chance?"

"I'd kill you first," said Belter with utter sincerity.

"Has it occurred to you that I might try the same thing, with the same amount of conviction?"

"It has," Belter replied promptly. "Only you wouldn't do it. You could not be driven to killing. Hereford, you pick the oddest times to indulge in dialectics."

"Not at all," said Hereford good-humoredly. "One likes to know where one stands."

Belter gave himself over to his controls. In the back of his mind was a whirling ball of panic. Suppose the power plant should fail, for example. Or suppose the Invader should send out a questing beam of a frequency which the camouflage unit could not handle. How about the meteor deflector? Would they be crushed if the ship located them and hurled them away with a repeller? He thought with sudden horror of the close-set wiring in the boat. Shorts do happen, and sometimes oxidation and vibration play strange tricks with wiring. *Do something,* his inner voice shouted. *Right or wrong, do something.*

They drifted up to the great silver hull, and the hole seemed to open hungrily to them as they neared it. Belter all but stopped the craft in relation to the ship, and nosed it forward with a view to entering the hatch without touching the sides.

"In the visirecord, didn't the camouflage disrupter at Outpost show up for a moment on the screen as it left the ship?" Hereford whispered.

"Yeah. So what? Oh! You mean the cam unit was shut off until the bomb was clear of the ship. You have something there, Hereford. Maybe we'd better shut it off before we go in. I can see where it would act like something less than camouflage, enclosed in a metal chamber and reradiating all the stray stuff in there plus the reflections of its own output." He put his hand out to the camouflage control. "But I'm going to wait until we're practically inside. I don't relish the idea of being flung off like a meteorite."

Handling the controls with infinite care, touching them briefly and swiftly with his fingertips, Belter tooled the boat through the hatch. He switched off the camouflage effect and had the boat fully inboard of the Invader before he realized he was biting his tongue.

Surprisingly, the chamber they entered was illuminated. The light was dim, shadowless, and a sickly green. The overhead and bulkheads themselves, or a coating on them, accounted for the light.

There was a large rack on the forward partition containing row on row of the disruption bombs, minus their warheads. Above each ended a monorail device which ran to a track ending in a solid-looking square door—obviously the storage space for the warheads. Another hoist and monorail system connected the hulls themselves with the open hatch. This trackage, and the fact that the chamber was otherwise untenanted, indicated that the bomb assembly, fuse setting, and dispatching were completely automatic.

"Camouflage again," gritted Belter. "This boat is enough like those bombs to fit sort of cozily in one of those racks. In this crazy light no one would notice it."

"This light is probably not crazy to those on board," said Hereford.

"We'll worry about that later. Slip into your suit."

From the after locker they drew the light pressure suits around themselves and secured them. Belter demonstrated the few controls—oxygen, humidity, temperature, magnetism, and gravity, to be quite sure the old man was familiar with them all. "And this is the radio. I think it will be safe to use the receivers. But don't transmit unless it's absolutely necessary. If we stick close together we can talk by conduction—touching our helmets."

It was the work of only a few minutes to grapple the weightless craft into the rack. It was a fair fit. When they had finished, Belter reached in and took out two blasters. He secured the escape hatch and turned to Hereford, handing him one of the guns. Hereford took it, but leaned forward to touch his transparent helmet to Belter's. His voice came through hollowly but clearly.

"What's this for?"

"Morale," said Belter briefly. "You don't have to use it. If we're watched, 'Two armed men' sounds better than 'Two men, one armed.'"

They groped to the inboard partition and followed it cautiously aft. The touch of the metal under his gloves brought a shocking realization to Belter of where he actually was, and for a moment his knees threatened to give way. Deep inside him, his objective self watched, shaking its figment of a head in amazement. Because he had secured a lifeboat equipped for the job, he had come. Because he had gotten inside the Invader's screens, he had approached the ship itself. Because he was close enough and a hatch was open, he had come in. *Just the way I got into the Army, and the way I got into politics,* he grinned.

They found a ladder. It led upward through a diamond-shaped opening in the overhead. The rungs were welded to the bulkhead. They were too narrow and too close together. There were dragging scuffmarks on each side, about eighteen or twenty centimeters on each side of the rungs. What manner of creature ambulated on its centerline, dragging its sides?

A Jovian.

He looked at Hereford, who was pointing at the marks, so he knew that Hereford understood, too. He shrugged and pointed upward, beckoning. They went up, Belter leading.

They found themselves in a corridor, too low to allow them to stand upright. It was triangular in cross-section, with the point down and widened to a narrow catwalk. A wear-plate was set into each side and bore the same smooth scuffs. The deck, what there was of it between the sharply sloping sides, was composed of transverse rods. A creature which could grip with claws and steady itself with the sides of a carapace could move quite freely in such a corridor regardless of gravitic or accelerative effects, within reason.

"Damn!"

Belter jumped as if stabbed. Hereford tottered on his magna-grips and clutched at the slanted bulkhead for support. The single syllable had roared at them from inside their helmets. The effect was such that Belter all but swallowed his tongue. He pointed at himself in the dim green light and shook his head. Hereford weakly followed suit. Neither of them had spoken.

"Lousy Jovians—"

Belter, following a sudden hunch, laid his hand on Hereford's shoulder to suggest that he stay put, and crept back to the bomb bay opening. He lay down, and cautiously put his head over the lip.

A long, impossibly black *something* was edging across the deck down there. Belter squeezed his eyes tightly closed and opened them wide, trying to see through the foggy green radiance. At last, he discerned a small figure pulling and hauling at the shadow, the bomb, the . . . the lifeboat.

A human figure. A man. A man who must have come through the Invader's defenses, even as he had. A man with a camouflaged boat.

But no one except a few Techs even knew that the boats had been completed. And the Council, of course.

The man below reached inside his boat and touched a control. It sank down to the deck next to the bomb rack as its magnetic anchors were activated. The man shut the escape hatch and shuffled toward the inboard partition, his blaster in hand, his head turning as he came.

Belter watched him until he discovered the ladder. Then he scrambled to his feet and, as fast as the peculiar footing would allow him, he scurried back to Hereford. His helmet receiver registered an angry gust of breath as the man below saw the short-paced ladder and the scuff-marks.

Belter slammed his helmet against Hereford's. "It's a Martian," he gritted. "You might know it'd be a blasted Martian. Only a Martian'd be stupid enough to try to climb aboard this wagon."

He saw Hereford's eyebrow go up at this, but the peace-man did not make the obvious comment. He was silent as he followed Belter forward to the nearest turn in the corridor. They slipped around it, Belter conning its extension carefully. There was still, incredibly, no sign of life.

Just around the turn there was a triangular door, set flush into the slanted wall. Belter hesitated, then pressed it. It did not yield. He scrabbled frantically over its surface, found no control of any kind. Hereford grasped his arm, checked him, and when Belter stepped back, the old man went to his knees and began feeling around on the catwalk floor. The door slid silently back.

Belter slipped in, glanced around. But for a huddled, unmoving mass of some tattered matter in the corridor, there was nothing in the room, which was small. Belter waved the old man in. Hereford hopped over the sill, felt on the floor again, and the panel slid shut.

"How did you know how to open that door?" he asked when their helmets touched.

"Their feet . . . claws . . . what-have-you . . . are obviously prehensile or they wouldn't have floors that are nothing more than close-set rungs. Obviously their door handles would be in the floor."

Belter shook his head admiringly. "See what happens when a man thinks for a living?" He turned to the door, set his head against it. Very faintly, he could hear the cautious steps of the Martian. He turned back to Hereford. "I suppose I ought to go out there and pin his ears back. Martians have nothing in their heads but muscles. He'll walk right up to the skipper of this ship if he has to wade through the crew to do it. But I'm mighty interested in just what he's up to. We couldn't be much worse off than we are. Do you suppose we could follow him close enough to keep him out of trouble?"

"There is no need for caution," said Hereford, and his voice, distorted by the helmets, was like a distant tolling bell.

"What do you mean?"

Hereford pointed to the huddled mass in the corner. Belter crossed to it, knelt, and put out a hand. Frozen substance crumbled under his touch in a way which was familiar to him. He shrank back in horror.

"It's—dead," he whispered.

Hereford touched helmets. "What?"

"It's dead," said Belter dully. "It's—homogenized, and frozen."

"I know. Remember the three Jovian capital ships?"

"They couldn't stand The Death," Belter murmured. "They opened all the locks."

He stood up. "Let's go get that fool of a Martian."

They left the room and followed the corridor to its end. There was another ladder there. They climbed it, and at the top Belter paused. "I think we'd better try for the control central. That'll be the first thing he'll go after."

They found it, eventually, before the Martian did, possibly because they were not being as cautious. They must have passed him en route, but such was the maze of corridors and connecting rooms that that was not surprising. They still eschewed the use of their transmitters, since Belter preferred to find out exactly what the Martian was up to.

They had just opened a sliding door at the end of a passageway, and Belter was half through it when he stopped so suddenly that Hereford collided with him.

The room which spread before them was unexpectedly large. The bulkheads were studded with diamond-shaped indicators, and above them and over the ceiling were softly-colored murals. They glowed and shimmered, and since they were the first departure from the ubiquitous dim green, their immediate effect was shocking.

In the center of the chamber was a pair of control desks, a V pointing forward and a V pointing aft, forming another of the repeated diamond forms. There was a passage space, however, between the two V's. In their enclosure was a creature, crouching over the controls.

It was alive.

It stirred, heaving itself up off the raised portion of the deck on which it lay. It was completely enclosed in a transparent, obviously pressurized garment. As it rose, Belter and Hereford shrank back out of sight. Belter drew his blaster.

But the creature was apparently not aware of them. It turned slowly to face the opposite corner of the room, and the sensory organ on its cephalothorax blushed pink.

There was a bold clanking from the corner of the room, which Belter felt through his shoes. Then the wall began to glow. A small section of it shone red which paled into white. It bellied momentarily, and then sagged molten. The Martian, blaster in hand, leapt through the opening. *And he could have opened that door,* thought Belter disgustedly. *Why does a Martian always have to do it the hard way?*

The Martian stopped dead when he was clear of the simmering entrance. He visibly recoiled from the sudden apparition of color, and stood awed before those magnificent murals. His gaze dropped to the center of the room.

"So there is a defense," he snarled. His transmitter was still blatantly operating. "Come on, Jupiter. I was wise to this whole stunt. Who did you think you fooled by poisoning your own forces on Titan? Invader, huh? Some stuff! Get out of there. Move now! I know you can understand me. I want to see that Death defense and the controls. And there's no sense trying to call your buddies. I've seen them all over the ship. All dead. Something saved you, and I mean to find out what it is."

He raised his blaster. The Jovian quivered. Belter crossed his left arm across his body and grasped the edge of the door. He rested his blaster across his left forearm and squinted down the barrel. Hereford reached over his shoulder and drew the muzzle upward.

Belter turned furiously to him, but the old man shook his head and, astonishingly, smiled. His hand went to his belt. He threw his transmitter switch and said in his deep, quiet voice:

"Drop that blaster, son."

The effect on the Martian was absolutely devastating. He went rod stiff, dropping his weapon so quickly that he all but threw it. Then he staggered backward, and they could hear his frightened gasping as he tried to regain his breath.

Belter strode out into the room and backed to the left bulkhead, stopping where he could cover both the Martian and the Jovian. Hereford shuffled over and picked up the blaster.

"P-peace Amalgamated!" puffed the Martian. "What in time are *you* doing here?"

Belter answered. "Keeping you from using your muscles instead of your brains. What do you think you're doing?"

"Recon," said the Martian sullenly.

"For who?"

"What do you think?"

"I think you're doing it for Mars," said Belter bluntly. "It would be just dandy if Mars had the Death defense now, wouldn't it? You guys have been chafing at the bit for a long time."

"We're not crazy," flashed the Martian. "We never did make peace with Jupiter, remember? We knew better. And now look." He gestured at the Jovian. "What a pretty way to knock slices out of all the Solarian defenses. Just play Invader for a few years and scare the bedizens out of humanity. Wipe out what looks tough, and take advantage of the panic. Heh! Treaties with Jupiter! Why in blazes didn't you exterminate them when you had the chance? Now, if Mars gets the Defense, we'll handle the thing right. And maybe when the smoke clears away we'll be magnanimous enough to let Earth and the Colonies work for us."

"All blast and brawn," marveled Belter. "The famous Martian mouth."

"Don't you brag about brains. I know for a fact that our councilman tipped off that camouflage boats were being made in secret. If you didn't act on it, it's your hard luck."

"In a way he did," said Belter. "Enough, I imagine, to keep his little conscience clear. I'm here, for all that."

"Not for long," snapped the Martian, making a long sliding step.

"Look out, Hereford!"

Belter snapped a fine-focus shot at the Martian but he was late. The Martian was behind Hereford, grappling for the blaster which the Peace delegate still held in his hand. Hereford tried to spin away but was unsure of his footing in the gravitic shoes and succeeded only in floundering. The Martian suddenly shifted his attack to the blaster at Belter's hip. He got it and danced clear. "I know the panty-waist won't shoot," he said, and laughed. "So it's you first, Belter, and then old 'Peace-in-our-Time.' Then I'll get the Death defense with or without the aid of the spider yonder."

He swung the weapon on Belter, and the chairman knew that this was it. He closed his eyes. The blaster-flash beat on the lids. He felt nothing. He tried to open his eyes again and was astounded to discover that he could. He stood there staring at Hereford, who had just shot the Martian through the head. The man's magna-grips held him upright as the air in his suit whiffed out, to hang in a mist like a frozen soul over his tattered head.

"I killed him, didn't I?" asked Hereford plaintively.

"To keep the peace," said Belter in a shaking voice. He skated over to the old man and took the blaster, which was still held stiffly out toward the dead man. "Killing's a comparative crime, Hereford. You've saved lives."

He went to the control table and put his hands on it, steadying himself against the broken sounds Hereford was making. He stared across the table at the great jelly-and-bone mass that was a Jovian. He would have given a lot for a translator, but such a machine had never yet been made portable.

"You. Jovian. Will you communicate? Spread that membrane for 'yes.' Contract it for 'no.' "

Yes. The creature was perfectly telepathic, but with humans it had to be one way. A translator could convert its emanations into minute electronic impulses and arrange them into idea-patterns for which words were selected.

"Is there anything on this ship which can resist The Death?"

Yes.

"You understand it?"

Yes.

"Will you share your knowledge with the Council?"

Yes.

"Can you deactivate all automatics on this ship?"

In answer the Jovian extended one of its four pseudoclaws, and placed it next to a control on the table. It was a small square housing, set so as to repeat the diamond motif. An orange pilot light glowed in its center, and next to it was a toggle. On the forward side of the toggle was an extremely simple symbol—two dots connected by two lines, each two-thirds of the distance between the dots, so that for the middle third they lay parallel, contiguous. On the after side of the toggle, the symbol differed. The dots were the same, but the lines were separated. It was obviously an indication of "open" and "closed" positions. The toggle slanted forward. Belter put his hand on it, looked at the Jovian.

The membrane spread affirmatively. Jovians did not lie. He pulled the toggle back and the pilot went out.

"This General Assembly has been called," Belter said quietly into the mike, "to clear up, once and for all, the matter of the Invader and the contingent wild and conflicting rumors about a defense against The Death, about interstellar drives, about potential war between members of the Solar Federation, and a number of other fantasies." He spoke carefully, conscious of the transmission of his voice and image to government gatherings on all the worlds, in all the domes, and on ships.

"You know the story of my arrival, with Hereford, aboard the Invader, and the later arrival of the Martian, and his"—Belter cleared his throat—"his accidental death. Let me make it clear right now that there is no evidence that this man was representing the Martian General Government or any part of it. We have concluded that he was acting as an individual, probably because of what might be termed an excess of patriotism.

"Now, as to the presence of the Jovian on the ship—that is a perfectly understandable episode. Jupiter is a defeated nation. I venture to say that any group of us in the same situation would commit acts similar to that of this Jovian. I can say here, too, that there is no evidence of its representing any part of the Jovian Government. What it might have done with, say, a Death defense had it found one aboard is conjecture, and need not enter into this discussion.

"I have before me a transcript of this Jovian's statement. You may rest assured that all facts have been checked; that fatigue and crystalline tests and examinations have been made of metallic samples taken from the vessel; that the half-lives of radioactive by-products in certain fission and disruption machinery have been checked and substantiate this statement. This is the transcript:

" 'For reasons consistent with Jovian philosophy, I took a Jovian-built camouflaged boat and departed with it before the improved drive had been submitted to the Joint Solar Military Council. I approached the Invader cautiously and found the camouflage successful. I boarded him. I put my boat in the Invader's bomb rack, where it was well hidden in plain sight, being the same size and general shape as the Invader's bombs. I went inboard, expecting a great deal of trouble. There was none. Every port and hatch was open to space except the warhead storage, which was naturally no hiding place due to radioactivity. I proceeded to the control chamber. I found the master control to all the ship's armament.

" 'But my most important discovery was a thought record. The Invaders were, like Jovians, of an arthropodal type, and their image patterns were quite understandable after a little concentration. I shall quote from that record:

" '*We are of Sygon, greater of the two planets of Sykor, a star in*

Symak. The smaller planet, known to us as Gith, is peopled by a mad race, a mistake of nature—a race which fights and kills itself and wars on its neighbors; a race which aspires to conquer purely for the sake of conquest, which hunts for hunting's sake and kills for pleasure. While it progresses, while it cooperates, it bites itself and fights itself and is never done with its viciousness.

" '*Its planet was large enough to support it, but it was not satisfied. Sygon was no place for these vicious animals, for they had to bring their atmosphere in bubbles for breathing, and Sygon's mass crushed them and made them sicken. Not needing Sygon still they were willing to fight us for it.*

" '*We killed them by the hundreds of thousands, and still they kept coming. They devised incredible weapons to use against us, and we improved on them and hurled them back. They improved on these, completely ignoring the inevitability of their end.*

" '*The ultimate weapon was theirs—a terrible thing which emulsified the very cells of our bodies, and there was no defense against it. The first time it was used it killed off most of our race. The rest of us threw all our resources into this, the Eternal Vengeance—this ship. It is designed to attack anything which radiates, as long as the radiations exhibit the characteristics of those produced by intelligent life. It will stay in Sykor's system, and it will attack anything which might be Gith or of Gith. Gith will strike back with its terrible weapon, and all of us on the ship will die. But the ship will go on. Gith will loose its horror and agony on Sygon, and our race will be dead. But the ship will go on. It will attack and attack, and ultimately will destroy Gith.*

" '*And if Gith should die and be born again and evolve a new race, and if that race shall reach a stage of culture approaching that of its cursed forebears, the ship will attack again until it has destroyed them. It will attack all the more powerfully for having rested, for between attacks it will circle Sykor, drinking and storing its energy.*

" '*Perhaps there will come a time when Sykor will cool, or flare up and explode, or become subject to the influence of a wandering star. Perhaps then the ship will cease to be, but it is possible that it will go wandering off into the dark, never to be active again. But if it should wander into a similar system to that which bore it, then it will bring death and horror to that system's inhabitants. If this should be, it will be unjust; but it will be only an extension of the illimitable evil of Gith.'*"

Belter raised his head. "That is what we were up against. What passed in that Jovian's mind when we burst in on it, with our quarreling and our blasters and our death-dealing, I can only imagine. It made no move to harm us, though it was armed. I think that it may have been leaving us to the same inevitable end which overcame Gith. Apparently a Jovian is capable of thinking beyond immediate advantage.

"I have one more thing to tell you. According to star photographs found in a huge file on the Invader, and the tests and examinations I mentioned, the Invader is slightly over fourteen million years old.

"There is a defense against The Death. You can't kill a dead man. Now, in more ways than one, I give you over to Hereford."

The Professor's Teddy Bear

"SLEEP," SAID THE monster. It spoke with its ear, with little lips writhing deep within the folds of flesh, because its mouth was full of blood.

"I don't want to sleep now. I'm having a dream," said Jeremy. "When I sleep, all my dreams go away. Or they're just pretend dreams. I'm having a real dream now."

"What are you dreaming now?" asked the monster.

"I am dreaming that I'm grown up—"

"Seven feet tall and very fat," said the monster.

"You're silly," said Jeremy. "I will be five feet, six and three eighth inches tall. I will be bald on top and will wear eyeglasses like little thick ashtrays. I will give lectures to young things about human destiny and the metempsychosis of Plato."

"What's a metempsychosis?" asked the monster hungrily.

Jeremy was four and could afford to be patient. "A metempsychosis is a thing that happens when a person moves from one house to another."

"Like when your daddy moved here from Monroe Street?"

"Sort of. But not that kind of a house, with shingles and sewers and things. *This* kind of a house," he said, and smote his little chest.

"Oh," said the monster. It moved up and crouched on Jeremy's throat, looking more like a teddy bear than ever. "Now?" it begged. It was not very heavy.

"Not now," said Jeremy petulantly. "It'll make me sleep. I want to watch my dream some more. There's a girl who's not listening to my lecture. She's thinking about her hair."

"What about her hair?" asked the monster.

"It's brown," said Jeremy. "It's shiny, too. She wishes it were golden."

"Why?"

"Somebody named Bert likes golden hair."

"Go ahead and make it golden then."

"I can't! What would the other young ones say?"

"Does that matter?"

"Maybe not. Could I make her hair golden?"

"Who is she?" countered the monster.

"She is a girl who will be born here in about twenty years," said Jeremy.

The monster snuggled closer to his neck.

"If she is to be born here, then of course you can change her hair. Hurry and do it and go to sleep."

Jeremy laughed delightedly.

"What happened?" asked the monster.

"I changed it," said Jeremy. "The girl behind her squeaked like the mouse with its leg caught. Then she jumped up. It's a big lecture-room, you know, built up and away from the speaker-place. It has steep aisles. Her foot slipped on the hard step."

He burst into joyous laughter.

"Now what?"

"She broke her neck. She's dead."

The monster sniggered. "That's a very funny dream. Now change the other girl's hair back again. Nobody else saw it, except you?"

"Nobody else saw," said Jeremy. "There! It's changed back again. She never even knew she had golden hair for a little while."

"That's fine. Does that end the dream?"

"I s'pose it does," said Jeremy regretfully. "It ends the lecture, anyhow. The young people are all crowding around the girl with the broken neck. The young men all have sweat under their noses. The girls are all trying to put their fists into their mouths. You can go ahead."

The monster made a happy sound and pressed its mouth hard against Jeremy's neck. Jeremy closed his eyes.

The door opened. "Jeremy, darling," said Mummy. She had a tired, soft face and smiling eyes. "I heard you laugh."

Jeremy opened his eyes slowly. His lashes were so long that when they swung up, there seemed to be a tiny wind, as if they were dark weather fans. He smiled, and three of his teeth peeped out and smiled too. "I told Fuzzy a story, Mummy," he said sleepily, "and he liked it."

"You darling," she murmured. She came to him and tucked the covers around his chin. He put up his hand and kept the monster tight against his neck.

"Is Fuzzy sleeping?" asked Mummy, her voice crooning with whimsy.

"No," said Jeremy. "He's hungering himself."

"How does he do that?"

"When I eat, the—the hungry goes away. Fuzzy's different."

She looked at him, loving him so much that she did not—could not think. "You're a strange child," she whispered, "and you have the pinkest cheeks in the whole wide world."

"Sure I have," he said.

"What a funny little laugh!" she said, paling.

"That wasn't me. That was Fuzzy. He thinks you're funny."

Mummy stood over the crib, looking down at him. It seemed to be the frown that looked at him, while the eyes looked past. Finally she wet her lips and patted his head. "Good night, baby."

"Good night, Mummy." He closed his eyes. Mummy tiptoed out. The monster kept right on doing it.

It was nap-time the next day, and for the hundredth time Mummy had kissed him and said, "You're so *good* about your nap, Jeremy!" Well, he was. He always went straight up to bed at nap-time, as he did at bedtime. Mummy didn't know why, of course. Perhaps Jeremy did not know. Fuzzy knew.

Jeremy opened the toy-chest and took Fuzzy out. "You're hungry, I bet," he said.

"Yes. Let's hurry."

Jeremy climbed into the crib and hugged the teddy bear close. "I keep thinking about that girl," he said.

"What girl?"

"The one whose hair I changed."

"Maybe because it's the first time you've changed a person."

"It is not! What about the man who fell into the subway hole?"

"You moved the hat. The one that blew off. You moved it under his feet so that he stepped on the brim with one foot and caught his toe in the crown, and tumbled in."

"Well, what about the little girl I threw in front of the truck?"

"You didn't touch her," said the monster equably. "She was on roller skates. You broke something in one wheel so it couldn't turn. So she fell right in front of the truck."

Jeremy thought carefully. "Why didn't I ever touch a person before?"

"I don't know," said Fuzzy. "It has something to do with being born in this house, I think."

"I guess maybe," said Jeremy doubtfully.

"I'm hungry," said the monster, settling itself on Jeremy's stomach as he turned on his back.

"Oh, all right," Jeremy said. "The next lecture?"

"Yes," said Fuzzy eagerly. "Dream bright, now. The big things that you say, lecturing. Those are what I want. Never mind the people there. Never mind you, lecturing. The things you say."

The strange blood flowed as Jeremy relaxed. He looked up to the ceiling, found the hairline crack that he always stared at while he dreamed real, and began to talk.

"There I am. There's the—the room, yes, and the—yes, it's all there, again. There's the girl. The one who has the brown, shiny hair. The seat behind her is empty. This must be after that other girl broke her neck."

"Never mind that," said the monster impatiently. "What do you say?"

"I—" Jeremy was quiet. Finally Fuzzy nudged him. "Oh. It's all about yesterday's unfortunate occurrence, but, like the show of legend, our studies must go on."

"Go on with it then," panted the monster.

"All right, all right," said Jeremy impatiently. "Here it is. We come now to the Gymnosophists, whose ascetic school has had no recorded equal in its extremism. Those strange gentry regarded clothing and even food as detrimental to purity of thought. The Greeks also called them *Hylobioi,* a term our more erudite students will notice as analogous to the Sanskrit *Vana-Prasthas.* It is evident that they were a profound influence on Diogenes Laërtius, the Elisian founder of pure skepticism....

And so he droned on and on. Fuzzy crouched on his body, its soft ears making small masticating motions; and sometimes when stimulated by some particularly choice nugget of esoterica, the ears drooled.

At the end of nearly an hour, Jeremy's soft voice trailed off, and he was quiet. Fuzzy shifted in irritation. "What is it?"

"That girl," said Jeremy. "I keep looking back to that girl while I'm talking."

"Well, stop doing it. I'm not finished."

"There isn't any more, Fuzzy. I keep looking and looking back to that girl until I can't lecture any more. Now I'm saying all that about the pages in the book and the assignment. The lecture is over."

Fuzzy's mouth was almost full of blood. From its ears, it sighed. "That wasn't any too much. But if that's all, then it's all. You can sleep now if you want to."

"I want to watch for a while."

The monster puffed out its cheeks. The pressure inside was not great. "Go on, then." It scrabbled off Jeremy's body and curled up in a sulky huddle.

The strange blood moved steadily through Jeremy's brain. With his eyes wide and fixed, he watched himself as he would be, a slight, balding professor of philosophy.

He sat in the hall, watching the students tumbling up the steep aisles, wondering at the strange compulsion he had to look at that girl, Miss—Miss—what was it?

Oh. "Miss Patchell!"

He started, astonished at himself. He had certainly not meant to call out her name. He clasped his hands tightly, regaining the dry stiffness which was his closest approach to dignity.

The girl came slowly down the aisle steps, her wideset eyes wondering. There were books tucked under her arm, and her hair shone. "Yes, Professor?"

"I—" He stopped and cleared his throat. "I know it's the last class today, and you are no doubt meeting someone. I shan't keep you very long . . . and if I do," he added, and was again astonished at himself, "you can see Bert tomorrow."

"Bert? Oh!" She colored prettily. "I didn't know you knew about—how *could* you know?"

He shrugged. "Miss Patchell," he said. "You'll forgive an old—ah—middle-aged man's rambling, I hope. There is something about you that—that—"

"Yes?" Caution, and an iota of fright were in her eyes. She glanced up and back at the now empty hall

Abruptly he pounded the table. "I will *not* let this go on for another instant without finding out about it. Miss Patchell, you are becoming afraid of me, and you are wrong."

"I th-think I'd better . . ." she said timidly, and began backing off.

"Sit down!" he thundered. It was the very first time in his entire life that he had thundered at anyone, and her shock was not one whit greater than his. She shrank back and into a front-row seat, looking a good deal smaller than she actually was, except about the eyes, which were much larger.

The professor shook his head in vexation. He rose, stepped down off the dais, and crossed to her, sitting in the next seat.

"Now be quiet and listen to me." The shadow of a smile twitched his lips and he said, "I really don't know what I am going to say. Listen, and be patient. It couldn't be more important."

He sat a while, thinking, chasing vague pictures around in his mind. He heard, or was conscious of, the rapid but slowing beat of her frightened heart.

"Miss Patchell," he said, turning to her, his voice gentle, "I have not at any time looked into your records. Until—ah—yesterday, you were simply another face in the class, another source of quiz papers to be graded. I have not consulted the registrar's files for information about you. And, to my almost certain knowledge, this is the first time I have spoken with you.

"That's right, sir," she said quietly.

"Very good, then." He wet his lips. "You are twenty-three years old. The house in which you were born was a two-story affair, quite old, with a leaded bay window at the turn of the stairs. The small bedroom, or nursery, was directly over the kitchen. You could hear the clatter of dishes below you when the house was quiet. The address was 191 Bucyrus Road."

"How—oh yes! How did you know?"

He shook his head, and then put it between his hands. "I don't know. I don't know. I lived in that house, too, as a child. I don't know how I knew that you did. There are things in here—" He rapped his head, shook it again. "I thought perhaps you could help."

She looked at him. He was a small man, brilliant, tired, getting old swiftly. She put a hand on his arm. "I wish I could," she said warmly. "I do wish I could."

"Thank you, child."

"Maybe if you told me more—"

"Perhaps. Some of it is—ugly. All of it is cloudy, long ago, barely remembered. And yet—"

"Please go on."

"I remember," he half whispered, "things that happened long ago that way, and recent things I remember—twice. One memory is sharp and clear, and one is old and misty. And I remember, in the same misty way, what is happening now and—and what will happen!"

"I don't understand."

"That girl. That Miss Symes. She—died here yesterday."

"She was sitting right behind me," said Miss Patchell.

"I know it! I knew what was going to happen to her. I knew it mistily, like an old memory. That's what I mean. I don't know what I could have done to stop it. I don't think I could have done anything.

And yet, down deep I have the feeling that it's my fault—that she slipped and fell because of something I did."

"Oh, no!"

He touched her arm in mute gratitude for the sympathy in her tone, and grimaced miserably. "It's happened before," he said. "Time and time and time again. As a boy, as a youth, I was plagued with accidents. I led a quiet life. I was not very strong and books were always more my line than baseball. And yet I witnessed a dozen or more violent, useless deaths—automobile accidents, drownings, falls, and one or two—" his voice shook—"which I won't mention. And there were countless minor ones—broken bones, maimings, stabbings . . . and every time, in some way, it was my fault, like the one yesterday . . . and I—I—"

"Don't," she whispered. "Please don't. You were nowhere near Elaine Symes when she fell."

"I was nowhere near any of them! That never mattered. It never took away the burden of guilt. Miss Patchell—"

"Catherine."

"Catherine. Thank you so much! There are people called by insurance actuaries, 'accident prone.' Most of these are involved in accidents through their own negligence, or through some psychological quirk which causes them to defy the world, or to demand attention, by getting hurt. But some are simply present at accidents, without being involved at all—catalysts of death, if you'll pardon a flamboyant phrase. I am, apparently, one of these."

"Then—how could you feel guilty?"

"It was—" He broke off suddenly, and looked at her. She had a gentle face, and her eyes were filled with compassion. He shrugged. "I've said so much," he said. "More would sound no more fantastic, and do me no more damage."

"There'll be no damage from anything you tell me," she said, with a sparkle of decisiveness.

He smiled his thanks this time, sobered, and said, "These horrors—the maimings, the deaths—they were *funny,* once, long ago. I must have been a child, a baby. Something taught me, then, that the agony and death of others was to be promoted and enjoyed. I remember, I—almost remember when that stopped. There was a—a toy, a—a—"

Jeremy blinked. He had been staring at the fine crack in the ceiling for so long that his eyes hurt.

"What are you doing?" asked the monster.

"Dreaming real," said Jeremy. "I am grown up and sitting in the big empty lecture place, talking to the girl with the brown hair that shines. Her name's Catherine."

"What are you talking about?"

"Oh, all the funny dreams. Only—"

"Well?"

"They're not so funny."

The monster scurried over to him and pounced on his chest. "Time to sleep now. And I want to—"

"No," said Jeremy. He put his hands over his throat. "I have enough now. Wait until I see some more of this real-dream."

"What do you want to see?"

"Oh, I don't know. There's something. . . ."

"Let's have some fun," said the monster. "This is the girl you can change, isn't it?"

"Yes."

"Go ahead. Give her an elephant's trunk. Make her grow a beard. Stop her nostrils up. Go on. You can do anything." Jeremy grinned briefly, and then said, "I don't want to."

"Oh, go on. Just see how funny. . ."

"A toy," said the professor. "But more than a toy. It could talk, I think. If I could only remember more clearly!"

"Don't try so hard. Maybe it will come," she said. She took his hand impulsively. "Go ahead."

"It was—something—" the professor said haltingly, "—something soft and not too large. I don't recall . . . "

"Was it smooth?"

"No. Hairy—fuzzy. *Fuzzy!* I'm beginning to get it. Wait, now . . . A thing like a teddy bear. It talked. It—why, of course! It was alive!"

"A pet, then. Not a toy."

"Oh, no," said the professor, and shuddered. "It was a toy, all right. My mother thought it was, anyway. It made me dream real."

"You mean, like Peter Ibbetson?"

"No, no. Not like that." He leaned back, rolled his eyes up. "I used to see myself as I would be later, when I was grown. And before. Oh. Oh—I think it was then— Yes! It must have been then that I began to see all those terrible accidents. It was! It was!"

"Steady," said Catherine. "Tell me quietly."

He relaxed. "Fuzzy. The demon—the monster. I know what it did, the devil. Somehow it made me see myself as I grew. It made me repeat what I had learned. It—it ate knowledge! It did; it ate knowledge. It had some strange affinity for me, for something about me. It could absorb knowledge that I gave out. And it—it changed the knowledge into blood, the way a plant changes sunlight and water into cellulose!"

"I don't understand," she said again.

"You don't? How could you? How can I? I know that that's what it did, though. It made me—why, I was spouting my lectures here to the beast when I was four years old! The words of them, the sense of them, came from me *now* to me *then. And* I gave it to the monster, and it ate the knowledge and spiced it with the things it made me do in my real dreams. It made me trip a man up on a hat, of all absurd things, and fall into a subway excavation. And when I was in my teens, I was right by the excavation to see it happen. And that's the way with all of them! All the horrible accidents I have witnessed, I have half-remembered before they happened. There's no stopping any of them. What am I going to do?"

There were tears in her eyes. "What about me?" she whispered—more, probably, to get his mind away from his despair than for any other reason.

"You. There's something about you, if only I could remember. Something about what happened to that—that toy, that beast. You were in the same environment as I, as that devil. Somehow, you are vulnerable to it and—Catherine, Catherine, I think that something was done to you that—"

He broke off. His eyes widened in horror. The girl sat beside him, helping him, pitying him, and her expression did not change. But—everything else about her did.

Her face shrank, shrivelled. Her eyes lengthened. Her ears grew long, grew until they were like donkey's ears, like rabbit's ears, like horrible, long hairy spider's legs. Her teeth lengthened into tusks. Her arms shrivelled into jointed straws, and her body thickened.

It smelled like rotten meat.

There were filthy claws scattering out of her polished open-toed shoes. There were bright sores. There were—other things. And all the while she—it—held his hand and looked at him with pity and friendliness.

The professor—

Jeremy sat up and flung the monster away. "It isn't funny!" he screamed. "It isn't funny, it isn't, it isn't, it *isn't!*"

The monster sat up and looked at him with its soft, bland, teddy-bear expression. "Be quiet," it said. "Let's make her all squashy now, like soft-soap. And hornets in her stomach. And we can put her—"

Jeremy clapped his hands over his ears and screwed his eyes shut. The monster talked on. Jeremy burst into tears, leapt from the crib and, hurling the monster to the floor, kicked it. It grunted. "That's funny!" screamed the child. "Ha ha!" he cried, as he planted both feet in its yielding stomach. He picked up the twitching mass and hurled it across the room. It struck the nursery clock. Clock and monster struck the floor together in a flurry of glass, metal, and blood. Jeremy stamped it all into a jagged, pulpy mass, blood from his feet mixing with blood from the monster, the same strange blood which the monster had pumped into his neck....

Mummy all but fainted when she ran in and saw him. She screamed, but he laughed, screaming. The doctor gave him sedatives until he slept, and cured his feet. He was never very strong after that. They saved him, to live his life and to see his real-dreams; funny dreams, and to die finally in a lecture room, with his eyes distended in horror while horror froze his heart, and a terrified young woman ran crying, crying for help.

A Way Home

WHEN PAUL RAN away from home, he met no one and saw nothing all the way to the highway. The highway swept sudden and wide from the turn by Keeper's Rise, past the blunt end of the Township Road, and narrowed off to a distant pinpoint pricking at the horizon. After a time Paul could see the car.

It was new and long and it threw down its snout a little as the driver braked, and when it stopped beside him it seesawed easily, once, on its big soft springs.

The driver was a large man, large and costly, with a gray Stetson and a dove-colored topcoat made of something that did not crease in the bend of his arms but rolled and folded instead. The woman beside him had a broad brow and a pointed chin. Her skin had peach shadings, but was deeply tanned, and her hair was the red gold called "straw color" by a smith as he watches his forge. She smiled at the man and she smiled at Paul almost the same way.

"Hi, son," the man said. "This the old Township Road?"

"Yes, sir," said Paul, "it sure is."

"Figured it was," said the man. "A feller don't forget."

"Reckon you don't," said Paul.

"Haven't seen the old town in twenty years," said the man. "I guess it ain't changed much."

"These old places don't change much," said Paul with scorn.

"Oh, they ain't so bad to come back to," said the man. "Hate to get chained down in one all my life, though."

"Me too," agreed Paul. "You from around here?"

"Why sure," said the man. "My name's Roudenbush. Any more Roudenbushes around here that you know of, boy?"

"Place is full of 'em," said Paul. "Hey, you're not the Roudenbush kid that ran away twenty years ago?"

"The very one," said the man. "What happened after I left?"

"Why, they talk about you to this day," said Paul. "Your mother sickened and died, and your pa got up in meetin' a month after you left an' asked forgiveness for treatin' you so mean."

"Poor old feller," said the man. "I guess it was a little rough of me to run out like that. But he asked for it."

"I bet he did."

"This is my wife," said the man.

The woman smiled at Paul again. She did not speak. Paul could not think up what kind of a voice she might have. She leaned forward and opened up the glove compartment. It was cram-full of chocolate-covered cherries.

"Been crazy about these ever since I was a kid," said the man. "Help yourself. I got ten pounds of them in the back." He leaned into the leather cushions, took out a silver cigar case, put a cigar between his teeth, and applied a lighter that flamed up like a little bonfire in his hand. "Yes, sir," said the man. "I got two more cars back in the city, and a tuxedo suit with shiny lapels. I made my killing in the stock market, and now I'm president of a railroad. I'll be getting back there this evening, after I give the folks in the old town a treat."

Paul had a handful of chocolate-covered cherries. "Gee," he said. After that he walked on down the highway. The cherries disappeared and the man and the lady and the car all disappeared, but that didn't matter. "It'll be like that," said young Paul Roudenbush. "It'll be just like that." Then, "I wonder what that lady's name'll be."

A quarter of a mile down the pike was the turn-off to the school, and there was the railroad crossing with its big X on a pole that he always read RAIL CROSSING ROAD. The forenoon freight was bowling down the grade, screaming two longs, a short, and a long. When he was a kid, two years or so back, Paul used to think it saluted him: *Paul . . . Roud . . . n'Bush-h-h . . .* with the final sibilant made visible in the plume of steam on the engine's iron shoulder. Paul trotted up to the crossing and stood just where the first splintered plank met the road surface. Engine, tender, Pennsylvania, Nickel Plate, T.&N.O., Southern, Southern, Pennsylvania, Père Marquette,

Canadian Pacific. Cars from all over: hot places, cold places, far places. Automobiles, automobiles, cattle, tank. Tank tank cattle. Refrigerator, refrigerator, automobiles, caboose. Caboose with a red flag flying, and a glimpse at the window of a bull-necked trainman shaving, suds on his jowls like a mad dog. Then the train was a dwindling rectangle on the track, and on its top was the silhouette of a brakeman, leaning easily into wind and velocity, walking on top of the boxcars.

With the train in one ear and dust in the other, Paul faced the highway. A man stood at the other side of the tracks. Paul gaped at him.

He was wearing an old brown jacket with a gray sheepskin collar, and blue dungarees. These he was dusting off with long weatherbeaten hands, one of which—the right—looked like a claw. There was no ring finger or little finger, and a third of the palm's breadth was gone. From the side of the middle finger to the side of the wrist, the hand was neatly sealed with a type of flexible silvery scar-tissue.

He looked up from his dusting at Paul. "Hi, bub." Either he had a beard or he badly needed a shave. Paul could see the cleft in his square chin, though. The man had eyes as pale as the color of water poured into a glass after the milk had been drunk.

Paul said, "Hi," still looking at the hand. The man asked him what that town was over there in the hollow, and Paul told him. He knew now what the man was—one of those fabulous characters who ride on freight trains from place to place. Ride the rods. Catch a fast freight out of Casey, which was K.C., which was Kansas City. They had been everywhere and done everything, these men, and they had a language all their own. Handouts and line bulls, Chi and mulligan and grab a rattler to Nollins.

The man squinched up his eyes at the town, as if he were trying to drive his gaze through the hill and see more. "The old place hasn't growed none," he said, and spat.

Paul spat too. "Never will," he said.

"You from there?"

"Yup."

"Me too," said the man surprisingly.

"Gosh," said Paul. "You don't look like you came from around here."

The man crossed the single track to Paul's side. "I guess I don't. I been a lot of places since I left here."

"Where you been?" asked Paul.

The man looked into Paul's open eyes, and through them to Paul's open credulousness. "All over the world," he said. "All over this country on freights, and all over the oceans on ships." He bared his right forearm. "Look there." And sure enough he had a tattoo.

"Women," said the man, flexing his claw so that the tattoo writhed. "That's what *I* like." He closed one pale eye, pushed his mouth sidewise under it, and clucked a rapid *chick-chick* from his pale cheek.

Paul wet his lips, spat again, and said, "Yeah. Oh, boy."

The man laughed. He had bad teeth. "You're like I was. Wasn't room enough in that town for me."

"Me either," said Paul. "I ain't going back there *no* more."

"Oh, you'll go back. You'll want to look it over, and ask a few questions around, and find out what happened to your old gals, and see how dead everything is, so's you can go away again knowin' you done right to leave in the first place. This here's my second trip back. Seems like every time I go through this part o' the world I just got to drop by here and let the old burg give me a couple laughs." He turned his attention right around and looked outward again. "You really are headin' out, bub?"

"Headin' out," nodded Paul. He liked the sound of that. "Headin' out," he said again.

"Where you bound?"

"The city," Paul said, "unless I hit somethin' I like better 'fore I get there."

The man considered him. "Hey. Got any money?"

Paul shook his head cautiously. He had two dollars and ninety-two cents. The man seemed to make some decision; he shrugged. "Well, good luck, bub. More places you see, more of a man you'll be. Woman told me that once in Sacramento."

"The—oh!" said Paul. Approaching the grade crossing was a maroon coupé. "It's Mr. Sherman!"

"Who's he?"

"The sheriff. He'll be out lookin' for me!"

"Sheriff! Me for the brush. Don't tag, you little squirt! Go the other way!" and he dived down the embankment and disappeared into the bushes.

Frightened by the man's sudden harshness, confused by the necessity for instant action, Paul shuffled for a moment, almost dancing, and then ran to the other side. Flat on his stomach in a growth of fireweed, he stopped breathing and peered at the road. The coupé slowed, all but stopped. Paul closed his eyes in terror. Then he heard the grate of gears and the rising whine as the car pulled over the tracks in second gear and moaned on up the highway.

Paul waited five minutes, his fear leaving him exactly as fast as his sweat dried. Then he emerged and hurried along the highway, keeping a sharp watch ahead for the sheriff's returning car. He saw no sign of the man with the claw. But then, he hadn't really expected to.

It could be like that, he thought. Travel this old world over. Gramps used to say that men like that had an itching foot. Paul's feet itched a little, if he thought about it. Hurt a little, too. He could come back years from now with a tattoo and a mutilated hand. Folks'd really take notice. The stories he could tell! *"I run down the bank, see, to haul this tomato out o' th' drink. She was yellin' her blond head off. No sooner got my hooks on her when* clomp, *a alligator takes off part o' me hand. I didn't mind none. Not when I carried this babe up the bank."* He shut one eye, pushed his mouth sideways, and clucked. The sound, somehow, reminded him of chocolate-covered cherries....

Another half mile, and the country became more open. He flicked his eyes from side to side as he trudged. First sign of that maroon coupé and he'd have to fade. *Sheriff! Me for the brush!* He felt good. He could keep ahead of the law. Bet your life. Go where you want to go, do what you want to do, come back for a laugh every once in a while. That was better, even, than a big car and a tuxedo suit. Women. A smooth-faced one in the car beside you or, *chick-chick,* women all over, Sacramento and every place, to tell you what a man you are, because of all the places you've been. Yup, that was it.

There was a deep drone from overhead. Paul looked up and saw the plane—one of the private planes that based at the airport forty miles away. Planes were no novelty, but Paul never saw one without an expressed wish that something would happen—not necessarily a crash, though that wouldn't be bad, but much rather something that would bring the plane down for a forced landing, so he could run over and see the pilot get out, and maybe talk to him or even help him fix the trouble. "Let me know next time you're at the field," the pilot would say.

Paul slowed, stopped, then went to the shoulder and sat down with his feet in the dry ditch. He watched the plane. It dipped a wing and circled, went off and came lower, made a run over the meadow. Paul thought he was going to—well, of course, he was going to land!

The wheels touched, kicked up a puff of yellow dust that whisked out of existence in the prop-wash. They touched again and held the earth; the tail came down, bounced a little, and then the plane was carrying its wings instead of being carried. The wings were orange and the fuselage was blue, and it was glossy in the sun. The wings wobbled slightly as the plane taxied over the lumpy meadow, and Paul knew that if he held out his arms and wobbled them like that he would feel it in his shoulders.

The motor barked, and the propeller blades became invisible as the pilot braked one wheel and turned the ship in its own length. The propeller, in profile, was a ghostly band and then a glass disc as the plane swung toward Paul. It snorted and wobbled across the meadow until it was within twenty feet of the fence and the ditch. Then, with a roar, it swung broadside to him and the sound of the motor dwindled to an easy *pwap-tick-tickety-pwap,* while the pilot did knowledgeable things at the controls. Paul could see him in there, plain as day, through the cabin doors. The plane was beautiful; standing still it looked as if it were going two hundred miles an hour. The windshield swept right back over the pilot's head. It was fine.

The pilot opened the door and vaulted to the ground. "Glory be! You'd think they'd have a field built in town after all these years."

"They never will," said Paul. "Nice job you got there."

The pilot, pulling off a pair of high-cuffed gloves, looked briefly at the plane and grinned. He was very clean and had wide shoulders and practically no hips. He wore a good soft leather jacket and tight breeches. "Know anybody in town, son?"

"Everybody, I guess."

"Well, now. I can get all the news from you before I go on in."

"Say—ain't you Paul Roudenbush?"

Paul froze. *He* hadn't said that. There were sudden icy cramps in the backs of his knees. The plane vanished. The pilot vanished. Paul sat with his feet in the dry ditch and slowly turned his head.

A maroon coupé stood by the ditch. Its door was open, and there, one foot on the running-board, was Mr. Sherman. *Sheriff! Me for the brush!*

Instead, he licked his lips and said, "Hi, Mr. Sherman."

"My," said Mr. Sherman, "you give me a turn, you did. Saw you sitting there so still, figured you'd been hit by a car or some such."

"I'm all right," said Paul faintly. He rose. Might as well get it over with. "I was just . . . thinkin', I guess."

Thinking—and now he was caught, and the thoughts raced through him like the cars of the forenoon freight; thoughts from hot places, cold places, far places. Stock market, car, claw claw plane. Women, women, cigarette lighter, landing field. Thoughts that were real, thoughts that he made up; they barreled on through him, with a roar and a swirl, and left him standing, facing the highway and Mr. Sherman, who had caught him.

"Thinking, eh? Well, I'm right relieved," said Mr. Sherman. He got back in the car, slammed the door, stepped on the starter.

"Mr. Sherman, ain't you—"

"Ain't I what, son?"

"Nothin', Mr. Sherman. Nothin' at all."

"You're a weird one," said Mr. Sherman, shaking his head. "Hey, I'm heading back into town. Want a lift? It's near eating time."

"No, thanks," said Paul immediately and with great sincerity.

Paul watched the maroon coupé move off, his mind racing. The car was going into town. Without him. Mr. Sherman did not know he was running away. Why not? Well, they hadn't missed him yet. Unless . . . unless they didn't care whether he came back or not. No.

No, that couldn't be! The car would go right past his house, soon's it got in town. Wasn't much of a house. In it, though, was his own room. Small, but absolutely his own.

The trouble with the other ways to go back, it took time to make a killing in the stock market and get married. It took time to acquire a plane. It probably took quite a while to get part of your hand cut off. But this way—

Suddenly he was in the road screaming, "Mr. Sherman! Mr. Sherman!"

Mr. Sherman didn't hear him but he saw him in the rear-view mirror. He stopped and backed up a bit. Paul climbed in, gasped his thanks, and sat still, working on his wind. He got it all back just about the time they turned into the Township Road.

Mr. Sherman glanced abruptly at the boy. "Paul."

"Yes, sir."

"I just had a thought. You, 'way out there on the pike; were you running away?"

Paul said, "No." His eyes were more puzzled than anything else. "I was coming back," he said.

Story Notes

by Paul Williams

"Maturity": first published in *Astounding Science-Fiction,* February 1947. Written before March 25, 1946 (when he told his mother, in a letter, that he had already sold it and been paid, $367.50). Substantially rewritten in early 1948, for inclusion in Sturgeon's first book, the story collection *Without Sorcery* (Prime Press, 1948). The version included in this volume is the later version, which the author strongly preferred. The text of the second half of the original magazine version is included here as an appendix, for scholars and the curious.

Sturgeon's introduction to the story in *Without Sorcery* follows: *Robin English, one of the most captivating characters ever to take a fictional bit in his teeth, appeared in an earlier version of "Maturity." Let the reader be enjoined, if he has read this earlier effort, to forget it; if he has not, to leave it alone.*

Halfway through the original version, I found that I had by the tail a very large beast indeed. Finding myself suddenly with neither information nor convictions, I completed the story by merely tying up plot-threads, and not by saying anything at all.

I have attempted here to erase this reprehensible act. The story now says much and concludes nothing. It may now, I earnestly hope, serve to generate a certain amount of directive thought on this curious subject.

Sturgeon's other major public statement about the story appeared in a book entitled *Maturity* (subtitled: *Three Stories by Theodore Sturgeon*) published in a limited edition of 750 copies to commemorate TS's appearance as Guest of Honor at a science fiction convention in Minnesota in April 1979. In the Editors' Notes to that book (Rune Press, 1979), editors Scott Imes and Stuart W. Wells III explain that, "Scott called Sturgeon and he agreed [to the idea of a limited edition book]. He had just the story for the book. He would rewrite and expand 'Maturity.' There was plenty of time, but he would start right away. . . . A few months come and go and February arrives. Deadlines draw nearer and nearer. How is the story coming? Sturgeon is reached and reveals that he started to rewrite the story but likes the original better. . . . The book is now too short. Sturgeon suggests that two stories be added on the same theme: 'Bulkhead' and 'The Graveyard Reader.'"

The first 60 percent of Sturgeon's 1979 Introduction to his book *Maturity* (the balance concerns the other two stories) follows:

"Maturity" was written in 1946, and appeared in Astounding Science-Fiction *under the editorship of the great John W. Campbell, Jr. It was preceded by two years of research—research which consisted of asking everyone I met—young people, old ones, rich, poor; strangers, loved ones, even faceless voices over the telephone: "What is maturity?"*

This story was, I think, the emergence of the "thing I say." James Blish and Damon Knight once produced the hypothesis that every writer has a thing he says, and he says it over and over again (in different ways, of course) every time he writes. I think they were right. Though I have since rephrased and refocused the "thing I say," this story is a good beginning. I'll tell you at the end of the book what it is now.

One interesting aspect my research unearthed is that a certain category of human beings backed off from my question. They were women over thirty-five. It wasn't until I pushed one of them into a wall and demanded to know where the reluctance came from that I learned that it had leaked out from ads in the newspapers and women's magazines. "For the mature figure" meant either fat, or old, or both.

The story tumbled into being without much effort until I was about two-thirds through, and then I began to have some doubts about my own definition of maturity. For a while I bogged down completely, and at last just finished writing the story, because by then I knew how to finish writing a story. But I was profoundly dissatisfied with it.

It appeared in the magazine in '47. In 1948, along came Jim Williams of Prime Press, wanting to do a collection. It would be my first, but the chief reason I jumped to say yes was that it would be a chance to rewrite this story. I did, and was better pleased, but not altogether.

In 1952 I became father of my firstborn son, and so I named him Robin, after the protagonist of this story; he is my "second rewrite." I thought he would either mature in ways where I could observe him, day by day, or he would not, and I'd find out why; either way, I could refine my concept of the nature of maturity. I write this on Robin Sturgeon's 27th birthday, and I can say with pride that the second rewrite is better than the first one. Tall, strong, talented, with a fifty-thousand candle-power smile, he plays guitar and trumpet, sings, composes, arranges, in and around Woodstock, New York. He is self-actualized and very alive, and he has done this for my definition of maturity: it isn't a condition, it isn't a place-to-arrive; like everything else in this universe, it's a way of going rather than a way of being. It's movement, flux, growth, change, development. This is the one thing that the first Robin couldn't quite grasp.

The relevant paragraphs of Sturgeon's Postscript to the 1979 book follow:

Maturity is not, after all, the name of my quest, the "thing I say." I look rather for the nature of the optimum human being—not a freak like Robin English or Superman, engaging as they may be, but humanity with a spleen and eyeballs and eardrums and all the other parts each working at the top of its capacity and in absolute harmony—a kind of perfect internal ecology. And along with that, of course, goes the optimum brain; and I deeply believe that there is no upper limit there.

Only the optimum human can save the species and populate the universe.

When Sturgeon spoke with David Hartwell in 1972 about his

"preoccupation with the optimum man," he affirmed that: *"Maturity" is the blueprint for this whole thing I've been talking about.*

In view of the plot of "Maturity," it is interesting to note that on April 29, 1938, noted bacteriologist Paul de Kruif wrote to Theodore Sturgeon (clearly in response to a letter from the young man), "Dear Mr. Sturgeon: Your spirit is certainly a laudable one, but at the present time I know of no institution which could avail itself of a human guinea pig for any of the diseases you mention." (Source: the papers of Theodore Sturgeon in the possession of his Literary Trust)

On Feb. 3, 1947, just after "Maturity" was first published, Ray Bradbury wrote TS a letter that began: "Ted, I hate you! Having just read your story 'Maturity,' I have every reason to hate you. It is a damned nice story. Your sense of humor, sir, is incredible. I don't believe you've written a bad story yet; I don't think you ever will. This is not log-rolling, by God; I only speak the truth. I predict you will be selling at least six stories a year to *Collier's* and *The Post* before long. You have the touch."

Also on Feb. 3, 1947, Robert Heinlein wrote, "Ted, my respectful congratulations on 'Maturity.' I recognized some of the autobiographical touches. You are probably the most accomplished Peter Pan ever to have survived three decades, more or less (except me, maybe, he added with a churlish pout). But don't let anyone monkey with your thymus gland; we like you the way you are. No kiddin', it was a swell story." One autobiographical touch: the biographical note in the back of Sturgeon books published by Ballantine in the 1950s says Sturgeon spent six years in high school and quotes him as saying, "I didn't graduate; I was released"—precisely what Robin tells Peg in "Maturity."

Two years after reading "Maturity," Heinlein began working on the novel that would become *Stranger in a Strange Land.* It is not difficult to see traces of Robin English's influence in the character of Michael Valentine Smith.

Sturgeon wrote to his mother (Christine Hamilton Sturgeon) on Feb. 9, 1947: *I am sending you the current* Astounding *and the current* Weird [with his story "Fluffy"]. *Both yarns have received quite a flurry of comment. I would particularly like a careful comment on "Maturity" from you. I've quite lost perspective on the yarn, and rather urgently want it back. (The perspective, not the magazine!) Maturity is, as I may have remarked to you before, a thing on which I am qualified to make objective observations....* (He also asked his ex-wife for her written comments on the story.)

Clifford Simak, a great science fiction writer who had been writing longer than Sturgeon, wrote TS on 2/14/47, "I'm sorrier than I can tell you, but I didn't care for 'Maturity.' ... The idea was a honey. It developed well up to about the middle of the yarn, although it seemed to me that you were holding yourself back, that you were positively laboring to make it subjective, determined that you would allow no dramatics and no overtones.... And the ending. By God, Ted, you didn't believe that yourself. A mature man, a really mature man would have done something other than follow the footsteps of normal humans.... I hope you aren't angry with me...." A further letter from Simak indicates that TS responded immediately, although no carbon survives in his papers.

Philip Klass (William Tenn) wrote TS on 12/30/48: "I have just finished reading the rewritten version of 'Maturity' which appears in your book.... Ted, accept my congratulations on your masterpiece."

Noted SF anthologist Groff Conklin wrote in 1954, about the second version of "Maturity": "In [my] opinion, this is one of the most poignantly real stories about the tragedy of a superman in our midst that has ever been written."

John W. Campbell's blurb on the first page of the story in *Astounding:* IT'S BEEN SAID THAT A MAN NEVER GROWS UP. THERE'S CONSIDERABLE EVIDENCE FOR THE LITERAL TRUTH OF THIS—AND A FASCINATING PROBLEM IN WHAT THE BEHAVIOR OF A TRULY MATURE HUMAN BEING WOULD BE.

"Tiny and the Monster": first published in *Astounding Science-Fiction,* May 1947. Probably written in the fall of 1946 (judging from the amount of time that usually elapsed between *Astounding* buying a story and getting it into print) or in February and March 1947 (based on a comment in a March letter that he "got a good start on the dog story").

In an interview with Paul Williams in February 1976, Sturgeon said, *"Tiny and the Monster" came out of a weekend I spent with* [science fiction writers] *Henry Kuttner and C. L. Moore, and that was the house that I visualized* [in that story]. *It was up in Hastings-on-Hudson. I really loved that house; I thought that was such a nice place to be. And the mother-in-law, who kind of took over the story ... she was a subsidiary character who took the bit in her teeth and just ran away with it. It's one of the many instances where one of my subsidiary characters has become so dimensional that I can't change it or eliminate it, and I'm not going to waste 6000 words of hard-earned copy, so I have to march up and down the road for a couple of weeks or months, or whatever it takes, to readjust the entire story to embrace this character without changing it. Which is nice, because if the author doesn't know how a story's going to come out, a reader couldn't possibly know. But that old lady and her little blue car, that was my mother and her funny little blue car that she had down in Jamaica. It was a fun story ... and it really had something to say, too, about ugliness as such. The monster itself was so hideous, and knew it, and didn't show itself, not only for reasons of security but because it knew the human reaction to it would be so violent.* [Arthur C.] *Clarke has used that* [in *Childhood's End,* written five years later, where the aliens hide themselves because they look like devils].

In July 1947, TS wrote his mother about showing an old friend his "treasures"; first on the list were: *the* [Edd] *Cartier originals* [drawings done to accompany the story in *Astounding*] *for "Tiny and the Monster."*

Of course, the St. Croix elements in the story derive from Sturgeon's residence on St. Croix in the Virgin Islands in 1944.

Magazine blurb: TINY WASN'T TINY—BUT THE MONSTER WAS DEFINITELY HORRIFIC. TINY, ON THE OTHER HAND, DISPLAYED A QUITE INCREDIBLE INTELLIGENCE FOR A DOG, AFTER ONE ENCOUNTER—

"The Sky Was Full of Ships": first published in *Thrilling Wonder Stories,* June 1947. Probably written in the fall of 1946. This has also been published (in *The Ancient Mysteries Reader,* 1975, and *Encounters with Aliens,* 1968) under the title "The Cave of History."

A radio adaptation of this story was broadcast on the *Beyond Tomorrow* program, April 11, 1950, under the title "Incident at Switchpath."

Your editor can't resist noting that it seems possible Bob Dylan read this story (or heard it on the radio) as a young man, which would explain the closing image in his 1968 song "Drifter's Escape": "Just then a bolt of lightning struck the courthouse out of shape/And while everybody knelt to pray, the drifter did escape."

"The Sky Was Full of Ships" can also be seen as a precursor of and possible influence on Arthur C. Clarke's 1951 story "The Sentinel," which in turn became the basis of *2001: A Space Odyssey.*

The angry prospector at the end of the story who says, *"I have a kid reads that kind of stuff, an' I never did like to see him at it. Believe me, he's a-goin' to cut it out as of right now,"* is reminiscent of Sturgeon's often-told-tale of his stepfather's hostility to science fiction. TS to Williams, 11/75: *My stepfather regarded them* [science fiction magazines] *with total scorn, and finally he forbade me to bring those things into the house.*

"Largo": first published in *Fantastic Adventures,* July 1947. Probably written late 1946.

The setting of this story is drawn from Sturgeon's experience at age 20 working for a month at a summer resort in Andover, New Jersey. His job and some things that happened to him there turn up in Vernon Drecksall's saga. On June 13, 1938, TS wrote to his mother (from the Hudson Guild Farm): *I am working as pot-walloper, vegetable groom, fire-tender, and general kitchen and dining-room factotum, from 6:15* A.M. *until 7:30* P.M.*... The pay is microscopic, but all in all I don't care. I have a splendid opportunity to regain and improve on my swimming, diving and tumbling; I have time to write, and best of all I can observe and enjoy a thousand and one types of the human animal.*

A month later, back in Manhattan, he wrote his mother about the people he met at the Farm, including *Patsy Freeman, the darkest white girl alive, and with the reddest cheeks and the blackest eyes, with whose understanding and whose casualness I fell in unprecedented violent love, so that I could hardly bear to be near her or touch her or speak to her ... who, when she left me, cried openly and unashamed, and then climbed into the truck and was gone, and I plunged off into the woods in an agony of emptiness with my guitar, and lay on the reservoir dam and beat the strings and played as never before; played her into a moaning swing composition I have called "Slip into a Minor Key" and another which is exactly suited to the phenomenal piano-style of her friend and, I think, fiancé; a Hungarian, Otmar Gyorgy, a man I am proud to know, and who led me to an immense emotional-ethical battle through the strength of my friendship for him and that of my love for Pat; his style ... rolling minor basses, treble cascading poundingly; that which I composed for him I doubt that he will ever play, for it is so much mine....*

Lucy Menger, in her biographical/critical chapbook *Theodore Sturgeon* (Ungar, 1981) cites "Largo" in a discussion of Sturgeon's "love of the English language," pointing out examples of "poetic devices" such as alliteration, consonance, assonance, and repetition in the paragraph that begins "Each night after Drecksall had scoured the last...."

Gretel in "Largo" bears a distinct resemblance to Cordelia in Sturgeon's 1948 story "The Martian and the Moron."

"Thunder and Roses": first published in *Astounding Science-Fiction,* November 1947. Written in January and February 1947.

TS wrote an introductory note called "Why I Selected 'Thunder and Roses'" for an anthology titled *My Best Science Fiction Story* (Margulies, Friend, editors, 1949):

There is good reason to believe that, outside of the top men in the Manhattan District and in the Armed Forces, the only people in the world who fully understood what had happened on August 6, 1945, were the aficionados of science fiction—the fans, the editors, and the authors. Hiroshima had a tremendous effect on me. I was familiar with nuclear phenomena; I sold a story in 1940 which dealt with a method of separating Isotope 235 from pure uranium ["Artnan Process"]. *Years before the Project, and before the war, we had used up the gadgets and gimmicks of atomic power and were writing stories about the philosophical and sociological implications of this terrible new fact of life.*

"Thunder and Roses" is the result of nearly a decade of preoccupation with the idea of atomic energy. It was written in 1947 out of a black depression caused by the uncaring reception of books like One World or None *by a public happy to goad the United Nations into a state of yapping uselessness.*

I wrote the words and music to the song in this story when I was seventeen. Mary Mair sang it at the Philcon in '47—remember?

The Philcon was the World Science Fiction Convention in Philadelphia in August, 1947; Mary Mair was a showgirl who became, briefly, Theodore Sturgeon's second wife, in 1949. The words to "Thunder and Roses" first appear in Sturgeon's work as a poem in a 1939 story called "Thanksgiving Again" (included in *The Ultimate Egoist,* Vol. I of *The Complete Stories of Theodore Sturgeon*). In late 1947 TS wrote to his mother that he was hoping that a phonograph record would be made of the song (*lyrics by THS,* he told her, *music by THS*).

Before "Thunder and Roses" was published in *Astounding* August Derleth read it in manuscript and selected it for his anthology *Strange Ports of Call,* published early in 1948. This contributed to the considerable impact the story had on science fiction readers at the time. William Lindsay Gresham (whose novel *Nightmare Alley* had been made into a film in 1947) wrote Sturgeon a very enthusiastic letter about "Thunder and Roses" in May 1948, after reading it twice in two days: "I couldn't do any of my own stuff all day for thinking about it. I think it stands with the great short stories of our time, up there with Kipling's 'Without Benefit of Clergy' and Paul Gallico's 'Testimony.' For one thing, you have done something so rarely attempted in fiction, and that is to hand the big slice of heroism to the girl."

James Gunn, in *Alternate Worlds, The Illustrated History of Science Fiction* (1975) notes that "Thunder and Roses" was a particularly poignant and powerful (and early) articulation of what the nuclear threat would come to mean to the human psyche for the rest of the century: "Here is science fiction pointing out the ultimate horror of holocaust—the horror is not just that so many will die so horribly and so painfully, but that they destroy the future of mankind—all the unachieved potential, all the untested possibilities, all the art and love and courage and glory that might be; it is not just that some idiot kind of total warfare might destroy the present, but that it might destroy eternity. In a metaphorical sense, science fiction might be considered letters from the future, from our children, urging us to be careful of their world."

(One wonders to what extent Carl Sagan's energetic campaigning to educate the public in the 1980s about the dangers of "nuclear winter" was influenced by his reading of "Thunder and Roses" as a young man.)

Although it's a very tiny part of the story and unrelated to its powerful theme, your editor notes that the lines—" 'What kind of a reproducer have you got?' 'Audiovid.' 'A disk.' "—now seem prophetic.

Magazine blurb: ATOMIC WAR CAN PRODUCE STRANGE SITUATIONS—FOR AN ATOMIC BOMB CAN EXPLODE MORE THAN ONCE. AND IT MAY BE THAT THE VICTIM OF THE ATTACK DARE NOT REPLY!

"It Wasn't Syzygy": first published in *Weird Tales,* January 1948, under the (editor's) title "The Deadly Ratio." Written January-February 1947.

In April 1953 Theodore Sturgeon wrote to Redd Boggs, editor of an excellent science fiction "fanzine" called *Skyhook,* to respond to an article in the previous issue by William Atheling, Jr. (James Blish), in which Atheling said, "I wonder what has happened to Sturgeon's gift for invention. Every story he has contributed to the field over the past two years has dealt in one way or another with syzygy...." Atheling was commenting on a Sturgeon story called

"The Sex Opposite" and asserted that Sturgeon had already handled the subject of syzygy "definitively" in his 1948 story "The Perfect Host." With Sturgeon's permission, Boggs edited his letter into an article called "Why So Much Syzygy?" which was published in the Summer 1953 issue of *Skyhook*, and reprinted in a 1977 book edited by Damon Knight called *Turning Points, Essays on the Art of Science Fiction.*

In his letter (and the article, but the quotes here are from the letter, a carbon of which survives in Sturgeon's papers), TS wrote: *Your (SKYHOOK's, that is) remarks on an apparent preoccupation I have with syzygy came as something of a jolt. One needs to be told about such things. No one knows what he thinks until it's crystallized for shipment, unspoken thoughts being the formless, tintless things they are. My first reaction is to deny such an allegation and say loftily that you guys haven't been reading enough Sturgeon, or you never could say such a thing.... My first-and-a-half reaction is to list some recent stories just to show you how wrong you are, and when I do, I find by God you have something there. It isn't the something you state, but it* is *something, and I hadn't realized it before: so thanks, see?*

He goes on to talk about other "thematic repetitions" he has been "accused" of, and says, *let's see if we can get an LCD* [lowest common denominator] *out of the tangle.... I think that in "Bianca's Hands" and "The Perfect Host" and* ["The World Well Lost"] *we have sufficient material for the tentative establishment of that denominator.... I think what I've been trying to do all these years is to investigate this matter of love, sexual and asexual. I investigate it by writing about it, because, as stated above, I don't know what the hell I think until I tell somebody about it. And I work so assiduously at it because of a conviction that if one could understand it completely, one would have the key to cooperation itself: to creative inspiration: to the marvelous orchestration which enables us to keep ahead of our own destructiveness.*

In order to do this I've had to look at the individual components. In "The Deadly Ratio" (that, *by the way, was the "definitive" syzygy story; its original title was "It Wasn't Syzygy") I had two lovers, only one of whom was real. In "Bianca's Hands" only one of them was human. In "Rule of Three" and "Synthesis"* ["Make Room for Me"] *I had (in reverse order) a quasi-sexual relationship among three people, and one among six so's it could break down into three couples and be normal. In "The Stars Are the Styx" I set up several (four, as I remember) different kinds of love motivations for mutual comparisons. In "Two Percent Inspiration" it was hero-worship, a kid and a great scientist; in "Until Death Do Us Join" it was the murderous jealousy between two personalities in a schizophrenic, both in love with the same girl. In "Killdozer" it was a choked-up worship for the majesty of a machine. By this time you get the idea.*

Now if we can ... return to the original question: why so much syzygy?—well, it's pretty obvious why a clear-cut method of non-reproductive exchange should be so useful in such an overall investigation. It's beautifully open to comparison and analog. It handles all sorts of attachments felt by any sensitive person which could not conceivably be sexually based. It does this almost as well as the general theme of symbiosis, of which I think you'll find more in my stuff than syzygy.

If you can understand non-reproductive love you'll be able to understand—and convey—those two kinds of awe, the one for Boulder Dam or an atom bomb, and the other for Grand Canyon or a nova. You'll understand why *Casals and Segovia and Landowska work with such exquisite devotion, and what's with the GI who falls on the live grenade to save his squad. A guy who could understand things like that could get to be a pretty fair writer.*

The opening lines of "It Wasn't Syzygy" are another striking example of Sturgeon's gift for projecting his readers into unexpected, unusual narrator-listener relationships. The scene that follows is another (probably the best) of his evocative tributes to love-at-first-sight. The first of many autobiographical tidbits sprinkled throughout this first-person tale of the ultimate love-induced identity crisis comes with the waitress who used to call Leo "The Hungry Fella." In an interview Dec. 6, 1975, Sturgeon told me, about his life in New York City in early 1945: *I went into some kind of funk at the time, it must have been a severe depression. I just slept all the time. Finally I got a job. . . . And then I went through another thing where I couldn't get enough to eat. I remember they used to call me at the restaurant the hungry fella. Anything I ordered they brought double orders of, and they served it on a platter instead of a plate.*

One of my favorite examples of Sturgeon prose-poetry occurs when Leo asserts his reality by describing memories he carries around that are "intimately my own." At my suggestion, Charlie Brown published this alongside Sturgeon's obituary in *Locus* ("The Newspaper of the Science Fiction Field"). Inevitably, some of Leo's "memories" seem to be drawn from his creator's own memory banks. Sturgeon was indeed "on the beach" in Port Arthur, Texas during his Merchant Marine days in 1937–39. He "pulled ropes" for the Barnes Circus in the summer of 1934. He did play guitar, though not professionally. The memories from Jamaica and Puerto Rico are presumably from the author's experiences when he lived on those islands in the early 1940s. And he did have a brother, Peter, who was slightly older than he.

In a letter (written but not sent) to his ex-wife soon after writing "It Wasn't Syzygy," Sturgeon said, *I was in love last December—hurriedly, deeply in love, with an urgency that was new to me.* Perhaps this brief relationship, with a woman named Marcia, played a part in inspiring this story.

When the story first appeared in a Sturgeon collection, *E Pluribus Unicorn,* in 1953, TS restored his original title in place of "The Deadly Ratio," which had been imposed against his will.

"The Blue Letter": unpublished until now. Written January-February 1947, during a productive month at a friend's home in Newcastle, Pennsylvania. On March 10, 1947, the day he got the exciting news that his 1939 story "Bianca's Hands" had won the thousand-dollar *Argosy* prize, TS wrote his ex-wife, Dorothe: *I spent a month away from New York, being by myself and writing. I wrote "Wham Bop" and "The Blue Letter" and "Thunder and Roses"* [which he'd begun before leaving New York] *and "It Wasn't Syzygy" and "The Place," and got a good start on the dog story. Two of these have sold; the* *rest are slicks* [aimed at non-science-fiction, better-paying markets] *and my agent* [Scott Meredith, as of 1/47] *tells me they're sure things. But they haven't sold yet. I got so I couldn't write, for waiting.* Later in the same letter he said, *I have written well since then* [last December]—*better than ever, notably in "Thunder and Roses" and "The Blue Letter," just because "Bianca's Hands" had been rewritten.*

The manuscript for this story was in the cache of papers Noël Sturgeon and I found in Woodstock in 1993, amidst a set of story fragments and pages on which TS talked to himself trying to develop story plots. The manuscript is untitled (but I feel certain it is the story referred to in the letter quoted above), and has pencil notes on the back indicating TS was considering rewriting or extending the story (*Tomorrow nite is different*). Amongst the many notes in this set of papers is one that says: *Work the Blue Letter into a yarn: the guy, in this hassle, is thrown into a different moral matrix ... maybe made to explain his emotions to aliens.* Sturgeon did successfully rework another 1947 mainstream story, "Hurricane Trio," in this manner in 1954.

(No manuscript for or other trace of "The Place" has yet been found.)

In spring 1945 Sturgeon did indeed receive an unexpected letter from his wife, after a separation of eight months and two thousand miles, asking for a divorce.

In Sturgeon's papers is a 15-page manuscript for an unfinished, untitled story about a man named Hamilton who, like Sturgeon, *decided it would be a good idea to go back East and get a job, and then send for his wife.... In the first week of the eleventh month of their separation, he got the short note asking for a divorce.* Also like Sturgeon, he moves into the apartment of a friend who is a ham radio operator. The unfinished story does introduce alien observers who are attempting to understand *the paradoxes in the moral code* of earthlings. One plot thread involves the mysterious atomic blasting of Newcastle, PA, which suggests the fragment was written during or after Sturgeon's month in Newcastle. Hamilton is described as *going to pieces* not just because of the divorce but because of his paralysis and that fact that *he would have to live with the memory of doing nothing about it.*

"Wham Bop!": first published in *Varsity* ("the young men's magazine," published by Parents Institute, apparently for high school boys), November 1947. This is its first book publication. Special thanks to Kyle McAbee who located this very rare Sturgeon story in the Library of Congress. Written January-February 1947.

This was the first (and one of the few) Sturgeon stories published in a non-science-fiction-or-fantasy magazine other than the early McClure Syndicate stories. He did sell a story called "Clock Wise" in early 1946; I believe this is probably the story published in *Calling All Boys,* apparently in 1948, under the title "The Clock." I have been unable to locate a copy of this or "Smoke" (which also appeared in *Calling All Boys*). If anyone is able to supply either of these stories, or any other story that seems to have been overlooked in these volumes, please do send us a copy and it will be included, out-of-chronology, in a future volume.

In April 1946 in a letter to his mother, TS wrote, *I met a fellow in Puerto Rico* [in 1943–44] *called Jeff. I picked him up because he played exquisite swing trumpet to my electric guitar.*

Magazine blurb: MANUEL HAD EVERYTHING IT TAKES TO BEAT THE SKINS IN THE BIG TIME—AND HE WAS SMART ENOUGH TO KNOW THAT YOU CAN'T GET AHEAD PLAYING SOMEONE ELSE'S DRUMS.

"Well Spiced": first published in *Zane Grey's Western Magazine,* February 1949. Written in mid-1947.

Don Ward, in his introduction to the 1973 collection *Sturgeon's West,* wrote: "When I suggested to a leading practitioner of science-fiction and fantasy that he write a Western story little did I suspect what would result. At the time I was editing *Zane Grey's Western,* a monthly magazine that enjoyed a substantial acceptance among the followers of the genre. I was also an enthusiastic reader of science-fiction. One night I read a wondrous tale, 'Maturity,' and its author was Theodore Sturgeon. I liked the humor and the significance, and, above all, the sheer humanity of it, so much that I wrote a letter to Sturgeon. I told him how much I enjoyed 'Maturity' and made that suggestion, wistfully—it would be a special pleasure for *ZGW* readers if he would do a story with some of those elements for that magazine. Several weeks later, the mail brought to my desk a Western story by Theodore Sturgeon: 'Well Spiced.' "

On July 4th, 1947, TS wrote to his mother: *I have just sold a swing-music story to a new Parents' Institute rag called* Varsity *and, at editorial request a western story to* Zane Grey Western Magazine. *I am very pleased with these two sales, as they represent complete departures from the sci-fantasy field. And about time. Don't worry—I shall never stop writing fantasy. But at the same time I am a commercial writer with enough on the ball, I think, to be able to write bread-and-butter stuff for many other markets. It's the only way I can stop living hand-to-mouth, and the only way I can hit the slicks, even though my friend Heinlein has sold four stf numbers to the* Satevepost *at something over a thousand per each.... In short, I think I am due for a flock of sales.*

"Hurricane Trio": first published in *Galaxy Science Fiction,* April 1955. Substantially written in summer or fall 1947; later revised and expanded, probably in 1954 or early 1955.

In a letter to his mother, Jan. 2, 1948, TS wrote, *Margaret Cousins of* Good Housekeeping, *which pays a minimum of $750 per story, has been profoundly impressed by my work. "The Professor's Teddy-Bear," a horror story which my agent sent to her for fun, scared the hell out of her; it was followed immediately by a slick story called "Hurricane Trio," which had three characters, two women and a man, and the entire action took place in bed ... all in the best of taste, of course, and very lushly written. She wanted to meet me after that, and did; I had a nice long chat with her; she gave me a collection of twenty-five* Good Housekeeping *stories and begged me to write something for her.*

Good Housekeeping never did buy a story from him; unfortunately. Ray Bradbury's prediction that TS would soon start selling a lot of stories to "the slicks," the high-paying magazine markets—

see "Maturity" notes—never came true, despite Sturgeon's frequently expressed desire for success of that sort. Science fiction critic and author James Blish alluded to this frustrating circumstance in a 1961 review of Sturgeon's novel *Venus Plus X* by saying, "[the] short sketches of contemporary life [included in the novel] are good enough to show, as did 'Hurricane Trio,' how expertly Sturgeon could write mainstream fiction given just one editor in that field with the wit to recognize the fact."

In his introduction to Sturgeon's 1955 collection *A Way Home,* Groff Conklin wrote: "The author has said that in its original form this story ['Hurricane Trio'] contained no element of science fiction, and perhaps some will consider that it should finally have been written that way. Mr. Sturgeon's point, however, is not that he used an alien *deus ex*—or rather, *in—machina* to resolve his plot, but rather to heighten the basic reality of the terrible human dilemma with which the story is concerned and its slow solution by the three people involved."

Science fiction author and anthologist Judith Merril, in her forthcoming memoir *Better to Have Loved* (quoted here by kind permission of the author), speaks of her affair with Sturgeon in the early months of 1947 and the week when he (and Merril) met Sturgeon's future wife Mary Mair: "On the 15th, Ted wrote to tell me Mary was still there, and he had made love to her. He was big on monogamy in those days and could hardly believe he now wanted both of us. He was, actually, in torment."

Poet Ree Dragonette, a childhood friend of Sturgeon's who lived with him in New York in 1946, told me in an interview in 1976 that a difficult moment in their relationship occurred when they were visiting Cape Cod in the summer of 1946 and found themselves confined indoors by the wind and rain of a nearby hurricane.

"That Low": first published in *Famous Fantastic Mysteries,* October 1948. Written in summer or fall 1947.

Fowler's need to *chip, chip, chip for a long, long time before he could ever call himself honestly broke again* is an echo of TS's own financial circumstances at the time. He wrote his mother in 1/48:

Mary and I want to marry. We decided at first to wait until my debts were paid, or at least until I was within a thousand or two of being honestly broke.

"Memory": first published in *Thrilling Wonder Stories,* August 1948. Written in summer or fall 1947.

"There Is No Defense": first published in *Astounding Science Fiction,* February 1948. Written in summer or fall 1947.

In the "In Times to Come" section in *Astounding* for 1/48, editor Campbell wrote, "The feature novelette next month is by a fellow we've heard from before—Ted Sturgeon. It's called 'There Is No Defense,' but it is *not* about atomic bomb warfare. It *does* contain a nice proposition, and it makes a fascinating yarn. There's an old saying 'It takes two to make a quarrel'; that isn't so at all. The fact that it takes only one to make a quarrel is proven in the beginning of this yarn—and in the end they find it takes nobody at all to make a quarrel!"

Sturgeon was not a newcomer to issues of militarism versus pacifism. In 1975, in a talk at a Unitarian church, he said: *Back in the late '30s, when I was a high school kid, I was organizing peace marches and condemning the armaments maker and so on. We used to march around to* [the song] *"Joe Hill" all the time.*

"The Professor's Teddy Bear": first published in *Weird Tales,* March 1948. Written in fall 1947.

The first piece of "horror" fiction written by Sturgeon after his long-rejected early story "Bianca's Hands" won the $1000 first prize in a prestigious short story contest in England in March 1947.

"A Way Home": first published in *Amazing Stories,* April 1953 (under the title "The Way Home"). Written in fall 1947.

In his 1/2/48 letter to his mother quoted in the "Hurricane Trio" notes, TS said that the *Good Housekeeping* editor had also been shown: *another of my stories called "A Way Home," which was written immediately after the "Teddy Bear" to prove that one person could write two stories so extremely different from one another that they couldn't possibly have been written by the same person.*

This became the title story of Sturgeon's 1955 short story collection *A Way Home.* In his introduction to that collection, Groff Conklin wrote: "There is one tale in this book that is not science fiction at all. The title story, 'A Way Home,' originally appeared in a science-fiction magazine, but it is in reality a poignant study of boy psychology. Since boys and girls are by nature spinners of fantasy, dreamers by day as well as night, the story carries with it an atmosphere of fantasy, but closer examination will reveal that it is a thoroughly real incident in a child's development.

The About the Author page in the back of the book concludes: "Of his writing, Mr. Sturgeon says, *I write what I write to find a way home. "Home" in this sense is what one wants. It is what one wants to be. In one context it is love; in another, truth. It can twist itself about and simply be an other-place; a place any time away from here. A way home can be a long way or a very short way. Sometimes it is a long way of finding out what the short way is. Home is also what one believes, and those very other things, what one believed and what one is coming to believe now, for later. So I write long stories and short stories and angry stories and funny ones so that they can be homes for me, that I had, that I have, that I wish."*

Corrections and addenda:

The story "August Sixth, 1945" included in Killdozer!, *Vol. III of* The Complete Stories of Theodore Sturgeon *was described in the Story Notes for Vol. III as "unpublished." This is incorrect. I have since learned that the full text was published as a letter from Theodore Sturgeon in the "Brass Tacks" letter column in the December, 1945 issue of* Astounding Science-Fiction. *My thanks to Charles Morris for providing this information.*

Appendix

The Original Second Half Of "Maturity"

[Because the second half of "Maturity" was substantially rewritten for Sturgeon's first book in 1948, the original text is made available below. There are no significant changes in the book version prior to the paragraph that begins this appendix (see page 33 in the rewritten version).]

But not from the thoughts of a few people. Drs. Wenzell and Warfield compiled and annotated Robin English's case history, with as close a psychological analysis as they could manage. Ostensibly, the work was purely one of professional interest; and yet if it led to a rational conclusion as to where he was and what he was doing, who could say that such a conclusion was not the reason for the work? In any case, the book was not published, but rested neatly in the active files of Mel Warfield's case records, and grew. And then there was one Voisier, himself a mysterious character about whom little was known except his aquiline features and unbuttoning eyes and his wealth, all of which were underestimated. Voisier thought about Robin a great deal; and because he was Voisier, he was able to gain scraps of information not available to most people. The conclusions he drew from two or three of these, one afternoon, led to the ringing of Peg's phone.

"Dr. Wenzell?"

"Yes?"

"Voisier speaking. Do you know Robin English?"

"Voisier, the producer? Oh, how do you do? Yes, I—have met Robin English."

"Do you happen to know where he is?"

"Does anyone?" she countered. "I understand that his lawyers—"

Voisier's soft chuckle slid over the wire and came out of the receiver like little audible smoke rings. "I have encountered his lawyers. Dr. Wenzell, I have to find out where he is."

"What has that to do with me?" Peg asked cautiously.

"There is some connection between you and Robin English," said Voisier smoothly. "Just a moment—I'm not trying to find out what it is, and I don't care. I know only that it is a matter of professional interest to you and a Dr. Mellet Warfield; and I *don't* care what it is. I'll be frank with you; I must see him purely on a business matter. It will be to his advantage—all of his dealings with me have been, you know. After all, I discovered him."

"You discovered him the way the atom bomb was discovered by the mayor of Hiroshima," said Peg tartly.

Voisier laughed urbanely. "Very good." Peg was figuratively conscious of the swing of his boom as he changed his conversational tack. "Please, Dr. Wenzell—let's not get off on the wrong foot. I'm sorry if I seem to pry. Will you take lunch with me tomorrow?"

"I'm sorry. I'm busy tomorrow."

"Dinner this evening, then. That would be better."

"I am completely tied up, thank you," said Peg, over the rustle of silk in his voice. "And besides, I do not know where Robin English is or what he is doing. Goodb—"

"I know what he is doing," said Voisier quickly.

"You—"

Through a smile, Voisier's easy voice said, "Of course. I don't know where he is, that's all. I thought that with what I know and what you know we might be able to locate him. For his own good, of course. I gather that you would like very much to know where he is."

"What's he doing?"

"I *can't* tell you over the phone!" he said, in the voice in which one says "You *mustn't* play with Daddy's watch!"

"I wish you—" said Peg sharply, and then sighed. "When can I see you?"

"Thank you *very* much, doctor," he said abjectly, and was that a touch of relief in his voice? "Dinner tonight, then—unless you are busy, in which case ... ah ... cocktail time is practically here. I could meet you this afternoon, if you could—"

"Thank you," she said, and startlingly, she blushed at the eagerness she heard in her own voice. "How soon can you get here?"

"Very soon. I know where it is. I'll see you in a moment. And thanks again."

He hung up, and Peg sat looking at the bland cornerless bulk of her cradled telephone. Robin, Robin English. She formed his name with silent lips, and smiled a little. "Robin," she whispered, "I'm going to catch you by the ear and stand you in a corner for doing this to me." Robin was a child—such a child.

Her assistant came in. "A Mr. Voisier to see you doctor."

"Thank you, Helen. Ask him—*Voisier!* Good heavens, I didn't expect him so quickly! Yes, show him in. Show him right in!"

Voisier appeared at the door, rather as if he had been projected there. He looked over the office, more rapidly than he appeared to be doing it, and then let his gaze slide to rest on her face. He smiled.

"Mr. Voisier?"

"I am very glad to meet you, doctor." He came forward, and she noticed that the Homburg he carried was not black, but a very dark brown. Like his eyes.

"You got here very quickly, Mr. Voisier."

"I was just downstairs when I called."

She frowned briefly, realizing that she had been told that he had come to the hospital perfectly confident that he could talk her into seeing him. She wondered why she didn't mind too much. "Sit down a moment," she said, "I'll be ready to leave in a second."

He thanked her, and surprised her by not taking the chair she indicated at the end of her desk and close to her, but one in the corner. He sat down, ignoring the magazines on the end table next to him, and rested a part of the weight of his eyes on her as she worked, stacking the reports on her desk and putting them away.

When her desk was clear she paused a moment, thinking, and

then dipped into the file drawer and brought out her copy of Robin's case history. She did not open it—she knew every line in it—but sat running her fingers over the binding, wondering whether to bring it with her.

"Bring it along," said Voisier, his eyes on the ceiling.

"I knew someone else who acted telepathic," said Peg with a little quirk of the lips. "All right."

The way he helped her on with her coat and handed her through the door made her feel like reaching for a lace trim to drape over her arm as she walked. They did not speak as they went down in the elevator. She wanted to study his face, but he was studying hers, and strangely, she did not want to meet his eyes.

Parked in front of the hospital was a low-slung limousine, beautifully kept, not too new. A chauffeur with a young, impassive face opened the door and Peg got in, feeling the lack of a velvet carpet and a fanfare or two. Voisier followed, and the car slid silently into traffic. Voisier gave no orders to the chauffeur, which was another indication to Peg of how sure he had been that she would come out with him. She wondered if he had made reservations wherever they were going. She never knew, because they pulled up in front of Lelalo's, and both the doorman and the head waiter greeted Voisier effusively and she realized that they would at any time, reservation or no reservation. They were shown to a very comfortable corner table. Peg asked for an Alexander; Voisier did not order at all, but a silvery cocktail was brought and set down before him.

Finally she met his eyes. He seemed relaxed, but watchful, and his gaze was absolutely unswerving. She gritted her teeth and said lightly, "Have you read any good books lately?"

His eyes dropped to the case history lying on the table between them. "No," he said.

"Tell me what you know."

He drummed idly on the table with long, flexible fingers. "Robin is in the trucking business," he said.

"Oh?"

"Yes. And in insurance. Air freight. Distilling. Drugs. A few others."

"For goodness sake! But that doesn't sound like Robin!"

"What doesn't sound like Robin?"

"Robin is almost exclusively a creative person. Business—organizing, money-making itself—these have never had any interest for him."

"They have now," said Voisier in a slightly awed tone.

"If he did go into business," said Peg carefully, "it would be like that—diversification, and excellent results in everything he tried. That is, if he's still ... I mean, if he hasn't changed. How do you know this?"

"I can't understand how he's doing, it," Voisier said, ignoring her question. "He has bought out a bunch of independent truckers, for example. Standardized their equipment, rerouted and scheduled them, put in the latest equipment for servicing all the way, so that he has practically delay-proof service. He pays his employees eight per cent more than ... than other firms, and works them four less straight-time hours per week. Yet his rates are twelve per cent per hundredweight under those of any of his competitors. Am I boring you?"

"You are not."

"He has hit the insurance business in an unusual way. He has a counseling service made up of insurance men so carefully chosen and so highly paid that his agency is a factor to be reckoned with by every company in the East. His specialty is in advising clients—the thousand-dollar policyholder to banking insurance—on ways and means of combining policies to get the maximum coverage from the smallest premium. His charge is nominal; it doesn't seem to be a money-making proposition, much, at all. But he is getting an increasing power to throw large blocks of insurance business any way he wants to. He does it to the benefit of the policyholder and well within the law. In other words, what he is machinating for is influence. And since nobody can possibly predict what he is going to do next, the agency is a Damocletian sword over us ... uh ... over the insurance companies."

"Mr. Voisier—wait. How do you know all this?"

"The most amazing thing of all is what he is doing in the drugs business. He has tapped a source of hard-to-get biochemicals that is something remarkable. Some sort of synthesis . . . never mind. I'm running along like a *Wall Street Journal* excerpt and I'm not going to start reciting things from the *Journal of the Chemical Institute.*"

"Have you seen him?"

"I have a picture of him. He spoke at a trucker's union meeting with his independent chain proposal recently. It's a good shot, and though he's changed a little since I last saw him, there's no mistaking him. He was using the name of Reuben Ritter—not that that's a matter of any importance, since elsewhere he is known as Schwartz, Mancinelli, Walker, Chandler, and O'Shaughnessy. Where he goes after the meetings and an occasional dinner he attends, no one knows. He only goes out on business and he always leaves a highly competent authority behind to handle the details."

"May I see the picture?"

"Certainly." Voisier took out a fine-tooled Moroccan wallet and leafed through it. He pulled out a four-by-five print and handed it to her.

"It *is* Robin," she said instantly, shakily; and then she pored over the picture, her eyes tearing down into it. A slight sound from Voisier made her look up; he was regarding her with a quizzical grin. She went back to the picture.

It was Robin, all right; and he stood before a flat table obviously in a loft which was converted to a meeting hall. He was half-leaning against the table, and his head and one arm were raised, and his face was turned to the right of the camera.

Yes, it was Robin, all right; but Robin subtly changed. His features were—was it older? They were the features of a young man; but there was a set of purpose about the profile that was unfamiliar to her. Two slightly out-of-focus faces in the background, watching him with something approaching raptness, added to the completely authoritative, unselfconscious pose of the speaker. And Peg knew that from that picture alone, something within her would never again let her speak of Robin as "that child." It was a jarring realization, for "Robin" and "Childishness" were all but inseparable associations in her mind.

She became conscious of Voisier's long white hand hovering in front of her. She looked up and clutched the picture. "You want it back?"

"I'd . . . oh, I have the negative. Go ahead." The quizzical smile appeared again.

Peg slipped the picture into her pocketbook, closed it tightly, and only when she felt Voisier's amused eyes on her hands did she relax her grip on the clasp. She said, "How do you think I can help you locate him?"

Voisier put the tips of his fingers together and eyed her over them. "In that book of yours," he said, indicating the thick binder of prognosis carbons, "you probably have information which would help us to predict at least what sort of surroundings Robin English would find for himself. I know what businesses he's in, and pretty much how he's conducting them. Certainly we could draw some pretty shrewd conclusions." He paused, and looked thoughtfully at the second joints of his fingers, one after the other. "All I have to do is see him once. Just once," he said as if to himself. "When I do, I can find out where he is living, what he is doing every hour, where he is liable to str . . . ah . . . jump next."

"You almost said 'where he will strike next,'" Peg said.

"Did I? I didn't know. That's ridiculous, of course."

"I suppose it is," she said slowly, watching his face. "Mr. Voisier, you have a remarkably easy way about you."

"I? Thank you."

"You're easy to talk with, and you talk easily. You divert the conversation to your chosen ways so *very* easily. You have still not told me why you want to locate Robin English."

"Everyone wants to know where Robin English is. Don't you read the papers?"

"I doubt, somehow, that you are motivated by intellectual curiosity. I don't think you want to produce another play of his, particularly, or sell a story to the press and scoop the town, or—obviously not this—give him pointers on his new business ventures. I hate to be blunt with anyone," she said with a sudden rush of warmth, "but

I must ask you—what are you after?"

He spread his hands. "I like the boy. Brilliant as he is, he is getting himself into a little hot water with certain of the interests with which he is competing. In the business world, as in the world of nations, there is room enough for everybody, providing everybody will cooperate. It is impossible to cooperate with a man who cannot be reached."

"It is impossible to retaliate, also."

Voisier held up a deploring hand. "Retaliate is too strong a term. Active as he is, it is inconceivable that he can keep himself hidden much longer. It is infinitely more desirable that I get to him before any of the others—I who have demonstrated so conclusively that I have his interests at heart. I like the boy."

"You like the boy." The picture of Robin in the union hall rose before her eyes. That was no boy. "Mr. Voisier, you are telling me that he is in danger, aren't you?"

He shrugged. "He *is* playing a dangerous game."

"Dangerous game? Danger from what?"

"I have not made up a roster, doctor."

She stared at him. "Mr. Voisier—just what business are you in?"

"I'm a producer. Surely you know that."

"Yes. I have just remembered that I heard you once mentioned in connection with the trucking business, and again, there was something to do with drugs—"

"You have a proclivity," said Voisier casually, "of connecting yourself, in one way or another, with remarkable people. I, like Robin English, am a man of some diversification."

She sat quietly for a moment, and thought. As Voisier had predicted, little pieces were beginning to fit here and there. Robin's progress had been so carefully charted, and prognosis made in such detail, that the information Voisier had given her was highly indicative. If she could talk it over with Mel—

"I can't piece all this together on the spot," she said.

"Why don't you get in touch with your associate, Dr. Warfield?"

"You *must* be psychic," she said wryly. "Let me phone him.

Without seeming to move quickly, Voisier was on his feet and assisting her out of the chair before she knew she was moving. "By all means," he said. "And if you can impress the urgency of the matter on him, it will be to Robin's benefit."

"I'll see," she said.

She went to the phone booth and called, and Mel was out, and when she returned to the table Voisier was gone. So was his limousine. So was Robin's case history.

"Mel, I don't know how I could have been such a fantastic idiot," she said brokenly.

She was in his office, hunched up in a big wing chair, and for the first time in years looking small and childish and frightened.

"Don't blame yourself, Peg," said Warfield gently. "No one would expect that kind of prank from a man like that."

"It w-was awful," she almost whispered. "He made such a *fool* of me! I called the waiter immediately, of course, and he acted surprised to see me at all. He absolutely denied having seen such a thing as that case book at all. So did the head waiter. So did the doorman, They simply looked at me as if I were crazy, exchanging wondering glances at each other in between times. Mel ... Mel, I don't *like* that man, that Voisier!"

"I wouldn't wonder."

"No—aside from that slick little piece of larceny. There's something evil about him."

"That's an understatement, if ever I heard one," Mel said. "I don't know much about that man—no one does—but the things I know aren't too good. I wonder if you knew that Chickering Chemical was his?"

"That drug firm that was peddling hashish as a tonic?"

"Not a tonic. A facial—mud pack, I think it was. It didn't harm the skin. Didn't do it any good, either. It was sold in small and adulterated quantities at a fantastic price, but it was hashish all right."

"But all the officers of that company are in jail?"

"All they could get anything on."

"How do you know this?"

"One of their lab assistants went to pharmaceutical school with me. Silly fool he was, but a very likable character. He could be bought, and he was. He was paid well, and he didn't care. I did what I could to help him when the whole mess happened, but he was in too deep. He had no cause to lie to me, and he told me that Voisier was the man behind the whole rotten deal."

"Why didn't he give some evidence against Voisier?"

"No evidence. Not a scrap. Voisier's much too clever to leave loose ends around. Witness the trick he pulled on you. And besides—my imbecile of a friend rather admires him."

"Admires him—and Voisier got him into the penitentiary?"

"He blames only himself. And it seems that Voisier has a certain likable something about him—"

Peg thought of that saturnine face, and the compelling eyes of the man. She remembered his tactile glance, and the incredible flexibility of his voice. "Oh." She shook herself. "I can't afford the luxury of sitting here and saying how awful it all is," she said firmly, putting away her handkerchief. "What are we going to do?"

"Why do anything? Robin English is no longer our responsibility, if it's Robin you're worried about. As far as the book is concerned, I have the original, so that's a small loss."

"When does your responsibility to a person end?" she demanded hotly.

"That depends," he said, looking at the ceiling, "on what the person in question means to you. If it's a patient, and that patient, of sound mind, decides to go to another doctor or to stop treatment altogether, there is no law or ethic which demands that I try to hold him. If, on the other hand, the person is a ... well, of personal interest, it's a different matter."

"And you feel that Robin can look out for himself?"

"He's demonstrated that pretty well so far, He must include self-preservation and the ability to act on it among his other talents."

"Mel—this isn't like you!"

"Isn't it, though!"

"Mel!" she cried, shocked. "If it weren't for us he wouldn't be in all this trouble! He's hooked up with Voisier in some way, and—"

Mel put his hands on her shoulders and pushed her back in her chair. He looked at her somberly and then sighed. "Peg," he said finally, "I've got to say this. I deeply regret the day I ever set eyes on Robin English. You haven't been yourself since the day you met him."

She thought of the extraordinary statement Robin had made at tea that day, about Mel Warfield's desire to kill him. She looked up at Warfield with horror in her face.

"Listen to me," he said. "You're all tangled up in your emotions, and you can't think straight. You think Robin's mixed up with Voisier in some business way. Isn't it obvious what Robin is doing? You know that Voisier is mixed up in a dozen different businesses, two-thirds of which are shady in some way or another. You were told by Voisier himself that Robin is engaged in some of these same fields. I think you'll find that Robin is engaged in all of them. I think that if you are fool enough to mix yourself into anything this big and this dirty, you'll discover Robin is out to undercut everything the man is doing."

"Why? Why on earth should he do that?"

"I wouldn't know. Probably because he recognizes Voisier as his own brand of genius, with many years' start on him. Without doubt he feels crushed by Voisier—feels that the world isn't big enough for both of them. The 'why' of it isn't important. The fact remains that if he is not doing such a fantastic thing, he isn't in any danger and you needn't worry about him. If he is, then he must be outdoing Voisier on the dirtiest of his rackets."

"No, Mel—no! Robin wouldn't do that!"

"Someone is. How many new addiction cases has your hospital admitted in the past three months?"

"Well, there is a decided upswing, but what has that—"

"Robin *could* be responsible. It would have to be a one-source deal—someone previously unknown, without a record that can be checked, with a tremendous organizing ability and personal compulsion, and a lot of scientific skill. Most of the drugs found on these poor devils are synthetic."

"But Robin never did an evil thing in his life!"

"He has done many things recently he never did in his life. I tell you, Peg, the responsibility I feel in this matter is a far greater one than anything that could happen to Robin English. If I'm right in all this, I have been instrumental in loosing something rather terrible in the world. And if I'm right and he's tackling Voisier by playing the man's own game, the odds are pretty strong that Voisier's too big for him. In which case—good riddance." He lowered his voice. "I'm sorry, Peg. Truly I am. I've been going round and round in smaller and smaller circles over this thing, and I've had enough."

Peg was feeling absolutely bewildered. "But I have only just told you about Voisier and this—"

"I've known about it for weeks, Peg. Let the thing take its course."

She rose, trembling. "You're wrong, Mel," she whispered. "You've *got* to be wrong."

"I'm afraid not," he said sadly. "I sincerely wish I were."

"I've got to see him."

"No, Peg! He might . . . he . . . can't you see that he's turned into a man who takes what he wants?"

"Does that make a difference?" Peg asked in a strange voice. "I can't let this happen to him. I'm going to find out where he is and see him. I'm responsible for this whole horrible thing and so are you. But through your stupid mulish jealousy you've argued yourself into blaming him!"

Warfield went white. "Responsible? He had the seed of this in him all along. He simply never had the courage to do an honestly evil thing until we so generously matured him. Maturity is a strange thing, Peg. Like other riches, it is dangerous in unskilled hands. It isn't something that can be achieved all in a lump. We gave him a kind of maturity which gathered all the loose threads of his personality into something monolinear—something productive. But we didn't give him the power to use the years of experience he had had before we got to him. He's a bulldozer with a skilled idiot at the controls. But he is no longer a glandular case. If you want me to change my attitude at all, prove to me that he is still suffering from imbalance of any kind. That's in my field. That I can handle."

"I'll have to see him."

"Do you know where he is?"

"Nobody does. But I'll find him."

"I know where he is. But I will certainly not tell you."

"*You* know?"

"He came to see me four months ago." Warfield wet his lips. "He—had a word or two to say about you. He was apparently suffering from some sort of a delusion. He explained carefully to me that he had no use for you, that there was no longer any reason for me to want to ... to kill him, and ... you don't seem surprised."

"He told me about that the last time I saw him," she said, shaken.

"You *knew* about that?"

"*Did* you try to kill him, Mel?"

"It was an accident, Peg. Really it was. And he compensated for it. Splendidly. I don't know how he found out about it—the man's incredibly sharp."

Peg felt turned to ice, and her voice was ice as she said, "It was the post-pituitrin excess, wasn't it?"

"Yes, but that couldn't have anything to do with this Voisier business. I tell you it was an accident. I didn't realize that I'd made a mistake in the solutions until after he'd left the office that particular day. It didn't affect his progress, except temporarily; and when he stopped his treatments, he was practically normal." He stopped and wet his lips again, and then suddenly ran to her. "Peg! Peg, what's the matter?" For she had suddenly turned white, and was rocking on her feet. He put an arm about her shoulders and led her back to her chair. She slumped down, shook herself, and looked up at him with a swift, scornful glance that was almost a physical force.

"How do you *dare* to call yourself a doctor?" she breathed. She opened her handbag with shaking fingers and took out the photograph Voisier had given her. She handed it to him without glancing at it. "Look at that and tell me he's not still glandular," she said.

He looked, and then stared. "It's Robin, all right," he said, and then, with a ghost of his old grin, "Getting to be quite a glamour boy in his old age, hm-m-m?"

"He is? Have you noticed why?"

"What am I supposed to look for?"

"Look at his jaw."

"Nice jaw."

"You don't remember Robin. You don't remember that round baby face."

"I wasn't in love with the man," Warfield said nastily.

"He didn't have much jaw," she said, her voice quivering. "Can't you see what's happening? That used to be *Robin,* with the charming, chinless face!"

Warfield's breath sucked sharply. He walked over to the window and for a long moment stood with his back to her, staring out.

"What do you diagnose, doctor?" she said acidly.

"Ac—" he began, and couldn't make it. He swallowed and coughed. He cleared his throat. He said, "Acromegaly."

"Acromegaly," she echoed sweetly. "His pre-pituitary has gone wild, he's suffering from hypertrophy of the chin and probably of the hands, and you say he's not glandular." Suddenly she was across the room, had spun him about and was clutching his lapels. "What are you going to *do?* Are you going to let him go on doing whatever crazy thing a glandular imbalance is forcing him to do, so that he'll be killed by Voisier? Or are you going to stand by while he gets around Voisier some way and then turns into a monster and dies?"

"I have to think," said Warfield. "Oh, Peg. Peg—"

"You can't think," she said wildly. "Why do you suppose Voisier stole that book? With what he knows, and with what that book contains, he'll track Robin down in a matter of hours! Do you really know where he is?"

"Yes," Warfield whispered. "A piece of his strange kind of braggadocio. He was defiant, and yet he seemed afraid of me. He promised to keep in touch with me whatever he did, so that if I ever wanted to . . . kill him I could come and face him with whatever it was. He swore to keep away from you. He has moved four times since he stopped taking the treatments, and each time he has called or written to give me the address. I don't know why." Warfield raised his eyes to hers. "I don't know anything about any of this," he said brokenly. "It's all mad. We're being played like chessmen, Peg, by a lunatic against a devil."

"Is he in town?"

Warfield nodded.

"Well?"

Warfield looked at her. She was a statue now, a dark-crowned bloodless figure. "I'll go with you."

"I'll see him alone."

"I'll go with you all the same, then, and wait."

"Very well. Only hurry."

Warfield slipped out of his laboratory smock and into a coat without another word. Outside the office he stopped and said, "Peg . . . please—" but she walked steadily down to the elevators, and he shrugged and followed her.

They caught a cab almost immediately, and Warfield gave the driver a Riverside address. Peg sat staring blindly ahead of her. Mel slumped in a corner and looked at his wrists, dully.

Peg broke the silence only once—to ask in a deceptively conversational voice if anything had been learned that she didn't know about the treatment of acromegaly. Warfield shook his head vaguely. She made a sound, then, like a sob, but when Warfield looked at her she still sat, dry-eyed, staring at the driver's coat collar.

They pulled up in front of one of those stately old cell-blocks of apartment houses that perch on the slanted, winding approaches to the Drive. They got out, and a doorman, a bit over life-size, swung open both leaves of a huge plate-glass-and-bronze door to let them into the building.

"Mr. Wenzell," said Warfield to a wax-faced desk clerk.

"What?" said Peg

"He . . . it amuses him to use your name," said Warfield, as if he were speaking out of a mouthful of sal ammoniac.

"Mr. Wenzell is out," said the clerk. "Can I take a message?"

"You can take a message right to Mr. Wenzell, who is not out," said Warfield. "Tell him his two doctors are here and must see him."

"Tell him," said Peg clearly, "that Margaretta Wenzell is here."

"Yes, Mrs. Wenzell," said the clerk with alacrity.

"Why must you make this painful as well as unpleasant?" gritted Warfield. Peg smiled with her teeth and said nothing.

The clerk returned from the phone looking as if he had learned how to pronounce a word he had only seen chalked on fences before.

"Fourteen. Suite C. The elevators—"

"Yes" growled Warfield. He took Peg's elbow and walked her over to the elevators as if she were a window-dummy.

"You're hurting me."

"I'm sorry. I'm—a little upset. Do you have to go through with this weird business?"

She didn't answer. Instead she said, "Stay down here, Mel."

"I will not!"

She looked at him, and said a thousand words—hot-acid ones—in the sweep of her eyes across his face.

"Well," he said, "all right. All right. Tell you what. I'll give you fifteen minutes and then I'm coming up." He paused. "Why are you looking at me like that? What are you thinking about?"

"That corny line about the fifteen minutes. I was thinking about how much better Robin would deliver it."

"I think I hate you," said Warfield hoarsely, quietly.

Peg stepped into the elevator. "That was *much* better done," she said, and pushed the button which closed the doors.

On the fourteenth floor she walked to the door marked "C" and touched the bell. The door swung open instantly.

"Come in!" grated a voice. There was no one standing in the doorway at all. She hesitated. Then she saw that someone was peering through the crack at the hinge side of the door.

"Come in, Peg!" said the voice. It was used gently now, though it was still gravelly. She stepped through and into the room. The door closed behind her. Robin was there, with a gun. He put it away and held out both hands to her. "Peg! It's *so* good to see you!"

"Hello, Robin," she whispered. Just what gesture she was about to make she would never know for she became suddenly conscious of someone else in the room. She wheeled. There was a girl on the chesterfield, who rose as Peg faced her. The girl didn't look, somehow, like a person. She looked like too many bright colors.

"Janice," said Robin. It wasn't an introduction. Robin just said the one word and moved his head slightly. The girl came slowly across the room toward him, passed him, went to the hall closet and took out a coat and a hat and a handbag with a long strap. She draped the coat over her arm and opened the door; and then she paused and shot Peg a look of such utter hatred that Peg gasped. The door closed and she was alone with Robin English.

"Is *that* the best you can do," she said, without trying to keep the loathing out of her voice.

"The very best," said Robin equitably. "Janice is utterly stupid. She has no conversation, particularly when I want none. What she has to recommend her, you can see. She is a great convenience."

A silly, colorful little thought crept into Peg's mind. She looked around the room.

"You're looking for a smörgasbord tray," chuckled Robin, sinking into an easy-chair and regarding her with amusement. "Why won't you look at me?"

Finally, she did.

He was taller, a very little. He was much handsomer. She saw that, and it was as if something festering within her had been lanced. There was pain—but oh the blessed relief of pressure! His face was—*Oh yes,* said Dr. Wenzell to herself, *pre-pituitary. Acromegaly.* She said. "Let me see your hands."

He raised his eyebrows, and put his hands in his pockets. He shook his head.

Peg turned on her heel and went to the hall closet. She dipped into the pockets of an overcoat, and then into a topcoat, until she found a pair of gloves. She came back into the room, examining them carefully. Robin got to his feet.

"As I thought," she said. She held up the left glove. The seam between the index and second fingers was split. And they were new gloves. She threw them aside.

"So you know about that. You would, of course."

"Robin, I don't think this would have happened if you had continued your treatments." He slowly took out his hands and stared at them. They were lumpy, and the fingers were too long, and a little crooked. "A phenomenal hypertrophy of the bony processes, according to the books," he said. "A development that generally takes years."

"There's nothing normal about this case. There never was," said Peg, her voice thick with pity. "Why did you let it go like this?"

"I got interested in what I was doing." Suddenly he got to his feet and began to stride restlessly about the room. She tried not to look at him, at his altered face, with the heavy, coarse jaw. She strained to catch the remnants of his mellow voice through the harshness she heard now.

He said, "It was all right during those months when I wrote *Too Humorous To Mention* and *Festoon* and invented the back out drills and all that. But everything got too easy. I could do anything I wanted to do. All of the things I had ever dreamed about doing I could do—and so easily! It was awful. I tried harder things, and they came easy too. I couldn't seem to apply myself on anything that couldn't be seen or touched, though perhaps, if I had been able to go into higher mathematics or something purely abstract like that, I wouldn't be—well, what I am now.

"I began to be afraid. The one thing I couldn't whip was Mel Warfield. I was afraid of him. He hated me. I don't think he knew it, but he hated me. I wanted you. There was a time when I could have—but I was afraid of him. He had too much power over me. Too much thumb-pressure on that hypodermic of his, or the addition of some little drop of something in a test tube, and he could do anything he wanted with me. I'd never been afraid for myself before. Maybe it was part of that maturity you were talking about."

"I imagine it was."

Robin sat down heavily, clasped his hands, stared at them, put them in his pockets again. "I was glad to take the risk, mind you. It wasn't that. Anything in my condition that was suddenly too much for his skill to cope with—any accident like that couldn't frighten me. It was knowing that he hated me, and somewhere underneath he wanted me out of the way—preferably dead. Anyway—I got out. I kept him informed as to where I was, because I was ready for him. I was ready to kill him first if he came after me. But no hypodermics. No solutions. So—I went on with my work, and then it all got old, right away. I could do anything I wanted to do. Peg—can you imagine how horrible that can be? Never to know you might fail? To have such a clear conception of what the public wants in a play or a poem or a machine, that you can make it and know from the start that it will be a success? I knew a man once, who had photography for a hobby. He got to be so good that he stopped printing his negatives. He'd *know* they were perfect. He pulled 'em out of the hypo and dried 'em and filed 'em. Often he sold them without looking at them. It killed his hobby. He took up electronics, which was more his speed. But I'm that way about everything."

"You got bored."

"Bored. Oh, Peg, if you only knew the things I tried! Finally I dropped out of sight. I got a kick out of the papers then. For a while. Know what I was doing when the whole world thought I was doing something fantastic? I was reading. I was holed up in the back room of my Westchester place with all the books I had ever wanted to read. That's all. They let me get out of myself—for a while. For a while." He stopped and wiped sweat off his lip. "But it happened again. It got so that a page or two would tell me an author's style, a paragraph or two told me his plot. Technical books the same; once I got the basics the whole thing was there. Or maybe I thought it was. Maybe I just lost interest. It was as if I were being pursued by a monster called Understanding. I understood everything I looked at or thought about. There was nothing I could see or say or do or read or think about where I couldn't predict the end result. I didn't want to give anything any more, either, the way I did with the Whirltoy. Do you know what I wanted? I wanted to fail. I didn't think I could. I don't think so now. If I purposely botched a thing up, that would be a success of a sort. So for a long time I did nothing."

He fell silent. Peg waited patiently. She had had dozens of questions to ask, and half of them were already answered.

"Then I began to think about Voisier. You know Voisier?"

She nodded. "Robin—wait a minute. You hate Voisier. I think you're trying to ruin him. But you hated Mel Warfield. Why didn't you try to—"

"Warfield? By then, he wasn't big enough. Voisier was the only man I ever met whom I thought could beat me." He sighed. "Now I think he won't do it." And suddenly, Robin smiled. The smile sat badly on that heavy face. "Peg, there's an alternative to unquenchable, inevitable success. That is to play a game in such a way that you never can know how it ends. That's what I'm doing."

"Voisier's trying to find you."

"Is he now? How do you know?" For the first time Robin's face and voice showed real animation. All the twisted ravings of the past few minutes had come out of him like toothpaste out of a tube.

Peg told him about Voisier's calling the hospital, and what had happened at Lelalo's, where he had stolen the case history.

"Good," said Robin. "Oh, fine. This means that things are shaping up better than I thought. Faster. Uh—excuse me a moment."

He went to the desk in the corner, sat down, and began to write rapidly.

"This maturity thing," he said, phrasing between the lines he was writing, "I think you and Warfield overlooked something. I'm the patient. Do doctors listen to patients?"

"They do."

"You realize, don't you, that humans die before they're fully mature?"

"You mean in the sense that their bones do not completely ossify?"

"That's it. And there's a psychological factor, too." He paused, thought a while, wrote for a moment, and then went on. "Puppies and kittens and lion cubs—they're terribly foolish, in a pretty kind of way. They have their mock battles and they chase their balls of paper and get wound up in milady's yarn, don't they?"

"They do, but—"

"Humans, with few exceptions, *always* are puppyish, to a degree. There is even a parallel in the proportions of head to body, even allowing for the larger brain pan of *homo sapiens*. An adult human being has proportions comparable to a half-grown colt or dog in that respect. Now—did you ever hear of a full-grown gorilla acting kittenish? Or a bison bull, or a lion? Life for them is a serious business—one of sex, hunger, self-preservation and a peculiar 'don't tread on me' kind of possessiveness.

"Peg—let's face it. That's what's happened to me. I can't go back. I don't see how I can go on this way. I'm mature now. But I'm mature like an animal. However, I can't stop being human. A human being has to have one thing—he has to be happy, or he has to think he knows what happiness is. Happiness for me is unthinkable. There is nothing for me to work toward. All of my achievements are here"—

he tapped his head—"as good as done when I think of them, because I know I can do them. No goal, no aspiration—the only thing left is that little game of mine, the one where, according to the rules, I can't ever really know the result."

"Voisier?"

"Voisier." He picked up the phone, dialed rapidly. He listened. "Come on back," he said. He hung up. "That was Janice. She'll be here in fifteen minutes. You'd better go, Peg."

The door buzzer began to shrill. Robin leaped across the room; the gun was in his hand again. He opened the door and stood behind it, peering out at the hinge side as he had before. Mel walked in.

"Peg—are you all right?"

"A little bewildered."

"Of course she's all right," said Robin in a tone that insulted both of them. Mel stared at him. Robin went over to the desk, picked up the sheets he had written and, folding them, handed them to Peg. "Promise me you won't read these until you get back to Mel's office."

"I promise."

Mel spoke up, suddenly—and with great effort. "English—You know what that condition is?" He indicated Robin's face.

"He does, Mel," said Peg. "Don't—"

Warfield pushed her hand off his arm impatiently. "Robin, I'm willing to do what I can to arrest it, and there's a chance ... not much, you understand—"

Robin interrupted him with a sudden, thunderous guffaw—quite the most horrible sound Peg had ever heard. "Why sure, Mel, sure. I'll be a bit busy this afternoon, but say tomorrow, if we can get together?"

"Robin!" said Peg joyfully. "You *will?*"

"Why not?" He chuckled. "Don't make an appointment today. Call me tomorrow." He took the note back from Peg, and scribbled on it. "Here's the number. Now go on. Beat it, you two. Maybe I ought to say something like 'Bless you, my children' but I— Oh, beat it."

Peg found herself in the hall and then at the door. "But Robin—" she said weakly; but by then the door was closed and Mel was guiding her into the elevator.

At Mel's office a few minutes later, she unfolded Robin's note with trembling fingers. It read:

> Peg dear,
> Here is where a mature human being gets kittenish, if he has to kill himself in the attempt.
>
> What I have been doing to Voisier is to drive him crazy. He's a bad apple, Peg. Very few people realize just how bad. I knew today would be the payoff when you told me how he had stolen the book and all that. He played you for bait. I told you he was almost as clever as I am. He knew that if he could worry you enough, you'd find me some way. My guess is that he simply had you followed until you found me. Then he'd wait until you had gone—he's waiting as I write this. When he's sure there are no witnesses, he'll come and finish his business with me.
>
> This is my game, Peg. The only one I can think of where I'll never know who won. If you call the police about now, chances are they'll find him here. Make it an anonymous tip, and *don't* use this note as evidence of any kind. Voisier is going to get his; Janice is here and besides, the place is equipped with a very fine wire recorder. I'll handle all the dialogue. I'm sorry about all those dope fiends I had to supply to undercut his rotten racket. Take care of 'em.

And down in the corner, where he had ostensibly written his phone number, were these words: "Sorry I can't keep that appointment. The condition is already arrested."

Peg phoned the police. The police found Robin English dead. Robin English left everything he had to Peg and Warfield equally. And in due course Voisier was electrocuted for the murder. The recording found in his apartment, coupled with the testimony of one Janice Brooks, was quite sufficient. Voisier's defense, that Robin was torturing him, held no water; for where is a law that specifies mental torture as grounds for justifiable homicide?